PRAISE FOR
HER SKY COWBOY

"Beth Ciotta's *Her Sky Cowboy* is pure charm. This is a must read for anyone who loves the genre—or hasn't even tried it yet. You'll be hooked!"

—*New York Times* bestselling author
Heather Graham

"A wildly inventive, action-packed steampunk adventure! Lady inventors, sexy renegade lawmen, airships, acid rock, and flying horses—*Her Sky Cowboy* has it all!"

—Zoë Archer

WHEN HEARTS TAKE FLIGHT

"Put your arms around me and hold tight."

Amelia did as he asked, and her heart nearly burst through her cinched wool corset. She'd never embraced a man before, except for Papa and her brothers, but this was vastly different. Perhaps it was hero worship, but quite simply, the Sky Cowboy scrambled her senses. Beyond tall, fit, and devilishly handsome, he possessed confidence and charisma and, by jiminy, a rocket pack!

He buckled a strap around her waist, cinching them close as pages in a book. "Ready?"

She smiled up into his bourbon-colored gaze, stomach fluttering like a flock of wrens. His mouth was most distracting. How bizarre that she was thinking of kissing him just now instead of flying. Embarrassed, Amelia glanced skyward. "Oh, yes."

HER SKY COWBOY

THE GLORIOUS VICTORIOUS DARCYS

BETH CIOTTA

A SIGNET ECLIPSE BOOK

SIGNET ECLIPSE
Published by New American Library, a division of
Penguin Group (USA) Inc., 375 Hudson Street,
New York, New York 10014, USA
Penguin Group (Canada), 90 Eglinton Avenue East, Suite 700, Toronto,
Ontario M4P 2Y3, Canada (a division of Pearson Penguin Canada Inc.)
Penguin Books Ltd., 80 Strand, London WC2R 0RL, England
Penguin Ireland, 25 St. Stephen's Green, Dublin 2,
Ireland (a division of Penguin Books Ltd.)
Penguin Group (Australia), 250 Camberwell Road, Camberwell, Victoria 3124,
Australia (a division of Pearson Australia Group Pty. Ltd.)
Penguin Books India Pvt. Ltd., 11 Community Centre, Panchsheel Park,
New Delhi - 110 017, India
Penguin Group (NZ), 67 Apollo Drive, Rosedale, Auckland 0632,
New Zealand (a division of Pearson New Zealand Ltd.)
Penguin Books (South Africa) (Pty.) Ltd., 24 Sturdee Avenue,
Rosebank, Johannesburg 2196, South Africa

Penguin Books Ltd., Registered Offices:
80 Strand, London WC2R 0RL, England

First published by Signet Eclipse, an imprint of New American Library,
a division of Penguin Group (USA) Inc.

First Printing, November 2012
10 9 8 7 6 5 4 3 2 1

PUBLISHER'S NOTE
This is a work of fiction. Names, characters, places, and incidents either are the product of the author's imagination or are used fictitiously, and any resemblance to actual persons, living or dead, business establishments, events, or locales is entirely coincidental.
   The publisher does not have any control over and does not assume any responsibility for author or third-party Web sites or their content.

ALWAYS LEARNING   PEARSON

*To my husband, Steve, the inspiration for all my heroes,
and the love of my life. Thank you for building this world
with me and for inspiring a flying horse with heart!*

ACKNOWLEDGMENTS

Creating an alternate steampunk world for *The Glorious Victorious Darcys* was a challenge and a thrill, and I'm delighted with the results! The Victorian Age meets the Age of Aquarius. What fun! There's nothing more exhilarating or satisfying than allowing my imagination to run wild and then, ultimately, sharing those flights of fancy with readers.

Although writing is often a solitary affair, it takes many people to coordinate the finished product. I'd like to express my heartfelt gratitude to everyone at New American Library who had a hand in bringing *Her Sky Cowboy* to life! The art, marketing, and editorial departments. The sales team. I appreciate your creative efforts and support and delight in the amazing results!

A very special thank-you to my amazing editor, Jhanteigh Kupihea. Your vision, enthusiasm, and keen editorial eye energizes and inspires!

My sincere gratitude to my copy editor, Tiffany Yates Martin, for her sharp and thoughtful touch.

My heartfelt thanks to my agent, Amy Moore-Benson, for her never-ending and always inspiring guidance and support. What a ride!

A special and fond shout-out to my critique partners on this project, my sister and fellow author Elle J. Rossi, and my cherished friend and fellow author Cynthia Valero. Rather than gush publicly, I'll just say . . . You know how I feel.

My supreme and sloppy appreciation to authors Heather

Graham and Zoë Archer for reading *HSC* and then providing me with such wondrous quotes! I am blessed.

To my many wonderful and supportive friends and family, loyal readers, and enthusiastic Facebook friends—thank you for brightening my days and enriching my life. To the hardworking bloggers and reviewers who help to spread the word—thank you for your thoughtful time and energy. And to all of the wondrous librarians and booksellers who live and breathe and promote literature—thank you for being.

PROLOGUE

"Could you have been any more rude?"

And here I was congratulating myself for being so astonishingly polite. "Apologies, Mother." Repressing her frustration, Miss Amelia Darcy endured her mother's disapproving glare—she was well used to it—and moved to the rear of Loco-Bug, the family's one-of-a-kind steam-powered automocoach. Stoking the coal in the firebox, she simultaneously praised her papa's ingenuity and cursed the extraordinary and unreasonable price of gasoline.

Since the Peace War, only the very rich could afford petrol for everyday use. Others, like Papa, hoarded such fuel for special occasions or, in his case, special projects. She supposed she shouldn't complain about their fickle and sluggish mode of transportation. If her mother, who resisted anything relying on cogs, pipes, and belts, had her way, they'd be traveling by horse and buggy. The woman feared progress as though it were the plague. The only thing that vexed her more was her daughter's emancipated mind-set.

Whilst Amelia replenished the boiler's water supply, her mother stood by, tugging on her fur-lined gloves, tightening the sash of her ridiculously frilly bonnet, and arranging her thick traveling cloak to accommodate her portly frame. "I spent two months cultivating a relationship with the dowager Viscountess Bingham," she grumbled under her breath, "and you managed to ruin my matchmaking efforts in less than two hours."

"Proof of my restraint. Otherwise we would have earned the boot much sooner." Not that Lady Bingham had physically shown them the door, but she'd certainly expedited their exit.

Speaking of which, Amelia glanced over her shoulder and saw the dour-faced woman in all her straitlaced glory standing on the front steps of the magnificent country estate alongside her son—the Viscount Bingham. Decorum dictated that they oversee their guests' departure, no matter how tedious the process. Whereas Lady Bingham was no doubt scandalized by Amelia's determination to fire up and drive a horseless carriage like an unrefined commoner, she could feel Lord Bingham studying her every move. She knew he was fascinated by her passion for aviation and flair for mechanics and somewhat amused by her father's Frankenstein version of an automocoach. Influenced by sketches of Bollée's La Mancelle and a time-traveling Mod's psychedelic Beetle Bug, Papa's hybrid, built from available scraps, was a visual curiosity. However, to someone like Amelia, who had not experienced life before the invasion of the Peace Rebels, Loco-Bug just was.

What really irritated Amelia was Lord Bingham's keen fascination with her bountiful bosom. Even the modest and hideously constricting visiting gown she'd donned to appease her mother had not detracted from her bothersome "fine figure." Most women would have been flattered by his attention, she supposed, especially since Lord Bingham was a man of great wealth and influence. But he was also an arrogant and crafty sod, and it was for that reason that Amelia had striven to alienate Lady Bingham and her son with her fervent utopian ideals. Influenced by the cautionary tales of the Mods, she took her role in policing the fate of the world most seriously.

The steam engine finally puffed to life and Amelia burst with joy. The sooner she distanced herself from Wickford Manor and the pompous Binghams, the better. She'd been duped into believing Lord Bingham was a fellow utopian, a New Worlder. After an hour in his company Amelia suspected he was, in fact, a Flatliner, someone who cared only for his future—and not the future of mankind.

Learning that he'd employed an entire staff of domestic automatons had singed Amelia's bustle. How insensitive to purchase robotic domestics at a set cost when so many living, breathing Vics were desperate for employment! It was just one of the things that had soured Amelia on the man her mother had envisioned as her husband. Not that Amelia had any intention of marrying. Ever. Why tie herself down when there was so much of the world to see? Why bend to a man's will and agenda when she possessed her own dreams and goals? As she lived and breathed, someday she would pilot her own airship and experience grand adventures! She imagined her exploits being reported alongside the colorful escapades of the Sky Cowboy, an American outlaw who flew the fastest airship in all of Europe. If only her mother would match her with that fearless aviator. Horrid husband material to be sure, but since she had no designs on being a wife—ever—she cared not about his notorious and scandalous reputation and only for his superior knowledge in aeronautical engineering.

Sighing, Amelia shoved aside that whimsical scenario and helped her mother up into the rear seat of the six-person cab. As the prim woman fussed and fidgeted, Amelia gathered her own bothersome skirts, compounded by the added layer of her leather duster, and climbed aboard the open-air driver's throne. She pulled on her leather gauntlets and tinted fur-rimmed goggles, then tugged her worn top hat, a gift from Papa, over her blond coiled braids. Unfashionable perhaps, but comfortable. Sensible as well—which was more than she could say for bustles and bonnets. Grasping the steering wheel, she rolled back her shoulders, feeling deliciously in control. Why anyone would prefer the role of passenger to pilot was beyond her imagination. Loco-Bug vibrated and puffed, primed for action—same as Amelia. She would have smiled were she not conscious of Lady Bingham's scorn and her own mother's disappointment; were she not repelled by Lord Bingham's lecherous attention, damn his eyes. "Are you going to glare at me for the entire journey home, Mother?"

"Quite possibly."

At least she knew what to expect. Unlike with Lord Bingham. She'd expected—or, perhaps more accurately, hoped for—a tour of his collection of aerostats and aeronefs—flying machines of all manner, each a technological marvel—but she'd never gotten farther than the drawing room, and tea and watercress sandwiches. Her own fault, true. Still . . . *Blast*.

"You are a beautiful young woman, Amelia, in spite of your peculiar taste in fashion. Well educated. Charming, when you strive to be. Yet you are twenty summers old and without a husband."

Smiling now, Amelia breathed in the crisp winter air and engaged the clutch, setting them on a course for home. "Life is good."

"Why in heaven's name did you even agree to this meeting, only to sabotage it? You could have saved me the humiliation by simply refusing."

"If I had refused you would have pressured me until I relented," she said reasonably as they rolled through the ornate iron gates. "I know this, since you have tried to match me six—"

"Seven."

"—times before. This time I bypassed prolonged misery by giving in at the outset."

"I would have preferred an outright refusal. At least it would have saved me the embarrassment of being tossed from the grounds." Her mother sniffed, and Amelia knew without looking that she was using a dainty handkerchief to dab away tears. "Honestly!" she said, choking back a dramatic sob.

Since her back was to the woman, Amelia indulged in a disrespectful eye roll. She'd never outwardly insult her mother, but blooming hell, it was difficult to hide her frustration. Anne Darcy possessed the extraordinary skill of crying at the drop of a hat. It was a weapon she used quite often against Amelia's father, Reginald Darcy, a baron by happenstance, an inventor by choice, and it drove Amelia to distraction, because her papa always relented. Always. Whatever Anne wanted, which was faithfully more than was reasonable, given the family's status and moderate wealth, her dear, sweet, brilliant, yet ofttimes scatterbrained husband strove to deliver.

Amelia, who could scarcely remember the last time she'd cried, rarely put stock in her mother's tears. This time, however, she acknowledged a morsel of guilt. True, she'd hoped to circumvent her mother's nagging by giving in and agreeing to at least meet with the viscount. But she'd also been driven by her desire to see and to perhaps climb aboard his magnificent zeppelin.

Oh, to pilot an airship of superior design, one that stayed afloat for longer than thirty minutes. Amelia had been obsessed with flying since she was a little girl. Thanks to her papa, who shared her obsession, she'd had the opportunity to sample the skies in his assorted flying machines. Unfortunately, like most of his inventions, his aerostats malfunctioned with extraordinary regularity, and her flights were thus often quite short.

"He was perfect for you, Amelia."

Meaning Lord Bingham. Although she wished her mother would dismiss the thought, she could not wholly disagree. His worldviews, or lack thereof, aside, she supposed he was perfect in that she could discuss aviation with him for aeons and he wouldn't grow bored. He could expose her to advanced technology and she would be mesmerized, but other than that, she saw no sense in the union. She did not love, nor was she even physically attracted to the man—in spite of his handsome features. Not to mention their extreme social and political differences. She didn't bother to explain those differences to her mother. She wouldn't understand. As an Old Worlder, Anne expected Amelia to conform to convention. She had no interest in technology or saving the future from chaos and destruction. She wanted everything to move forward with the natural march of time, the way things used to be, before the Peace Rebels.

As they chugged along, the vibrations from the engine invigorating Amelia's good senses, she cursed herself for giving in to her mother. For giving over to her curiosity regarding Lord Bingham's personal air fleet. Instead, she could've spent the morning assisting Papa, who, day by day, had become almost psychotic in his mission to fly to the moon. Although he'd promised not to tinker with *Apollo 02* (his second attempt at a futuristic rocket ship) until she returned, she didn't wholly trust his word or judgment of late.

"Can't you make this thing go any faster?" Anne asked, sounding suddenly anxious to return home.

"Regrettably, no," Amelia said as Loco-Bug's iron wheels rolled over the pitted, snow-dusted road. As with most of the shires, Kent had fallen upon hard times, and the much-traveled roads had fallen into ill repair. Not to mention that Loco-Bug was simply not made for great speed. "For what it's worth, the journey would have been half the duration if we had taken Bess." Her papa's one-of-a-kind kitecycle. Unfortunately, among other things, Anne Darcy was aerophobic.

"If people were meant to fly," she said with a sniff, "we'd have been born with wings."

If only, Amelia thought with a wistful sigh.

They fell into a sullen silence. Really, what was there to say? Old Worlder and New Worlder, fatalist and utopian, repressed and emancipated. They would never see eye to eye. For the next hour they rode in tense silence—Amelia contemplating her papa's moonship obsession whilst her mother no doubt plotted her next marriage match.

A short mile from their home, Loco-Bug stalled for the second time in thirty minutes.

Anne ridiculed her husband's automocoach as Amelia hopped out to inspect the engine. Unlike her mother, she had faith in Papa's inventions. Sometimes it just took a lot of positive thinking and a bit of elbow grease. And in this case, a hair ornament. Pulling a decorative comb from her braided hair, Amelia probed and unclogged a valve. Though pleased when Loco-Bug coughed back to life, she glanced at the sky, thinking how much more enjoyable it would have been to soar the seamless air as opposed to driving along rutted roads.

A deafening boom blasted her eardrums, tripping her pulse and stealing her breath.

Pushing her goggles to her forehead, Amelia gaped at a large plume of smoke and fireworks marring the near horizon—a mushrooming cloud littered with fragments of brass, iron, and clockwork.

It came from Ashford. The Darcy estate.

Her mother gasped. "What in heaven's name?"

Apollo 02, Amelia thought, stifling a scream as she imagined Papa tinkering, then . . .

Please, God, no.

Refusing to think the worst, Amelia scrambled back into Loco-Bug, intending to push the machine to its limits. Upon reaching Ashford, she would find Papa singed and discombobulated but very much alive. She willed it with all her heart.

Amelia refitted her goggles, then engaged the clutch. "Hang on to your bonnet, Mama."

CHAPTER 1

The *London Informer*
January 5, 1887

MAD INVENTOR DIES IN QUEST
FOR GLORY

The Right Honorable Lord Ashford, lifelong resident of Kent, blew himself up yesterday whilst building a rocket ship destined for the moon. Ashford, a distant cousin of the infamous Time Voyager, Briscoe Darcy, was rumored to be obsessed with making his own mark on the world. Fortunately for the realm and unfortunately for his family, Ashford's inventions paled to that of Darcy, earning him ridicule instead of respect, wealth, or fame.

Amelia's heart pounded with fury as she read the irreverent newspaper article for the zillionth time in four days. She should have shredded the infernal report upon first reading. Her brothers had suggested setting the rag aflame, but morbid obsession had seized her good senses. Quite simply, she was astonished by the audacity of their lead reporter, known as the Clockwork Canary. The *London Informer*, and indeed the Canary, frequently leaned toward sensationalism rather than dignified journalism, but this was downright cruel. It ridiculed not only her father but also mocked her twin brothers, Jules and Simon, who, like Papa, were visionaries. Each time she read the printed poppycock, her soul cried out against the unfairness, the injustice, the outright lies!

"Papa was not mad," she ranted whilst pacing his beloved though cluttered workshop. "He was inspired, driven. Creative!"

She paused in front of her enhanced pet falcon, Leo, who'd perched upon a stargazing telescope. So beautiful, even though he'd been hideously disfigured. "Who else would have thought to replace your annihilated legs and beak with iron prosthetics?"

Whilst immense energy and thought went into reconstructing—or, as in the case of automatons, constructing—people, few techno-surgeons cared about the plight of deformed animals. Shot from the sky, the young falcon had suffered ghastly injuries. Amelia, who'd found and carried the wounded bird home, had begged Papa to save his life. The softhearted man had toiled for days devising artificial parts that moved via releases and springs. He'd applied said parts with the help of their local physician. That had been three years ago. After an adjustment period, Leo had learned to operate his new talons and beak with remarkable skill. Leo was, in fact, Papa's greatest success, although no one, aside from Amelia, acknowledged the significance. "Crikey," she said to her feathered friend, "you're better than new!"

Leo, who always seemed to understand her moods and commands, puffed out his feathery chest as though very proud of his enhanced status indeed.

"And look at all these other inventions," she said, turning to the messy worktables. "The toaster contraption and stun gun. The instant photo camera and telecommunicator." Everything influenced by the rants and renderings of the Mods—the twentieth-century faction of the Peace Rebels who never would have invaded this time were it not for Briscoe Darcy. How could her father—or any inventor, for that matter—outshine the man who'd discovered a way to breach dimensions?

Amelia pocketed the damnable article, then lovingly fingered each object. "I confess, many of these prototypes did not work, but some did, even if only for a while. Perhaps Papa never accomplished great things, but he certainly aspired to greatness." The enormity of his loss boggled and vexed. If only he had concentrated on one effort, but Papa's mind had constantly burst with ideas. She'd always been in awe of his vast knowledge and interests. She had but one interest. One passion.

Flying.

She wondered, not for the first time, whether that was why he'd been so obsessed with building his moonship: because he wanted to afford her the ultimate flight. A flight through space. To the moon. According to the Book of Mods, it had been done before. In their time, a man had walked on the moon. She couldn't imagine . . . but she did. Whether Papa had been more influenced by the Mods or by his brilliant, innovative cousin, she did not know. Nor did it matter. All that mattered was that he'd had a vision. How dared the *Informer* sully his efforts!

"You look as content in this environment as he did."

Amelia glanced up and saw her brother Jules, older than she by a decade and a year, standing on the threshold of their father's workshop. So deeply and darkly intense, the exact opposite of his twin, Simon, a gregarious, carefree sort. Jules, the elder of the twins by three and a half minutes, had lived in London for the last several years making his living as a science fiction writer, and before that he'd been abroad with the military. He was worldly and mysterious, a source of fascination for Amelia. And a source of irritation for their mother, who fixated overly much on his rumored decadent pastimes.

Now Jules was the head of the family, the master of Ashford, although she couldn't imagine her complex brother relocating to this simple, remote country setting. Nor would Simon, a civil engineer and skilled artisan, abandon his lofty pursuits. Which meant Amelia would be living here alone with their mother—a notion that chafed for numerous reasons.

"Did you know," she said to Jules, "that Mother asked me to clear this carriage house of Papa's contraptions? Said it's a painful reminder of his wasted life." Her heart hammered with defiance. "Whereas I see every grease-smeared gear, spring, gizmo, and gadget as a testimony."

"Do not mistake Mother's cold words for a lack of caring, Amelia. She mourns the loss of Papa as greatly as you do, albeit in her own way."

Amelia sighed. "As someone who witnessed her harping and ridicule on a daily basis, I find that difficult to believe. You have not lived here for more than a decade. You do not know—"

"I know far more than you think, little sister, and I am far less biased."

"What is that supposed to mean?"

"It means," he said reasonably, "that although I loved Papa, I did not worship the ground he tinkered upon." Utilizing his walking cane, Jules moved slowly and deliberately (as was his way since the operations) into the workshop, filling the already crowded space with his bigger-than-life aura. Amelia scarcely noticed his limp anymore, although she knew his war injury was a great source of curiosity to many. Details revolving around the skirmish that had earned him a medal and early retirement from the military were classified. Jules never spoke of his service to the Crown, nor the incident, nor his extensive rehabilitation. He was a man of few words and many secrets. Women were mad for him, stilted gait and all.

As he moved closer, Amelia noted his impeccable attire.

Unlike her, he was dressed in conventional Victorian garb—tailored black trousers and frock coat, a burgundy waistcoat, stark white shirt, and an impeccably tied cravat. Of course, he'd been attending to formal matters whilst she'd taken refuge in her room, and now here. If he disapproved of her boyish trousers, grease-smudged shirt, and leather tail vest (an ingenious combination of corset and cutaway skirt), he didn't show it. He simply regarded her with a tender, big-brotherly gaze.

"I understand why you kept your distance at the funeral, Amelia. I respect your reluctance to sit through the reading of Papa's will, but you need to know the outcome."

Given his ominous tone, she anticipated dire news, although she couldn't imagine how things could get worse. Almost a week later and the air still reeked with the smells of the massive explosion. She wondered whether the noxious, nightmare-inducing fumes would forever taint her nostrils and dreams—a horrific reminder that Papa was gone. As a way of calming her nerves, she gathered miscellaneous gears and springs, sorting the parts into labeled cans. She'd left the house specifically to avoid that meeting with the solicitor. She didn't want to face reality. That involved acknowledging Papa was gone *forever*. She couldn't do that. Aside from his mangled pocket watch, no trace of his person had been found. Officials blamed the intensity of the explosion. Logical. Yet fanciful scenarios played in Amelia's head. Wishful thinking that, so far, had kept her from falling apart.

"Hear me out, Little Bit."

The nickname, used only by her brothers and Papa, nearly brought her to her knees. Stiffening her spine, she stood strong, her throat clogged with grief. "How's Mother?"

"Distressed."

"All will be well," she said in general.

"In time, yes. Presently, however . . ."

Jaw clenched, she gathered nuts and bolts, separating them into two jars. "Stop trying to scare me."

Leo flapped his wings in response to her agitation.

"The farthest thing from my mind." Jules smoothed a steady hand over the falcon's ruffled feathers. "Nevertheless, we have monsters to slay."

She continued sorting, organizing. "All right then, speak plainly. I've no patience for mollycoddling." Unlike their mother, who seemed to thrive on it.

"Papa invested the bulk of the family's fortune in Simon's latest venture."

"I was unaware."

"As were we all, until a few moments ago."

"A daring and somewhat risky maneuver," Amelia conceded. "But in the long run, wise." Simon had designed a fuel-efficient, cost-efficient public railway intended to operate *above* London's overcrowded streets as opposed to below, like the Underground. His vision, his reasoning, his sketches were brilliant. Surely, in time he and all those who'd invested in the innovative project would be rich beyond their dreams.

Jules rubbed the back of his neck. "Simon's venture failed, the project damned by financial and political corruption."

Her stomach flipped. "What? When?" Simon had traveled directly to Ashford upon news of the moonship debacle. He'd said nothing of his own catastrophe.

"Five days ago."

The same day as the explosion. Her mind raced to follow Jules's unspoken thoughts. "What are you saying? That Father invested in a doomed project? That we are now destitute?"

"We are . . . at a disadvantage. Temporarily," he added with a soft smile. "Do not concern yourself. Simon and I will do what we must to secure a future for you and Mother."

Guilt gnawed at her. She could have secured their future,

and thereby Ashford and Papa's inventions, by taking a conventional approach and encouraging Lord Bingham's attentions. Had she known . . .

No.

There had to be another way without relying solely on her brothers. But in the current repressed society, and given the family's eccentric notoriety, now reinforced by the *Informer*, what could they do to raise funds?

"Simon must be devastated," she said, feeling as though she'd been hit in the head with an iron bar. "Not just because of his failed project, but . . ." Her thoughts took an ugly turn. "Did Papa know?"

Jules dragged a hand over his whiskered jaw. "Simon sent a Teletype that morning."

Amelia dropped into a chair as several awful and weighty scenarios seeped into her brain. "Papa must have been terribly upset and distracted. If I'd been here, working alongside him instead of indulging Mother's matchmaking efforts and my curiosity . . ." She trailed off, unable to voice her most sickening thought: *I could have saved him*.

Leo screeched and Jules pulled Amelia out of the chair and into his arms. "Such musings are madness."

Yet such musings tainted her soul. Tears burned her eyes, though they did not fall, and it felt as if a rusty gear were lodged in her throat. To her dismay, she trembled with grief and angst as Jules stroked a comforting hand down her rigid spine.

"No one is to blame," he said as if reading her thoughts. "Not you. Not Simon. Together we will survive this. Mark my words. The Darcys will prevail."

"Got a bad feeling about this skytown, Tuck. They're flying the flag of the Peace Rebels. Means they welcome Mods and Freaks."

"I know what it means, Axel." Tucker Gentry noted the banner featuring the infamous circle and two-legged stick billowing from the end of the central zeppelin. What had once been a symbol of peace was now a badge for chaos and rebellion. Change. A notion Old Worlders feared. A reality Tuck accepted, but on his own terms.

Relinquishing the controls of the air dinghy to StarMan, his chief navigator and copilot, Tuck angled his Stetson to shadow his eyes from the stark moonlight, then turned to his highly competent yet superstitious ship's engineer, Axel O'Donnell. "When's the last time you saw a Mod in the flesh?" he asked as the big man raided their weapons box. "As for Freaks, I don't hold to judgin' a man purely based on his race. That includes altered races."

Axel spit a stream of tobacco juice over the starboard side while clamping a stun cuff around his left wrist. "I ain't judging no one. Just sayin' they're more dangerous than most."

"He's afraid a Freak will read his mind," StarMan said dryly while steering the air dinghy toward the floating pleasure mecca.

"Don't figure they'd find much of interest," Tuck joshed.

"Go ahead and make fun," Axel said, "but they ain't called Freaks for nothing."

Shunned by polite society, the offspring of nineteenth-century Vics and twentieth-century Mods possessed supernatural abilities. Their gifts and the level of their skills varied. In Tuck's experience, like most living creatures, some Freaks were good and some bad. "If I were you," he said while dipping into the weapon box himself, "I'd be more worried about running into that murdering smuggler we crossed a week back. Heard Scotland Yard cut him loose."

"Bought his way out, did he?" Axel spit again. "Don't worry. If Dogface Flannigan comes gunnin', I'll take him on myself, Marshal."

"Call me that after boarding that mecca, Axel, and you're courtin' trouble for sure and certain."

"It's not like they won't know who you are," Axel said, jerking down the brim of his slouch hat. "Thanks to them dime novels, penny dreadfuls, and the *London Informer*, you're as famous over here as you were in America."

"Point is," Tuck said, hitching back his greatcoat in search of his astronomical compendium, "I'm no longer the law."

"Except on the *Maverick*," StarMan said with a grin.

"'Cept that." Manned by a skilled and loyal crew, Tuck's customized airship was one of the fastest boats in Europe. Handy, given his new vocation as sky courier—speedy delivery for a premium price. Essential when outrunning sky pirates or circumventing the occasional air constable intent on confiscating the *Maverick*'s sometimes unsanctioned cargo.

Three dirigibles of various sizes cruised by as Tuck consulted his compendium, a navigational instrument combining a compass, sundial, lunar and solar dials, and a few hidden trickeries. "As for my notoriety," he said, after verifying their position, "that's what gets us the bulk of our work, boys. That's why we're here tonight—business, not pleasure. Remember that when you're tempted by the hawkers." These colorful, persuasive sorts most commonly found in the shopping districts of major cities had infiltrated the decks of skytowns as well. Also known as costermongers and street vendors, they called out to passersby, advertising their wares or luring them into establishments. Half the time the prey ended up hornswoggled, or at the very least extensively, though pleasurably, detained.

With the *Maverick* anchored a safe distance away and manned by the rest of his crew, Tuck concentrated on his raucous destination—a safe haven for illegal substances and activities and, in this case, supernatural misfits. Between his past profession and personal interests, he'd seen his share of gambling halls, saloons, pubs, circuses, bordellos, theaters, dancing halls, coffeehouses, and social clubs. He was no stranger to alcohol and soiled doves, and frequently indulged in sports such as billiards and boxing—although poker was his game of choice. Though he wasn't a practitioner, he was acquainted with opium dens and, because he rubbed shoulders with criminal types, was well aware of the current drugs of choice—both legal and illegal, including laudanum, opium-laced cigarettes, cocaine, speed, and weed.

What he couldn't get used to was seeing all these forms of entertainment under one collective sail: fleets of four to five dirigibles connected by swinging gangways enabling patrons to move freely and quickly from one entertainment venue to another. Like the boomtowns of his native American West, skytowns seemed to appear overnight, and within hours teemed with customers. Transient in nature, like a traveling circus, this particular skytown presently straddled the borders of Surrey and Kent, just south of London proper. Since these floating meccas were "above the law," they attracted all manner of men and women, from laborer to aristocrat, Vic to Freak, Old Worlder to New Worlder—all of them looking for a good time, with random miscreants looking for trouble.

Once upon a time in America, Tuck had been appointed to police disorder. But since the day he'd been wrongfully accused of theft and murder and forced to flee his own country in order to escape the gallows, Tuck turned a blind eye to criminal activity. Mostly. These days, his number one objective was to make money, and lots of it. Buying back his old life might not be an option, but securing a new future was. He needed a damned hefty bankroll in order to grease the right palms, which would enable him to reunite with his sister and secure pardons for his men. The way Tuck saw it, which bordered on arrogantly optimistic, lassoing some form of justice was only a matter of time—one step at a time.

Tonight he was hoping to rustle up the crew's next job. As was his practice, he'd seek out the gambling house and join in a game of poker or faro. StarMan and Axel would work the saloon in their own manner, and as word spread about who they were and what they did, someone would approach the Sky Cowboy about precious or contraband cargo in need of transport. All that was left was for Tuck to accept or decline.

While StarMan hitched the air dinghy to an available post, Tuck and Axel slipped Disrupter 29s, the latest black-market version of a McCabe Derringer, into their ankle holsters and checked the Remington Blasters wedged into their shoulder rigs. No one openly flashed his hardware in a skytown, but everyone carried a concealed weapon— whether it be a knife, gun, or stun mechanism. Which was why Tuck preferred not to be called by his former title of marshal. Contrary to Axel's opinion, not everyone knew about his fall from grace and current "wanted" status. Being mistaken for the law in unlawful territory was a misconception he'd just as well avoid.

The night air sizzled with energy and exploded with the boisterous sounds of laughter, applause, mechanical whir-rings of amusement rides, scattered tussles, and what was either gunshots or backfire. As added ambience, a song Tuck hadn't heard in aeons, a song passed on by the Peace Rebels some thirty years back, a song that had yet to be written by an icon who'd yet to be born, wailed on the crisp winter wind.

Axel groaned, obviously recognizing the song as well, or at least the style—something called acid rock.

Smothering a smile, Tuck grabbed a brass crash helmet and shoved it against Axel's massive chest.

"What's this for?" he asked.

"See anyone comin' toward you wearin' those love beads, you put on that helmet," Tuck said. "Metal blocks their tele-pathic brain waves."

Clutching the helmet, Axel asked, "Really?"

Swinging onto the gangway, Tuck winked at StarMan, then strode toward the sound of outlawed music.

CHAPTER 2

Though she had no wish to rise and face a new day in her new reality, the day did indeed come. Amelia heard her curtains being wrenched open, saw sunlight behind her closed lids, and felt a hand upon her shoulder.

"As you requested, Miss Amelia. The newspaper, first thing."

She bolted upright and grabbed the inked rag from Eliza's hands. Every morning their housekeeper and her husband, Harry, Ashford's groundskeeper, rode into town to procure fresh food, the mail, daily newspapers, and, when available, the latest fashion and scientific periodicals. Amelia had specifically requested a copy of the *Informer*. As it was one of London's most popular newspapers, she wanted to know whether they'd printed a hideous follow-up on Papa, or perhaps Simon. Upon reflection, Amelia had been perplexed by the lack of publicity regarding the corruption surrounding her brother's high-profile project. In particular, why would the Clockwork Canary forgo a chance to sing of the further failures of the Darcys?

"Thank you, Eliza." Amelia shivered against the morning chill while focusing on the front page.

The older woman moved to the fireplace, using a bellows to fan the burning coals. "Your brothers are dressed and in the dining room, miss."

"I'm not hungry."

"Regardless, it would be polite...." Eliza trailed off as Amelia shot her a venomous look.

"You mean it is expected." Had she not buckled so easily regarding her mother's conventional matchmaking agenda, Papa would still be alive. Amelia would have been there to make sure of it. "As I live and breathe, never again will I cross my sensibilities and bend to polite or expected behavior."

"As you wish, miss." Clearly confused, the housekeeper hastened to leave.

Blast. "Wait." In the fifteen years that she'd been with the Darcys, Eliza had shown Amelia nothing but kindness. Embarrassed by her curt manner, Amelia softened her tone and expression. "I apologize for being churlish. Be assured my discontent does not lie with you, Eliza."

"You are in mourning, Miss Amelia. We all are. Some withdraw while others lash out. I suspect that will be the way of things for a time." With a kind smile and a nod, the woman withdrew, leaving Amelia alone with the morning news.

She got no further than the lead article on the front page.

The London Informer
January 10, 1887

ROYAL REJUVENATION—A GLOBAL RACE FOR FAME AND FORTUNE

In celebration of Queen Victoria's upcoming Golden Jubilee, an anonymous benefactor has pledged to award a colossal monetary prize to the first man or woman who discovers and donates a lost or legendary technological invention of historical significance to her majesty's British Science Museum in honor of her beloved Prince Albert. An additional £500,000 will be awarded for the rarest and most spectacular of all submissions. Address all inquiries to P. B. Waddington of the Jubilee Science Committee.

Blinkin' hell!

Unable to believe her eyes, Amelia read the article twice. Last night, between bittersweet dreams of working alongside her father and heart-wrenching nightmares of dreams going up in smoke, she'd tossed and turned, praying for a miracle that would bring Papa back, scrambling for a way to replenish the family fortune. Now this! Amelia launched out of bed, pulled on a dressing gown and slippers, then dashed downstairs. Heart racing, she burst into the dining room, a cramped area made even smaller by her twin brothers' bigger-than-life presence. Forgoing pleasantries, she waved the paper and blurted her news. "I know how to rescue the family name and fortune!"

"By discovering a lost invention?" Jules asked.

"Winning a global race?" Simon added.

"How . . ."

Each of her brothers flashed a missive.

"'Given your family's reputation as innovators, adventurers, and visionaries,'" Jules read aloud from his letter, "'you have been specifically targeted and are hereby enthusiastically invited to participate in a global race for fame and fortune.'"

"'Royal rejuvenation,'" Simon said, skimming his own missive. "'Colossal monetary prize . . . legendary technological invention . . .'"

"Yes, yes!" Amelia smacked the rolled newspaper to her palm. "It's all here. In the *Informer*!"

"As well as the *London Daily*," Jules said, tapping the newspaper next to his plate.

Simon held up a third newspaper. "And the *Victorian Times*."

Encouraged, Amelia paced between the ornately carved china cabinet and the matching ten-seat dining table, the paper now tucked beneath her arm. "So the contest *must* be authentic." Unlike the *Informer*, the *Daily* and the *Times* were respected newspapers. They'd verify the story, and they wouldn't embellish the facts. "How extraordinary!"

"Indeed," Jules said.

"Even more extraordinary is the fact that you both received personal invitations," she went on. "But from whom?"

"That, dear sister, is a mystery," Simon said. "No signature. No return address."

"Just a contact name," Jules said. "P. B. Waddington."

Amelia stopped in her tracks as a vexing thought occurred. "As a member of this family and something of an adventurer myself, why did I not receive a personal invitation?"

Her brothers glanced at her seat at the table. There, next to her place setting—an envelope. Amelia beamed as she retrieved and read the formal invitation addressed specifically to her. "When did these letters arrive?"

"This morning," Simon said.

"This is a *gift*!" Amelia exclaimed. "The answer to our misfortune. Were any one of us to succeed, we would bring glory to the Darcy name, restore honor to Papa's memory, and be set monetarily, all of us, for life! How can you be so blasé?" she asked Jules.

"Have you ever known him to show exuberance?" Simon asked.

"I sent a Teletype to Waddington," Jules said, "inquiring about specifics. I also contacted a friend within the science museum. I'm reserving my exuberance based on their responses."

"If Ashford had a modern telephone, as does most every household in England," Simon said, "you could have spoken to them directly."

Her brothers, accustomed to the advanced technology still thriving in London, in spite of the queen's efforts to suppress it, had also remarked upon Ashford's use of gas

lighting when the house had been recently wired with electricity. Perceiving electricity as evil technology perpetuated
by the Mods, their mother persisted in resisting the transi-
tion. As for the telephone . . . "You speak as though we live
in the Dark Ages," Amelia snapped, "whereas we simply
live in the country. Yes, we have dodgy service, but the
blame lies with the long-distance wiring, not our telephone."

"Merely an observation," Simon said.

"Unless you can talk sense into Mother where modern
conveniences are concerned," she went on, "or work mira-
cles with the long-distance company, stuff your observa-
tions, Simon."

He laughed, though his normally vibrant personality
seemed muted by a cloud of gloom. "I believe she's grown
extremely willful this past year," he said to Jules.

"She has always been willful."

Amelia ignored them both, noticing for the first time
that, though her brothers were drinking coffee, they'd
barely touched their porridge. Odd, given their usually rav-
enous appetites. "Why aren't you eating?"

"Eliza prepared the morning meal," Simon said.

Eliza, though an excellent housekeeper, floundered in
the kitchen. "Why?" Amelia marched to the sideboard and
frowned at the porcelain tureens boasting undercooked
eggs and burned bacon. "What happened to Concetta?"
Their cantankerous cook of nine months. Amelia had never
warmed to her as a person, but as a cook, she had most
impressive skills.

"Dismissed," Simon said.

Amelia looked to Jules, who'd inherited their father's
title and troubles. "I understand we can no longer afford
certain luxuries, but could you not have at least given her
the standard month's notice?"

"I didn't do anything. It was Mother who trimmed the
fat, so to speak, and she did offer Concetta notice, in addition to excellent references."

"Unfortunately for us," Simon said with a nod toward the watery eggs, "Concetta's prideful. I venture she is packing as we speak. I heard her venting earlier, and though I am not fluent in Italian, I'm almost certain she mentioned going home."

"To Italy?" Although Amelia was not truly surprised. Concetta consistently dithered about British ways. Why she'd remained in a country she abhorred was an utter mystery.

A bell sounded, announcing an incoming Teletype. Papa had fixed several key rooms with amplifying mechanisms so that one could be alerted promptly of incoming messages. Ingenious, if you asked Amelia. Pocketing her anonymous invitation, she scrambled for the library, her favorite room in all of Ashford, save for the carriage-house workshop, with Simon alongside her and Jules lagging behind. She slid over the parquet floor in her haste to reach the customized Teletype machine. Noting that the message was indeed addressed to Jules, she stepped aside and waited. Never would she tell him to hurry, but blast, she wished he'd make greater haste.

Simon perched on the edge of Papa's rosewood desk, also waiting. He dragged a hand through his hair, longer and lighter than Jules's, though they sported identical mustaches and beards. Closely trimmed. Impeccably groomed. His attire, however, was somewhat more casual than his brother's, whimsical in comparison. As was his mind-set. Simon the freethinker. Jules the deep thinker. Two very different cogs in a clock, as Papa had been fond of saying.

Jules leaned his brass-tipped walking cane against a bookcase and pulled the paper from the machine. The tilt of his mouth, the angle of his head, and the gleam in his eye said it all.

"It is a legitimate contest," Amelia said.

"With a daunting deadline," Simon added. "Less than five full months to locate and deliver a prize-worthy lost invention."

Amelia pounded a determined fist to her palm. "Between the three of us, one of us will succeed."

"You mean between the two of us," Jules said. "This is no venture for a lady."

Amelia huffed. "I'm not a lady. I'm . . . a member of this family. And, as I was influenced by Papa and his obsessions, an expert of sorts on inventions." She glanced at Simon. "Speak sense to him. Our chances are greater if—"

"Sorry, Little Bit. I stand with our brother. Your place is here at Ashford with Mother."

"That is so very . . . Old World!"

"It is sensible." Jules offered a tender smile.

"But I received an invitation," she persisted. "A personal invitation!"

"Curious, that," Simon said.

"And very New World," Jules said. "To invite a female to participate in a potentially dangerous mission."

Amelia harrumphed. "I call it fair. I am qualified."

"You are also our sister," Jules said. "How do you expect Simon and me to function properly if we are worried about you out in the world getting into God knows what trouble?"

"But—"

"It is settled."

When pigs fly. Rather than argue the point, which would get her nowhere, Amelia clenched her fists and bit her tongue. Meanwhile her mind fixated on a very special invention indeed. Historical. Legendary. Thanks to her obsession with Leonardo da Vinci and his investigations into flight, Papa's extensive catalog of scientific journals, and a secret letter, she knew exactly—well, almost precisely—where to find it. Or at least where to search. Unfortunately (or fortunately, considering it would entail a grand adventure), it meant traveling to Florence, Italy.

"Time is of the essence," Simon said.

Amelia's thoughts exactly.

"I have a significant object in mind," Jules said.

Simon nodded. "As do I."

That makes three of us!

"So we'll—"

"Absolutely. And upon occasion—"

"Naturally."

"Twin conversations are both vexing and rude," Amelia pointed out. Although they did not look exactly alike, Jules and Simon frequently knew each other's thoughts, and therefore unfinished sentences were all the rage between them.

Mouth quirked in a semblance of a smile, Jules nabbed his walking cane and ambled toward the door. "After speaking with Mother, I'll leave directly for London. Harry can drive me to the station in Loco-Bug. Coming with?" he asked Simon.

"No. I'll be taking—"

"Of course. Good luck with that."

Amelia refrained from pulling out her hair. "Good luck with what?"

"The *Flying Cloud.*"

"What?" Amelia fairly pounced on her big, fairer brother's back. She had planned to utilize the *Flying Cloud*—a salvaged and modified clipper ship fitted with a hot-air balloon and steam-engine components. An airship constructed by Papa and occasionally flown by Amelia, it rarely traveled far without breaking down, but she had new ideas on how to amend that.

"You won't be needing her," Simon said with a brow raised in warning. "Although I do not doubt your determination and resourcefulness, Amelia, your strength and calm are needed here at Ashford. Mother is fragile."

Amelia started to argue the point, but was forced to concede that Anne Darcy was indeed stricken low. Learning that she was a widow, and then, worse, a disgraced, penniless widow, had thrown her into a severe tizzy, sending her bouncing between sobs and rants and dramatic swoons. As she was someone who cared greatly about keeping up appearances, the fact that her mother had dismissed a valuable servant was testament to her desperate mood. Although Amelia was most often at odds with her mother, in this instance she was very much attuned to the woman's misery.

All the more reason for Amelia to triple the Darcys' chances of winning that astounding jubilee prize. Amelia's alleviating the family's financial woes would serve her mother far better than would her vexing company. No, she would not debate their mother's mind-set. She would attack from another, wholly reasonable direction. "Although you are a skilled enough pilot, Simon, the *Flying Cloud* is unreliable."

"She won't be after the upgrades." He kissed Amelia's forehead, then hurried after Jules.

"What upgrades? Where are you taking her? Where are you off to? What invention . . . ?" Her questions went unanswered as the household flourished with activity. She knew most certainly and dreadfully that within the hour her brothers would be on their way and she would be left behind, feeling helpless and frustrated beyond measure. She could not bear it!

Never would she voice these concerns, but Jules was hindered by his bum leg, and Simon, despite his calm demeanor, must be distracted by the guilt of his failed project, the project that had compromised the family funds. She, however, was in prime condition physically and mentally, and, as Simon had pointed out, determined and resourceful. Twiddling her thumbs at Ashford was not an option.

Amelia paced the library, her mind spinning. She could not afford to purchase transport on one of the upscale public dirigibles. Only the very wealthy could.

Thanks to Simon, the *Flying Cloud* was no longer an option. Loco-Bug would take her only so far before she'd have to purchase water passage across the channel and then a train ticket across France and beyond to Italy. It all seemed so costly and time-consuming. Also, a young woman traveling alone for such a long distance in the company of foreign travelers was risky.

Just then she had a vision of herself peddling across the skies. "Bess!"

Flying the kitecycle all the way to Italy would be a challenge, to say the least. But it would be most affordable, and if she tweaked the rocket blaster and steam engine, and if the winds and luck were with her, the journey would be more swift and less complicated. She would be in control, and she would not have to worry about propriety or unscrupulous traveling companions, as she would be traveling alone.

Except . . . the kitecycle required two pedalers. The dual-cycling mechanism enabled maximum thrust for lift. Once it was in the air, at least one person needed to pedal at all times. For such a long journey she required someone to share the workload. She needed a copilot. Additional manpower.

Blast!

A door slammed, causing Amelia to whirl toward the window. She'd thought to spy Simon striding off toward the aero-hangar. Instead she saw their former cook stomping along the garden path with her long, sturdy legs. Saw her lips moving as she blathered to herself, no doubt in her native tongue.

Eureka!

Amelia smiled as she hurried to catch up to Concetta. A copilot and, once upon Italian soil, a translator and guide. Her spirits lifted as she focused body and soul on a positive venture. Her pulse zinged at the prospect of soaring foreign skies and restoring Papa's reputation and the family fortune.

The Darcys would indeed prevail!

CHAPTER 3

Though a dense cloud bank obliterated what had started off as a sunny day, the winds were strong and blowing at the *Maverick*'s stern. The topsails and mainsails were fully engaged, and the augmented blasterbeefs were operating at optimum capacity.

"Smooth sailing," Tuck noted as he approached the ship's wheel.

"At this rate," StarMan said while navigating the airship over Kentshire, "we'll be in Paris by morning."

"The sooner, the better." Their venture into that skytown two nights past had afforded them a lucrative job, but not without risk. Sky pirates and corrupt air constables would kill to get their hands on his current cargo, a shipment of contraband alcohol that would earn a fortune on the black market. Were he less scrupulous and lacking vision, he'd be tempted to abscond with the cargo himself. Instead, Tuck focused on making the delivery, collecting the second half of their fee, and spending a few days in a Parisian dove's bed before moving on to the next job.

His lust stirred as he recollected the flexibility and enthusiasm of Chantel, a buxom brunette who operated out of Le Chabanais, a luxurious brothel near the Louvre. The last time he'd been in the City of Light she'd lit up his—

A horn blasted.

"Dig ahead!"

Tuck and StarMan looked up through the transparent thermoplastic shield surrounding the cockpit just as Bird-man Chang leaned over the side of the iron-grilled crow's nest. "Incoming!" he announced through the amplified dual-purpose megahorn. "Starboard bow!"

Tuck peered through his spyglass. "Hard to port!"

StarMan spun the wheel, veering the *Maverick* off a collision course at the same time as the two-person dirigible took a hard turn.

"What the hell?" Tugging down his Stetson, Tuck strode to the starboard, where Eli and Axel had already gathered to watch the show.

"Came out of nowhere." The flaps of Eli's aviator cap whipped in the frigid wind as he leaned over the gunwale for a better look. "What is that thing?"

Axel whistled around the unlit cigar clamped between his teeth. "Quart bottle of whiskey says they bite the dust."

Tuck focused his spyglass. Sure enough, what looked like a cross between a motorized tandem bicycle, da Vinci's glider, and an oversize kite bucked and reared, then took a fateful nosedive.

"Cut the blasterbeefs," Tuck shouted to StarMan. "Bring to and hoist the bally." Trading his Stetson for a fly cap, he turned to Eli. "Grab three packs."

The person seated in the rear of the flimsy flying apparatus bailed, and soon after a parachute opened and billowed. That harnessed sail wasn't the only thing flapping in the wind. Skirts and petticoats caught the men's eyes.

"Damn," Axel said, squinting through his goggles. "That's a woman."

"Looks like the pilot's going down with the ship," Eli noted as the three men buckled on steam-and-nitrogen-powered Pogo Packs.

"Fighting to regain control," Tuck said while adjusting his harness and tank.

"Crazy as a loon," Axel said, tugging on gloves and gripping the hand controls.

Tuck disagreed. "Ballsy." The three men fired up the deafening blasters and launched overboard. From what he could tell, that pilot had some impressive skills. Even so, the flying contraption continued a speedy descent. At the last second, the dirigible leveled off, but still hit the ground at a jarring speed, skidding, then rolling into a snow-covered embankment.

By the time the men touched down, that two-person flying machine was a tangle of twisted metal, hissing steam, ripped sails, and one ballsy pilot.

Hearing a whoosh and thud, followed by a stream of foreign ranting, the men turned and saw the woman who'd bailed, wrestling to escape the trappings of the ropes and canvas.

Eli shrugged off his still-hissing pack—"I'll get her, Marshal"—then trotted toward the caterwauling female.

"Least that one's alive," Axel said as he and Tuck moved in the opposite direction toward the crashed dirigible.

Tuck noted a pair of thick-soled boots sticking out of the mangled wreck, but no movement. As they drew closer he saw those boots were attached to some mighty shapely legs—legs clad in tight leather pants.

A feminine moan sounded from beneath the rubble, quickening both men's pace.

"Damn," Axel said. "That ballsy pilot's a woman?"

"Seems like." Tuck's respect for her flying skills doubled.

They unbuckled the cumbersome Pogo Packs in order to dig her out. Just as they reached for the bent frame, a bird screeched and swooped close to their heads before settling on the wreckage.

Axel spit away his cigar. "What the hell is that?"

"A falcon."

"Yeah, but look at its legs and beak."

"Interesting."

"Mechanical body parts on a bird? Seems a waste of ingenuity."

"Not for the bird." Goggles now dangling around his neck, Tuck tugged off his leather gloves and stuffed them in the pockets of his overcoat. Seemed to him that enhanced falcon was protective of the lady pilot. Fascinating. He edged closer and the falcon flapped and screeched.

Axel jerked his Remington Blaster from his holster. "Vamoose or roast, you iron-beaked pecker."

Rubble shifted as the pilot pushed into a wavering sitting position, some manner of a pistol aimed at Axel's private parts. "Harm one feather on Leo and I promise I shall roast another kind of pecker altogether."

Tuck grinned at that. "Just trying to help, ma'am."

Using her free hand to push her fur-rimmed goggles onto her forehead, she blinked to clear her vision. Her dazed blue gaze hopped from Tuck to Axel, then skyward, to where the *Maverick* now hovered. "Were you to steer your ship responsibly, I would not be in this predicament."

"Of all the sass," Axel remarked while holstering his piece.

Flygirl lowered her weapon as well and visually absorbed the wreckage. "Crikey," she complained, voice brittle. "Look what you've done to Bess."

Tuck assumed she was referring to her flying machine. He might have felt worse if she'd stop faulting him and his boat for her misfortune. "Plenty of time to sort blame," he said. "Let's get you out from under that mess, make sure you're in good workin' order." He stepped closer, soothing the falcon's angst with a gentle signal of peace. Leo shifted his weight, but stood down.

"I say, how did you manage that?" Flygirl asked.

"Marshal's got a way with animals," Axel said as he lifted away a mangled kite wing.

She winced as Tuck disengaged her boot from the twisted pedal. "I suppose you cannot be all that bad then, Mr. Marshal."

"Name's Tuck." Admiring her disarmingly pretty face, he helped the frank young woman to her booted feet. "Tucker Gentry."

Favoring her left leg, she slipped her pistol into the coat's pocket and gaped. "The Sky Cowboy?"

"In the flesh," Axel answered for him, nudging aside a bent wheel to retrieve a carpetbag and leather satchel from the snow.

"Did you twist your ankle?" Tuck asked. "Do you hurt anywhere else?"

"I'm fine." She licked her full lips, then glanced up. "So that's the *Maverick*?" she asked in an awestruck tone.

"It is." Tuck was captivated as well. Flygirl was beautiful. A tad young for his taste, but striking. Although her heart-shaped face was smudged with grease and red from the brisk cold, her complexion was flawless, her eyes as blue as the clear skies of Arizona on a dry, hot day. Her hair was hidden beneath a fleece-lined aviator cap, but given her fair brows, he guessed corn silk blond. As for her lips . . . damn, he'd like to kiss that rosebud mouth.

Staring up at his airship, she whispered, "Beautiful."

"She's something, all right," Tuck said, though he wasn't talking about his ship. Even though Flygirl wore a thick leather duster, mannish boots, and had two colorful scarves wrapped around her neck, he was well aware of her womanly form.

She met his gaze, causing lustful thoughts to scorch his brain. *Well, damn.* "Listen, Miss . . ."

"Darcy," Eli said, coming up from behind. "And this is Concetta, her traveling companion."

The dark-haired, olive-skinned woman shook a finger at Flygirl. "I knew this mistake!" she railed with a heavy accent. "You said you see me safely to *Italia*!"

Miss Darcy burst to infuriated life. "I would have if not for these sky pigs!"

"You sayin' we were hoggin' the sky?" Axel asked, outraged. "We were in the right. A mite dig like yours should have been flying at a lower altitude."

"The air current was better higher," Miss Darcy argued.

"You aimed on flying that winged bicycle all the way to Italy?" Tuck asked, astounded.

"I would have done it too, if not for you."

His blood burned. "Hold up."

"Now what am I supposed to do?" she asked, hobbling in a circle. "You've ruined everything!"

"We can take you as far as Paris," Eli said.

Tuck shot him a look.

The bighearted son of a former slave gestured to the isolated landscape. "We can't just leave them here."

Amelia's blue eyes sparked, and her sexy leather-clad body perked. "You're traveling to Paris, France? Spectacular. I accept."

Tuck tensed. No woman had ever boarded the *Maverick* in the midst of a job. The crew couldn't afford the distraction, especially with someone as distracting as Miss Darcy. How could he trust his men—the majority not having been at port in two weeks—to behave like gentlemen? Hell, how was he supposed to trust himself?

"Eli spoke out of turn," Tuck said.

"Damned straight," Axel said. "Talk about trouble."

"Eli," she said with a nod toward the big man, "is a gentleman. I am most grateful for his kindness." She smiled then at Axel and pointed up. "If you wouldn't mind putting our luggage aboard."

"Of all the—"

Concetta marched forward and snatched her carpetbag from the man's hands. "I will go nowhere with these outlaws," she said in broken English. "You are foolish like your *padre*," she told Flygirl. "Like him you will die."

The blue-eyed hellion flushed and Concetta bolted.

Eli looked to Tuck. "Give me the dinghy and an hour or so. There was a village a few miles back. I'll drop Miss Concetta there and return faster than chain lightnin' with a link snapped."

So much for being ahead of schedule. "An hour," Tuck said. Eli was right: They couldn't abandon these women to the elements and road ruffians.

Hollering for Concetta, who'd taken off on foot, Eli hefted his pack and hurried after.

"Good heavens," Flygirl exclaimed. "Is that a working rocket belt?"

"Pogo Pack," Tuck said. "Good for short vertical flights."

"I've never seen one."

"And you won't," Axel said, chomping on a new cigar. "Not on the open market."

Eli, who was arguing with the ill-tempered woman, finally lost patience and tapped her with his stun cuff. She wilted in his arms and ten seconds later they were airborne.

"Astonishing," Flygirl whispered as they blasted straight up and disappeared over the side of the *Maverick*.

Hoping she'd be willing to join Concetta for a dinghy ride back north, Tuck looked to the mesmerized woman, trying to ignore her infectious wonder. "Since your friend no longer requires your services, seems you've got no reason to visit Italy."

Awe turned to panic. "I have every reason!" She gulped air, then felled him with desperate eyes. "My grandfather lives there and he is dying. I must travel to Italy in haste." She gestured to her wrecked dirigible, then glared at Tuck. "You owe me."

"Hold on," Axel interrupted before Tuck could give her an earful. "Darcy?" He narrowed his eyes, then raised one condemning brow. "You related to that kook who blew himself up building a moonship?"

She fisted her hands. "If by kook you mean visionary, then yes."

Tuck blinked. A few days ago Axel, an irritatingly superstitious man as well as a fierce fan of that scandal sheet the *London Informer*, had shared the curious article with the gang over an evening meal. Which had led to a heated discussion regarding Lord Ashford's infamous cousin, time travel, and the Peace Rebels.

Axel swiped off his slouch hat and slapped it to his thigh. "If that don't cap the climax," he said to Tuck. "Told you she was a loon. Runs in the family."

Sore as a frog on a hot skillet, she launched herself at the burly Irishman, clipping him in the jaw just as Tuck grabbed her by the waist and hauled her back.

The falcon screeched.

"Damn!" Cringing at the earsplitting noise, Axel covered his assaulted ear with one hand and rubbed his jaw with the other.

"You asked for it," Tuck said, sensitive to the woman's distress. Christ's sake, she'd just lost her pa. And now her grandpap was fading?

Flygirl smacked at his arms. "Unhand me!"

Tuck ignored her and held tight. "Settle down."

"Not to mention she's related to Briscoe Darcy," Axel barreled on. "Thanks to him—"

"That's enough." According to diversified sources, the infamous Time Voyager was either a savior or an annihilator of mankind. Either way, Tuck grew more intrigued with Flygirl Darcy by the moment.

Still squirming, she flailed a fist at Axel. "Don't tell me you're an Old Worlder. Or worse, a Flatliner."

"Don't reckon my political or social views are your business, Miss Crazy Pants." He, too, shook a fist.

The falcon swooped, grazing Axel's knuckles with his talons, causing the man to yelp and draw his Blaster.

Miss Darcy cried out.

"Holster your weapon, Ax." Tuck squeezed Flygirl's waist. "Call off the bird."

"Leo!" She gestured and the falcon settled on a leafless tree branch.

Axel sucked his scraped knuckles and glared.

Miss Darcy turned in Tuck's arms, gut-twisting misery clouding those pretty eyes. "My family has suffered a great loss," she railed. "And now ... if you do not take me ... if I do not get to Italy in time ... I shall never forgive you."

He wasn't sure what swayed him: her beauty, her circumstance, or her fighting spirit. It sure as blazes wasn't her charm. "To Paris, but no farther."

"Damnation," Axel complained.

She blew out a sigh of relief as he set her on her feet. "Right then," she said, bolstering her shoulders as she turned to the ship's engineer. "I am sorry Leo hurt you, but he is most protective."

"Obviously."

"You would do well to mind your manners, Mr. . . . . Axel."

Tuck cut off the man's retort with a sharp look. "I'll take Miss Darcy. You get the luggage."

"And do what you must to hoist Bess aboard," she added.

"What the hell for?" Axel barked.

"To what purpose?" Tuck asked while buckling on his Pogo Pack.

"So that I may resurrect her, of course."

He eyed the destruction as Flygirl and her falcon prepared to board his airship. If she could repair that mess, Miss Darcy was a damned miracle worker. Then again, she *was* related to the Time Voyager.

"Put your arms around me and hold tight." Tuck's blood burned as she pressed against him and clung. She smelled of wind, leather, grease, and lilac soap. Not nearly as pretty as Chantel's French perfume, but somehow twice as enticing. Damn. "Ready?"

She smiled up at him, then at the sky. "Oh, yes."

Oh, hell. Were he charging for the ride, he would have asked for hazard pay. As far as cargo went, Miss Darcy was more dangerous than a crate of nitroglycerin.

CHAPTER 4

Astonishing how one miscalculation had obliterated her logical, if not perfect plan to reach Italy, losing her transportation and translator to boot. Amelia could hardly be blamed for concocting a ruse and manipulating the situation. She was, after all, desperate. Not to mention that this quirk of fate had landed her in the company of her aeronautical hero. Even his rumored crimes couldn't dampen her excitement. In her eyes, his past heroics and present exploits overshadowed the transgression that had pulverized his reputation and rendered him a wanted man. In her heart, she believed his claim that he had been falsely accused of stealing invaluable art from a powerful American judge and then murdering the man's daughter in order to cover the theft. *Crikey.* Anyone who'd read about Gentry's long history of valiant and noble deeds knew that atrocity went against the lawman's very nature.

A former United States air marshal, Tucker Gentry had policed wild territories and protected and saved countless lives. His courage and daring on the ground and in the air were as legendary as his flying skills. Amelia had been following his adventures as featured in the penny dreadfuls for years, and most recently through the *Informer*. True, that newspaper was not quality press, but the stories pertaining to Gentry had been in line with anything she'd ever read and offered a grittier peek into his life. Though accounts were assuredly embellished, she trusted they were rooted in truth and that he was indeed a good man.

Now here he was in the flesh.

Her mind spun with dazed reverence and wonder, causing her heart to flutter in a most bizarre fashion.

Perhaps she had sustained a severe head injury and this was indeed wishful, addled thinking. A grand hallucination. Yet she could feel the brisk wind upon her cheeks and a painful throbbing in her thigh. Could taste blood where she'd bitten the inside of her cheek upon impact. She could smell fuel, tobacco, and bay rum cologne. Surely this was real. As such, she intended to embrace the opportunity and to benefit from the knowledge, skill, and advanced technology of Tucker Gentry.

Amelia's stomach flipped and her heart pounded as he readied his Pogo Pack for launch. She chalked up the dizzy sensation to anticipation—her first rocket-pack ride—and not infatuation. Although she couldn't deny he was an absurdly attractive man.

At first she'd been too dazed to notice, struck dotty by the bone-jarring crash. Then too angry as his brawny, quick-tempered, thickheaded sidekick had threatened Leo with his enormous gun. Then, after seeing the wreckage that was once Bess, too distressed. The enormity of the debacle had made her physically ill. Papa had spent countless hours building that kitecycle, and though Bess wasn't perfect, she was proof of his extraordinary imagination and tireless efforts. Amelia had tried to save her, hoping to regain control and altitude, but she'd failed.

Miserably.

She knew Mr. Gentry doubted her ability to repair Bess, but she'd show him. And Papa.

"Put your arms around me and hold tight."

Amelia did as he asked, and her heart nearly burst through her cinched wool corset. She'd never embraced a man before, except for Papa and her brothers, but this was vastly different. Perhaps it was hero worship, but quite simply, the Sky Cowboy scrambled her senses. Beyond tall, fit, and devilishly handsome, he possessed confidence and charisma and, by jiminy, a rocket pack!

He buckled a strap around her waist, cinching them close as pages in a book. "Ready?"

She smiled up into his bourbon-colored gaze, stomach fluttering like a flock of wrens. His mouth was most distracting. How bizarre that she was thinking of kissing him just now instead of flying. Embarrassed, Amelia glanced skyward. "Oh, yes."

He thumbed a control and, with a rumble and roar, they shot straight up.

The inertia . . . the exhilaration . . . Amelia whooped with joy!

"Damn," the cowboy complained, and she realized she'd screamed in his ear.

She forced her head back to apologize but saw he was smiling. She smiled back. She couldn't help it. Few thrills compared.

It was over much too soon. In a heartbeat they were up and over the side of the massive airship and Amelia was privy to a new sensation. As she lived and breathed, she was aboard the *Maverick*! The wonder of it all—the collapsed masts and sails that had given way to a steam-powered balloon, the gleaming outboard blasterbeefs—almost made her forget about her throbbing thigh. Almost. She winced when her boots hit the deck.

"You all right?" Tucker asked while unbuckling the strap.

She'd just seen stars, but she shook off the pain, intent on showing no weakness in front of this man or his crew. "Splendid."

He didn't look convinced. He pushed his goggles to his forehead, raised one tawny brow. "You can let go now."

She realized with a start that she had a stranglehold on his neck. Mortified, she hobbled back, trying like the devil to ignore the searing pain in her leg. She noted several men of various ethnicities, most looking close in age to her brothers, all dressed in a combination of American West and Victorian England attire and displaying various degrees of Mod-influenced body art: pierced ears and eyebrows, intricate tattoos. She'd seen no such marks or piercings on the Sky Cowboy, which made her ponder the body beneath his clothes.

Cheeks burning, she averted her mind from those tawdry thoughts, self-conscious now as the unique collage of men moved in and took stock of her. Probably she should be nervous, given their scandalous reputation, given their intimidating presence, but she was quite simply intrigued.

Whilst the crew stared at Amelia, a man whom she guessed to be American Indian, given the color of his skin and his ink black braids, stepped forward to relieve Mr. Gentry of his pack. "Eli filled us in before he pushed off with that other woman," he said in a low voice. "You sure about this, Tuck?"

The devastatingly handsome man nodded and traded his aviator cap for a black Stetson. Now he truly looked like the Sky Cowboy of penny-dreadful fame, from his wide-brimmed, round crown hat to his billowing black duster to his pointy-toed boots. Amelia mentally cursed another attack of stomach wrens and focused on the soft-spoken Indian.

"A woman on board?" He glanced at the cowboy's vexing sidekick. "Surprised Axel didn't pitch a fit."

"Didn't give him the chance."

Axel grunted. "First thing goes wrong—"

"Never mind that." Tuck looked to the rest of the crew, then nodded toward Amelia. "This is Miss Darcy."

"Amelia Darcy," she said with what she hoped was a friendly smile. After all, she'd be traveling with these men for days. No need to tempt their bad favor. She'd already knocked heads with Mr. Brawn-Brain. "Pleased to make your acquaintance, Mr. . . . ."

"StarMan. No mister."

"Chief navigator and copilot," Tuck said.

His name and position explained the inked design slashing across one high cheekbone. "The Big Dipper," Amelia noted with wonder.

StarMan nodded, a hint of a smile tugging at his no-nonsense mouth.

"Blooming fantastic," she whispered.

Tuck diverted her attention, pointing out the other men and assigning names to faces. "Birdman Chang, Doc Blue. You've met Axel O'Donnell, Maverick's engineer, and Eli Boone, a tinker of many talents."

"What's that?" Chang asked, pointing over her shoulder.

"A menace," Axel said as he abandoned Amelia's satchel and shrugged off his pack.

"Leo," Amelia corrected, counting the small gold hoops piercing Chang's right ear from lobe to upper cartilage. *Six*.

"Mind your manners around Miss Darcy, boys," Axel warned with an eye roll. "Otherwise that iron-beaked pecker will rip you a new one."

"Don't reckon you should talk like that around a lady," Doc said to Axel.

Amelia smiled at the man. Maybe she had at least one ally on board. "So you're the ship's physician?"

"And cook."

"Fixes up food better than people," StarMan said, then looked to Doc. "Meant that as a compliment."

Doc Blue, who looked to be near her own age, just smiled. Of all of the men, he was the slightest in frame. Muscular, yet wiry. Pale enough to be Scandinavian, though not as tall as she imagined a typical Norseman to be, and his accent was most definitely American. His fair hair was cut in a choppy fashion, as if he'd sliced it willy-nilly with a scalpel. She wondered if his eyes, hidden behind tinted blue goggles, were blue as well. Hence his name? Each hand was inked with a different symbol, something Celtic perhaps.

She wondered at their meaning. Boyishly handsome, Doc struck her as a man of good humor and tolerance.

Birdman Chang was shorter in stature, though his clothes hinted at an impressive muscular physique. Of Chinese descent, he had dark eyes that danced with curiosity whilst he vibrated with a caged energy that made her skin itch. Although his hair was black as a starless night, it was not long and braided, as one might assume, but short and wild, like Doc's. His sleeves were rolled to his elbows, and she was mesmerized by the intricate designs that covered his forearms—wrists to elbow and perhaps beyond.

The other men were much taller. All intimidating, although some more than others. All handsome in a rugged, rebellious way. Again she marveled at the varied races. Indian, Oriental, Scandinavian. Eli Boone, though absent just now, had impressed her as a fine-looking black man with large, kind eyes. Axel had fierce features and an odd accent, although his surname and flaming red hair suggested Irish descent. She realized suddenly that every man was scrutinizing her as intensely as she was studying them.

Amelia detected a combination of interest and aversion. Unsettling on both counts. She decided then and there that a brazen demeanor would be her best defense.

"When you're done gawking at Miss Darcy," Tucker told his men, "help Axel upload her dig."

"You mean that mangled heap of rubble?" Chang asked.

Axel smirked. "She's gonna fix it."

I'll fix you, Amelia wanted to say, but she was suddenly too weary to fight. Her thigh hurt to distraction now, and when she shifted she yelped.

Doc frowned. "You didn't say she was hurt, Marshal."

"She said she was fine." Tucker crouched to inspect her ankle. "What the . . ."

"Boot's soaked with blood," StarMan noted.

Light-headed now, Amelia grasped the rail. "It's my thigh."

Tucker lifted away the hem of her duster. "Ah, Christ."

Doc leaned in, then just as quickly pushed off. "Take her below. I'll get my bag."

"My cabin!" Tuck called after the man.

Amelia tried to look but couldn't see. The injury was on the back of her thigh. "I thought it was a bruise."

"That ain't no bruise," Axel said, his unlit cigar dangling from his lower lip. "Damn, girl."

The other men whistled and shook their heads.

Panicked a little now, Amelia swallowed hard. "What is it? What's wrong?"

"Nothin' Doc can't fix," Tucker said. "Hush now, darlin', and don't fuss."

When Tucker rose, he lifted her up and over his shoulder. Before she could argue, he ordered the men to attend to Bess, then, toting Amelia like a sack of flour, carried her toward the stern and down a ladder. She tried to absorb her surroundings, but her upside-down vantage point was most disconcerting. From what she could tell, though, the *Maverick,* unlike the *Flying Cloud,* was in top form. Wood and brass gleamed, and the scents ranged from lemon polish to grease to engine fumes, coffee, and leather. At one point she thought she smelled fresh hay and licorice.

She tried not to think about the bloody awful pain in her leg, about what those men had seen and why they'd looked disconcerted. Surely it couldn't be that bad. She thought about poor Jules and how his leg injuries had resulted in a permanent limp. *There are worse things,* she told herself. She could fly with a limp. Although maybe not the kitecycle. What if she could no longer pedal?

"Is Doc really better at fixing food than people?" Amelia asked, cursing the wobble in her voice. "Not to offend, but he doesn't appear old enough to have much experience in the medical field."

"Doc's an enlightened soul and a man of many talents." Tucker kicked open an ajar door and moved into a dark-paneled room. The last light of day streaked through the windows in tandem with the artificial light beaming from at least three lamps. She pondered the brightness and realized the halls had been illuminated as well, though she hadn't smelled kerosene. Electricity?

"Put her on the bed," Doc said.

She spied a massively large mattress covered with an exquisite bone-and-black woven coverlet and several pillows. "Is that your bed?" she asked Tucker. "I cannot—"

"You can and you will."

"Need access to that wound," Doc said as he rifled through his black bag.

"Hold tight to me when I set you down, Flygirl, and don't put weight on your injured leg."

Amelia blanched as Tucker set her gingerly to the floor. "I'm not taking off my trousers." No man had ever seen her in her bloomers, and these particular homespun bloomers were somewhat snug and sparse in material—as was needed when wearing her formfitting flight pants.

"Then I'll have to cut away enough leather for Doc to work," he said.

She mourned the potential loss of her flight pants. "So be it."

Feeling woozier by the minute, she held on to the lapel of Tucker's coat, using one hand to aid him in ridding her of her scarves and coat. Beneath she wore her unconventional leather breeches and a wool brocade corsetlike bodice over a loose white blouse.

The Sky Cowboy's gaze fell to her bountiful cleavage but did not linger. She knew not whether to be insulted or impressed. Feeling exposed and vulnerable, she couldn't think straight—although she knew for certain that her mother would condemn her for lying upon this virile man's bed. Inappropriate. Scandalous. Amelia almost smiled.

He indicated the mattress, which sat quite high on an ornate frame. "Do you need help or can you manage?"

"I'll get blood on your coverlet."

"I don't care—"

"But—"

"Dammit, woman." He swiped away the quality piece and replaced it with an ordinary green wool blanket.

Doc turned and she noticed he had traded his tinted goggles for blue-tinted spectacles, although they resembled goggles, given their thick frames and wraparound fashion. "Do you prefer laudanum or chloroform?" he asked.

"Neither."

"Whiskey then."

"No."

This time Tucker got in her face. "It's gonna hurt like hell, Flygirl."

It hurt like bloody hell now. "Why?" she asked, swiping off her flight cap and pivoting on her good leg to lie across the bed. "What is it? A cut? Do I need stitches? I've had them before. I assure you I can stand the prick of a needle."

She was blustering a bit with that last part. Times before the physician had dulled the pain. Just now she needed her wits about her. Lord forbid she slip about her true mission due to a drug-induced stupor. She did not trust Tucker Gentry and his gang—or any man, for that matter—not to rob her of her invention of historical significance. Surely they knew about the jubilee contest and prize.

Tucker rounded the bed, shrugged out of his overcoat, and stooped so he faced her eye to eye. "You've got a metal shard lodged in your thigh, Amelia. Doc's gonna have to extract it. Then he's going to disinfect the wound and stitch it closed."

"Oh." She swallowed hard. "Right then. Be done with it."

He swore under his breath, then moved behind her. The mattress sagged with added weight, and her cheeks burned at the thought of sharing his bed. Next she felt big hands— Tucker's hands—on her leg, felt him cutting and ripping the leather. She squeezed her eyes shut, mortified and more than a little nervous.

She heard someone else enter the room.

"Your instruments, Doc. Fresh out of boiled water, as requested."

From the slight Asian accent, she assumed that was Birdman Chang.

Her mortification mounted. "Please go."

"Stay," Tucker commanded. Next thing she knew he'd rounded the bed once again. He took her hands, squeezed. "Look at me, darlin'."

The endearment was inappropriate, although, at this moment, oddly comforting. She should dissuade him from such intimacy, and she would. At some point.

"Hold her steady," Doc said to Chang.

She felt strange hands upon her person and wanted to die. The need to live, however, was much stronger. She needed to save her family from financial ruin, to resurrect their reputation, her papa's name.

"How'd you come by those other injuries?" Tucker asked. "The ones that required stitches."

She knew he was striving to distract her and blessed him for it. "Flying incidents."

His lip twitched just as she felt a painful tug at her leg. She bit back a yelp, and breathed deeply. "Tell me about the engines on deck. Do they power the blasterbeefs? Supply the ship with electricity? How did you . . . How does it work?"

She closed her eyes and gritted her teeth as Doc Blue pulled metal from muscle. Never had she felt such blinding pain. She jerked and moaned, but she did not scream or cry. *Show no weakness*. She focused on Tucker's steady words— something about steam turbines—but then Doc bathed her wound with something that stung like a thousand wasps.

"Blooming hell," she hissed, wondering how big and deep the cut was, how long it would take Doc Blue to stitch her wound, anticipating the needle piercing her skin, the thread tugging, tightening. . . . She felt ill.

She opened her eyes to stem the nausea, mortified that damnable tears blurred her vision. She thought she saw Tucker nod at either Doc or Chang. Light-headed with pain, Amelia felt a swift tap at her temple, then blissful peace.

CHAPTER 5

"It is settled."

"Dismal business, this."

"A small and necessary price for the reformation and salvation of mankind."

Nine men. One goal. Or so eight of them thought.

The Viscount Bingham, odd man out and referred to in this covert society as code name Mars, noted the others' grim expressions with morbid humor. Men of peace, yet they plotted to assassinate the queen.

Hidden away in a secret room, seated around a table once owned by Sir John Flamsteed, a seventeenth-century astronomer and Britain's first astronomer royal, nine titled men of science and industry raised their crystal goblets to seal the treasonous pact.

"To the Age of Aquarius."

"Aquarius," they all repeated, vowing their silence and commitment with the mention of the society's name, the clink of glass on glass, and a swallow of port.

An astrological cycle of change revered by the Mods, Aquarius ruled electricity, flight, freedom, modernization, astrology, rebellion, and—among other things the Vics had yet to experience—computers. Though the precise year of arrival was in dispute, to those in this room, and many outside these walls, the Age of Aquarius was now.

Unfortunate that Queen Victoria, a woman ruled by staunch morals and bitter heartbreak, seemed intent on halting progress. As if she could go back in time by slowing time. All in the name of love. Damn her royal eyes. Were she to lift the ban on building and perfecting time-traveling devices, she could reunite with her deceased beloved, or perhaps save him in some fashion by time traveling herself. But that would involve altering history—something Briscoe Darcy and then the Peace Rebels had already done. Something she was very much against.

One would think, at the very least, that given Prince Albert's voracious appreciation of science, the queen would honor her husband's memory by allowing Mod technology to flourish. Instead, she denounced the development and sales of marvels, including rocket packs, telecommunicators, and advanced weaponry, to name only a few. Unlike her husband, she had never embraced the fantastical futuristic knowledge of the Peace Rebels. She was not surprised when that advanced knowledge and a few corrupt Mods ignited a war and divided society. And she was famously bitter when that advanced knowledge had failed to save Prince Albert's life. Unlike the men in this room (and much of the altered world), Queen Victoria saw no advantage in cultivating twentieth-century technology—technology that, according to the Book of Mods, had steered mankind toward the brink of destruction.

New Worlders were of a different mind. Knowledge was power, and, knowing what could be, they would choose an alternate path, using technology only for good.

As a Flatliner, Bingham cared only about what futuristic knowledge could do for *him*. He saw himself as a visionary and entrepreneur, and as far as he was concerned, this assassination was long overdue. The difference between Bingham and the other eight plotters was that they approached this "elimination" with trepidation. In order to soothe their consciences, they'd adopted the noble mind-set that they were sacrificing the regal one for the good of the many. Bingham wanted the deed done, period. No regrets. Only a promise of a brighter future. *His* shining future. Rather than risk his freedom and life by orchestrating the assassination on his own, he'd sought out progressive souls (and potential scapegoats), tripping upon this society.

Jupiter set aside his goblet and initiated talk of possible locations for the unsavory deed. The attack would take place during the Golden Jubilee, a monumental event honoring the queen's fiftieth anniversary of her accession. There would be much pomp and circumstance over the two-day period, and in some instances chaos due to the clamoring masses—some adoring, some disenchanted.

But where did Aquarius stand the best chance of success? Where could they do the most harm and therefore the most good? Where should they strike? The train en route from Windsor to Paddington? Buckingham Palace? Westminster Abbey? Or perhaps the procession through London? They were privy to the chain of events and closely guarded details, thanks to having a man on the inside—a boon that had come at substantial cost. Now to use that information wisely.

Bingham listened with interest and disgust as his cohorts bickered. Their utopian mind-set was frivolous, but their objective—to unleash and embrace the advanced knowledge of several brilliant and reclusive Mods—served his purpose well. That advanced knowledge included specifics on how to construct futuristic wonders in the realms of transportation, weapons, and communications—knowledge that would make him a man of enormous wealth and power. He had finessed his way into this secret society with one goal—to monopolize the technological market worldwide. The British Empire would make a fine start.

Still, he did not trust these knobs not to falter in the moment of truth. To ensure his goals he'd set an additional plan into motion: the Royal Race for Rejuvenation—an event that he'd secretly coordinated with the Jubilee Science Committee. As the anonymous benefactor, Bingham would have full access to progress reports and discoveries pertaining to legendary inventions. He had cast a wide net in order to disguise the narrow scope of his intent—to locate the designs, prototype, or key component connected to a working time machine.

Because of his rumored close connection to Briscoe Darcy, Lord Ashford had been an obvious source of information. Yet fraternizing with that eccentric bumpkin and his idiotic wife had not produced the desired results. As for their daughter, though she was a tempting bit of flesh, Amelia Darcy's temperament proved a barrier. If she possessed valuable knowledge pertaining to time travel, she would not willingly share it with Bingham. Forcing information out of her might prove morbid fun, but what if his efforts proved unsuccessful? That particular venture struck him as risky and unwise; therefore he'd devised the Triple R contest.

Broadening his horizons had been crucial in his inspired quest. Were he to possess a working time-traveling machine, such as the one devised by Briscoe Darcy and copied by the Peace Rebels, futuristic intelligence would be his for the taking. Unfortunately, the construction of time machines had been outlawed. Of the two successful models, Darcy's was rumored to be stuck in the future and the Mods' destroyed, the engineering designs of both hidden or lost . . . unless someone recovered them. He cared not who, but Bingham's money was on a Darcy. To ensure that all three of Ashford's offspring participated in the global treasure hunt, he'd issued personal, albeit anonymous, invitations.

One way or another Bingham would be a global technological kingpin.

"What if this . . . *elimination* is the wrong path?" Venus said, jerking Bingham out of his musings and back to plan A.

Mercury raised a brow. "You voice doubt now that we have sealed the pact?"

"Playing devil's advocate."

"How can it be the wrong path when it is different?" Saturn asked. "Every change we make carries us farther from what will be if nothing goes unchanged."

"But the Peace Rebels already altered the course of history by traveling back in time and sharing their knowledge and infecting us with fear, greed, and wonder. What was to be will not be. At least not precisely so."

"The greater the change," Bingham said calmly, "the greater the chance of utopia." He fairly choked on the word, as if he gave a rat's arse, but the sparks in the others' eyes urged him on. "Had the Peace Rebels not intervened, the world would be destined for destruction in 1969, blown to smithereens by nuclear bombs. Thirty-one years after the Mods' invasion, we are not, as you said, what we had once been. In their history books, the four-year transcontinental Peace War did not exist, the American Civil War lasted four, not three years, and Prince Albert, rest his soul, died in 1861 instead of 1869. History has been altered. But has the course of mankind? Knowledge is power, and the more advanced we are, the wiser our actions. If we embrace twentieth-century knowledge now," Bingham said with more conviction, "we could be populating other planets by 1969. Discovery, not destruction, would be our focus. Living in hope, not fear."

"Hear, hear!"

They applauded his views, and, for their benefit, Bingham smiled in appreciation. On the inside he was laughing. How gullible these New Worlders were. "Now," he said, while he had their ear and favor, "as to where to strike, I have a suggestion."

CHAPTER 6

"Said it before and I'll say it again: A woman on board is bad luck."

Tuck pushed aside his plate of food, his appetite slim as a bed slat, and frowned across the table at Axel. "Near as I recollect, that's the sixth time you've mentioned that superstitious crock since we sat down to eat."

"Yeah, Ax," Eli groused as he peppered his stew. "Give it a rest."

The big man who'd escorted Concetta to the safety of a village had returned three hours ago, his normally jovial mood unusually prickly. Eli had yet to shake his irritation. Then again, Tuck thought, Concetta had been as thorny as a bramble, and now Ax was bitchin' up a dust storm.

"Thing is," Tuck went on, "that's a sailor's myth. We're not at sea. We're in air. We're not sailors; we're skymen."

"But this here is a ship."

"A flying ship," Eli clarified.

"Mark my words," Axel said while tossing a handful of salt over his hunched shoulder, "we're in for some rough weather, thanks to her."

"Not that I'm siding with Axel," Doc said, "but Miss Darcy could prove a distraction for the crew. Considering our cargo, we need to be extra vigilant."

Tuck couldn't argue with that. Amelia was distracting for a whole lot of reasons.

"All that sass irritates my bowels," Axel added, then drank deeply from his iron mug.

"That sass might be what makes her a tolerable guest," Eli said. "Least she's not fragile."

"That's for sure and certain," Doc remarked.

"Still think you're funnin'," Axel said as he tore off a chunk of brown bread. "That piece of metal was wedged deep. She didn't whine? Or give you hell when you did your mendin'?"

"Not once. No crying either. Nor would she allow me to numb the pain. As I've stated before."

Four times exactly, to Tuck's recollection.

"Impressive," said Eli.

To say the least. For the second time in a day, Tuck had been stunned by Amelia's courage and stubborn determination. He'd been the one to buckle. When he'd seen her blinking back tears, the sweat on her brow, the greenish tint of that creamy white skin, he'd given Birdman a silent order to put her under. Proficient in the Chinese art of acupressure, Birdman had used a mere tap to render her unconscious, putting both Amelia and the men out of their misery. Watching her suffer in unnecessary pain hadn't been easy.

"Much obliged," Doc had said, then attacked his work with steadier hands.

That had been hours ago. Presently, Amelia was sleeping in Tuck's cabin. In his bed. He tried not to dwell on that. Or the vision of her fine bare legs as he'd peeled off those trousers so that Doc could dress the wound. Ridding her of that corset had almost robbed him of his good sense and manner. She'd been clad only in that low-cut blouse and those brief bloomers. All that skin. The lean curve of her thighs and calves. The generous swell of her breasts. Distraction be damned—Amelia Darcy was fast becoming an obsession.

"She'll rally, right, Doc?" Eli asked.

"She'll rally."

Tuck agreed, but again held silent. He didn't want to talk or think about Amelia Darcy. Superstition had nothing to do with it. His gut warned of a large dollop of trouble, and his gut was always right. The one time he'd chosen to ignore it had cost him dearly. Family. Home. Reputation.

"Here's a question for you," Axel said. "You said Miss Darcy needs to get to Italy on account of a dyin' granddad. According to that article reporting her pa's accident, that girl has two older brothers." He raised a suspicious brow. "Why ain't they travelin' with her?"

"Inexcusable," Eli said in between bites. "Don't they care about seein' their dyin' kin and protecting their sister from scalawags?"

Axel shook his head. "Wouldn't leave my little sister to fend for herself. No way, no how."

Tuck didn't react. Not visibly. But everyone else around the galley table did. Forks and mugs stilled midmouth. No one spoke. No one moved. Tuck needed air and he needed it now. The legs of his chair scraped across the wooden floor, breaking the silence. "Time for me to relieve StarMan."

"Oh, hell. Damn, Marshal, I didn't mean—"

He cut off Axel with a raised hand. "I know."

"Nice going," Eli muttered under his breath.

Axel cleared his throat, then stood. "Guess I should be getting back to work, too. Turbine's been acting up. Thanks for the hot stew, Doc. Real treat."

"Sure." Doc stood and reached out as Tuck passed, then thought better of it. "Barely touched your food, Marshal."

"No reflection on the cook."

"Fruit and nut scones for dessert. Picked them up yesterday—"

"Maybe later." Tuck pulled on his overcoat and left the cramped and stifling galley, striving to keep his stride measured and calm. Typically he took his evening meal at the table in his cabin, a time of solace as he read through literature and periodicals of interest, but since Amelia was sleeping there . . .

He was nearing the ladder leading topside when he spied her: hobbling along at a slug's pace, shoulder against the wall for stability. She looked vulnerable and beautiful and two seconds from falling on her pretty face. He wanted to thrash and ravage her at the same time.

"What are you doing?" he asked, bolstering Amelia by the shoulders.

"Looking for you."

"To give me hell, no doubt. Something you can do in my cabin." He frowned when she stiffened under his touch. Obstinate as a mule.

"I do not wish to return to the cabin. I need fresh air." She felled him with those intense blue eyes. "And an explanation."

Well, hell.

At least she'd had the presence of mind to pull on her duster, covering the skin that tempted good men to do wrong. "Icy and windy on deck," he said, intimating that the duster alone was insufficient against the elements. Hoping she'd reconsider instead of risking her already compromised health.

She produced her fur-trimmed goggles and a black felt disk that, when popped, expanded into a worn top hat. Smirking, she pulled them on.

Tuck challenged her sass with a raised brow and a stipulation. "Only if I carry you."

"I don't—"

"Back to the cabin then."

"Insufferable sod," she mumbled under her breath.

"I've been called worse, darlin'."

Mindful of her bandaged thigh, he lifted her off her feet and up the ladder. To her credit, she didn't fuss.

Tuck hit the deck and cursed a primal twitch down south. Even the frigid night air failed to cool his illicit thoughts. She felt good in his arms. Right. Then again, he hadn't been with a woman in more than three weeks. Maybe any woman would feel right.

"I feel better already," Amelia said, breathing deeply.

"That makes one of us." He looked for a place to ditch his precious cargo.

"I'd prefer a view from the bow," she said as he prepared to set her on a rolled canvas.

"I've got better things to do than tote you around, Fly-girl."

"Then put me down. I'll have my say, then make my own way."

"You're just dyin' to bust open those stitches."

"I'll be careful."

"I doubt it." Irritated, he whisked her forward, ignoring StarMan's questioning gaze as they moved past the dimly lit cockpit.

"I don't know why you're so cross," Amelia huffed. "I'm the one who's been wronged."

"How so?"

"I specifically stated I wanted to be awake and aware, and you had me knocked out."

"I call the shots on this boat."

"Is that your idea of an apology?"

"No, darlin', it ain't."

"That's another thing. I insist you refrain from such intimacies. Endearments should be reserved for family and sweethearts, neither of which we are."

"Next?"

She narrowed her eyes. "You removed my trousers."

"Nothin' personal," he lied while settling her on a barrel that allowed her to peer over the gunwale. "Doc needed to bandage that leg proper-like. Don't worry. Birdman left the room prior to the . . . unveiling."

Her cheeks flushed and she looked away. "I can only hope you were gentleman enough to avert your eyes."

"Sorry to disappoint," he said, donning his own goggles against the strong winds. "I've never been one to turn away from a curiosity."

She cast him a furtive glance. "You considered my . . . my bare parts curious?"

His lip twitched at a hint of insecurity. A new and welcome twist. "Your legs are lovely, Miss Darcy. Your bloomers, what there was of them, are curious. Barely enough fabric to cover your lovely—"

"That's quite enough," she said, cheeks flushed. "And never mind my . . ."

"Unmentionables?"

"Precisely."

Her falcon swooped in and settled close by, as if sensing she needed saving—if only from an improper conversation. Tuck watched, mesmerized, as she smoothed delicate fingers over the bird's feathered head. He'd handled a canary and other such domesticated fowl, but never a falcon. He wanted to cover Amelia's hand with his own, to join her in stroking the majestic, albeit altered beauty, but he refrained. Her relationship with this falcon was personal. Tuck hesitated to intrude. Not to mention that holding Amelia's hand would be as inappropriate as discussing her bloomers. Still, he couldn't tear his gaze from the way she lovingly stroked that bird. He imagined those fingers stroking him and . . .

Christ.

"I know Leo is an oddity," Amelia said, breaking in on his randy thoughts, "but he is a valiant and good creature. Promise me Mr. O'Donnell won't hurt him."

Her quiet plea spoke to the deepest part of him. "Axel's more bluster than bite. Except in dire circumstances," he added. "Leo's safe." He'd see to it. Tuck had a long and deep appreciation of birds. As a boy he'd been obsessed with the way they glided through the air. He couldn't think of anything more thrilling than soaring through the open sky. Even now. However, Leo was a source of fascination for more than his ability to fly. Tuck wondered about his artificial parts. Who had made and applied them? How did they work? How did metal function with muscle? When the time was right, he'd ask. For the moment Tuck pulled back, reminding himself that Amelia, though feisty, was recovering from what would have been in the hands of a lesser pilot a fatal wreck. Instead of engaging her in deep conversation, he'd do better to snuff this meeting and escort her to bed. The only thing stopping him was her reverent appreciation of the view. Gazing over the bow, rosy lips curved in a smile, wind ruffling the tendrils that had escaped her messy coiled braids and tattered magician's hat . . . Amelia Darcy was a glorious sight.

"I've never flown at night. There is an added degree of danger," she said in a thoughtful voice. "As if navigating whilst wearing a blindfold."

"No different from sailing a ship on darkened seas." He moved in, his arm brushing hers as he pointed up. "We navigate by the stars and astronomical compendiums, an instrument that—"

"I know what it does, Mr. Gentry. I own one myself."

"Of course, you do."

"Probably not as fancy as yours."

"I'd wager not. Doesn't mean it's less dependable."

"Are you humoring me, sir?"

"Not at all, miss." He spoke close to her ear, breathing in her distinct scent. "In addition to conventional navigational means," he plowed on, "tonight we're blessed with the light of a nearly full moon. Truth told, we prefer travelin' when the sun's asleep. Less activity. Less chance of . . . unwanted encounters."

"You mean air constables." She quirked a wry grin. "Are you carrying illegal cargo, Mr. Gentry?"

"Never mind my cargo, Miss Darcy."

"According to the *Informer*, part of the reason you're able to circumvent 'unwanted encounters' is because of your customized blasterbeefs. I'm still uncertain as to how they operate."

"As am I."

She cast him a perplexed look. "But you designed—"

"With the help of an expert in the field. I'm a pilot, not an engineer."

"Is it true you outmaneuvered Frank and Jesse James in an aerial showdown?"

"Read a lot of dreadfuls, do you?"

"I also enjoy daily newspapers, scientific periodicals, and materials related to past and future aeronautics." She stiffened in offense and gave him her back. "I suppose you prefer your women docile and ladylike. The delicate sort who read about fashion and etiquette."

"I prefer my women spirited and curious." She didn't flinch, but he knew he'd shocked her. "And yes, it's true about the James brothers."

"Astonishing," she whispered.

He didn't know whether she referred to his taste in women or his air skirmish with the James boys. Didn't matter. What charmed him was her general sense of awe. Her fascination with aviation stimulated his sexual appetite like French champagne. He'd never known a woman pilot. Never encountered a woman so hungry for technological knowledge. Yes, she was beautiful, but it was Amelia's sharp and inquisitive mind that made Tuck randy as hell.

Breathing deeply, he fought an almighty urge to free those corn silk curls, allowing them to flutter around her mesmerizing face. She looked fetching enough in the moonlight as it was. Also, he didn't figure she'd appreciate the intimate gesture. For all her bluster and salty language, Miss Darcy struck him as an innocent. Or maybe she was frigid. He shouldn't care. He didn't care, except the better he knew their guest, the better he could anticipate how best to handle her presence on the *Maverick*.

"Just in case you were worried, Eli dropped your friend safely at a reputable inn."

"I wasn't worried. Mr. Boone seems most respectable."

"Many would argue that point."

"I'm well aware of your crew's reputation and your frequent brushes with danger."

"Yet you're not afraid to fly with us."

"I can take care of myself."

"With that peashooter you pulled on Axel earlier today?"

She squared her shoulders, but kept her gaze averted. "With whatever means available."

Tuck crossed his arms, studied her slight form, and pondered all that sass. "Seein' as you're acquainted with my colorful history, I assume you know I'm a wanted man." A fact that ate at his gut every day.

"Wanted in America. I know."

"For theft and murder."

"I know."

"You're not bothered by that?" He sure as hell was.

"I would be if you were guilty."

"According to the evidence, I am. What makes you think I'm innocent?"

"You said so four months back, in that interview with the Clockwork Canary."

Tuck thought back on the awkward meeting and the way that confounding reporter had pried into his innermost thoughts. Yes, he'd wanted to spread the news of his innocence, but he hadn't aimed on sharing the more sordid details of the case. Somehow, some way the Clockwork Canary had gotten Tuck to open up about his relationship with Ida Titan, the woman he'd been accused of killing. How they'd been past lovers and how he'd broken off with her when she'd become obsessive and delusional. He hadn't meant to speak ill of Ida, even though she'd plotted against her own father to secure a future for her and Tuck—a future that had been rooted solely in Ida's fanciful mind. Even though she'd threatened Tuck with his own gun when he'd refused to play her twisted game. No matter her transgressions, Ida hadn't been of sound mind.

Gut knotted with regret, Tuck shook off the sour memories of his last and fatal meeting with his twisted former lover and instead focused on the feisty ingenue in front of him. Amelia's unquestioning belief in his innocence was humbling ... and worrisome. The case against Tuck had been built by Ida's father—a vengeful man and a powerful judge. The evidence (though mostly concocted) had been damning and well publicized in respected publications throughout the world. Yet Amelia took Tuck's word as reported by one sensationalized newspaper? Never mind that it was true. "Believe everything you read?"

"Of course not. Certainly not everything written by that disreputable reporter, but in your case ..." She finally looked his way again, and even with those goggles on he could see the bald admiration in those big blue eyes. "You are incapable of such an atrocity, Mr. Gentry."

Though he was indeed innocent of the aforementioned crime, he'd sinned plenty in his efforts to uphold the law. Her admiration was misplaced and it galled. "You have no idea what I'm capable of."

"Are you speaking of the criminals you killed in the line of duty? Unfortunate. But sometimes good men have to do bad things to obliterate evil."

Just when he'd thought Amelia was a naive innocent. Swear to God, he'd never met a woman of such contradictions. Tuck shook his head and rubbed the back of his neck. "I'm beginning to think Axel's right about you. No sane woman would willingly board a ship manned by reputed outlaws. I don't care if you have some romanticized notion about us. We're still healthy men with carnal needs."

"No need to be crude. Or cruel," she said, no doubt in reference to her mental stability. "I told you: I am desperate to get to Italy."

"I read the newspapers too, Miss Darcy, and I have to wonder why your brothers aren't accompanying you on this journey."

She turned her pert nose to the stars. "Otherwise engaged. Matters of grave importance."

"Graver than a dying grandpap?"

"They'll join me as soon as they are able. Trust me when I say family is uppermost in their minds."

"They had no reservations about you traveling all that way alone?"

"I wasn't alone." She cut off his next words with a gasp. "Look at all that water." She glanced over her shoulder and caught his eye, causing his goddamned heart to pound. "Is that the English Channel?" she asked in wide-eyed wonder.

And just like that their tense conversation was over. "It is."

The moon sat high, lighting their way and casting a brilliant glow over the coast of Sussex and the vast waters rippling between England and France. Over the past year he'd flown this path several times, enough times that the impressive landscape had lost its shine. Amelia looked as if she'd just gotten her first glimpse of diamonds. "You've never seen the channel?"

"With the exception of one excursion to London to visit my brother Jules, I have never been outside of Kent."

A sheltered country girl with a thirst for adventure.

His gut blared louder than Birdman's megahorn.

Left to her own devices, Amelia Darcy was an all-fired beacon for trouble.

Even now he could sense all eyes on deck assessing the woman gracing their bow like a living figurehead.

"What are you doing?" she asked when he whisked her off the barrel.

"Doc'll tan my hide if you catch pneumonia." Granted, her good health was of concern, but mostly this was an excuse to get her below and out of sight.

"I assure you I am quite hardy."

"No doubt." A woman who'd sustained more than a few injuries due to flying incidents. A woman who'd intended to pedal a flimsy kitecycle over the damned English Channel. It wasn't Amelia Darcy's constitution that Tuck questioned. The burr under his saddle pertained to a suspicion that this young gal possessed more sass than sense. Between her pretty face, enticing curves, and infectious sense of wonder, she'd have his men twisted up in less than three days. At a time when he carried a hold full of the banned hallucinogenic liquor known to the French as *la fée verte*. He envisioned a crew of sky pirates absconding with his precious green-fairy cargo, his crew in shackles due to being distracted by a spitfire in leather.

"I insist you put me down."

"Noted." He shouldered open his cabin door, and as much as he wanted to fling this obstinate filly on the bed, he set her gently on the mattress and stepped away. Distance was key. Every time he touched her, all of his thoughts went south of his waistline.

Shifting his position to hide another damned hard-on, he gave her a stern look. "Let's get one thing clear, Flygirl. This is my boat. I give the orders, not you. As our guest, you'll be afforded protection, food, and board until we reach Paris. In return, you'll keep out of our way, belowdecks and out of sight as much as possible."

She folded her arms and narrowed her eyes. "Why don't you just confine me to quarters?"

"Don't tempt me."

"I need to work on Bess."

At least it would keep her occupied. "I'll set you up a workplace."

"And I prefer my own sleeping compartment."

"I prefer you here." Safest place for her. He could curb his randy desires. Chantel, in all her flexible glory, was only a day away. And *she* wasn't a virgin.

Red-faced, Amelia pushed herself to her feet, clinging to the bedpost for stability. "If you think—"

"Farthest thing from my mind."

She blinked. "Really? Why?"

For the love of . . . "Contrary to what you may have read or heard, Miss Darcy, I don't cotton to seducing innocents."

"I'm not . . . That is to say . . ." She palmed her forehead as if wrangling stray thoughts. "I didn't mean to offend. I just . . . It's been an unusual day."

"Won't argue that." Restless, he moved to the threshold. "It's late and I've got a four-hour watch in front of me. If you need anything—"

"I won't."

"I'll ask Doc to bring you some food and to check your bandages. Make sure you didn't foul up those stitches. Make yourself at home." He gestured toward his spacious lodgings. "Good view from those windows. Plenty of reading material. Scientific periodicals and the like."

She blew out a breath and sagged to the bed as if she'd spent her last ounce of energy. "You're a complex and somewhat infuriating man, but you do have your moments."

"That your way of saying thank-you?"

"No, it is not." She managed an exhausted smile that tugged at his heart. "Fly safe, Mr. Gentry."

"Sleep well, Miss Darcy."

CHAPTER 7

Amelia roused herself through a bleary fog, heart heavy, mind discombobulated. Perhaps she would skip today altogether, whatever day this was. Exhausted, she turned her face into her pillow, wishing away the void. Wishing Papa home. She'd slept fitfully, tortured by dreams of the man who'd filled her life with affection and wonder. The same visions that had plagued her since the demise of *Apollo 02*.

At first the dreams were pleasant pieces of memories — happy memories; then they'd melded into something she hadn't even experienced. His last hours, as she imagined them. His last minute. His last breath. The explosion. So horrific she couldn't breathe. Only last night, when she'd choked on cogs, gears, and fragmented metal, he'd reached down from heaven to ease her anxiety. Last night she'd felt less alone.

Not that she was alone now, as evidenced by the smell of . . . bay rum?

Tucker Gentry.

Amelia burst through the last wisps of nocturnal fog, acutely aware of her surroundings and circumstance. His airship. His cabin. His bed. She half expected to find him stretched out alongside her. The air vibrated with the man's charismatic presence.

Upon keen inspection of the dimly lit quarters, she noted she was, in actuality, quite alone. Odd that her heart sank. A respectable woman would be relieved. In spite of her unconventional approach to life, Amelia was indeed chaste. She'd experienced a brief infatuation a time or three in her twenty years, and had even allowed Phineas Bourdain, a military acquaintance of Jules's, to steal a kiss. But the infatuations, like Phin's kiss, had fizzled. More curious about aeronautics than lovemaking, she'd never been tempted to explore more scandalous pleasures.

Until last night.

Peering over the bow of the *Maverick*, seeing the vast English Channel glittering below them, she couldn't imagine anything more exhilarating. Then she'd turned and caught Tucker staring at her. Those intoxicating eyes simmering with ... curiosity? Desire? Whereas she'd easily assessed Lord Bingham's moral character and lecherous intent, the Sky Cowboy was an enigma. Near as perplexing was her reaction to the man and the moment. The more he tried to frighten her away, the greater her attraction.

She had no illusions. Tucker Gentry was a dangerous man. Not because of his ability or willingness to kill in extreme circumstances, but because of the sensations he evoked with a mere brush of his hand, a sensuous look, an inappropriate statement. She'd experienced all three and she'd nearly expired from the heady rush. Heat had singed her cheeks and radiated between her legs. She'd ached in the most curious manner, yearning for things she couldn't precisely describe. It was the first time she'd felt the full force of her sheltered upbringing, making her bitter and defensive. Then, when he'd assured her he had no intention of seducing her, she'd been perplexed and more than a little disappointed. She'd been so certain he fancied her, or at least her curvaceous figure, as most men did. After half a day in his company and an evening of skimming his personal library, she was fast learning Tucker Gentry was not like any man she'd ever known. She wanted to know him better ... and she didn't.

A knock on the door dashed her musings. Pulse racing, Amelia smoothed her hair from her face and clutched the coverlet to her chest. "Yes?"

"It's Doc Blue, Miss Darcy."

"Oh." She cursed her disappointed tone and forced a smile even though he couldn't see it. "One moment, please." She pushed out of bed, ignoring stiff muscles and the twinge in her thigh. Cinching her dressing gown tight, she clasped the bedpost for support, then invited him inside.

The door swung open and, with only a brief nod of greeting, the young doctor strode across the room carrying a breakfast tray. "How did you sleep?"

"Very well," she lied. She'd spoken to no one of the nightmares and had no intention of doing so. In the light of day she managed to lock away the images, the grief and guilt, and as a result kept her wits and heart, if not whole, then at least functioning.

Doc cut her a glance that said he didn't believe her, which meant she must look a fright. Instead of arguing, he gestured to the array of food he'd placed on the table. "An assortment of cakes, breads, jams, and fresh fruit. Plus a pot of hot tea, a hearty blend from East India. Sound good?"

"Sounds lovely. Thank you." Last night he'd brought her a delicious dinner, not that she'd had an appetite, but she'd eaten so as not to offend. After sampling the stew, she'd understood why StarMan had raved about his cooking, and why Tucker had declared him a man of many talents. "I feel bad that you're serving me in this manner. Is there a common dining area?"

"Marshal insists you take your meals here. How's that leg?"

"Mending."

Doc grinned while pouring her tea.

"What?"

"Told Axel you were tough. Now I get to tell him again."

"Mr. O'Donnell is a cantankerous man."

"Socially inept, but essentially a good man. So the marshal keeps telling me."

"I sense you don't care for the ship's engineer."

"Don't care for his uneducated views and suspicious nature. Other than that . . ."

"He's a good man," Amelia said, repeating Tucker's opinion of Axel. Doc seemed unconvinced. Amelia had her own reservations about the surly engineer, but another knock averted her attention. Her face burned red when she spied Birdman Chang on the threshold, partly because he'd held her firm when the pain had been at its worst, but mostly because he'd knocked her unconscious with a finger tap. Something called acupressure, according to Doc. "As an apology for assaulting my person," Amelia blurted, midthought, "you can teach me how to do the same. Render someone unconscious, that is."

He raised a dark brow. "I can?"

"I insist."

"For what purpose?"

"Defensive purposes."

"Seems reasonable," Doc said.

"A fair exchange," Amelia said.

"Perhaps." Chang pulled a shiny gadget from his coat pocket: a brass knob attached to a four-inch rod. "Eli made this for you. Would've given it to you himself, but he's dealing with a mechanical problem."

She stared. It looked like a gavel or maybe a hammer of sorts. "What is it?"

"A walking stick. He saw the marshal carrying you on deck last night. Thought you could use some help. You'll mend in no time under Doc's care, but until then . . ."

She flushed. "I appreciate the gesture, but . . ." She shook her head. "Surely you can see it's far too short—"

Chang pressed a rivet at the base of the knob. *Snick, snick, snick.* Joints popped and clicked into place at astonishing speed. Amelia stared as the four-inch rod expanded to a full-fledged walking cane.

"Works on the same principle as our retractable masts," Chang said.

"I . . . Goodness. That was thoughtful. Please thank—"

"Of course." He handed over the impressive gadget, then left.

Amelia pressed the rivet. *Snick, snick, snick*. Six sections retracted to one. "Amazing."

"Eli's a machinist by trade. I swan, that man can craft a working mechanism out of two bolts and a scrap of metal."

She swallowed hard, remembering how Papa had constructed Loco-Bug and Bess out of available scraps. Indeed, most of his inventions were two parts materials, one part imagination. Suddenly Amelia wanted nothing more than to indulge in a lengthy conversation with Eli Boone.

"Ingenious, really," Amelia said whilst admiring his work. "A pocket cane."

"And a handy weapon." Doc mimicked conking someone using the heavy knob, then followed through with a stabbing motion.

She depressed the rivet, felt the power of the sections snapping into place, and then noted the tip of the cane—perhaps not pointy enough to pierce skin, but surely a good jab would do some damage. She smiled. "Indeed."

"Allow me to check your wound before you dress for the day."

Her smile faded. She'd had quite enough of men viewing her bare legs and brief bloomers. "I assure you I am fine."

"Have a degree in medicine, do you?"

She'd not meant to insult the man. She would be a shrew to do so, considering his bountiful kindness. "Remarkable that you have a license to practice at such a young age," she said whilst pulling aside the folds of her dressing gown. "You look no more than my twenty summers."

He stooped to inspect his work. "I'm twenty-one."

"Still—"

"A child prodigy."

"Indeed?" She felt him unwinding the tight bandage, felt him covering her wound with his palm as he had last night, and felt the same comforting warmth and vibrations radiating through the affected area. She wanted to ask about the odd sensation and also about the tattoos on the backs of his hands—so intriguing—but his actions were hurried this morning, his manner brusque in comparison to the day before.

Within seconds, he'd replaced the bandage and distanced himself. "Looks good, but don't overtax yourself today, Miss Darcy. If you must leave the room, please rely on Eli's cane."

She thought about the way Tucker had ordered her to stay below and out of sight and felt an overwhelming urge to defy him posthaste. "Is Mr. Boone topside?"

"I believe so, but—"

"Not to bother you further, but I'd like to bathe." She glanced at the screened panel that shielded a claw-footed slipper tub. "Do you suppose—"

"Best not to get those stitches wet, but I can provide a basin of hot water and soap."

"Thank you, Doc Blue."

"Just Doc is fine."

"Then you must call me Amelia."

"Marshal wouldn't approve. Told us not to get familiar."

Hence Doc's more formal behavior. Why was Tucker so intent on isolating her? Did he worry that one of his crew would make an inappropriate advance? Or that she'd distract them from their chores? All in all his restrictions implied she was a hindrance. The notion rankled. Arms crossed in defiance, Amelia challenged the good doctor with a raised brow. "Do you obey all of former Air Marshal Gentry's directives? Even the ridiculous ones?"

"His boat. His rules." Adjusting his peculiar spectacles, Doc nabbed his tray and strode toward the threshold.

"I can take care of myself," she grumbled.

"Don't know if it's you he's worried about so much as us."

"What does that mean?"

"Ask the marshal," Doc said, then shut the door behind him.

Irritated beyond reason, Amelia hobbled into action. "Indeed I will."

"Told you this would happen," Axel complained as Tuck joined him at the starboard turbine. "Yesterday there was a problem with the auxiliary oil pump. Last night the masts jammed, and since we've yet to free them, we've been forced to fly under decreased speed, relying mostly on the bally. Not long after, the control valve on the port turbine clogged, and now this."

Tuck knew about the masts. He'd been at the wheel when they'd failed. Figured between Eli and Axel they'd have the problem solved in a timely manner. When they'd hit a stone wall, he'd inspected the mechanisms himself but couldn't find fault. Even now Eli was concentrating his efforts on righting the problem. These kinks in the turbine added insult to injury. He pushed back the brim of his hat and studied the steam-belching machine that not only supplied an extra burst of power to the blasterbeefs but also generated electricity for the entire ship. He saw nothing amiss. "What am I looking for?"

"Listening for."

"Specifically."

"The clanking."

"What clanking?"

"In the coils. You don't hear that?"

Sleep-deprived and distracted, Tuck realized his senses weren't as sharp as usual. Listening harder he did indeed hear an ominous clank. "Sounds like the coupling is getting ready to seize." Which would cause an even greater delay.

"Not the coupling," Axel argued. "Problem's in the stator coils. Been trying to fix it all morning but I'll be damned if I know what's wrong. Ain't never had so many malfunctions in such a short time." He shook a wrench at Tuck. "Dump that woman in Dieppe, or we'll never make it to Paris."

"Holster your superstitions, Ax. Miss Darcy didn't bring this on. The *Maverick*'s in need of extra maintenance, is all. We'll gussy up in Paris. Just keep her runnin' till then." If anyone could, Axel could. Tuck forced an easy smile. "Think of it as a challenge."

The man grunted, then, after a double take, cursed. "Don't let her near this turbine, Marshal. The whole thing might blow."

Tuck looked over his shoulder and cursed as well. Limping toward them with the aid of an odd-looking walking stick was the woman who'd kept him awake all night. He'd returned to his cabin at half past midnight and bedded down on the floor, but damned if he could sleep with Amelia tossing and turning in a fitful bout of dreams. Her pitiful moans had grown louder, tangling his heartstrings. He'd intended to rouse her, but then he'd noticed her tears and he'd frozen.

She'd plummeted out of the sky, crashed her beloved kitecycle, but hadn't cried. A damned hunk of metal had skewered her leg. No crying. Though tears had filled her eyes when Doc mended that wound, not one tear had fallen. So what the hell tortured this courageous gal in her sleep? Tears had turned into choked sobs and then she'd gasped for air. On instinct he'd soothed her brow, stroked her hair, and made tender shushing sounds. Within seconds, she'd settled and drifted into a more peaceful rest. Intrigued and concerned, Tuck had watched over her till the break of dawn; then he'd left to catch some winks on deck. That hadn't panned out either. He'd ended up bringing Peg topside for a bout of exercise, then taking another crack at the jammed masts.

As Amelia approached, his senses sharpened. Her face was scrubbed pink. Her eyes, though shadowed, sparked with defiance. The long, soft curls he'd stroked were now braided and coiled in a whimsical fashion. Her delectable body was hidden beneath her duster—thank God for small favors. He noted two colorful scarves—one red, one purple—looped around her neck, and the clunky boots, and almost smiled.

But then she was toe-to-toe, in his face. The impact of her presence knocked him off balance—not a feeling he welcomed.

"Good morning, Mr. Gentry."

"Miss Darcy." He lassoed his emotions, battling for control. "You've met Axel."

She cast the engineer a look. "Wish I could say it was a pleasure."

"Same here," Axel said, then turned his back.

Amelia fixed her devastating blue gaze on Tuck. "I need to speak with you."

Conversation was the last thing on his mind. He imagined pulling her against his body, kissing those rosebud lips, tracing his thumb along her prominent cheekbones. . . . "Go on."

"Perhaps someplace quieter. It's hard to think with all this noise."

"I'm working on it," Axel groused.

"Say your piece," Tuck said. *And move along before I sweep you off your feet and whisk you to my bed.*

She blew out a breath. "It occurs to me that you are unhappy about my presence on your ship."

"There's an understatement," Axel mumbled.

"I'm not keen on being where I am not wanted."

"Wouldn't want the lady feeling uncomfortable," Axel said to Tuck as he poked and prodded the turbine. "Drop her in Dieppe."

"Where's Dieppe?" she asked Tuck.

"Coastal town in France."

She shook her head. "Though I am an inconvenience,

since you are traveling in that direction anyway, I must insist you honor your commitment and take me as far as Paris. The closer to Italy, the better. Plus it will allow me more time to reconstruct Bess."

"No way in hell are you gonna rebuild that dig before we reach Paris, darlin'."

"How much time do I have?"

"Not enough."

"That will have to do."

Her stubborn determination gave Tuck a hard-on and a goddamned pain in the neck. "Travel would be swifter and for sure and certain safer if you purchased passage from France to Italy on a commercial airship."

"Do I look as though I am made of money?"

"The train then."

Though she maintained fierce eye contact, she lowered her voice to a ragged whisper. "My family is . . . We recently learned . . ." She cleared her throat. "There is no money to squander on commercial travel."

"You sayin' your family's down and out?"

"Financially challenged. Temporarily."

Tuck noted the pride in her voice and his natural inclination to help. Seemed to him this gal had suffered a whole lot of heartbreak as of late. Maybe it was a culmination of personal debacles that tortured her dreams. The urge to somehow right her world was almighty, but it wasn't his place. Nor could he afford the distraction. He had his own family to worry about.

Specifically his sister, Lily.

With an ocean between them it had become next to impossible to monitor her well-being. Since the day they'd been orphaned, Tuck had considered Lily his responsibility. Even though she'd ended up living most of her life with their aunt, he'd seen to her financial needs, maintaining a long-distance relationship in order to shelter her from his dangerous profession.

After his rise to fame as the Sky Cowboy, he'd done his almighty best to keep Lily's existence out of the press. Luckily, the dime novels had focused mostly on his adventures. When things had turned sour, reporters had started digging into his personal life, and Tuck had sent Lily and their aunt to live with a distant cousin in New York City.

In the past year, their aunt had died, and now, more than ever, Tuck regretted leaving his sister behind in the States, even though it had seemed the right thing at the time. He no longer trusted the family she was living with, suspecting they were poisoning Lily against him and mishandling her finances. Tuck had to get to his sister or get her to him.

Way he saw it, he had two choices: appease or bribe Judge Titan so that he dropped the twisted charges against Tuck, clearing his name and his path to home, or . . . secure a fortune, enabling Tuck to smuggle Lily out of America, after which he'd set them both up with aliases and a new life in Europe.

"How long before we reach Paris?" Amelia asked again, diverting talk of funds, or lack thereof.

Though, like his sister, Amelia was young and somewhat gullible, Tuck reminded himself that she had two capable and older brothers on this continent, neither of them wanted by the law. Neither of them currently indulging in a dangerous and disreputable profession. She wasn't entirely on her own, so why was Tuck compelled to ease her troubles? He glanced up at the steam-powered balloon, then frowned at the lowered masts and compromised blaster-beefs. "At this rate it'll be another hour before we reach the coast."

She turned her face to the south. "Given the strong winds, we'd make greater haste with the sails."

"That's a fact." Her profile was stunning. Her knowledge of aviation stimulating.

"So why not deflate the balloon and hoist the sails?"

"Problem with the retracting mechanism on the masts."

"Oh." Amelia regarded the engineer and the turbine with a frown. "It would seem you are plagued with several problems this morning."

Axel glared over his shoulder. "How about that?"

"Your tone suggests I am somehow at fault," Amelia shot back.

"The *Maverick* was in tip-top shape till you boarded."

"Are you suggesting I somehow sabotaged—"

"No, he is not," Tuck said firmly. He should've told Axel to shut the hell up sooner, but he'd been impressed with Amelia's reaction to his surly engineer. The woman held her own. Maybe it was because she had two older brothers, but she was not easily intimidated. He liked that. He liked her. *Hell.* "Was there something else, Flygirl?"

"What?" Brows scrunched, she massaged her temple, then focused back on Tuck. "Oh, yes. If you would be so kind as to show me to Bess . . . Good Lord," she complained, "the infernal clinking."

"Clanking," Axel growled. "I'm working on it."

Amelia grabbed the wrench out of his hand and knocked it hard against the coils. The ominous sound stopped.

Tuck and Axel stared.

Amelia shrugged. "Sometimes it just takes a good whack."

Axel grabbed back his tool. "Can't be that easy."

"Sometimes it is. I have a lot of experience with malfunctioning machinery. Papa's inventions, though brilliant, were unfortunately plagued by flaws."

Axel narrowed his eyes. "Prone to bad luck, was he?"

On that note, Tuck grasped the woman's arm and steered her away. "A word in private."

"That was my intention in the first place."

On second thought, privacy would prove disastrous. Privacy would tempt indulgence. He burned to kiss this feisty girl senseless. Instead, he finessed her toward the companionway, out of earshot but within sight of StarMan. "I asked you to stay below."

"Sorry to disappoint, but in addition to wanting to initiate repairs on Bess, I have someone to thank." She flashed her walking cane. "Could you point me to Mr. Boone?"

He should've recognized Eli's handiwork. "I'll pass on your appreciation."

"I'd rather do so in person."

"Miss Darcy—"

"Mr. Gentry—"

"Ahoy! Incoming!"

What now? Tuck wondered, just as a cannonball whizzed over the hull. "What the hell?"

"Pirates!" Birdman called from his post in the shrouds.

"All hands, battle stations!" Tuck hauled Amelia into his arms.

"What are you—"

"Hush." He whisked her down the ladder, adrenaline pumping. Hurrying toward his cabin, he envisioned his illegal cargo hidden two decks below. Cargo that, once delivered, would advance him toward his means of returning home to America. To Lily. Unless some low-down sky pirates stole his booty. "Goddammit."

"You can outrun pirates," Amelia said, her voice now high-pitched and breathy. "You've done it before. I once read in the *Informer*—"

"Sails down. Blasterbeefs at quarter capacity. No running from this one." He kicked open the door to his cabin and set her on her feet. "If you value your life, lock the door behind me and stay quiet as a church mouse."

Her eyes were huge, alight with fear and, damn it all, excitement. "But maybe I can help," she said. "I can shoot—"

He shushed her with a kiss. Not smart or timely, but dammit, her offer torched his blood. He nipped, sampled, and consumed. She tasted of nectarines and sunshine. More intoxicating than whiskey. Addictive as opium. Though passionate, the kiss was brief, leaving her breathless and him wanting more. "You can help by staying safe."

They shared a look sparking with mutual lust. He heard an explosion, felt the ship rock. At this moment, he wasn't sure what had suffered the hit—the *Maverick* or his heart. Unbalanced twice in one day, Tuck pushed away with a growl. "Lock the damned door," he said, then swung into the hall.

Eli jogged up from behind, tossed him a .357 Annihilator. "Ready to tussle, Marshal?"

Hopped up on a nectarine kiss, Tuck broke into a run. "Let's kick some scurvy ass."

CHAPTER 8

Amelia stood, stunned and reeling from Tucker Gentry's kiss. Not so intimate nor intrusive as Phin's fervid assault, but twice—no, aeons more powerful. She wanted more. She wanted Tucker.

The ship shook with an explosion, shattering her sensual daze and prodding her into action. Cowering in his cabin, hiding quiet as a mouse? She couldn't imagine. From what she'd seen this airship operated with a skeleton crew. Surely she could help. An unknown variance? A wild card of sorts?

Tucker would not appreciate her presence. And what if Doc or Eli tried to protect her instead of the airship? What if their crewmates suffered? No, if she joined this fight, better to blend with the men. Heart pounding, she hobbled to the massive chest pushed against the starboard wall. Yes, it was rude to poke about in someone's belongings, but she assumed good manners were moot in times of danger. Rooting through her host's clothing, she quickly settled on a worn greatcoat with an attached cowl. She traded her own coat for Tucker's—overly large and long on her petite frame, all the better to disguise her womanly curves. She wrapped one scarf around her neck, hiding the lower portion of her face, then pulled on her goggles and Papa's top hat. Feeling somewhat anonymous, she procured the stun pistol from her satchel and slid it into the voluminous coat's pocket, then nabbed her walking cane and limped toward the door.

Thud. Thud.

Though helpful, the brass stick knocked against the planked floors and could well alert someone of her approach. Amelia retracted the cane and stuffed the mechanism into her other pocket. She'd have to deal with the limp.

Breathing deeply, she lifted the long hem of Tucker's coat and braved the hall, creeping forward as silently as possible. Her own ears rang with the boisterous activity above: shouting, gun blasts, tussling footfalls. A battle raged, filling Amelia with fascination and dread. She'd craved adventure and she'd gotten it. *Crikey*.

She neared a ladder and paused, startled by sudden chilling silence. Had someone surrendered? Was everyone dead? Swiping her clammy hands down Tucker's wool coat, she steeled her spine, then crept up the rungs. Nearing the top, she heard voices and froze in place.

"Ye're ootnumbered and ootgunned, Sky Cowboy."

"But not outsmarted."

The other man laughed, a grave and haughty sound that caused Amelia to frown in disgust. His arrogance would be his undoing. Was he unaware of Tucker's history? His reputation? Did he really think he'd bully a man who'd tangled with the most notorious outlaws in the American West?

"I'll match my Boomer Cannons and Stormerator against yer wits anytime, mate."

"I'm not your friend, Dunkirk."

"That's Captain Dunkirk to ya," a third voice barked.

The Captain Dunkirk? Amelia wondered. Scottish Shark of the Skies? *Bloody hell.* Perhaps there was reason for concern.

"Ya holding a grudge because I beat ya in faro last month, cowboy?"

"Easy to win when you're a low-down cheat," Axel said.

"I'm pissed," Tucker said, "because you blew a hole in my bally."

"Prepared to dae worse if ya dinnae give me what I want."

Amelia reached in her pocket and palmed her gun. She couldn't imagine Tucker and his men giving over anything to these plundering, murdering scoundrels. She braced for a fight. As soon as chaos commenced, she'd sneak on deck and stun the living daylights out of someone. Unless the gun malfunctioned. Highly possible, since it was a prototype of Papa's. She considered the retracted cane. She might do better with a blow and a jab.

"Hand over the lass," Dunkirk said, "and ya and yer men live to see another day."

Amelia blinked. Was he referring to her?

"No women on this boat," Eli said.

"Bad luck," Axel said.

"True, that," Dunkirk said. "But worth the risk with almost a million pounds at stake. What say you?" he asked in a louder voice, causing several men—his crew?—to cheer.

Amelia's brain reeled as she tried to make sense of the circumstance. How did Captain Dunkirk, an infamous air pirate of international skies, know that she, an inconsequential citizen of Kentshire, was aboard the *Maverick* and in pursuit of the jubilee prize money? Overcome with curiosity, she peeked out of the windowed hatchway.

"Lookee here," a gruff voice said, hauling her up on deck by the scruff of her coat's cowl.

"Bollocks." The crude word slipped from her lips, the severity of the situation dashing all semblance of decorum. Wide-eyed, she took in the ominous sight. Tucker and his men were surrounded by a gang of leather-clad ruffians wielding swords and revolvers of various enormity. Outnumbered and outgunned indeed.

Equally disconcerting was the pirate airship floating alongside with its menacing weaponry, the attached zeppelin balloon painted to resemble a great white, hence its moniker—the *Flying Shark*. Glancing up she noted that the *Maverick*'s steam-powered balloon was badly damaged. With the mast and sails still lowered, if Mr. O'Donnell didn't get the airship's blasterbeefs operating full-out, and soon, the compromised *Maverick* would plummet to the ground along with all on board.

The foul-smelling oaf who'd plucked her from the ladder hauled her forward. The stench of gunpowder triggered thoughts of *Apollo 02*. The explosion. The destruction. *Papa*. Amelia swallowed bile and focused her attention on the towering brute facing Tucker. Though the *Informer* described Captain Dunkirk as devilishly handsome, between his sin black hair, unkempt beard, the jagged scar marring his right cheek, and his piercing obsidian eyes, Amelia saw nothing but a wicked scoundrel.

He removed Amelia's hat, revealing her coiled braids, then smirked at Tucker. "Ya thought to disguise Miss Darcy as a lad?"

"How do you know me?" she blurted.

"Common acquaintance," he said, turning his disconcerting focus on her.

"You've been hornswoggled, Dunkirk," Tucker said in an even tone. "You can't squeeze blood from a stone. Her family can't pay a thousand pounds for her return, let alone a million."

"Ransom is not my objective. Like ya, I intend to capitalize on her knowledge of a hidden treasure."

Amelia swallowed hard and braved Tucker's gaze. Up until this moment he had not known her true objective. His eyes crinkled with confusion. Was it possible he was unaware of the global contest? A heartbeat later, she sensed his fury. No matter the details, he'd been duped.

His expression, however, betrayed nothing as he focused back on Dunkirk. "You should know," he said, casually bumping up the brim of his Stetson, "that Miss Darcy is a fanciful sort."

"Crazy as popcorn on a hot skillet," Axel said, crossing his arms over his brawny chest.

"Loco," StarMan added solemnly.

She noticed then that Tucker and crew had been stripped of their weapons. Blood stained the ripped sleeve of Chang's shirt, and Mr. O'Donnell had a nasty gash on his Neanderthal forehead. Dunkirk's men sported injuries as well, but they didn't glare at her as though she were at fault.

"Damaged goods," Doc threw in, and Amelia felt as though he'd just stabbed her heart with the shard he'd removed from her thigh. "Hope you have a good physician on board, Captain Dunkirk. Otherwise she may not make it as far as the Swiss border."

Amelia blanched further. What the devil was he talking about? She was mending, not failing.

Dunkirk looked her up and down, then focused on her mouth, telegraphing lewd thoughts with a wicked smile. How mortifying!

"What did she offer ya for yer courier services, cowboy? A percentage of the prize? Twenty percent? Thirty? A dive in the dark?"

Tucker said nothing, and Amelia started to sweat.

"Ahoy!" someone shouted from the enemy airship. "ALE, dead ahead!"

Dunkirk ordered his men back to the *Flying Shark*. "Interfere with our retreat, cowboy, and I'll blow ya oot of the sky."

Tucker raised his hands in surrender. "Truth told, you're doin' me a favor, Dunkirk. That filly's brought nothing but bad luck."

Amelia stared at her hero in unabashed disbelief. Surely he wouldn't let her go without a fight. Even if he was irritated with her, he wouldn't allow these pirates to whisk her away to God knew what end? She thought about the cargo he refused to talk about. Was it worth so much? Was he willing to risk her life in order to save his booty?

Panicked, she thought back on something Tucker had said to her the night before: *You don't know what I'm capable of.*

Damnation! Her head and heart pounded with rage. If he wouldn't save her . . . She pulled her stun pistol, only to have it knocked away by Dunkirk.

"Feisty lass." He laughed, then hauled her up and over his shoulder. "This should be fun, yeah?"

"Bastard!" she yelled at Tucker, then pummeled Dunkirk's back, calling him every obscene name she'd ever heard her brothers utter as the air pirate dashed over the gangway linking the two airships. Out of the corner of her eye, she saw Leo swoop down to attack, heard a blast, then, seeing feathers fluttering down from the sky, screamed and walloped Dunkirk in the side of his head.

"No time fer this shite," he growled, passing her off to another ruffian after jumping aboard the *Flying Shark*. "Stow her below, Cromwell."

Chaos erupted in tandem with the shattering of Amelia's heart. Was Leo dead? Dying? She damned Tucker Gentry, who'd promised to keep her falcon safe. She damned him for stealing a kiss, then quashing her illusions. Even as this Cromwell scoundrel locked her inside a cramped, dismal cabin, she plotted her escape. She would survive this, and she would prevail.

"Bad luck, my foot!"

Tuck's blood burned as he handed Leo over to Doc. "Make this right."

The gifted healer nodded and ran off, cradling the wounded falcon in his arms.

Trusting the man's extraordinary skills, Tuck holstered his Blaster and retrieved the .357 Annihilator that had been kicked out of his reach while keeping one eye on Dunkirk's retreat. In kind, his men scrambled for their weapons while Axel made a beeline for the engines. The *Maverick* listed just as a voluminous cloud mushroomed out of nowhere and consumed the *Flying Shark*. "What the—"

"Leaving same as she flew in, Marshal," Birdman said.

"Concealed in a cloud. That's why I didn't spy her until it was too late."

"Not a typical cloud," StarMan said as the towering vertical mass shimmered with lightning, then miraculously blended into the cloud bank.

"Supernatural shenanigans," Eli said.

"Some Freak's doin'," Axel shouted across the deck. "Did you notice? Dunkirk's flying two banners now. The Jolly Roger and the Peace Rebel flag."

"I noticed." Tuck used his spyglass to pinpoint the approaching ALE dig. Same as in the States, some Air Law Enforcers were trustworthy, some crooked. In this case he was double damned, since his cargo was unsanctioned. Either they'd arrest him and confiscate the liquor or confiscate the liquor and sell it on the black market, threatening to make his life hell if he breathed a word of the robbery. "Birdman. Need Doc to look at that wound?"

The squat ball of energy squinted through his goggles at the incoming dig. "No time for that," he said, knotting a kerchief around his bloodied arm.

Tuck nodded. "Take the mizzenmast. Ready the sails."

"Masts still down," StarMan said.

"Pessimism begets failure, my friend." Birdman smacked the somber navigator's shoulder, then trotted off. "Think positive!"

Tuck pulled on his gloves. "Get the damned blasterbeefs up to speed, Axel. StarMan, take the wheel. Eli, we need sail power. You take the foremast; I'll take the main."

"StarMan's right, Marshal. Mechanism's still jammed. I've tried everything."

"Did you whack it with a wrench?"

Eli frowned but took off toward the bow.

Doc ran up behind Tuck. "Leo's resting. What about Miss Darcy?"

Tuck ignored him and hurried toward the mainmast.

"We can't leave her to Dunkirk's mercy."

"One crisis at a time, Doc."

"But—"

"Can't help her if we're dead in the air." He glanced at the ALE dig, short minutes from contact. "Or locked in the hoosegow."

The young doctor stepped back, and Tuck inspected the retracting mechanism. He blew out a breath, shrugged. "What the hell?" Using the butt of the .357, he gave it a hard whack. He heard a metallic chink and groan, and on a whim cranked the rotor wheel. The telescopic inner core extended with ease and speed. He shook his head and laughed. "Eli," he shouted over his shoulder. In tandem he saw the foremast shooting up and Eli waving a wrench in victory.

"Blasterbeefs at full capacity!" Axel yelled.

"I'll be damned."

The engines roared and belched. Sails snapped and billowed. Steam, rocket, and airpower surged through the previously compromised ship.

Tuck grasped StarMan's shoulder. "Taking the wheel."

"About time."

The *Maverick* burst forward and Tuck took control as ALE gave chase. Adrenaline surged as he outmaneuvered and outran the less sophisticated airship. Yes, the zeppelin cruiser was equipped with steam turbines, but they couldn't compare to the additional power of the *Maverick*'s outboard blasterbeefs. As he circled into a mass of midlevel clouds, then out the other side, breaching the channel's shoreline and taking an alternate route, as dictated by his navigator, Tuck's mind fixed on the mishaps that had plagued his normally tip-top dig overnight. All three masts, for chrissake, and the blasterbeefs. Malfunctions that coincided with Amelia's presence. He wasn't a superstitious man, yet as soon as she was off the *Maverick* his luck had turned for the better. Just like that the masts and blasterbeefs were in good working order, and he'd secured the safety of his cargo by fleeing, not fighting, his preferred method of dealing with the law—crooked or otherwise.

"All clear," Birdman yelled down from his elevated vantage point.

Pocketing his astronomical compendium, StarMan moved in beside Tuck. "That was close," he said in a hushed voice.

Tuck eyed his trusted friend. "Too close."

"Miss Darcy is an enigma," StarMan added.

"You mean a liar."

"We're better off without her."

"Absolutely."

"Going after her, aren't we?"

"We are."

Concern had twisted Tuck's gut when Dunkirk's man had hauled her into the fray. Her nectarine kiss still sweet on his lips, her fiery passion simmering in his blood, all he could think about was her reckless spirit and vulnerability. Bad enough when he'd thought Dunkirk considered her a tasty boon to his intended theft. But when he'd learned the air pirate was specifically after Amelia and not his illegal shipment of absinthe, concern had turned to confusion, then anger. What the hell was Flygirl playing at? She'd claimed she was bound for Italy to visit her dying grandpap. Instead she was involved in some treasure hunt? The hell if he wasn't intrigued and furious at the same time.

"Observation," StarMan said.

"Go on."

"With the ship operating at full power, maybe we should make haste for Paris, deliver our shipment, and collect our due while good fortune smiles upon us. Then set off on this rescue mission. You know as well as I do that Dunkirk will not kill her, not if she can lead him to a million pounds."

"Ain't killin' I'm worried about," Tuck said. He'd seen the way Dunkirk had leered at Amelia. Even though she'd concealed her figure under his all-weather overcoat, there was no hiding that pretty face, that tempting mouth.

StarMan dragged a hand over his face and sighed. "You like her."

"Of course I like her. She's worth a fortune." Though it wasn't Tuck's top reason for wanting to rescue Amelia, the notion *had* seeped under his skin and burrowed into his brain.

"So it's the treasure you're wanting, not Miss Darcy."

"A million pounds? Windfall like that'll pave the way to freedom, StarMan."

"Yeah, but are we talking gold? Diamonds? A priceless artifact? Dunkirk asked what Miss Darcy offered for your courier services. So she planned on tricking us into delivering this hidden treasure to . . . who? Where? What are we getting into, Tuck?"

"I intend to find out. Take the wheel. Skirt the clouds till you're certain ALE's not tailing." They were out of the Brits' jurisdiction now, but that didn't mean the law enforcement agency wouldn't alert the French, negotiating for a cut.

"Destination?"

"Paris. For now." Tuck gave over the wheel, shouted a few dictates, then called for Doc. "Come with me."

The younger man trailed after as Tuck strode toward his cabin. "What you said about Miss Darcy's wound . . . You told me she was on her way to bein' right as rain."

"She is. I thought if Dunkirk considered her a liability, maybe he wouldn't take her. Or maybe he'd take me along to look after her. At least then I could've afforded Miss Darcy some protection."

Tuck glanced over his shoulder. "Smart. Although, no offense, Doc, you ain't much of a match for Dunkirk and his kind. They have no compunction about killin' a man. You do."

"Yes, well, I am a healer."

"Among other things." Tuck pushed into his cabin. "That cloud," he said while shutting the door behind them. "That was a cumulonimbus. Indicative of thunderstorms."

"Dunkirk mentioned a Stormerator. Something that generates storms?"

"That'd be my thinking." Tuck snatched Amelia's satchel and tossed it on his bed, striving for a casual tone as he entered sensitive territory. "Sense any Freaks amongst Dunkirk's men?"

When Doc didn't answer, Tuck pushed. "Flying the PR flag," he said as he sifted through Amelia's belongings. "Means they welcome Mods and Freaks."

"I know."

"Could a Freak be responsible for that supernatural cloud?"

He heard Doc shifting his weight, knew he was considering his words. "There's been talk of a few who can . . . modify the weather."

"Conjure rain on a sunny day? Summon clouds out of nowhere? That kind of thing?"

"Don't know much about it, Marshal. Just heard talk."

"Ain't askin' you to rat out one of your people, Doc. Just need to know what we're getting into when we go after Miss Darcy."

The younger man blew out a breath of relief. "So we're going to steal her back."

"I've got a bone to pick with that gal and a score to settle with Dunkirk."

"Surprised you let him take her in the first place."

"Weighed the options. Considered the outcomes. It was the wiser choice at the time."

"And now?"

Tuck grinned. "Now we stack the odds in our favor."

"That why you're invading Miss Darcy's privacy, looking through her things?"

"Justifiable search, Doc." He tried like the devil to ignore her saucy unmentionables. He sure as hell didn't linger. One thing was sure and certain: Amelia Darcy could pack a load of belongings into one moderately sized valise. Tightly rolled blouses, trousers, some sort of combined vest and cutaway skirt, a canvas bag stocked with tools and assorted cogs and bolts, hair combs, an astronomical compendium (basic, but sufficient; old, but interesting). Intrigued by the colorful collection of items, Tuck almost forgot he wasn't alone.

Doc cleared his throat, moved closer. "Yes, there's at least one Freak among Dunkirk's crew," he finally conceded. "Didn't see him, but I felt him. The ripple of two opposing dimensions."

Tuck looked over his shoulder. "So it's possible Dunkirk's Stormerator could be a man as opposed to a machine."

"Mingled with a few of my people when we were at port a few weeks back. Heard tell of a brewing rebellion among Freaks." Doc adjusted the band of the tinted wraparound specs that shielded his modified eyes. Freaks, the children of Mods and Vics, people from two different times and dimensions, were born with multicolored eyes. It was like looking into a kaleidoscope. Those who wished to conceal their mutant race wore specs or corneatacts—modernized lenses designed to fit directly over the cornea. Though corneatacts created the illusion of normal, singular-colored irises, they couldn't be worn for more than a couple of hours without causing extreme discomfort. More drastic and permanent measures involved surgery, which was what Doc's parents had chosen for him early on. Unfortunately, it was a risky and imperfect procedure.

"Everyone's fed up with being treated like monsters or curiosities or second-class citizens at best," Doc said. "While some incorporate peaceful steps in their march toward equality, others plot more aggressive measures. Some, it's rumored, are going renegade, hiring out their special gifts to the highest bidder, not caring if that gift is used for ill."

"So Dunkirk's Stormerator could be one of these mercenaries."

"Which makes him very dangerous and Dunkirk quite powerful."

"I'll keep that in mind, Doc."

"You didn't hear it from me."

Tuck raised a brow. "We have a pact. Don't intend to break it." Given Doc's mysterious gift for accelerated healing, and the fact that he never removed his tinted specs or goggles, Tuck was pretty sure most of the crew suspected the man's true origin. The fact that no one called Doc out on it proved that they were accepting of the man and tolerant of his race. As far as Tuck knew, Axel was the only one aboard who got spooked by Freaks. Regardless, Doc chose to live his life as a Vic, and Tuck had promised to keep his secret. Knowing the hell the kid's parents had gone through, as well as his brother's ongoing dilemma, Tuck couldn't blame Doc for being cautious.

Would the world forever be divided by racial and religious unrest? According to the Book of Mods, yes.

Jaw clenched, Tuck dipped back into the satchel and discovered a false bottom. "Here we go." He pulled out a glob of damaged clockwork, a pouch of money, two folded pages of a newspaper, and one letter.

Doc pointed to the mangled gold. "What's that?"

"Looks like it used to be a pocket watch." He passed the timepiece to Doc.

"Been through hell."

"Or a fiery explosion." Tuck read the contents of the first article, then passed that to Doc as well.

"The article announcing the death of Miss Darcy's father." Doc shook his head. "Terrible thing. The accident and the cynical report. Implies her father and brothers are incompetent eccentrics."

Eccentric certainly described Amelia, but Tuck held silent, immersed in the second article. "'Royal Rejuvenation,'" he read aloud. "'A Global Race for Fame and Fortune.'" He read the rest to himself, then handed the article to Doc.

The man adjusted his specs and frowned. "So you think Miss Darcy knows the whereabouts of a"—he referred back to the article—"a 'lost or legendary technological invention of historical significance'?"

"Dunkirk's under that assumption." Amelia hadn't argued the pirate's claim. Instead she'd looked guilty as hell. "Must be some truth to it. This letter relates the same information as the newspaper."

"A personal invitation to join the contest?"

"Seems like." Tuck's mind turned, latching onto pieces and working the puzzle.

"Seein' as she's related to Briscoe Darcy, perhaps she possesses or has access to information about his time machine," Doc mused. "Talk about an invention of historical significance. Although it can't be the actual machine she's after, since it's locked in the 1969 version of the British Science Museum. A prototype, maybe?"

"Or a replica."

"The Peace Rebels' Briscoe Bus?" Doc shook his head. "Destroyed in 1856, soon after the time travelers arrived. Documented fact, Marshal. A story I heard time and again while growing up. They wanted to ensure no one from this century would travel to another and muck up their efforts."

"Mucked up their own efforts," Tuck noted, thinking about the Peace War and the escalated racial and political unrest that lingered.

Doc shifted uncomfortably.

"No offense intended toward your kin," Tuck said. "Besides, I wasn't referring to the vehicle itself. Rumors have been circulating for years that one of the Mods salvaged the clockwork propulsion engine and hid it away. Put that engine in the right hands and you've got a next-generation time machine."

"It would take a genius."

"Heard tell there's a few in this world. Maximus Merriweather could do it. He's got the twentieth-century know-how."

"No one's heard hide nor hair from Professor Merriweather for twenty years. Probably dead."

"Maybe," Tuck said. A lot of the original Peace Rebels were. He'd never been one to dwell on the time-traveling radicals and how they'd screwed up what, up until then, according to his parents, had been a normal world. He'd been one year old at the time of the invasion. The world as it was now simply was. Normal as he knew it. Like most folks, he just wanted to move forward. That wasn't to say he wasn't grateful for the technological information leaked by corrupt Mods—information that had escalated advances in transportation, weaponry, and communication. Those advances had helped to enable his modifications for Peg, and the designing of the blasterbeefs. It had armed his men with Annihilators and Pogo Packs. He had no wish to digress or even slow down, a difficult bullet to dodge, given the fears of Old Worlders, specifically Queen Victoria.

"Just thinking out loud," Tuck said while returning the items to their hiding spot. "Miss Darcy is an enigma, and this supposed treasure . . . hell, it could be anything."

"Whatever it is," Doc said, "it's in Italy. Don't suppose there's a map in that satchel?"

He quirked a wry grin. "That would make it too easy."

"You plan on coercin' Miss Darcy into sharing the location of her potential treasure?"

Sobering, Tuck hastened to return topside. "Ain't nothing compared to what Dunkirk'll do to get the information."

CHAPTER 9

London had twisted Bingham into a knot of seething resentment. The masses craved progress, yet the queen maintained her recent repressive rule. The sooner she disappeared, the sooner his rise to global industry kingpin. Thus frequent visits to the capital were vital, if only to keep the members of Aquarius inspired and on track. He had business interests as well. His pet project of late: a London-based commercial air fleet—exclusive transcontinental sky travel for the upper echelon. Although he acted more in an advisory capacity, Bingham reaped a hefty portion of the profit.

Since returning to Wickford, he'd depleted his frustration by ravishing a voluptuous automaton in various sordid ways. If only she would've fought him or had the ability to show fear, his satisfaction would have doubled. Whilst taking the man-made love slave from behind, Bingham had flashed upon Amelia Darcy, knowing she would fight, knowing he would dominate. The fa-ntasy had fueled his release.

So as not to obsess on the vexing Miss Darcy, Bingham had immersed himself in his master plan. He'd been scanning the latest reports from two of his Mod trackers, contemplating their incompetence when he'd received the telegraph from that Italian domestic. But, of course, Concetta had failed in her mission. He'd been a fool to expect more. He'd seduced the woman, enlisting her services months prior after learning she'd hired on with the Darcys. For what he considered a pittance, she served as his eyes and ears within that curious household. Though Lord Ashford was a distant cousin to Briscoe Darcy, he was still blood and there had been an association. Bingham had thoroughly researched the matter.

In 1851 Darcy had been thirty summers old to Ashford's eighteen, but they'd shared a common passion for science, and that passion had enticed both men to attend the Grand Exhibition. On an evening that later proved a historical milestone, Briscoe Darcy had unveiled his invention and then disappeared in a rainbow of light. Ashford, along with thousands of others, had witnessed the miraculous event. Over the years, Ashford (and the rest of the extended Darcy clan) had denied any knowledge of the time machine's construction or any insight into its design. Bingham did not believe this claim and had purchased Wickford Manor, a large estate in a remote portion of Kent, which afforded him closer proximity to Ashford, as well as greater privacy to experiment with banned technology. He'd clung to the possibility that the bumpkin inventor was in possession of information, even a morsel of insight, regarding the creation of his cousin's extraordinary time machine. But Concetta had learned nothing to verify this. Even Bingham's own efforts had failed. To think he'd suffered through several dinners with that scatterbrained buffoon and his obnoxious, domineering wife. Patience spent, he'd employed drastic tactics, establishing himself as the anonymous benefactor of the Race for Royal Rejuvenation. Unbeknownst to the Jubilee Science Committee, they'd aided Bingham in pushing Lord Ashford's offspring, as well as multitudes of other adventurous or greedy souls, into action. Yes, Bingham believed one or more of the Darcys to be his best bet, but in reality any number of people could possess vital knowledge pertaining to the outlawed time machine. Surely the promise of a fortune was worth risking royal persecution. Someone bloody well knew something, and someone would produce!

Bingham's boot heels clicked against the multicolored marble floor as he moved across the crimson drawing room to peer out the window. He willed control. Summoned focus. Hands clasped behind his back, he gazed across the vast, lush lawn, now white with a dusting of snow, and beyond to the aero-hangar where he shielded *Mars-a-tron*—his spectacular modified zeppelin—and various other dirigibles from the elements. Had his initial meeting with Miss Darcy gone otherwise, he would have toured her about, seducing her with his superior aerostats, perhaps stealing a touch when she'd been distracted by his state-of-the-art gyrocompass. But alas, the woman had surprised both him and his mother with her utopian balderdash and sharp tongue. Oh, to curb that tongue with his own.

Control! Focus!

"Any news yet, son?"

"Not yet." Bingham nodded in greeting as his mother moved in beside him. Upon learning Concetta's disappointing news, he'd confided in the dowager viscountess, as was often his practice. A valuable sounding board, his mother had a mind as keen and a goal as lofty as his. He would succeed where other men of great vision, yet inferior determination, had failed. Global technological and industrial domination. One world under one business mogul. It could be done, and he would do it. "Dunkirk assured me he would find and procure Miss Darcy." After Concetta's coded telemessage informing him Amelia was now with the Sky Cowboy, a disgustingly moral man in spite of his alleged crime, Bingham had reached out to Captain Colin Dunkirk, an associate of dubious reputation.

If indeed Amelia was in pursuit of an outlawed time machine, an invention that had been declared a threat to the natural progression of mankind, Gentry might somehow interfere, thwarting Amelia's search or preventing her from sharing the discovery. Dunkirk would act according to Bingham's orders, ensuring Amelia reached her destination and then bypassing the science committee and delivering the treasure directly to Bingham. As to Amelia, her fate depended on the ferocity of her adventurous spirit. She had only to abandon her utopian mind-set, and Bingham would allow her to jump dimensions with him in order to build his empire. She could do so as his lover or his wife—he cared not which. But she would do as he bade, in life and in bed.

"Perhaps I should've striven harder to smooth the way toward a union between you and Miss Darcy and thereby a more . . . pleasurable means to your triumph, but I will not apologize. There are other ways to get what you deserve, my dear. Marrying that headstrong New Worlder is too great a sacrifice. Not to mention," she added with a sniff, "she is below your station."

Bingham afforded his conservative mother a quick glance. "At present Miss Darcy is indeed unacceptable, although not because of her station. Were she to alter her views and embrace my goals . . ." He shrugged, preferring to keep his more salacious thoughts to himself. "Let us just say I have not dismissed the possibility of uniting with Miss Darcy." He was in fact keen on her high intellect and daring spirit. Having her in his home and bed, enabling him to indulge his insatiable fetishes at will, would be an additional and welcome boon. His cock hardened as prurient thoughts stormed his mind.

For now Amelia Darcy was in Dunkirk's hands. *Do what you must*, he'd told the man, *to secure and deliver her lost invention*. Above the woman, Bingham prized a functioning time machine. The engineering plans alone would escalate his chances of visiting the twentieth century in order to gather the futuristic knowledge that would enable him to monopolize the technological market of his own time.

Meanwhile, in order to cover every angle, he'd coerced

another associate to report on Amelia's brother Simon. Jules Darcy was another matter—a man who lived in the shadows and was, therefore, difficult to track. Still, Bingham had ears and eyes everywhere. In times when so many were desperate for coin, or vulnerable because of their genetic aberrations, information was easily attained. If any one of the Darcy siblings attained the master designs or a prototype or any other pertinent information that would allow the re-creation of Briscoe Darcy's machine, he would know it.

"I worry about your obsession with the Time Voyager."

Though the remark cut, Bingham calmly poured them each a sherry. "Obsession is a harsh and erroneous assumption."

"You've exhausted and promised enormous resources hoping to find or re-create a similar machine that will catapult you to the future."

"You say that as if you think I'm intent on a frivolous jaunt. What I seek is advanced knowledge in order to build my empire."

"You could get that here, in our time, through those infernal Mods."

"Not just any Mod. Certainly not a creative artist or militant activist." Upon their arrival, the Peace Rebels had numbered sixty-nine-plus, a mix of Brits and Yankees, a combination of men and women—mostly men—and a few smuggled babies (who constituted the plus). All rebellious fanatics of peace from several fields of expertise, all under the umbrella of the arts and sciences.

"A physicist or an engineer," she said. "Someone of keen intellect."

"As you know, many were killed in the Peace War. The corrupt ones—those we have to thank for the few anachronistic advances we do have—were assassinated by their own kind. The stubborn pacifists have been in hiding for years, several, according to my trackers, now dead. As far as constructing a working time machine, there is but one Mod who can aid me in my mission."

"Professor Maximus Merriweather. Yes, yes. I know." His mother grunted. "More myth than man."

"Hence all the more difficult to locate." But Bingham was not averse to a challenge. He had a goal and he would stop at nothing to reach it. He'd purposely plotted options in his quest to obtain twentieth-century knowledge. Merriweather, a twentieth-century physicist/cosmologist, would be a wealth of information if coerced or bribed. Unfortunately, the brilliant professor had thus far escaped Bingham's Mod trackers. Rumors had placed Merriweather in the Highlands of Scotland, then Switzerland, and then Tibet. Presently he was off the map, although Bingham had issued orders to track the professor to the end of the world.

Another source, hidden somewhere in this century, was the legendary Aquarian Cosmology Compendium—the collective notes of the scientific faction of the Mods. And last, the designs or components of a time machine, the century and make of which were unimportant as long as it functioned properly.

To pave the way, he'd even finessed his way into Aquarius, encouraging the secret society's nefarious plan to ease technological restrictions. Obsession be damned. He was methodical.

Just as he passed a glass of sherry to his mother, someone announced his or her presence with a curt knock. Bingham turned to find his newly acquired housekeeper, Renee—an automaton with a fetching face and figure specifically designed to his liking—hovering on the threshold. "Yes?"

"Mr. P. B. Waddington of the Jubilee Science Committee to see you," she announced in her tinny, monotone voice. A voice that grated, though her body pleased.

"Show him in," Bingham said. He'd been waiting for this detailed report for two days. Respecting his wish for anonymity, and grateful for an invitation to tour Bingham's collection of airships, Waddington had agreed to visit Wickford.

"I'll leave you to your business," his mother said as she swept out of the room. She must've assumed he'd fill her in later. He was not so sure he would. Her censure of late chafed.

Waddington entered and Bingham shook his hand. "Thank you for traveling to Kent, good sir."

"My pleasure, Lord Bingham. Thank you for the invitation."

Anxious, he cut to the chase, though he did, for the sake of pretense, affect an amiable smile. "What news of the contenders?" he asked whilst pouring the man a drink.

Waddington smiled back. "I daresay the race is off to an extraordinary start. Your generosity and dedication to preserving and celebrating mankind's technological genius is unparalleled. You do Prince Albert proud."

"I only wish to serve queen and country," Bingham lied as he passed the man a sherry. After settling in for their clandestine meeting, he proposed a toast whilst quelling a sneer: "Long live the queen."

CHAPTER 10

"The captain requests the pleasure of yer company for dinner and insists ya dress for the occasion." Cromwell tossed a delicate gown and slippers upon the narrow bunk of Amelia's appointed cabin.

"What occasion is that?" she asked.

Cromwell smirked. "The pleasure of the captain's company."

Amelia saved the eye roll until after he left. She had no intention of antagonizing Dunkirk or any member of his crew. A lone woman amongst twenty-something men? Unsavory pirates? She was smarter than that. In fact, in the last hour she had striven to think like Jules, who was indeed brilliant. What would he, a decorated military man, do in this circumstance?

First, he would keep his head and try to outwit them. She was sure of it.

She had something Dunkirk wanted. Or at least she would once she reached her destination—although in truth there were no guarantees. Amelia was operating on history, optimism, and her memory. Long ago, in a moment of unguarded fancy and too many glasses of port, Papa had shared a story with her involving a secret note and a secret room—secrets revealed to him by Briscoe Darcy. She'd listened in wide-eyed wonder.

"Why can we not go there and see for ourselves, Papa?" she'd asked.

"Because it is dangerous."

"I'm not afraid."

"You should be." Then Papa had lectured her on human nature. He'd quoted from the Book of Mods and explained the importance of moral responsibilities. None of this had quelled her desire to see the two marvels hidden within that secret room, but the lecture did indeed influence Amelia's political and social views. Panicked that he'd burdened his ten-year-old daughter with such a volatile secret, Papa had begged her to forget their conversation. Not wanting to upset him, she'd agreed, but the best she could do was stifle the knowledge. She had cherished and guarded that secret for ten long years.

Amelia tamped down a flutter of guilt. Reginald Darcy would not approve of this venture. But she would be careful and, above all, responsible. She would not tamper with the marvel Papa had feared. She would not touch it. She would not even look upon it. She was, in fact, obsessed with the other invention. The one that could do no harm and only bring glory to the Darcys.

A working Leonardo da Vinci ornithopter.

The mere thought of the ancient flying machine gave Amelia shivers. She'd been studying the designs and theories of da Vinci since she was a child. Although she admired the Italian Renaissance genius's paintings as well as his studies regarding civil engineering, optics, and mechanics, she was most fascinated by his sketches and theories on flight.

Whilst several of his theories proved impossible, it was believed that at least one of his flying contraptions took to the air—even if momentarily and with calamitous results—in 1506. The suggestion was documented in his own hand in the "Codex on the Flight of Birds."

The great bird will take its first flight on the back of Monte Ceceri. . . .

Mount Ceceri, a breathtaking summit close to da Vinci's home in Tuscany, was her destination. She intended to manipulate Captain Dunkirk into delivering her close to the mark. She refused to feel bad about employing dishonest means, as he was, after all, a dishonest man.

Frowning, Amelia fidgeted with discomfort as she examined the gown she was to don for dinner: a provocative evening gown with a barely there bodice and layers of scalloped, flowing skirt. She'd never seen anything like it. Sin black and bloodred. Silk and lace.

Scandalous.

She refused to care.

Because of Tucker Gentry, she could not afford to care. Because of him, she no longer had access to Bess, such as she was, nor her belongings: her clothing, tools, and stash of money. Mostly she mourned the loss of Papa's pocket watch. *Bloody hell!* Each time she recalled how Tucker had allowed Dunkirk to kidnap her without so much as an argument or plea she wanted to wrestle him to the ground. When she thought about Leo injured—or worse, dead—she wanted to crush his soul. Blast the Sky Cowboy and her romantic illusions! She'd thought him noble. Trustworthy. She'd thought him smitten, just a little, with her. He'd *kissed* her. He'd toyed with her affections, dallied with her heart. Never had she felt so gullible. So ... foolish. Perhaps she couldn't soothe her pride or save poor Leo, but she could still save her family. She'd wear the disgusting gown, and by God, she would ensure her passage to Tuscany.

Amelia had never been one for aimless chatter, but she could think of no better way to dissuade Captain Colin Dunkirk from his obvious ploy of seduction than by prattling on about aerodynamics, the theories of lift and thrust, and fixed wings versus flapping wings whilst filling his head with empty flattery by pronouncing the *Flying Shark* a remarkable airship, superior in countless ways to the *Maverick*.

He'd smiled throughout the candlelit dinner, responding now and then, but mostly he'd watched her. No matter how hard she tried to divert his prurient attention, he persisted in eyeing her as a starving man eyed a bountiful meal. She blamed the damnable gown. It was a tad too small, so her waist was horribly pinched and her bosoms fairly spilled over the plunging décolletage. She supposed that one might consider her leather flight pants and favored corseted tail vests revealing, but somehow this frilly gown was far worse, perhaps because it was so decadently feminine. In addition, Dunkirk had insisted she wear her hair down, making her feel even more dreadfully exposed.

She could have refused, of course. But then she would've spent the evening locked in her suffocating cabin, and Amelia was intent on gaining the upper hand, being treated as partner as opposed to prisoner.

Unfortunately, somewhere between the chestnut soup and roasted pheasant she began to worry that Tucker and crew had good reason to question her sanity. Had she truly believed she could manipulate the Scottish Shark of the Skies? From the moment she'd confidently entered his large and somewhat risqué cabin he'd undermined her bravado. His cunning and dark charm made her skin prickle and her palms sweat. As did the sight of his fur-covered bed, only partially hidden behind an ornately painted Asian dividing screen. Stubborn will kept her seated and calm. She did not wish to anger him. Nor to bore him. Nor to placate him. She'd never straddled a more precarious fence.

Amelia realized with a start that she'd fallen silent, lost in anxious thoughts whilst the pirate drank deeply from his wine goblet, devouring her with his blatant, hungry stare. Cheeks burning, she cleared her throat, tempted to cover her cleavage with the faded cloth napkin. "Where was I?"

"Ya were listing the components needed to construct a new . . . what did ya call it? Oh, aye. Kitecycle." He angled his head. "Silence is infinitely more interesting."

Stunned by his rudeness, she frowned. "Do I bore you, sir?"

He grinned. "Ya amuse me, Amelia. May I call ya Amelia?"

"You may not. And why do I amuse, Captain Dunkirk?"

"Ya strive to be brave when ye're scared shiteless. The endless chatter. A nervous tell, yeah?" He gestured to her untouched plate. "No appetite. Ghostly complexion."

"You confuse fear with disgust. I never eat fowl." Her stomach had turned the moment his cook had served the roasted bird. Ever since she'd adopted Leo, she couldn't stomach the thought of eating his feathered friends. To add insult to injury, she assumed one of Dunkirk's men had shot Leo from the sky. Swallowing bitter fury, she pushed the plate aside and focused on her host. "No offense."

"None taken." He arched a wickedly suggestive brow. "We all have our predilections, yeah?"

There was no mistaking his train of thought, and it only fueled her anxiety. The man obviously thought to impress and seduce. He'd bathed and changed into brown leather trousers and a flowing white shirt, open at the collar and showcasing his bronze chest. If the display of muscle was supposed to make her swoon, he'd failed.

He'd shaved his beard and tamed his dark, wild mane into a queue, drawing attention to the hard planes of his face, which oddly enhanced his rugged good looks. Only the scar across his cheek detracted, a reminder that he lived dangerously. That he was a scoundrel, an infamous thief who thought nothing of blowing airships to bits whilst absconding with their booty.

Amelia had read nearly as many tales about Dunkirk as she had about Gentry. She supposed she should be fascinated by the pirate's exploits and flattered by his attentions. She was not.

Head held high, she kept her voice steady but firm. "Captain Dunkirk, I do wish you would look me in the eyes when addressing me rather than ogling my . . . blessings. Your lecherous regard is most unseemly."

"Blessings, eh?" He grinned, then met her gaze, which only heightened her unease. "Indeed, ya are blessed with a fine face and form, lass. No wonder Gentry was taken with ya."

Amelia's heart fluttered at the notion, pounded in memory of that knee-quaking kiss and then, as Tucker's betrayal flashed in her mind, thudded with monumental disappointment. "Mr. Gentry couldn't wait to be rid of me."

"Ya dinnae know the man well."

"Nor do I want to."

"Saving yerself for me then?"

"I'm not saving myself for any man."

He smiled and she blushed. Perhaps he'd misconstrued her intent. "Let us cut to the chase, shall we?" Anxious to end this discussion, Amelia used the napkin to cover her plate, hiding the poor, wretched pheasant from her sight. "You intend to plunder my hidden treasure."

He laughed. "Aye, lass, I do."

She failed to see the humor, but plowed on. "You cannot steal it if you do not know where to find it, and I refuse to disclose the location unless we come to an arrangement."

He raised a brow. "A partnership?"

Now she was getting somewhere. She forced a smile. "Yes."

"Ya wish to bargain with me, lass?"

Although he looked somewhere between amused and astounded, she continued to smile. "Yes." She needed passage to Italy, and she needed a way to transport the invention, once found, back to England. This airship would do, and as a miscreant, surely Dunkirk could be bought. "If you aid me in my quest, and if I win the jubilee prize, I will compensate you with a percentage." There. That sounded reasonable.

He stood, then rounded the table and topped off her wine, even though she'd barely imbibed. Setting aside the decanter, he leaned in and toyed with one of her long curls. "What if I be wanting something else?"

His close proximity rattled her composure, as did his wondering gaze. Naturally, he focused on her breasts. "I, uh . . ."

"Point of interest, Amelia, I dinnae bargain. I take."

She knew then that she'd been an infernal twit, thinking she could somehow manipulate this infamous rake and ruffian. He'd been toying with her. Whether by seduction or force, Dunkirk meant to have her and her treasure. For the first time since she'd defied Jules and Simon and embarked on this quest, Amelia felt out of her depth and very much in danger. She imagined her brothers' guilt and fury should she suffer harm or humiliation. They'd forever blame themselves for her ill fate. She couldn't let that happen. She'd gotten herself into this muddle and she would bloody well get out.

Then she saw it—*him*—through the window beyond the captain's shoulder. Shrouded in black. Face illuminated by moonbeams. Mode of transportation unknown.

The Sky Cowboy. *Her* Sky Cowboy.

Amelia fought the urge to swoon. She had never swooned in her life, yet at this moment she felt positively light-headed. Dizzy with relief and, good Lord, *infatuation*. *Blast and damnation!* Even though he'd betrayed her, she was still smitten with the man who'd given Jesse James an airborne run for his tainted money.

From her angle, Tucker appeared to be floating on the winter wind. He pointed at her, then pointed up. He wanted her on deck.

Since she wanted to escape Captain Dunkirk, and since she'd never once felt physically threatened by Tucker, she set aside her grievances with the cowboy, opting for the lesser evil. Forcing her gaze from the window, she touched a palm to her forehead. "I . . . I fear I am unwell, Captain."

Dunkirk raised a brow. "If ya mean to now capitalize on Doc Blue's insinuation that ya are gravely ill . . . too late."

She didn't blame him for doubting her. She'd been feisty

and fit since they'd met. She realized now that she hadn't even limped when she'd entered his cabin. Indeed, she felt no pain in her thigh at all. Not even a twinge. Odd. Switching tactics, she gestured to her goblet. "The wine—"

"Ya barely drank."

"Yes, but it is overly warm in here and . . . this gown. It's crushing my ribs. I need air." Since she wasn't sure she could fake a swoon, instead she beseeched him with the same look that had swayed Papa and, upon occasion, her brothers. "Please. Let us continue our negotiations on deck."

"Ya still think to bargain with me." He chuckled, then aided her to her feet. "Ya intrigue me, lass."

"I thought I amused you."

"That, too."

Since she'd claimed to feel faint, she couldn't shrug off his touch as he half carried her from the cabin and through the dank, dimly lit passage. She noted two things as he whisked her topside.

First, unlike with Tucker, Dunkirk's touch did not incite delicious sensations and knee-quaking desire. The thought of lying with this man frosted her blood. Further incentive to jump ship.

Second, the *Flying Shark*, though in good working order, lacked the spiff and shine of the *Maverick*. It also stank of stale tobacco, kerosene, and unwashed bodies.

Once on deck, Amelia panicked. What now? What was she supposed to do? Say? Where in the devil was Tucker? Was he alone? One man against Dunkirk and crew? She thought about the retracted walking stick she'd managed to stuff within her layered stockings and thick boot. If she acted swiftly and surely, she could conk Dunkirk on the head with the brass knob, rendering him unconscious. Acupressure wouldn't require such muscle. If only she'd had time to learn Birdman Chang's trick.

At that moment an explosion ripped through the dead of night. Startled, she bit back a scream, her stomach churning as images of *Apollo 02* battered her mind. She turned in tandem with Dunkirk, spying flames at the stern, hearing shouts from the crew.

"What the . . . ?" Dunkirk stashed Amelia behind a protective barrier. "Stay here."

Another explosion. This one from above. The zeppelin. "Holy . . ."

"Fook!" The captain took off, shouting orders while chaos commenced.

Was this Tucker's plan? The element of surprise and distraction? She'd seen him through a portside window. She was now indeed portside. She took a chance and hurried to the rail just as the cowboy drifted up within eyesight. Her heart caught in her throat. "Crikey."

"Jump."

She didn't think. If she did she'd argue that they were a great distance above the earth. That she had no more than a sliver of moonlight and the fire from the explosions to light the dark and vast sky. That if she jumped and missed, she had no parachute to slow her descent. Instead, she gathered her skirts and climbed up on the rail.

Tucker extended a hand. "Show some sass, Flygirl."

From behind, she heard a shout. Heard a gunshot, then a screech that sounded very much like Leo's. She started to turn, but the airship listed. Adrenaline surging, Amelia reached out, jumped, and landed on what felt like the back of a horse with a force that jarred her entire body.

Tucker glanced over his shoulder. "You okay?"

Her pulse raced; her lungs seized. Instead of plummeting to the ground, she'd landed safely on Tucker's curious mode of escape. A flying horse? Her mind strained to make sense of it. Meanwhile, she took comfort in Tucker's presence, in his courage and strength. He gave her hand a reassuring squeeze, and her blood stirred in a most curious manner, making her chest ache and her body tingle. *It is the circumstance, not the man*, she told herself. One daring rescue couldn't possibly mend the romantic illusions he'd shattered mere hours before. Yet her heart was full, her mind crowded with the memory of his knee-melting kiss. Gobsmacked, she managed a nod.

"Hold tight." Snapping the reins, he nudged the horse— or rather, the bird-horse—into action. Massive wings flapped, propelling them away from the burning airship.

A Pegasus.

As she lived and breathed, the Sky Cowboy owned a mythical horse. Straddling the ebony beast, feeling its body heat and quivering power, she knew it to be real—not a figment of her imagination or a mechanical configuration— even though her mind screamed, *Impossible!*

Just then thunder boomed and lightning flashed. Amelia shivered as an ominous cloud mushroomed around them, seemingly devouring the *Flying Shark*. Tucker urged the horse faster, cutting through the perimeter of the cloud as a hard rain pelted them.

Seconds later they were clear of the storm, soaring through the night air with the ease and grace of a bird. Dazed, Amelia clung to Tucker, front plastered to his strong back, arms wrapped like a vise around his waist, legs draped over his thighs so as not to hinder the creature's wings. She half expected a cannonball to blow them out of the sky. But there was no gunfire, no more explosions. Only the sound of the wind, the pounding of her heart, and massive wings buffeting the current.

She realized then that they blended into the night sky. As far as she could tell their mount was pure ebony, and Tuck was dressed in head-to-toe black. In kind, Amelia's gown was deeply subdued. Only her golden curls threatened to give them away. She considered ripping fabric from the hem of her skirt and wrapping it around her head like a turban, but that would mean letting go of Tucker. She felt unbalanced as it was.

"How did you find me?" she shouted near his ear.

He gestured to the left.

"Leo!" Her beloved falcon was alive and well and flying alongside them. She burst with joy and a million questions, but emotion clogged her throat. Though her hair whipped and obscured her vision, though the wind stung her face and burned her eyes, she refused to bury her face against Tucker's broad shoulders. Refused to miss one moment of the glorious experience. Yes, Leo had flown alongside Bess and the *Flying Cloud*, but this was different. This time Amelia almost felt as though she had wings herself. She'd thought the Pogo Pack rocket ride had been a rush. Nothing would ever compare to this thrill.

Moments ago she'd anticipated death. This moment she'd never felt more alive. Amelia's soul danced as they sailed amongst the stars. She hugged Tucker, silently thanking him for this dream come true, breathing in the scent of bay rum, wool, horse sweat, and . . . licorice?

"Home, boy," Tucker said to the horse.

Peeking around the man's shoulder, Amelia spied flickering lights and the silhouette of a ship. The *Maverick*.

Blast.

She ached to ask Tucker to circle the airship, to fly her to the moon and back. The man owned a mythical horse. Surely he was capable of such magic. Unfortunately, she was clearheaded enough to realize that they could still be in danger because of Dunkirk. She couldn't expect the *Maverick* and its crew to lie in wait like sitting ducks whilst Tucker showed her the stars via Pegasus.

Sighing, she hugged the man who vexed and inspired and, damn him, ignited desire and tender affections that befuddled and annoyed her emancipated self. Grateful for the unique and wondrous experiences of the past two days, Amelia swallowed her pride and spoke her heart. "Thank you."

CHAPTER 11

Peg's hooves hit the deck of the *Maverick* and, for the first time in more than an hour, Tuck breathed easy. His plan had been risky, damned by most of his crew; even so it had worked. But instead of feeling boastful or proud, he was pissed.

Knowing Dunkirk's style, he'd assumed an elaborate seduction. He just hadn't anticipated Amelia succumbing. The sight of her in that revealing gown, smiling and flirting with that bastard in his goddamned *cabin*, had torched Tuck's blood. It had also doubled his conviction to steal her back pronto, since clearly the woman didn't have a lick of sense.

After pinpointing her whereabouts, he'd planted the detonators, then returned to signal her to rendezvous. For a moment he wondered whether she'd ignore or betray him. She'd made her fury evident when she'd cursed him to "bloody hell" after he'd allowed Dunkirk to carry her off. Maybe she'd decided any airship traveling to Italy would suit her purpose—even the airship of an unscrupulous pirate. Maybe she thought she could handle her abductor. But then she'd feigned sickness, and Tuck knew she'd opted to escape the Scottish bastard.

He didn't want to focus on the relief he'd felt when she jumped onto Peg. Or the pounding of his heart when she'd clung to him like a honeysuckle vine. Or the lump in his throat when she'd hugged tight and whispered her gratitude. He sure as hell didn't want to focus on the jealousy that had ripped through him like a blistering sandstorm at the thought of her in Dunkirk's bed.

"Take us out of here," Tuck called to StarMan as he handed Amelia down to Doc. "What are you looking at?" he asked the younger man while vaulting out of the custom-made saddle.

Doc tore his gaze from the woman's tantalizing curves. "Nothing. I . . . That is—"

"Ask Eli to see to Peg." Eli was the only man he fully trusted regarding the delicate mechanics of the horse's wings. Tuck patted his beloved stallion's neck, offering a licorice treat before trading the reins for Amelia and spiriting her from appreciative eyes. Axel and Birdman were drinking in their fill as well. "You men have your orders!" he snapped, then whisked her down the ladder.

"Where did you ever find a creature like that? A Pegasus. As I live and breathe. How—"

"Later."

"And Leo. I was certain he'd been shot. I distinctly saw—"

"Doc."

"It would seem he has a magical touch. Do you know my leg feels fully healed?" she went on as he hurried her through the darkened passage way. "No discomfort at all. So soon. How can that be? How—"

"Consider yourself lucky."

"Yes, but . . ." She tried to shake off his hold, then peered over her shoulder. "Why the urgency?" she asked in a breathless voice. "Do you think Captain Dunkirk will come after us?"

"Safe bet." He squeezed her waist. "I've got something he wants."

"But you set his airship afire."

"Storm put out the flames. Trust me: He'll rally. Did you tell him what he wanted to know?"

"What?"

"The location of the treasure."

"Do I look vapid?"

"Don't ask me what you look like just now, Amelia." He steered her into his cabin and slammed the door. Wanting the *Maverick* to remain as invisible as possible, he opted for a kerosene lantern over an electric lamp. The soft glow illuminated the petite woman in all her tantalizing splendor. Windblown waist-length curls. Flushed cheeks. A silk-and-lace gown that left little to the imagination. Full hips, small waist, delectable breasts. Face of an angel, body of a goddess. "Christ."

She crossed her arms, trying to hide her bountiful bosom. It didn't help. Angry now, she stiffened her spine, which only heaved the pale globes higher. "Don't look at me like that," she huffed.

"Then take off that damned dress."

"What?"

He wrenched off his coat and flight cap. "Take it off or I'll rip it off."

She gasped. "What is wrong with you, Mr. Gentry?"

"You're what's wrong with me, Miss Darcy." He whirled and pinned her against the wall. Volatile emotions walloped calm thinking: jealousy, possessiveness, desire. Add to that the lingering adrenaline from attacking Dunkirk and the *Flying Shark* solo.

This was bad.

Walk away. Clear out.

He stood his ground. "Have you no shame?"

She blanched. "If wearing this hideous gown meant getting the upper hand with Captain Dunkirk, then it seemed a small price to pay."

"You thought to manipulate Colin Dunkirk?"

"I . . . Well, yes."

"The way you manipulated me? By playing a part?"

"Excuse me?"

"With me you were the damsel in distress. The feisty virgin in desperate need of passage to Italy to see your dying grandpap."

"Yes, well . . ."

"With him a saucy treasure hunter in desperate need of reaching Italy to obtain hidden riches." He leaned in, lowered his voice, and grazed her ear with his mouth. "How far were you willing to go, Flygirl?"

"Of all the . . ." She placed her palms on his shoulders and shoved.

He easily resisted, though there was surprising muscle behind that push. Point taken, he allowed her some breathing space.

In gratitude, she swung out and slapped his face.

Damn.

"You're the one who allowed that scoundrel to kidnap me," she railed. "You said I was bad luck. 'Good riddance.'"

"Tactical call." He braced his hands on his hips and glared. "If you would have stayed in this cabin like I told you—"

"The thought of hiding whilst you and your men faced peril was unacceptable. I had Papa's gun. I thought maybe . . . I wanted to help. Silly me," she added in a mocking tone.

Tuck dragged a hand through his hair. She sounded so earnest. This woman tied his senses in knots so he didn't know up from down. Only one thing was sure and certain: When given the option, she'd chosen him over Dunkirk. "You didn't actually think I'd leave you at the mercy of air pirates?"

Still furious, she threw up her hands in frustration. "I do not know what you are capable of, remember? From your words and actions I assumed you'd rather the pirates abscond with me than your illegal cargo. Then I saw . . . I heard . . . I thought Leo had been shot after you promised to keep him safe."

"You thought I betrayed you, so you sought to get even by sleeping with Dunkirk?"

"Yes. I mean, no. I was striking a bargain."

"A roll in the hay for safe passage to Italy?"

She swung out again; only this time Tuck caught her wrists. She kicked and thrashed and, dammit, nearly clipped his family jewels. Patience spent, he wrestled her to the bed. Pinning her arms over her head, he looked hard into those furious blue eyes. "You can't bargain with a man like Colin Dunkirk, Amelia."

Chest heaving, she looked away. "I know that now. I misjudged. I thought . . . That is, you are an outlaw and I trusted *you*. I . . . I felt safe."

This was worse than bad. Lust and affection lassoed his being, hog-tied logic and propriety. His gaze skimmed the blush of her cheek, the curve of her jaw, the length of her neck, the swell of her . . .

Christ.

He struggled to be a gentleman, even though he was no longer convinced she was chaste. "We're both outlaws, true. The difference is, I won't take what isn't willingly offered or honestly earned."

She slowly turned and met his gaze. "Meaning?"

"I won't seduce you with dinner and wine. I won't make promises or offers or bargains. I'll tell you straight up: I want you, Amelia. Naked and writhing beneath me. I want to kiss you senseless, make you tremble with desire. But I won't make a move unless you ask. Way I see it, given the natural pull between us, it's only a matter of time." He stroked his thumbs over the insides of her wrists, pressed his erection against her silky skirts. *Flee or soar, Flygirl?* "Still feel safe?"

She reared up and kissed him—a closemouthed kiss that sent a shock of lust to his already throbbing shaft. *Well, hell.* He nipped her lower lip; she nipped back. He suckled; she suckled. He sensed inexperience, yet a passion that would scorch the ocean dry. A heartbeat later she dropped her head back and stared up with blatant desire.

"That your way of askin', Miss Darcy?"

"Are you deaf, Mr. Gentry?"

"You're playing with fire."

"I live for adventure."

"I can't give you forever."

"Thank God."

Amelia held her breath as Tucker flipped her over and un-laced the bodice. Somewhere between being seduced by a pirate and rescued by a cowboy, Amelia had decided she would lose her virginity to the man of her choice. At the moment of her choosing. She chose Tucker Gentry, and she chose now.

Never had she craved a man's touch such as she craved Tucker's. His hands upon her flesh as he slid the capped sleeves from her shoulders set her entire body afire. Years of hero worship combined with spontaneous combustible desire obliterated inhibitions and rational thought. The longer he took to rid her of the abominable gown, the tighter the sensuous coil in her stomach. "What is taking you so long, sir?"

"Savoring the moment, miss."

Bothersome, that. She didn't want slow—all the more time to lose her nerve. Unpracticed in the art of seduction, she expedited the matter by getting straight to the point. "I am not naked. Nor am I writhing," she said, jerking up so that he rolled aside. "Allow me to help you with the first portion." Now that he'd loosened the laces, she easily wiggled out of the bodice. "What are you waiting for?" she asked whilst shimmying out of the skirts. "Take off your clothes."

She didn't stop to think or look, for fear she would grow skittish. She simply continued to disrobe, sitting on the edge of her bed in her skimpy bloomers and chemise in order to unlace her boots.

"What, no dainty slippers?"

"I had to draw the line somewhere." Dunkirk had sup-plied a pair of delicate red satin slippers, but they were too small. Much like the ridiculous gown, though, she had not been able to squeeze her feet into those narrow, knobby-heeled shoes. She hadn't cared at the time, but just now her clunky boots made her feel like a big-footed clod. Striving to connect with her feminine side, she tossed her long curls over her shoulders and glanced at Tucker. The hungry look in his eyes cast her heart aflutter with dread and anticipation.

Quelling a whisper of panic, she gestured to his still-clothed body. "Must I do everything?" Seduction was not her forte, shrinking violet not her style. Amelia grasped two handfuls of Tucker's ebony shirt and yanked it over his head. Before she could fully enjoy the astounding view of his muscled torso, he nabbed her and flipped her onto the bed.

"Anxious, are you?" he asked with a wicked gleam in his eye.

"Quite." She wrestled off his trousers. Her heart hammered. *Good Lord.* He resembled an exquisitely chiseled statue—corded sinew, etched perfection. And his member—so large and rigid.

Her womanhood pulsed whilst her brain scrambled. She'd overheard titillating gossip and read a scientific piece on the mating rituals of animals. She had two older brothers who spoke frankly when unaware of her presence. Amelia knew the basics of lovemaking. She knew what went where, but, bloody hell, how?

Then suddenly Tucker was on top of her, kissing her, urging her to open her mouth. Thoughts blurred as his tongue plundered and suckled, as his hands pushed under her chemise and smoothed over her quivering stomach. She gasped as his fingers brushed her bare breasts, then moaned as he ridded her of her bloomers, spread her legs, and skimmed her slick womanhood.

She was, she conceded in dazed euphoria, out of her element.

He smiled against her cheek. "Anxious and ready."

She cupped his devilishly handsome face and kissed him, wanting him to shut up and hurry. As he'd wished, she was trembling with desire. She ached with wants and needs, yet knew not what precisely to ask for. She'd never been one for trial runs or cautious advance. Just like the first time she'd pedaled Bess off the end of a dangerously high ramp, she simply wanted to fly. Delirious from Tucker's kisses, she barely registered the moment the tip of his shaft grazed her folds. But then she felt a painful intrusion.

She tensed and he froze.

"Good Christ, you *are* an innocent." Before he could retreat, she grasped his buttocks and pulled him down whilst pushing her hips up and ... "Oh!"

"Easy, darlin'." He dropped his forehead to hers, breath labored, voice gruff. "No turning back now."

She adjusted to the strange and wondrous intrusion. "I ... I do not wish to turn back. I want ... I want ..." Something she could not describe.

He withdrew ever so slightly, then eased back in. He brushed his mouth over her forehead, her cheeks—soothing, enticing. "Relax, Amelia. Give yourself over and let me do the rest."

She breathed, nodded. Astonishing, but she was actually thankful for his vast experience in this matter. She gave over, relished the feel of his strong hands stroking and caressing as he slowly moved within. Pain soon gave way to a sensual friction, and then delicious sensations that rolled ever so slowly throughout her being. She gripped his shoulders, body quaking, pulse pounding. "I can't breathe."

"Let go." He quickened his pace, the pressure. His fingers stroked, kneaded. "Come for me, Amelia. Come with me."

She moaned, arched. Excitement surged as she edged toward the unknown.

"Let go and soar." He coaxed her with a searing kiss, shattered her control.

Oh, the sensations!

She screamed his name—chest aching, muscles burning. White light exploded behind her closed lids, breaking apart into a zillion twinkling lights. "Stars," she whispered as she felt Tucker tumbling after her. Dazed and delirious, she said nothing as he rolled aside with a colorful curse, pulling her into his arms and holding her close. Her body tingled and her brain buzzed in the sensual fallout. Without a flying contraption of any sort, including a Pegasus, Tucker Gentry had shown her the stars.

CHAPTER 12

Tuck lay silent as he warred with his conscience. As his body recovered from an explosive climax that had left him light-headed and bleary eyed. He hadn't been that quick on the draw since he was fifteen, when he'd lost his virginity to Wanda Mae, a local dove with a fondness for breaking in young bucks. An expert in her field, the buxom beauty had brought him back around in a matter of minutes and then taught him a few lessons on stamina that he'd cultivated over the years. Tuck took a lot of pride in pleasuring a woman thoroughly before indulging in his own release.

That had not been the case with Amelia.

Her kisses alone made him randy as a bull. Then when she'd stripped ... he hadn't expected that. Nor had he expected to be aroused by the sight of her cotton unmentionables paired with thick striped socks and mannish boots. The way she'd barked orders and tugged off his shirt, he'd abandoned his assumption that she was chaste. Unrefined in the art of lovemaking, but not innocent. She'd been so damned slick with want, he hadn't paid attention to how tight she was until he'd felt resistance. In the moment his mind screamed, *Retreat*, she'd robbed him of the chance. He wanted to thrash her for putting him in the damnable position of having to behave like the bastard that half the world believed him to be. An honorable man would offer marriage. Under normal circumstances, even though he felt somewhat duped, he would've done the right thing. But Tuck's circumstances were far from normal. By manipulating the carnal alliance, Amelia had tainted her reputation and hammered his conscience. At the same time, he felt primal jubilance in being her first. That said and considered, her first time was all wrong.

Now she was curled alongside him in his arms, limbs heavy from exhaustion. He could feel the rapid pounding of her heart and her uneven breathing. He could not, however, guess her thoughts.

"You misled me, Amelia."

She stiffened, her soft curls tickling his nose as she dipped her head into the crook of his shoulder, angling her face from view. "It seemed unwise to admit to an outlaw that I was in pursuit of a great treasure," she grumbled into his collarbone. "How could I trust you wouldn't steal it from me?"

"I'm not talking about the treasure right now, although that is another bone of contention." He grasped her chin and gently drew her attention. When her dazzling blue eyes locked with his, he had to temper his pulse all over again. "Between your aggressiveness and nonchalance you intimated you were an experienced woman."

"I did not say one way or another, and you did not ask. What you chose to believe is not my fault."

Fair enough. "Why?"

"Why what?"

"Why me?"

She lowered her lashes, though she didn't pull away. He assumed she felt awkward now, naked but for her skimpy chemise. "Previously lovemaking held no interest for me. Tonight it did. You make me . . ." She breathed, sighed. "You inspire vexing yet thrilling yearnings. I wanted to experience, to explore. I refuse to feel bad."

"I'm not asking you to feel bad, darlin'. Just trying to understand."

"What if there is no tomorrow?" she asked in a quiet voice.

He frowned down at the top of her head. "What do you mean?"

She shrugged. "I could have perished in the kitecycle crash or at the hands of Dunkirk. I could have jumped for Peg and missed, plummeting hundreds of miles to the earth. If tomorrow never comes I wish to die with no regrets. No missed opportunities."

He thought about that newspaper article. About the unexpected and horrific death of her father, a man she obviously revered. He suspected Lord Ashford's death haunted her dreams and motivated her reckless actions. He understood, but couldn't say he approved of her derring-do attitude. "Living like there's no tomorrow. Risky business, Flygirl."

"My business," she insisted.

"Do what you please and everyone else be damned?"

"I didn't say that."

"Your brothers don't know about your Italian excursion, do they?"

She didn't answer.

"What about your ma? Did you sneak off in the middle of the night? Leave her a note? Bet she's riddled with worry."

"The only thing she's riddled with is misery regarding our dire straits. She knows not my destination, but knows my goal. I have her blessing."

"You don't sound happy about it."

"I'm delirious," she snapped, then shifted to glare down at him. "Shouldn't you join your men? Won't they be waiting?"

"They know what to do."

"But if Dunkirk—"

"If they need me they'll call." She thought to end this discussion, but he'd only just begun. "I've got business here. With you. But first we need to change the linens and wash up."

She blinked, caught off guard by the change of subject, then flushed as she realized his meaning. "Oh, I . . ." She peeked under the coverlet. "Blast."

Tuck smoothed Amelia's tousled hair from her face and noted the intensity of her embarrassment. "Stay here." He swung out of bed, at ease with his naked state, although he felt her stunned gaze burning into his backside as he crossed the cabin.

"Your tattoo," she said in blatant awe. "It's magnificent."

And here he'd thought she'd been impressed by his naked body. "Compliments of an artist I met in an Irish sky-town seven months back." Once in a blue moon Tuck got news from home, and it always knocked him on his ass, causing depression and fury. He often numbed the pain with booze and smoke, only that night someone slipped him an opium-laced cheroot and he'd ended up getting tattooed by a Freak, a brilliant artist shunned by the mainstream because of his mongrel race. Now Tuck was branded with a work of art that spanned his entire back and shoulders. Not that he minded much, since the body art honored Peg.

"Did it hurt?" Amelia asked.

"Didn't feel a thing." Nor did he remember much of the event. He was lucky he hadn't ended up tattooed with a Mod slogan—*Make love, not war*—or some damned neon-colored flower-power symbol. Grimacing, he pushed aside the partition that hid the cast-iron-and-porcelain tub and a gleaming seven-foot tank. He tripped a spigot and steaming water flowed. "Eli and I devised a compact electric water heater," he said, distracting her with a newfangled invention. "Damned convenient."

"I've heard of such a thing," Amelia said, knees clutched to her chest, eyes wide. "You do much with electricity on this airship."

"Electricity, steam, gas. We've been experimenting with solar power as well. Diversity's key, given the astronomical cost of gasoline."

"So you do have an understanding of science and me-chanics."

He raised a brow at her accusatory tone.

"Earlier today, you said you were unsure as to how the blasterbeefs function, precisely. I do believe you misled me, Mr. Gentry."

"As for misleading you, Miss Darcy," he said while test-ing the temperature of the water, "those blasterbeefs are one of a kind. I intend to keep it that way."

"You think I'd steal your technology?"

"I don't know what you're capable of."

"I suppose I've given you little reason to trust me."

"No reason at all." He gestured to the tub. "Climb in before it cools."

She looked longingly at the steaming water. "Doc ad-vised me not to get these stitches wet."

"What stitches?"

She reached beneath the coverlet, unwound her ban-dage, then a heartbeat later gasped. "They're gone. The stitches disappeared!"

"You said you felt fully healed. I assumed the stitches dissolved. They usually do. Doc uses special thread."

"Amazing."

He strode to an armoire he'd brought all the way from Wyoming territory, and rifled a shelf in search of fresh lin-ens. "Water's getting cold."

"Will you be leaving the room?"

"No." Back turned, he heard her make a dash for it, heard the gentle sloshing of water as she eased into the deep, high-backed tub he'd purchased in Paris. Heard her blissful sigh, and smiled. "Find the soap?"

"Yes, thank you."

She soaked and washed in thoughtful silence as he made quick work of the bed.

The silence was short-lived. "I'm dying to know about your flying horse."

"I'm sure you are."

"Where on earth did you find a Pegasus?"

"I didn't. Peg's a Friesian stallion. Had him since he was a colt. Bought him off of a European breeder who relocated to California."

"But he has wings."

"Detachable wings."

"But how—"

"It's complicated."

"One of a kind?" she groused. "Another trade secret?"

"A combination of technology and heart." Linens changed, he moved to the tub. The sight of Amelia soaking neck-deep in sudsy water, her golden hair slicked back from her flawless face, stirred his lust quicker than Wanda Mae's practiced touch. Sporting a rock-hard erection, he squeezed her shoulder. "Scoot up."

She scrunched over and concentrated on her finger-nails—perpetually stained with grease, which he found oddly charming. "Why?"

"So as not to waste hot water. Only so much in the tank."

"I'll get out."

"Don't bother." He moved in behind her, forcing her to make room. "Relax, darlin'. We shared a bed; we can share a bath."

She sat rigid, nestled between his legs.

Ignoring the discomfort of his throbbing arousal, Tuck took the soap from her clenched hand and lathered her tense shoulders. "Tomorrow we drop our cargo near Paris. *Maverick*'s in need of fine-tuning. Figure my crew can use a respite, given that we haven't been at port in a while. Day or two; then we'll move on to Italy."

She glanced over her bare, glistening shoulder. "You said you'd take me to Paris but no farther."

"Changed my mind."

"Because you want my treasure?"

"Won't deny I'm curious about it." Tuck wrestled with

his annoying conscience and lost. What the hell? He'd take the honest high road and lay his cards on the table. "Because of my legal quandary I'm in need of a bargaining chip. For the time bein' I'm focused on building my bankroll. Figure we can work out a deal."

Amelia chewed her lower lip, causing his blood to stir. "I'll think about it."

"You do that." He knew better then to press just now. Sensed she'd shut down. She'd gone through more in one day than most women did in a lifetime. He'd do better to take it slow, catch her off guard, but damn, Tuck wanted her to put a name to that treasure. An invention of historical significance, somewhere in Italy. What the hell could it be? As suggested by Doc, he couldn't shake the feeling that it had something to do with her kin's time machine— which posed a bit of a moral dilemma. Tuck had no interest in trading now for the future, and tampering with the past could well worsen the present. The way he saw it there was no adventure as grand as living in the moment. Unfortunately, there were plenty of folk who'd jump at a chance to dip their toes into another dimension, consequences be damned. Reintroducing a working time machine into society—even into the hands of the British government—struck Tuck as dangerous. Still, a percentage of that monumental prize money would go a long way toward financing his personal goals of reuniting with his sister and properly compensating his men for saving his neck.

"What is it?" Amelia asked. "What's wrong?"

Tuck blinked out of his gloom.

"You drifted away."

"Doin' some thinkin' of my own, is all." He rinsed her long, thick tresses, then pulled her back against him, kneading her shoulders, her arms. "How do you feel?"

"Exhausted."

"Sore?"

"Not in the way I think you mean," she said softly. "But my entire body aches. It's been a tense and most active day."

As irritated as he was with the situation, as much as he didn't trust Amelia Darcy, he sure as hell liked the feel of her. Hell, he liked *her*. He thought about the way she'd whacked the blasterbeefs, clearing the stator coils, and almost laughed.

Feeling the tension ease from her limbs, he continued to massage her muscles—shoulders, arms, thighs. She sighed and he took advantage, skimming his fingers between her legs, over her womanly folds.

"What are you—"

"Shh." He nipped and suckled her earlobe, pleasured her with his fingers—stroking, rubbing. She moaned, her legs parting wider. "That's it, honey." His other palm slid up and over her taut stomach, teased the underside of her full breast, then closed over the firm mound. He ached to suck her buds but rolled them between his fingers instead. Plucking, pinching.

Her moans grew louder as he continued to stroke her to orgasm. She tensed and trembled, and he urged her to let go. She bucked with a climax, and swear to God, he nearly lost control—simply from the intense pleasure of watching Amelia come apart under his touch.

She let out a shaky breath. "Are there no limits to your talents?"

He smiled close to her ear. "Just part of what you hurried me through before."

"Then I regret my lack of patience."

He considered the woman in his arms, wondering whether she'd be so bold as to allow another man to broaden her sexual horizons. The notion rankled. At the same time he had no right to judge or censor. "Just so we're straight on this, Amelia, I can't offer marriage."

"I wouldn't accept if you did. I have no desire to be shackled to any man."

"But you want to know the pleasures of a man's touch."

"I wish I hadn't rushed you."

Tuck pondered the next few days, tried to sort through his jumbled feelings regarding this complicated and infinitely fascinating woman. For once he couldn't think ahead with any clear direction. He decided to fall back on Amelia's current mind-set: living in the here and now. One day at a time. No missed opportunities. If any man broadened her sexual horizons, he wanted it to be him.

He finessed Amelia so that she was facing him, ignored the stutter of his pulse as he looked into those hypnotic eyes—eyes that viewed the world with never-ending wonder. "You want to explore? Learn the extensive pleasures of lovemaking? I'll show you the stars and introduce you to a few planets, but there'll be no promises or ties beyond your being true to me as long as we're keepin' company. That agreeable?"

She furrowed her brow. "Seems a little one-sided."

"How so?"

"If I am to be faithful, then you should be true to me as well. For as long as we're keeping company."

Her candor and sass never failed to amaze. He quirked a brow. "Think I can handle that."

Teeth chattering from the cooled water, she offered her pruney fingers. "Shall we shake on it, Mr. Gentry?"

He grasped her hand and pulled her up with him, lifting her from the tub and wrapping her in a towel. Carrying her to his bed, he winked down at the brazen minx. "I can think of better ways to seal the deal, Miss Darcy."

CHAPTER 13

Amelia stirred but clung to the last vestiges of sleep, her hazy mind and achy body assessing and acknowledging her scandalous behavior the night before. She felt no regret, only wonder. What did that make her exactly? Emancipated? Progressive? A rebel? A hussy?

Face buried in her pillow, she calmed her rising anxiety and dug deep. According to gossip, her brothers had bedded many a companion, and yet their reputations as honorable men remained intact. Granted, she was a woman, and the social and moral rules of conduct were vastly different, not that they made sense to Amelia. Why should she be judged harshly purely because of her gender? At heart she was the same person as before, just . . . more worldly. Although she aspired to a great many things, mostly having to do with flying, lovemaking had never been on her must-do-or-die list.

It was now.

No denying the realization, the relentless yearning. Now that she'd sampled the arousing delights of Tucker Gentry, she longed for more. More kisses. More caresses. More shockingly intimate stimulation.

Dazed with desire, she'd allowed Tucker to touch her in the most brazen and illicit ways. By the time he'd entered her the second time, she'd been shameless, begging for more, begging for release. They'd peaked at the same time, falling into sated, silent exhaustion.

She didn't remember falling asleep. But she remembered

him holding her close, the mutual pounding of their hearts, the possessive feel of his hand upon her hip, of her palm upon his shoulder. Then suddenly she was dreaming. Fragments of her life, good and bad. Papa cheering her first flight. Pulling her from the wreckage. Offering courage whilst the doctor stitched the gash in her leg. She'd dreamed about the day Papa had presented her with the modified version of Leo. About the story he'd told her time and again, rehashing the day he'd attended the exhibition at the Crystal Palace. The day he'd seen his cousin Briscoe disappear in a rainbow of light via his time machine.

And the one time he'd mentioned the secret letter.

She'd dreamed about her brothers and her mother struggling to resurrect the family's reputation and finances. She dreamed about Papa dying. Heart-wrenching, and yet there'd been an intangible sense of comfort. For the first time since Papa's death, she'd greeted the dawn with a sense of hope as opposed to depression.

Amelia slowly opened her eyes, mourned the absence of Tucker for a brief second—he had an airship to captain, after all—then disengaged herself from the tangle of blankets. Hurrying toward the blessed water heater, she decided to embrace the new day with a nonchalant air. She would face Tucker and his men as she had the previous days, with confidence and a dash of bravado, as if nothing had changed. Even though her heart and mind were full of their wondrous lovemaking, she would focus on the future. On her goal. Although Tucker had agreed to transport her to Italy, she intended to rebuild Bess—partly because she preferred an alternative mode of transportation, should the need arise. Partly because she burned to keep one of Papa's inventions alive.

Thirty minutes later, Amelia approached the cabin door, her hair braided and coiled in her own unique fashion, dressed in her mended leather flight pants—stitched back together courtesy of Doc—a cotton blouse, and her leather tail vest. Bracing for the brisk winter winds, she'd donned her duster and scarves, goggles and top hat—everything as normal. "I am the same, yet better. Worldly."

Breathing deeply, she stepped into the hall. It occurred to her suddenly that Doc had not yet appeared with breakfast. Not that she expected to be served, but thus far all of her meals had been taken in Tucker's cabin. As she navigated the hall, she was also aware of the unusual silence and warmer temperature. Smelling licorice and hay, she hesitated, contemplating whether or not to seek out Peg. He must be stabled on this deck or just below. Admittedly she was bursting with curiosity regarding that winged horse, but at the same time the undeniable sense that they were no longer in flight propelled Amelia topside. She scaled the ladder and climbed on deck, noting the bright sunshine and lack of wind.

Peeling off her hat and goggles, she looked up and saw that the sails and masts were lowered. The clouds were sparse and floating high above. The blasterbeefs were abnormally quiet. Looking ahead over the bow, instead of sky she saw trees. As she'd suspected, somewhere between last night and this morning, they'd taken refuge in a densely wooded area. Landing in the secluded clearing had taken great skill, and she bemoaned the fact that she'd missed the event.

At that moment, Leo flew out of a copse of trees, swooped in, and perched on the rail. Smiling, Amelia rushed to his side. "Greetings, my friend."

Smoothing a hand over his back, she inspected the wondrous creature for bandages or stitches but saw no sign of injury, even though she was certain he'd been shot. Again, she marveled at Doc's methods. She wanted to thank him for his efforts and wondered at his absence. Come to think of it, she'd yet to spy even one of the crew this morning. Pulse tripping, she searched the vicinity, then, spying a manmade trail that cut through a swath of trees, peered beyond.

In the distance, set amidst a breathtaking mix of woods and meadows, she saw a massive estate that more closely resembled a palace. Even Lord Bingham's luxurious mansion paled in comparison to the grandeur of this country residence.

"Something, ain't it?"

Amelia turned, bracing as the ship's engineer joined her at the starboard gunwale. She noted the unlit cigar dangling from his mouth, the Blaster holstered in his shoulder rig, his grease-stained hands, and the bandage covering the wound he'd sustained during the tussle with Dunkirk. She wondered whether he blamed her for the injury. He certainly blamed her for everything else.

"The Château de Malmaison," Axel said with something that resembled a rusty smile.

She wasn't sure what surprised her more: that they'd landed near the home that had once belonged to Napoléon Bonaparte and Joséphine de Beauharnais, and then later Napoléon III, or that Axel O'Donnell had addressed her with a modicum of civility. Grateful, she peered back at the estate. "Even at this distance," she noted in awe, "the opulence is astounding."

"Why anyone would want to live in that ostentatious monstrosity beats the stuffing out of me. Although I wouldn't mind a gander at the gardens. Heard tell zebras and kangaroos roam about the rosebushes. Never seen a kangaroo."

Presently an eccentric duke of excessive wealth owned Malmaison and, like Joséphine, had populated the magnificent gardens with exotic wildlife. Amelia had read an exposé in the *Informer* that focused not only on the menagerie but on his legion of automocoaches and a small collection of aerostats. "I'd prefer a tour of his aero-hangar."

"Ain't you got any interests beyond flying, girl?"

She did now, but she wasn't about to mention her new obsession with lovemaking to the *Maverick*'s engineer—or anyone else, for that matter. Ignoring his question, she asked one of her own. "Why are we here?"

"Business."

She put two and two together and whistled low. "Transporting illegal cargo for a famous nobleman. Whatever you smuggled, he must be paying a fortune."

"Ain't nothing compared to the booty you're tailing. Elsewise Dunkirk never would've left the *Maverick* without searching her hold."

Amelia turned and regarded the hulking man with a furrowed brow. "What precisely are you transporting?"

"What precisely are you tailing?"

"I'd rather not say."

"Same here."

Sensing a hint of hostility, Leo screeched.

Axel narrowed his eyes on the falcon. "Who fixed that bird up with mechanical parts?"

"My father," she answered with pride.

"Surprised they work."

She bristled. "Contrary to that article in the *Informer*, Papa was not an inept lunatic. He was, in his own way, quite brilliant."

"If you say so."

"I knew your civil humor was too good to be true."

"Marshal asked me to be nice to you. I tried, but the effort wore thin fast."

For a fleeting moment she wondered whether Tucker had mentioned their intimate liaison, but then she realized it was not the sort of thing a man bragged about, unless he wanted to risk gossip that could result in her brothers forcing him down the church aisle. He'd stated clearly he could not marry; therefore surely her secret was safe. This was simply Axel being Axel. He'd disliked her upon first meeting. "You are a vexing man, Mr. O'Donnell."

"You're a pain in the ass, Miss Darcy. Frankly speaking."

"I do not recall making a nuisance of myself."

"First you slowed us by almost crashing into the *Maverick*, then insisting we haul your wreck aboard."

"Yes, well—"

"Then we were delayed by Dunkirk and in turn had to outrun ALE."

"Not my—"

"Last night we flew out of our way, then cooled our rudders while the marshal risked his life and delayed our valuable shipment in order to rescue you."

"I can see how—"

"Since you boarded we've experienced one misfortune after another."

"I am not bad luck."

"Maybe not. But you are trouble. Thanks to you we ticked off ALE and Dunkirk, and one or both is tracking our hides. We should be lying low for a spell. Instead we're vamoosing to Italy. That is, after we fit this boat with repairs. Not that anything was wrong with the *Maverick* before—"

"—I boarded. Yes, yes. I follow your warped line of thinking." Her own patience snapped. "Where's Mr. Gentry?"

Axel nodded toward the château. "Takin' care of business."

Amelia gawked at the burly engineer. "He left the ship?"

"Along with rest of the crew."

"I cannot believe . . . Why wasn't I invited along?" Surely Tucker knew she'd consider a visit to the Château de Malmaison a once-in-a-lifetime thrill. She thought she'd made her decision to explore rare opportunities quite clear.

Axel grunted. "What? So you could muck up the delivery? Tuck may be softhearted when it comes to you, but when it comes to money he's a hardheaded bastard."

"Yet he risked a substantial payday, putting his ship and cargo at risk by stealing me away from Dunkirk." She wasn't sure why she felt the need to remind him of his own words, except that it made her feel less the fool. She was beginning to wonder who had manipulated whom regarding her intimate liaison with the Sky Cowboy.

Axel quirked a sardonic brow. "According to Dunkirk, you're worth a fortune. Guess the marshal considered you a smart risk. A man can buy anything with enough money. Including freedom."

Amelia didn't care for his insinuation one whit. Then again, she was pretty sure the narrow-minded lunkhead would say or do about anything to alienate her from Tucker and hasten her departure. As it happened, Tucker had freely stated his financial concerns the night before. Exasperated, she whirled and paced toward the stern, hands on hips. Of all the men to be stuck with. She would've preferred the company of any one of the other crewmen. She could've asked Doc Blue about his seemingly magical skills. Birdman Chang owed her a lesson in acupressure. She was most eager to question Eli Boone about the intricacies of the retractable masts and walking stick. She suspected he also had knowledge of Peg's amazing detachable wings. But no. Tucker had left her with this superstitious, cranky, pea-brained oaf.

Furious, she paced back to said oaf. "Where's Bess?"

"Two decks below. Near the stern. A heap of mangled canvas, wood, and metal. You can't fix her!" he shouted as she stalked away.

"*Can't* is not in my vocabulary, Mr. O'Donnell."

Once Amelia had retrieved her tool bag and Axel had shown her to the cavernous storage room that housed the remnants of her kitecycle, she'd waited until she was sure he'd returned topside before skipping out in search of Peg. The scent of hay was stronger than ever. She simply followed her nose to the opposite end of the ship. Peg's stable was nearly as big as her temporary workspace. Spacious and well lighted. Cozy and clean. Remarkably ventilated. Peg, however, was not in residence. Amelia assumed Tucker had ridden or flown the horse to the great estate. Surely the mighty creature enjoyed freedom, fresh air, and exercise. She remembered Tucker's tender manner with the steed, his gentle touch with Leo. She remembered Axel's words: *Marshal's got a way with animals.*

Her heart swelled. A fine quality indeed.

Intrigued, she inspected the tidy stall and tack area, the generous mound of sleeping straw, the bales of hay and barrels of oats. She sniffed out the licorice stash. She'd never known a horse to eat licorice. Then again, she'd never known a horse to fly. She noted the organized tack, the grooming supplies, and a massive cabinet. She tried the doors. Locked. Was that where they kept Peg's detachable wings? Aside from the obvious—Peg was well tended, in fact perhaps spoiled—there was little more to learn here, and Amelia was beginning to feel like a snoop. Were Tucker to find her now, would he accuse her of trying to learn his secrets? Of studying the mechanical wings in hope of reproducing them or selling the designs?

Probably.

In truth she was merely dying of curiosity. How could a horse fly? Could a similar design work for a man? Or, more precisely, a woman? Soaring the skies upon Peg had been wondrous, but soaring the skies on her own? Like the fabled Icarus? Only, unlike the winged man of Greek mythology, she would not fly too close to the sun. Not that she thought Peg's wings were constructed from wax, although they could be. The feathers had looked and felt real enough, but how were they affixed to the framework, and what constituted the frame? Metal and hinges? How did the wings attach to Peg? How did Peg make them flap or know when to glide?

Blast.

The mystery of it all taxed her being. Needing to focus on something else, Amelia hurried back to her workspace. Upon a second and more intense look at the mangled heap, she blew out a breath, acknowledging the great challenge before her. "What a bloody mess."

Whilst sorting through the rubble, she wondered how her brothers were faring in their quest, then just as quickly shoved them from her mind. She wished them success. Truly she did. One significant find was all the family needed. But that did not dim her personal determination. Surely the Darcys weren't the only ones vying for the jubilee prize. What if the Jubilee Science Committee was ultimately presented with a dozen inventions of historical significance? Or fifty? Or a hundred? Who determined the scale of significance? The committee? The queen? Unlike Prince Albert, rest his soul, Her Majesty was not a great proponent of science. Would she recognize the importance of a da Vinci ornithopter?

Amelia snuffed that line of thought. Second-guessing her invention of choice was fruitless. Besides, the ornithopter was of vast interest and significance to her. And she knew where to look for it. Peeling off her scarves and coat, she pushed up her sleeves, nabbed her tool bag, and immersed herself in the resurrection of Bess. Her restless mood instantly settled.

Sunlight poured through two concave windows, spreading warmth and light. Time passed in an intense blur. She had no grasp of the hour or the physical toll. She simply worked. Although there was nothing simple about the process.

Amelia sat back on her haunches at one point, acknowledging a throbbing at her temples, an ache in her back. Her brain hurt as badly as her body. She'd drawn on memories. Her father's words and musings. Her recollection of the building process. Since she hadn't been present during all of Papa's working hours, she was not aware of his every move. Thus she felt as though there were missing pieces to this puzzle. Not to mention she was working with damaged goods. Although Mr. O'Donnell had provided her with some pristine raw materials.

Amelia had no illusions. The engineer had not acted out

of kindness so much as desperation. He probably thought that if she did reconstruct Bess, she'd abandon the *Maverick* and fly off under her own power and command in order to privately secure her "treasure." *Good riddance*, she could hear him say. As it happened, she did not relish having to share even a percentage of the jubilee prize, and truth be known, part of her harbored the ugly possibility that Tucker might try to steal the invention for himself. What had Axel said? *When it comes to money, he's a hardheaded bastard.* Bothersome, that. Still, she'd rather contend with Tucker than Dunkirk. Also, the *Maverick* would travel much faster to Italy than her kitecycle. It would provide greater protection were Dunkirk to sniff out her trail. All that considered, Bess was merely Amelia's mode of escape should there be an emergency.

Exhausted, she dragged a hand over her face, disgusted with her pitifully slow progress. She'd tinkered and corrected damage to the main engine, and because of Mr. O'Donnell, she had new canvas for the wings. But the wrought-iron frame of the tandem velocipede was bent beyond her personal ability to repair. As were the iron tires. The wooden spokes of the wheels and the skeletal frame of the kite wing had suffered severe fractures. "Crikey."

"Twin-cylinder double-acting engine?" Tucker hunkered down beside her and pointed out various parts. "What about those connecting rods?"

Caught up in her frustration, she hadn't heard his approach. Now his presence filled every particle of the spacious room, making her nerves jangle and her heart dance. She could scarcely breathe. "Designed to run directly to the rear axle."

"Fire tube boiler?"

"Originally fitted behind the rear seat. Doubles as a water tank."

"Heat?"

"Provided by crushed coal. Kept a backup supply in augmented saddlebags." She shrugged, sighed. "Those appear to be missing."

"Easily replaced. You mentioned rocket fuel."

"Auxiliary power. Used for extra thrust. Takeoff only."

"Clever."

"Papa's idea. He—" Her breath caught; her chest ached. "I don't know how to re-create that part. I don't . . . The frame and wheels . . ."

"Also replaceable."

"Arrogant to think I could salvage Bess working with these original parts alone."

"Not arrogant. Optimistic. Hopeful. I admire that."

She cast him a sideways glance. "You do?"

Tucker nodded, then indicated the engine. "Impressed with what you've done."

"You're patronizing me."

"Not my style." He grasped her hand and pulled her to her feet. "You didn't sleep well last night. You must be exhausted."

Had she tossed and turned with her nightmares? She didn't ask. She had no desire to discuss the troubled dreams regarding her father. "I don't know what you mean—"

"Then never mind." He gestured to Bess. "You've accomplished enough for today. Make a list of supplies and I'll see you have what's needed."

She looked up into his mesmerizing gaze, her body tingling in recollection of their lovemaking. "You're making it difficult for me to be angry with you."

He quirked a grin and stroked her burning cheek. "What have I done to earn your ire this morning, Flygirl?"

"It's what you didn't do. An invitation to accompany you to Château de Malmaison would have been appreciated."

"But unwise. The fewer people who know you're with me, the greater our chances of outwitting Dunkirk." He studied her with an enigmatic expression. "And anyone else who may have designs on you."

"No one else knows of my agenda. Mother and Concetta know of my general destination, but they do not know what I'm after."

"Doesn't matter. Anyone who reads the newspapers knows about the global contest honoring Queen Victoria. You're related to the Time Voyager; hence assumptions will be made. Figure that puts you in a dicey position."

Amelia tensed. "You think I know the whereabouts of something having to do with a time machine?"

"Briscoe Darcy's time machine or some aspect thereof. Given who you are, Amelia, it's a natural conclusion."

She snorted, feigning astonishment whilst scrambling to snuff his suspicions. From the preachings of Papa, not to mention the upheaval instigated by the Peace Rebels, Amelia well knew the detrimental effects of time traveling. She felt bound by a duty to mankind as well as a promise to Papa to make sure that aspect remained hidden.

"So I'm wrong?" Tucker prodded.

"Briscoe was long gone by the time I was born."

"He could have shared relevant information with your father—"

"He didn't." She waited for lightning to strike her down and cursed her burning cheeks.

"Perhaps another member of the family."

"I wouldn't know."

He angled his head. "Alienated from the rest of the Darcy clan?"

Not a comfortable subject, but preferable to time travel. "I've never met my aunts or uncles." Or cousins or any of their offspring. They did not visit; nor did they write. A black sheep of sorts, Papa had lost touch with extended family long ago. It was a subject that had made her normally gregarious father sad, so Amelia had written off her relatives. To her knowledge, her brothers had done the same. Odd how she'd never felt isolated until this moment.

"Sensitive topic?"

"Not really," she lied, then avoided his gaze by returning her tools to her pocketed canvas bag. "After the invasion of the Peace Rebels and learning that Briscoe had indeed appeared in the future only to disrupt our time, life for a Darcy—every Darcy—became most complicated." She frowned, feeling prickly regarding their infamous relation—someone Papa had admired. Someone who had cast a shadow over Papa all of his inspired but unremarkable life. "Let us just say that those related to the Time Voyager quickly tired of being hounded. Either people damned us for playing an unwitting part in the Peace War, or they tried to coerce or bribe us into sharing pertinent information regarding Briscoe's time machine. Various factions of those related to my father's distant cousin scattered to the four winds years ago in search of serenity, Mr. Gentry. So, yes, I am alienated from the rest of the Darcy clan."

"I've upset you."

Before she could respond, he pulled her into his arms and kissed her. A tender apology then as she melded against him—a kiss meant to arouse. Cradling the sides of her face, he teased open her mouth and suckled her tongue, causing her brain to spin and her body to burn. Delicious wanton desire. Bliss.

Caught off guard by the intensity of her needs, Amelia tangled her fingers into Tucker's hair and kissed him with fervor. He'd promised to show her more intimacies, various planets, incredible stars. *What if tomorrow never comes?* She wanted him. Here. Now. Filling a dark emptiness and satisfying a ferocious hunger.

Feeding off her escalated passion, Tucker slid his hands down her back, cupped her backside, and pulled her closer, his own arousal enormously apparent.

Instinctively, Amelia sprang off her tiptoes and wrapped her legs around his waist, grinding her pelvis against his erection. She broke the torrid kiss, heady with want. The demand on the tip of her tongue died as she noted the absurd. "You have grease on your face."

"That's because you have grease on your face."

Mortified, she noted that her hands were also stained. *Crikey.* "I'm sorry."

"I'm not. Something erotic about you and mechanics. Bit of a mystery."

Heat sizzled and zapped like a live wire. She intrigued a man who'd experienced numerous adventures. She'd never felt more special. Entranced, on fire, Amelia nipped his beautiful mouth. "Take me."

"My cabin—"

"Here. Now."

"Someone could walk in."

"Lock the door."

"Amelia—"

"You started this."

"I'm trying to be a gentleman."

"Lock the door." She kissed him with all the passion burning inside her, her legs still locked around his back as he engaged the dead bolt. "Show me something new. Something adventurous." *Something I'll never do again with another man.*

As if he were reading her last thought, Tucker's actions grew more fervid, the kiss deeper, wilder. He finessed her to her feet, and next thing she knew he was tugging her flight pants to her ankles, turning her around, and bending her over a polished table.

"What are you doing?" she asked in a husky whisper—a little panicked, but mostly excited. The thrill of the unknown. The thrill of Tucker's touch.

He leaned over, front pressed to her back, brow resting against the back of her head. "Too soon for this," he said in a conflicted tone.

"No. I want this." Whatever *this* was. She squirmed with anticipation. "Please."

He shifted, and she moaned with wonderful, miserable yearning as he kissed the back of her neck, suckled her earlobe. Could a person go mad from unquenched lust?

He smoothed his palm over her exposed backside, then between her legs, feeling her slickness. "Do you trust me?"

Her heart pounded. "In this matter, yes."

He smiled against her ear. "Sassy *and* sexy." Then he slid into her from behind. Slowly. Inch by inch. All the while kissing her neck and shoulders, his hands gliding and caressing. "Relax."

Difficult, that. The sensation thrilled even as her inexperience screamed. Her mind and body warred but a second. Shocking, yes, but she felt no discomfort, no guilt. With Tucker, everything felt right. Even this. He rocked against her, growing bolder with her lustful moans, increasing his rhythm as she begged for release.

Her stomach coiled; her body trembled, every muscle aching as she soared higher and higher until . . . she exploded and shattered, vaguely aware of Tucker's sweet words of seduction as she floated down to earth.

His touch was gentle, his body tense, his manhood still rigid and pulsing as he slowly withdrew. Dazed, she whispered, "But you didn't—"

"Not now." He brushed a kiss over her cheek. "That was for you."

Her heart pounded, a deafening thud in her ears. Even though she felt vulnerable now, half-naked and sated in a storage room, she was quite certain, to her absolute horror, that she'd just fallen in love.

Tucker put them to rights, somehow muting the awkward moment. Fully dressed, he pulled a bandanna from his pocket and gently wiped grease from her face. His eyes twinkled, and she wondered whether he was contemplating finding satisfaction with her later in his cabin. Instead he angled his head. "How would you like to go to Paris, Amelia?"

Body tingling in the sensual aftermath, pulse racing with emotions that scared her more than leaping from an aerostat without a parachute, for the first time in her life Amelia felt utterly feminine. Besotted. *How awful.* She quirked a dopey smile. "What girl wouldn't want to see Paris?"

CHAPTER 14

Every time Tuck turned around these days, someone threw a wrench in his plans. That someone being a pretty little thing with a tough-as-iron persona, keen mind, and guarded heart. Blasterbeef malfunctions. Jammed masts. The run-in with Dunkirk and ALE. Deflowering a virgin. The only thing that had gone off without a hitch these last few days was his meeting with Gaston, Duke of Anjou. Then again, Amelia hadn't been present. Not that he believed she was bad luck, but damn, when in the mix, she put a chink in the cogs of life, the latest glitch occurring just moments before.

Even though he'd promised a tour of the sensual universe, Tuck hadn't planned on taking Amelia in a damned storage room—from behind, no less—given her inexperience. The woman drove him to it. He had limited willpower when it came to her passion and curiosity. Her adventurous streak was infectious, affecting him almost as deeply as her internalized sadness.

She'd cried again last night in her sleep—mumbled, too. He was pretty sure her nightmares were associated with her pa. He'd sensed that same bone-deep sorrow when he'd walked in on her trying to fix Bess. Then again when she'd talked about being estranged from the Darcy clan. There seemed to be bad blood between her and her ma, and she'd taken on this jubilee quest behind her brothers' backs. He knew nothing about Jules and Simon Darcy. Good men? Bad men? With her pa gone, was Amelia, for all intents and purposes, alone in the world?

Bonding with her physically had taken a unique toll, especially given her trust in sexual matters. Each touch, every kiss fueled a mounting possessiveness—a need to protect and preserve. Becoming emotionally involved with this woman was a mistake of almighty proportions. Tuck knew it. Felt it. Yet he couldn't cut himself off from Amelia. Not yet. Reminded him too much of abandoning his sister. He'd had his fill of guilt and regret. Hence the invitation to Paris.

After discussing a plan, Tuck had whisked the flushed and disheveled woman out of the storage room and one deck up. He had to admit, with the lucrative absinthe delivery behind him, he was looking forward to their mutual ruse, his mind ticking off Parisian points of interest specific to Amelia. They were midway down the hall to his cabin when he saw one of his crew approaching. His always calm and in-control navigator nodded in greeting.

"Miss Darcy. Marshal."

Even though his expression betrayed nothing, the intuitive Cheyenne knew. *Damn.* Tuck released Amelia's elbow. "Head on in, honey. I need a word with StarMan."

Spine straight, she clutched her bag of tools to her chest, smiled meekly at StarMan, and rushed into the cabin.

Neither man spoke until they were topside and alone at the stern. Tuck broke the silence. "Spit it out."

The man Tuck had known and trusted for thirteen years looked to the toes of his boots, weighed his words, then met Tuck's gaze. "Dallying with an innocent—"

"I'm not dallying."

"So you've offered marriage?"

"You know that's impossible."

"You've compromised her honor."

"What are you, my conscience?"

"If I have to be."

Tuck looked up at the cloudless sky and breathed deeply. "I know you mean well."

"I know you're a good man."

He met StarMan's gaze. "If doin' the right thing wouldn't cause more harm than good, I'd do it. First of all, she ain't willin'."

"Did you ask?"

"No. She made it clear she didn't want to be—how did she put it?—shackled to any man. And, not that it's any of your business, but I made it clear I can't offer forever. We have an agreement. You need to let this go."

StarMan pursed his lips and raised a brow. "That an order?"

"Yes."

The man nodded.

Tuck locked down the guilt niggling into his soul. He looked over his shoulder and caught sight of the rest of the crew performing various tasks. "I won't be going with you when you dock the *Maverick* in the duke's aero-hangar. I'm taking Amelia into Paris."

"I thought you wanted to keep her hidden."

"We'll be hiding in plain sight."

"Meaning?"

"You know that skytown we spotted north of here? Typically those pleasure meccas feature at least one transformation center. Be someone else for a night. Wardrobe, hair, a complete metamorphosis, fictitious ID."

"You're going to purchase an identity change for Miss Darcy?"

"And myself. One night only." He leveled the no-nonsense man with a no-nonsense look. "The woman wants to see Paris. Got any better ideas?"

StarMan sighed. "I do not."

"Then we're done here. Miss Darcy and I will take the air dinghy. We'll be back in the morning. You oversee the ship's transfer to Gaston's aero-hangar; then you and the men are free to seek your pleasure as discussed earlier. Just avoid your favorite haunts."

Though an eccentric, the Duke of Anjou had won Tuck's

approval upon first meeting. He'd not only paid Tuck the amount agreed upon but a bonus for speedy delivery. Gaston had a healthy dislike of corrupt officials and irrational prohibitions that interfered with his lifestyle. As a libertine and patron of the arts, the green-fairy liquor was the duke's choice of cordials for private soirées. He was also a collector of fine modes of transport and kept two expert mechanics on staff. So when he'd suggested Tuck leave the *Maverick* in their care overnight, Tuck had agreed—with the stipulation that Axel oversee the proceedings. The blasterbeefs were off-limits. Other than that, why not take advantage of the duke's generosity? A private country residence. Well guarded. Miles from Tuck's usual Parisian port, should anyone be looking for him in the usual places. The *Maverick* needed tending, and his men needed a break before resuming their new quest to Italy.

"I'm thinking about staying behind with Axel," StarMan said. "He's anxious about strangers tinkering with the *Maverick*. What if he takes exception to their methods and gets into a tussle? Someone should stick around as mediator. Besides, I've seen Paris. Ain't never seen a kangaroo. Aim to take the duke up on his invitation to walk that garden."

Tuck raised a brow. "What about that pretty Oriental woman we saw tending to those exotic hedges on the front lawn? The one who couldn't take her eyes off of you? Plan on taking her up on her invitation as well?"

"Got a problem with that?"

Unlike a lot of people, Tuck had never had a problem with folks of varied nationalities mixing. Smiling, he gripped StarMan's shoulder. "Enjoy the kangaroo."

"First you lose Miss Darcy. Now you're demanding more money to continue the search?"

"Aye."

Bingham glared at the Scottish pirate, his chest burning with rage. Incompetence. He was surrounded by knobs who bumbled their assignments, and this one expected further compensation. He should've ignored the man's request to meet him over the French coast, but it was safer than meeting on English soil. Wanting answers and results, Bingham had roused his personal navigator and engineer and taken to the air. The Scottish Shark of the Skies had rendezvoused via a stolen aerostat.

"Because of Miss Darcy," Dunkirk said calmly, "my ship sustained severe damages. Costly damages."

"Not my responsibility."

"It is if ya be wanting me to act swiftly. I dinnae have the resources handy to replace the core thrust propulsion system. Ya do." He glanced around the spacious and ornate gondola of Bingham's pride and joy, shrugged. "Or ya can loan me your zeppelin to complete the mission, yeah?"

Bingham grunted. "As if I'd trust the likes of you with *Mars-a-tron*."

"When it comes to going up against the Sky Cowboy and securing Miss Darcy's treasure, the likes of me is the best you've got, Lord Bingham."

The truth of that statement vexed him like the devil. Dunkirk's aviation skills were legendary, as was his cunning. When the man had contacted him, informing him that he'd been the victim of foul play, then admitting he'd lost Amelia, Bingham had been stunned. Then, soon after, furious. He refused to be outwitted by that rebellious chit and a former air marshal, an American who, although accused of being a criminal, continued to exhibit disgustingly high morals. "You're sure it was Tucker Gentry?"

Dunkirk clenched his jaw. "Aye."

"And you're certain Miss Darcy made no mention, gave no hint as to her specific destination whilst in your care."

"I'd only just begun my . . . interrogation."

Bingham drummed his fingers on the brass rim of his gyrocompass and considered his options. Dunkirk was still the best man for this specific assignment. "I'll send an alert to my league of trackers and informants. Gentry will have to dock at some point for supplies, fuel. His fame will be his downfall. Someone will recognize him and someone will report. When they do, you'll have your direction. Meanwhile" — he rolled back his shoulders, harnessed his rage — "I'll provide you with the means necessary to repair your ship."

Dunkirk smiled, though the gesture lacked good humor. "Ye're going to great trouble and expense in pursuit of a mystery treasure, yeah? I've been thinking—"

"Don't tax yourself, Dunkirk."

"And reading the papers—"

"You read?"

The fearsome-looking pirate crossed his arms over his broad chest. "The man who possesses a time machine would be a powerful man indeed."

Now Bingham smiled, the full extent of his own menace burning in his gaze. "Powerful men crush those who hinder."

Dunkirk had the balls to laugh in the face of ruthless nobility. "And reward those who help, yeah?"

"Bring me what I seek and we'll talk." Bingham turned his back on the man lest he lunge and wring his bloody neck.

Still chuckling, the pirate took his cue and left. "I'll be in touch, matey."

The insolence! Once he had what he wanted, Dunkirk would pay for his cheekiness. At least the informant he'd set upon Simon Darcy was much easier to control. Pitifully, beautifully easy. Bingham stared out the window of his superior zeppelin, eyed the distant, sporadic air traffic, and considered his glorious future. If perchance the younger of the twin Darcy brothers procured the invention that would secure Bingham's dream, then he would know it. Miss Wilhelmina Goodenough would not bumble. She had too much to lose.

*   *   *

"Astonishing." Amelia could scarcely contain her excitement as Tucker steered the air dinghy toward the floating island of ships. She counted five sizable dirigibles connected by rope-banistered gangways and kept aloft by twin steam-powered balloons—massive and colorful. Several small transports were anchored to nearby floating docks. Even from this distance, she could hear music. Her own sheltered heart sang. She was about to embark upon another adventure.

She'd heard Jules mention the growing popularity of skytowns. She suspected from the looks her brothers traded that they both frequented the meccas of scandalous, outlawed pleasures. She'd read gossipy insinuations in the *Informer* regarding a certain noble indulging in a certain decadence in a certain airborne establishment. She knew they existed, even though they were only whispered about. Europe's dirty little secret.

"Remember what I told you," Tucker said.

"'Do not gawk like a foreigner. Do not succumb to the too-good-to-be-true-so-it-is hawkers.'" With her back to him, she gave a mock salute and openly gawked. "No worries, Marshal."

"And don't call me Marshal. I'm no longer the law, and I don't want anyone in a skytown thinking I am."

"Must tax your sensibilities something terrible," Amelia said whilst adjusting her goggles. "Being in the midst of illegal activities and not having the authority to quell it."

"Most of the pastimes aren't illegal so much as restricted or frowned upon. Try as she might, your queen can't erase the social and cultural influence of the twentieth-century Mods. New Worlders need a place to indulge and let off steam. Freaks need a place to socialize without being policed or judged."

Struck by his ardent tone, Amelia glanced over her shoulder. "Are you a New Worlder, Mr. Gentry?"

"Don't cotton to labeling myself, Miss Darcy."

"But you have an opinion on the preachings of Peace Rebels and whether or not to accept or change our destiny."

He didn't answer.

Her pulse flared. "Please assure me you are not a Flatliner. Surely you must care about the fate of the world and—"

"Word of advice: Don't invite or engage anyone, and I mean anyone, in a political or religious discussion in a skytown."

She faced front and rolled her eyes. "No gawking, no succumbing, no engaging. Understood." She dropped the subject. For now. Though she knew it was wrong to judge a person based solely on his or her beliefs, she couldn't imagine spending a lifetime in an intimate relationship with a man who possessed a vastly opposing worldview. She wasn't one to bite her tongue or bury her head in the sand. Not that she planned or wanted to spend a lifetime with Tucker. Not that he'd offered. In fact, he had been most forthright about his inability to sustain a permanent relationship. Which led her to believe he was indeed a New Worlder, or at least someone who leaned toward the freethinking, freeloving nature of the Mods. Otherwise he would have insisted upon doing the right thing regardless of his vagabond, outlaw status.

Unless, of course, he was promised to another, or perhaps secretly married.

"Absurd."

"What's absurd?" Tucker asked as they neared the outer docking isle.

Her cheeks flushed. "I, uh . . . I was thinking about what you said about Freaks needing a place to socialize. Absurd that they're shunned by the mainstream. Since when is being different a crime? Were that the case I would have been locked away long ago."

"Come here."

Amelia swiveled and shifted closer to the man at the wheel.

He cupped the back of her neck and pulled her in for a swift but knee-melting kiss.

Breathless, she quirked a bewildered grin. "What was that for?"

"Being you." Smiling, Tucker tied off the air dinghy and escorted Amelia across the narrow gangway.

"Dodgy construction," she noted in a tight tone.

"Temporary, but safe. Just don't look down."

She wasn't afraid of heights, but the walkway was more like a swinging bridge than a stationary gangway. Surrounded by fluffy white clouds, she truly felt as if she were walking on air. The unstable sensation incited a case of the stomach wrens. Or perhaps it was the realization that she was stepping into another world. She'd heard about and read about Mods and Freaks her entire life, but Mods lived in seclusion, and Freaks preferred the bustle of major cities. Easier to get lost in, she supposed. Although she'd heard they leaned toward psychedelic bohemian Victorian fashions, a trend called ModVic, and had kaleidoscope eyes. How could they possibly blend? She glanced up at the Peace Rebel flag waving from one of the masts. Once a sign of peace, now a symbol of chaos. "I've never met a Freak."

"Not that you know of," Tucker said as they stepped upon the deck of the first airship.

A man moved into their path and greeted them in French. To Amelia's surprise Tucker responded in kind. Fluently. She blinked at her escort, then back to the greeter, who switched to English.

"My name is Doobie. Welcome to Skytown, miss," he said with a nod toward Amelia. "We have but one law: Make love, not war."

A credo of the Peace Rebels. Amelia vibrated with excitement. She tried not to stare as the colorfully garbed man explained the layout of the "town" and its most popular venues. Difficult, that. Doobie was a curiosity indeed. Medieval tunic embroidered with flowers and accentuated with studs. Long, unkempt hair. An Indian-type band around his forehead and a sprig of daisies behind his right ear.

He looked to Tucker. "What's your pleasure?"

"Got a transformation center on this mecca?"

"The Fantasy Factory on Prankster Street. Next dig over, one deck down." He squinted through his rose-colored spectacles. "You look familiar."

"No, I don't."

Doobie nodded. "My mistake." He glanced to Amelia and smiled. "Have fun, chickadoodle." He bade her good-bye as Tucker pulled her away, but not with a wave.

"Did you see that?" she whispered, stunned. "Doobie gave me the two-finger! Was he a Mod? He looked too young, but— "

"Not a Mod."

"A Freak? Except I saw his eyes over the rims of his spectacles when he bowed his head. Plain brown, but— "

"A Vic dressed up like a Mod, honey. An actor. Part of the appeal and atmosphere. Just like the rest of these hawkers," he said without making eye contact with any one of the colorful people they passed.

Amelia, however, tripped twice, distracted by sights she'd seen only in the Book of Mods. Men and women dressed to the nines in threads of the Love Generation. One played a guitar, singing about "blowing in the wind." One smoked an odd-smelling cigarette, offering a "toke" to Amelia as they passed. Another was passing out free necklaces— "love beads." She accepted two colorful strands with a smile. "Thank you."

A doe-eyed woman with a diamond stud in her nose gestured to a doorway. "Hemp headbands and bracelets, incense, leather cuffs . . ."

The woman's words faded as Tucker steered Amelia away. "Come on, Flygirl, before she sells you a bong."

"What's a bong?"

"Never mind."

They crossed another swinging gangway. Dig number two—Prankster Street. "I'm surprised by how deserted this skytown is. More hawkers than patrons," Amelia noted as they descended a deck.

"That's because it's early. Skytowns come alive after sundown."

"Must be something to see."

"Paris is something to see. Unless you've changed your mind."

"Oh, no." She tugged him to a stop, wide-eyed, adrenaline racing. What if she didn't win the jubilee prize? What if her brothers failed? What if she was doomed to live out her days with Mother at Ashford, or someplace even *more* remote? Or to marry some wealthy conservative, someone like Lord Bingham? What if this was her one shot at freedom? She gripped the Sky Cowboy by the lapel of his greatcoat. "I want to experience it all, Mr. Gentry."

He wrapped his hand around hers and squeezed. "Then you will, Miss Darcy." He glanced at the sign hanging above a curtained doorway.

THE FANTASY FACTORY

Tucker cocked a brow. "Ready?"

A free license to forget her troubles? To pretend and cavort with this man for one night? In the City of Light? She smiled up into his eyes. "Oh, yes."

CHAPTER 15

The Fantasy Factory was divided into two emporiums—gender specific—each staffed with a costumer, coiffeur, cosmetic artist, and a certification forger who provided each slicked-up customer with his or her customized identification card—not legal, but official-looking enough to ensure a twenty-four-hour fantasy. Hefty deposits were required and refunded upon return of the elaborate costume. Some folks indulged for pure escapism or sexual fetishes. Others took advantage of the temporary transformation as a means of momentary anonymity. It had seemed an easy solution to enable Tuck to show Amelia the Parisian sights without having to look over their shoulders for Dunkirk, corrupt air constables, or international bounty hunters on the prowl for foreign outlaws. Posing as man and wife also afforded another sort of freedom altogether.

Two hours later, Tuck and Amelia walked out of the Fantasy Factory hand in hand as Mr. and Mrs. Digger and Cherry Peckinposh, aerial stuntmen presently employed by a start-up flying circus. As soon as they cleared the exit, Tuck pulled his "wife" into a private alcove. "Your hair is pink."

"Temporarily."

"Bright pink. Like a Caribbean flamingo."

"You've been to the Caribbean?"

"On second thought, more like a Japanese cherry blossom."

She grinned. "When I told the coiffeuse I wanted to be a

daring and evocative circus performer, she suggested a hair color to go with my chosen fantasy name and persona. She said vibrant hair colors are all the rage with the performance artists who frequent Paris. She said no one would give me a second look."

"Except every breathing man within half a kilometer."

She furrowed her brow and toyed with a pink-tinted loose and wild curl. "Are you suggesting men will find this color and style attractive?"

He skimmed her low-cut pink satin blouse and red brocade corset, the flouncy, lacy layers of short skirts, and the striped hose that accentuated her shapely legs. Instead of her clunky black boots, she wore white, pointy-toed, midcalf button boots with spiky heels. She looked good enough to eat. She even smelled of cherries and peppermint. "The whole package is attractive, darlin', in a whimsical, exotic way."

"You're staring at my décolletage, Mr. . . . . Peckinposh."

Not that Amelia was showing more cleavage than any fashionable lady dressed in the latest evening wear, but the ensemble itself more closely resembled the costumes worn by the dancing girls in the cabarets of Montmartre. The free-spirit persona coupled with those lovely bosoms gave a man wicked thoughts. "They're sparkling."

She shrugged. "Felicia said all circus performers sparkle."

"Mmm."

Snorting, she gestured to his colorful ensemble. "You're not exactly the picture of subtlety yourself."

At least he'd talked the costumer out of the formfitting metallic breeches. Tuck drew the line at flashing his package. Instead he wore black wool trousers with black satin stripes. His shirt was also black satin. The waistcoat was metallic red-and-black brocade. The frock coat was cranberry red. The bowler hat wouldn't have been too bad except the red band was accentuated by a damned gauzy black rose the size of his fist.

Then there were the accessories.

Elaborate bronze-and-iron wrist cuffs adorned with clockwork, a reversible locket-style Beetle Bug pocket watch, five ornamental rings, and red-tinted goggles with attached magnifying loupes.

"I haven't seen that much jewelry on a man since, well, ever." She fluttered her glittery lashes. "Spectacularly pretty getup, Mr. Peckinposh."

He grunted, remembering how the costumer had wanted to replace his working Blaster with some showy prop gun: the Particle Beam Combobulator. The damned thing shot sparkly confetti. So, yeah, it could've been worse.

She narrowed her kohl-lined eyes. "This was your idea. Said our best way to avoid unwanted attention was to go incognito." She perched her hands on her hips. "I'll have you know I would never wear such revealing, frilly clothes; nor would I fancy pink hair, allowing the bothersome curls to blow willy-nilly; nor would I apply glitter to my cheeks and bosom or red lip rouge to my mouth. These bloody boots are cramping my toes, and just look at this ridiculous overnight satchel. Zebra stripes with pink trim? Honestly!"

Tuck laughed. Her outrage highlighted the humor of the moment. The brilliance of their absurd, dandified appearance. "I apologize, Mrs. Peckinposh. The transformation is indeed impressive." He inspected her hands and lowered his voice. "Not a trace of grease. Don't reckon your own ma would recognize you."

She raised a newly defined brow and matched his hushed tone. "Mother would faint were she to see me in this absurd getup. Actually, first she would accuse me of being shameless, scandalous, and rebellious. Then, after chastising me for ruining my chances of ever marrying a respectable man, she'd burst into uncontrollable sobs. Then she would faint."

"Sounds dramatic."

"Manipulative, mostly. Annoying." She plopped her zebra valise on the floor. "Anne Darcy can cry at the drop of the hat. I suppose you could call it a talent, being able to summon tears, whilst I . . ."

"What?" Tuck asked while helping her into the coordinating coat.

She shrugged. "I can't remember the last time I cried."

He could. Last night and the night before that. "Not even when your pa passed?"

"I grieved. I still . . . grieve," she said, voice tight, "but I see no need to dissolve into a weeping idiot."

"Sometimes tears are cathartic, Amelia."

"Cherry," she reminded him, then turned and met his gaze. "One of the many tales I read about you in the penny dreadfuls mentioned that you lost both of your parents years ago. As a point of interest, did *you* cry?"

"Considered myself too old to cry—thirteen goin' on fourteen—but yeah." After the burial. Not when they'd been shot and killed in the stagecoach robbery. That moment he'd been too riddled with shock and rage, vowing to make it his life's mission to hunt down murdering thieves. Now he was accused of being the very thing he hated.

After a tense moment Amelia broke eye contact and pulled on red kid gloves, focusing diligently on each finger. "Were I to give in to what I am feeling, Mr. Peckinposh, I fear I would lose the ability to function for weeks. I would be paralyzed by the guilt and—" She shook off her thoughts. "We should go."

He caught her by the elbow, sensitive to that bone-deep sorrow. Grief intensified by guilt? Talk about an almighty burden. "What's gnawing at your conscience, Flygirl?"

She worked her jaw. "How do the blasterbeefs work? How does Peg fly?"

"That your way of telling me to mind my own business?"

"Why should I entrust you with my deepest personal feelings and thoughts whilst you refuse to share even one secret with me? Or perhaps you would prefer to confess something about your personal life?"

"Like?"

"Never mind."

She hurried ahead of him down the narrow hall and up the ladder leading topside.

He strapped his leather satchel over his chest, nabbed the ridiculous zebra valise, and followed. When Amelia hit the deck, she headed back toward their air dinghy.

"You're going the wrong way, Mrs. Peckinposh."

She swiveled on her white heels and stormed back. "We're not going to Paris? Just because we . . ." She looked around, noted passersby, and reined herself into character. "Just because we had a lovers' tiff?"

He stroked a pink curl out of her wide eyes. "We're going to Paris, sugarplum, but not in the Sky Cowboy's air dinghy. I rented a special transport, docked at that rig over there on Black Panther Lane. Something more suitable for Digger and Cherry Peckinposh, international stuntmen and stars of Professor Dingle's Flying Circus."

She pursed her painted red lips. "Should I be worried?"

"You should be thrilled."

"Why's that?"

"I'm going to let you pilot."

Amelia hadn't appreciated Tucker's interest in her mourning process. She preferred to think of Papa in the present tense. As if he were still alive. She preferred to pretend. The truth of the matter led her down a miserable lane where she experienced all manner of horrible thoughts and feelings. Perhaps she would wallow after she won the jubilee prize and restored honor and respect to the Darcy name, but until then she would stand strong. She would pretend. Adopting Cherry Peckinposh's frivolous, adventurous persona, even if only for one day, soothed her injured soul. As did Tucker's invitation to pilot their rented dig. As apologies went, it was a doozy.

Unfortunately, five minutes into their flight, her excitement had twisted into damnable anxiety. The horror! Amelia couldn't remember ever being so nervous. Not when she and Papa had first taken Bess for a ride. Nor the first time she'd captained the *Flying Cloud*. It wasn't so much that this flying contraption differed from anything she'd ever manned; the experience was complicated by the presence of the Sky Cowboy, a man whose aviation skills she worshiped. A man who'd erased her innocence and stolen her heart. Even his outrageous guise as Digger Peckinposh could not detract from his charismatic aura. She was as sensitive to his magnetic pull as she was to his opinion of her flying skills. The latter proved supremely distressing. Papa and her brothers had always thought her overconfident, reckless even, yet this moment her nerves jangled like those of a fledgling aviatrix.

Did Tucker sense her trepidation? Did he guess he was the cause? Her cheeks flushed and her fingers tightened on the controls as she flew in between an air taxi and a commercial zeppelin. A bit dicey, but doable. Should she have gone the long way around instead? Not wanting him to know he had the power to make her question her judgment, Amelia offered another reason for her discomfort. "I've never flown amidst such traffic." This was, in fact, true. All manner of dirigibles navigated the skies over Paris. Private and commercial. Primitive and advanced.

Tucker, or rather Digger, squeezed her shoulder. "You're doin' fine."

His touch instilled pride, but it also distracted. She ignored the sensual tingle between her thighs and focused on the matter at hand. "The last time you saw me piloting a dig, I crashed. Are you not nervous?"

"I am not."

"Why?"

"Because you're good."

If she weren't already dreadfully head over heels for this man, that statement would've pushed her over the edge. "But I crashed."

"Impressed the hell out of me. You could've bailed like your friend Concetta, but you fought to pull that kitecycle out of a dive. You've got courage and heart. Skill. Unfortunately, you were operating an inferior piece of machinery."

She would've taken exception to his negative view of Papa's design, but she was too stunned by his praise of her character and talent. She should probably thank him, and as soon as she found her voice she would.

"What do you think of this dig?" he asked whilst stoking the firebox. "Compared to Bess, I mean."

The mention of Bess made her pounding heart ache. She cleared her throat and rolled back her shoulders. "She's all right, I suppose. The steam engine is more advanced, and the gondola is a luxury. Still . . ."

"You'd prefer an exposed chassis as opposed to being more protected from the elements?"

The two-person gondola was certainly more comfortable, but still . . . "Although the windows are generous they are still windows. There's something inspiring and invigorating about the open air."

"There's also comfort in clinging to the sentimental, no matter how flawed."

"Bess wasn't flawed," she snapped.

Tuck didn't argue.

Amelia sighed. "Fine. Bess was flawed. Massively flawed. I do not recall ever being aloft for more than fifteen minutes without some malfunction. Still, she was a product of Papa's imagination and determination. A gift. For me. Flawed, but cherished."

"I'll keep that in mind." He pointed out the starboard window. "See that park? Set her down there."

"You want me to land?"

"That a problem?"

"No. It's just . . . I'm not ready."

"Thought you wanted to see Paris."

"I am seeing Paris. I find this vantage point vastly engaging. Surely nothing on the ground can compare to soaring the skies." If she could fly forever, she would. Up here she was beholden to no one. Free of conventions, restrictions, and expectations. *Bliss*.

Tucker cocked his head. "Most women would be anxious to sample the gourmet pastries and exclusive fashions. Then again, you're unlike any woman I've ever known."

She flushed. "Is that a good thing?"

"It's interesting." He tempered that cryptic statement by leaning forward and grazing her cheek with a kiss. "Trade places."

His lips, his touch, his infernal magnetism incited a tremor of delight. *Crikey*. Throwing herself at him whilst in flight would probably be a bad idea. She cleared her throat. "Why?"

"You want a scenic tour of Paris? I'm gonna give you one. It'll work better if I'm in control. I know where I'm going; plus, you can gawk to your heart's delight through those windows you hate so much."

She wasn't keen on being a passenger, but she would enjoy the tour. Amelia shifted as Tuck slid into the pilot's seat. Even though he sported Digger Peckinposh's fancy clothes, the moment he took control of the small aircraft he radiated a manly intensity that turned her knees to pudding.

"Buckle in, Flygirl. I'm taking some shortcuts."

She settled into the passenger seat, secured the leather safety harness, and within seconds Tucker was soaring at an accelerated speed, edging past larger transports, skimming rooftops. She grinned like an idiot as she did indeed gawk out the window.

Paris, France, second largest city in Europe, directly after London. Amelia's time in the British capital had been brief but the impression long-lasting. Mostly she'd been stunned by the overcrowded streets—pedestrians, personal automocoaches, public transport, even horses and buggies clogged the narrow streets. At times she'd felt invigorated. At other times suffocated. Even the sky had been congested with an astonishing amount of traffic. How the pilots could see clearly amidst the film of grimy smoke that coated the air, she had no idea.

The skies of Paris were less congested and not nearly as polluted, but, looking down, she saw the city itself appeared nearly as choked with humanity. As was typical of this altered age, the Industrial Revolution had melded with bits and pieces of twentieth-century technology. Steam power thrived, yet electrical power gained momentum by the day. Amelia noted the endless industrial smokestacks and the factories that housed enormous electric generators. She thought about the chaos below. The hordes of people. The overpowering scents and sounds. This was by far a more pleasurable means of exploring the vast metropolis.

Tucker pointed out the several cultural locations. The Arc de Triomphe at the western end of the Champs-Élysées. The Louvre Museum on the right bank of the Seine. He talked about the advanced thinking and heated debates amongst forward-thinkers whilst drinking or gambling or partaking in the visual delights of any one of a hundred revues and risqué cabarets: wireless communication, quantum theory, computers. She'd read about such wonders in the Book of Mods, but she'd never engaged in thoughtful conversation regarding these matters with anyone other than her father and brothers. Once again, she felt the vexing hindrance of her sheltered life.

"I confess I'm beginning to feel a bit intimidated about mixing with the progressive Parisians."

"This from a woman who tried to manipulate the Scottish Shark of the Skies."

"That was different. At least we spoke the same language. I don't speak French."

"I do."

"I noticed." She'd been impressed and more than a little

smitten. "I don't suppose you speak Italian as well?" she
joked.

"Sì, bella."

Her stomach fluttered and a smile teased the corners of
her mouth. Did he just call her beautiful? He'd definitely
said "yes." "You speak French and Italian?"

"Plus a few other languages," he said matter-of-factly.
"Always had an ear for foreign speech and dialects. Spanish,
Chinese, different American Indian tongues. Not fluent in
all, but versed enough to get by. Came in handy when I was
an air marshal. America the melting pot. Now that I'm in
Europe . . ." He shrugged. "Simplifies things to converse in
an associate's native tongue."

Was there no end to this man's talents? Beyond impressed, she thanked her lucky stars. Tucker could not only
transport her to Italy, but translate for her once there. "Astounding."

"Here's the deal," he said, pushing the dandified bowler
to the back of his head. "I'm going to circle the city once
more, and by the time I land, you're going to have at least
one place in mind that you'd like to go."

Crikey. The City of Light. The most progressive city in
the world, given the Parisians' more liberal stance on morals and Mod technology. Art, architecture, industry, inventions. So much to experience and so very little time. How to
choose?

Tuck glanced over his shoulder. "About Peg."

"Sorry?"

"I can't explain how he knows what to do when it comes
to flying, except to say he was born with the instinct."

If she hadn't been buckled in she might have fallen out
of her seat. He was going to share something about one of
his guarded secrets. "How do you mean?" she asked tenta-
tively.

"I've had Peg since he was a yearling. Bought him off a
breeder who'd threatened to put him down because he was

too wild. Jumped corrals. Went loco when harnessed. But I didn't sense a mean streak. I sensed a gentle spirit in need of open spaces and a patient hand."

"Axel said you have a way with animals. I saw it with Leo. It's as if you speak their language, too."

"Just put myself in their shoes, so to speak. I had a ranch in Wyoming territory. Lots of land, and Peg got the run of it. That freedom soothed his temperament. Still, I knew early on he was different. I'd catch him peering up at the sky—sometimes for a second, sometimes for a spell. Realized after a while that he was fascinated with birds. I'll never forget the day I saw him take off across the pasture like a bat out of hell. Then he leaped, stretching his body and legs as if to soar, hooves pawing the air."

"He was trying to fly?"

"That's how it looked. Body of a horse. Heart of a bird. Though I didn't understand how an animal could yearn to go against his nature, I did understand the intense desire to fly. We bonded in that way, and my chest ached every time he took that running leap and hit the ground."

Amelia's own heart bloomed. "You decided to find a way to make Peg's dream come true."

"I was working a case in San Francisco. Art theft. In the course of the investigation I had reason to examine some sketches of Leonardo da Vinci's."

Amelia's heart pounded. "Did you say da Vinci?"

"Yeah. Why?"

"No matter. Go on." *Thud. Thud.*

"There were drawings of one horse jumping over another, body and legs stretched, just like Peg. Then there were sketches of a flying contraption—wings strapped to a man—and I thought, Why not wings strapped to a horse? I researched da Vinci's notions on flight. Researched birds. I devised a special harness and a set of wings mimicking the anatomy of a bird. Consulted a techno-surgeon on the skin-replication techniques used on automatons. As an afterthought I created a sensor of sorts meant to detect Peg's heartbeat, tap into his power—more symbolic than anything—an iron disk embossed with the image of a Pegasus that fits over his heart." Tucker shook his head. "I swan, it was like magic, Amelia. I don't know how it works; it just does. Near as I can tell, the wings are fueled by Peg's unique passion. Out of curiosity, I've harnessed other horses with the wings and sensor."

"But it didn't work."

"Not once."

"Which makes Peg quite rare and unique." Amelia's mind raced. "Were someone to discover his gift, they might try to steal him and profit from his extraordinary ability. Or worse, conduct experiments in hopes of discovering his secret. How awful!" She placed her hand on Tucker's shoulder. "Please know that Peg's secret is safe with me. As much as I would like to boast about my wondrous flight upon his back, never will I divulge his unique gift. I know you do not trust me—"

He covered her hand with his own. "On this, I do."

Amelia's heart danced; her soul settled. If only for a moment. If only on this matter. As Tucker maneuvered the dig toward an aeropark near the Seine, she was overcome with a sense of calm and resolve. "I know where I want to go," she said as the wheels touched down. "The library."

CHAPTER 16

The Bibliothèque Nationale. The most important library in France—according to their hired driver—and one of the oldest libraries in the world. As much as he enjoyed reading, Tuck had never visited this majestic literary monstrosity. When in Paris he indulged in the marvels of Montmartre, exploring decadence, not cerebral stimulation.

Given Amelia's unpredictability, he shouldn't have been surprised that she'd chosen a library over a famous monument or museum. He hadn't expected a request to tour the fashion district, but he had anticipated a visit to the Musée des Arts et Métiers, home to a unique collection of inventions. He would've understood a request having to do with any aeronautic or technology-based establishment. But the Bibliothèque Nationale?

"I'm specifically looking for books pertaining to Leonardo da Vinci and his studies whilst in Tuscany," Amelia whispered as they entered the grand foyer. "Sketches, maps, journals."

"This have to do with Peg?"

"Only as a coincidental connection. You shared a secret. Now I shall do the same."

Hell's fire. Da Vinci? Tuscany? Italy. Did this have to do with the invention of historical significance? He'd hoped that by his relating the story behind Peg, Amelia would confide in him regarding her guilt about her pa. He hadn't expected this. This was the damned mother lode. Did this mean that Amelia trusted him? *Implicitly?* Knowing he meant to benefit from her secret treasure and being twice as intrigued knowing it might be related to da Vinci, Tuck wrestled with guilt. He interlaced his fingers with hers, giving a supportive squeeze as she gawked at their impressive yet overwhelming surroundings. At the very least, he could help to ease the anxiety he sensed simmering below her surface.

"What collection do you suppose we should locate? Arts? Science and technology? Crikey," she said as they moved into a vast room containing floor-to-ceiling shelves. "Where to begin?"

Where indeed? And this was just one room. Centuries old, this multilevel library contained thousands upon thousands of periodicals, books, maps, sketches, and documents. Multiple and extensive collections. The burgeoning stacks were tight as a tick. "We need a librarian."

Amelia pointed to a woman standing behind a desk.

Dressed in a conservative gown, she wore gloves and a set of complicated spectacles with several magnifying loupes similar to the lenses attached to Tuck's Fantasy Factory goggles, only he suspected hers actually functioned. Her nose was buried in a massive tome. As if sensing she was being watched, the studious woman looked up, traded one loupe for another, and frowned across the marble floor at the extravagantly colorful Peckinposhes.

"I say, I don't think she likes the look of us." Amelia hurriedly fastened her crimson coat, duly hiding Cherry's provocative bodice. "Probably thinks we're pesky foreigners or obnoxious show people."

"Obvious assumption. Have you forgotten your pink hair?" Adopting a friendly expression, Tuck approached the librarian, quickly winning her over with quiet charm and his exceptional language skills. Minutes later, after escorting them to a table in the cavernous and impressive reading room, Mademoiselle Galibru rolled a brass cart over. She explained that four pertinent books were loaded into the biblio-capsule and demonstrated the mechanism that would allow them to review one book at a time.

"She said this should get us started," Tuck translated for Amelia. "If we want to examine original documents, we'll have to make an appointment."

Amelia nodded and smiled at the woman, who all but scowled at her bouncing pink curls.

Tuck winked at Mademoiselle Galibru. "*Merci*," he said, causing her cheeks to flush and inciting a hasty retreat.

As soon as the flustered librarian turned her back, Amelia shed her coat and pushed the button that initiated the release of the first book. A mechanical arm delivered the thick journal from capsule to table. Tuck studied the mechanism while Amelia ran a reverent hand over the cover of a reproduction of da Vinci's "Codex Leicester." "I do hope at least one of these books is written in English; otherwise you'll have to translate."

"Speaking and reading a foreign language," Tuck said. "Two different animals. We could be in trouble. And if you expect me to crack any documents written in da Vinci's own hand, we could be here all night."

"You mean because he tended to pen his notes backward?"

"Or upside down."

"Some say it is because he was left-handed and it was simply easier for him to write and read right to left."

"Nothin' simple or easy about Leonardo da Vinci, darlin'." Between that art theft case and his obsession for helping Peg fly, he'd read a powerful amount of material on the Renaissance genius.

"I already possess significant information," she whispered, then looked over each shoulder to make sure no one was eavesdropping. "It just occurred to me that I might find additional details or clues within this library's expansive and historical collection. Papa's resources were . . . limited," she said while carefully skimming and turning pages. "Also,

I wanted to show you what we are looking for. Ah." She smiled. "Here."

"An ornithopter." A flying machine that soared by flapping its wings—like a bird or bat or some manner of insect. Da Vinci had sketched several versions, and Tuck had studied as many reproductions as he could clap his eyes on. He glanced at Amelia, who was staring hard at the detailed drawings. "So you have knowledge of what? The whereabouts of a lost design? Buried blueprints?"

"A working model. One constructed by da Vinci himself."

The notion glanced off his brain. "Impossible."

"This from a man who owns a flying horse."

Suddenly conscious of the other patrons hunkered over books at nearby tables, Tuck maneuvered his chair closer to Amelia and lowered his voice to barely audible. "Da Vinci studied birds and the theory of flight for almost twenty years. Sketched detailed designs of various ornithopters. Even constructed a few, but none of them flew."

"'The great bird will take its first flight on the back of Monte Ceceri . . .'" she recited in a reverent tone.

"From his 'Codex on the Flight of Birds.'" A collection of eighteen folios. Da Vinci's detailed examination on the mechanics of flight, air resistance, and the effects of wind on wings. "I'm familiar with the codex and the legend associated with various versions of that quote, Amelia. Supposedly one of da Vinci's associates test-flew one of his designs, launching from Mount Ceceri. Even if that were true, legend claims the associate suffered a ruinous fall. That ornithopter was faulty, not to mention destroyed."

"There is a prototype. I know not its dimensions nor its precise design," she said, indicating various versions. "I simply know it exists and where it is hidden, although I'm not altogether certain how to get to it."

Crazy as a loon, Tuck could hear Axel saying. *Like her pa.* "Not that I consider myself an expert on all things da

Vinci, but how is it I never heard or read about this working prototype?"

She looked at him as if he were daft. "Because it's been hidden for centuries in a secret extension of the workshop."

He refrained from smacking his head on the table. "If it's a secret, how do you know about it?"

Gaze riveted on a drawing, she tucked bright pink curls behind her ears and chewed her red-stained lower lip. At long last she blew out a breath and cast him a glance. "You were right. Briscoe Darcy did indeed pass on a bit of information to my father."

Tuck stared. His heart hammered against his ribs. She knew something about the Time Voyager, and the Time Voyager had known something about Leonardo da Vinci. A secret. An invention of almighty historical significance. How? What? Why? A dozen questions bombarded his reeling mind, as did one soul-wrenching notion.

If it did indeed exist, he could buy back his life with that ornithopter. As a rabid collector of precious art and rare antiquities, surely Judge Titan would agree to anything in order to possess a functioning, one-of-a-kind da Vinci ornithopter. It was perhaps the one thing that could replace the priceless collection of miniature paintings Titan had accused Tuck of stealing. *Christ almighty.* Potentially, Amelia had the power to solve all of Tuck's problems. Although that would entail sacrificing her own goals and compromising the financial future of her own family. How the hell could he ask or expect her to do that?

Unless he could think of a compromise.

Poleaxed, Tuck dragged his hands through his hair, trying to corral his thoughts.

Amelia must have read something in his eyes, because she eased away and opened a second book.

He kept his tone casual. "You gonna enlighten me with details, Flygirl?"

"I'm contemplating the wisdom in that. For now."

Wary. *Smart*. "Fair enough." He sure as hell didn't want to push and scare her off. "How can I help?"

She took a deep breath and nodded. "I realize now that I cannot do this alone. I'm sure we can come to some sort of business arrangement, but I don't want to waste time sorting that out now. I'm going to trust that I can trust you."

Damn. "I'll do what I can."

She smiled, squeezed his hand, then focused on the book.

He coldcocked his conscience. *Get the facts, then ponder the solution, Gentry.*

"Mount Ceceri is our destination. Da Vinci had a workshop in the stone quarry." She placed her palm on the book. "We're looking for any mention of the workshop. It's the portal to a secret room, a vault of sorts. I know that much, but I do not know how to access that vault. There must be a code or a trigger."

"Nothing more invigorating than solving a mystery."

"Solving this mystery will restore honor to my father's reputation. Solving this mystery will secure a comfortable future for my family. I must succeed, Tucker."

Shoving aside his own selfish inclinations, he focused on Amelia's genuine need. Hell or high water, he'd think of a solution to their mutual quandaries. "The Darcys will triumph, darlin'. Mark my words."

Six books and several hours later, Amelia was bleary eyed and brain-fatigued. She wanted nothing more than to leave this impressive and oppressive library, even though they hadn't discovered any hints or clues pertaining to the secret vault. She was spent, mentally and physically.

"Don't despair," Tucker said as he helped her from her seat. "We're dealing with da Vinci. The clue wouldn't be obvious. I'm guessing something will click when we're in the workshop. A connection between something we actually see—a painting, a symbol, an object—and something we read here or somewhere else. Something that will trigger the opening of the secret room."

"So you believe me now?" Amelia asked whilst refastening the buttons of Cherry's coat. "You think the ornithopter Briscoe mentioned exists?"

"I think it's worth investigating. I hope it exists."

Something in his tone, his manner. An urgency. She'd sensed it when she'd first mentioned the connection between the Time Voyager and the da Vinci ornithopter. It had stopped her from revealing further details. She could hear Tucker's mind turning but couldn't guess his thoughts. "If we find it, you won't pinch it from me, will you?"

"I won't steal it. You have my word."

The promise did not temper the flutter of unease. Then again, she could attribute the attack of stomach wrens to two things: fear of failure — what if she was wrong about the ornithopter or couldn't locate the secret room? — and the constant sensual awareness of Tucker — she had but to look into his eyes and she was sucked into a spectacular vortex of desire.

She was also suddenly and incredibly famished.

"I don't know about you," Tucker said whilst pulling on Digger's bowler, "but I've worked up quite an appetite. What would you think of dinner, then a boat ride down the Seine, Mrs. Peckinposh? Unless you'd rather attend the theater. I saw an advertisement for — "

"Newspapers and periodicals!" Distracted, Amelia followed the arrow to another reading room. "I wonder if they stock the *Informer*."

Tucker moved in behind her as she scanned scores of major city newspapers. "If you want to know what's happening in London, you'd do better to consult the *Daily* or *Times*. The *Informer* leans toward sensationalism."

"Precisely why I want to catch up on the last few days. I'm curious as to whether the Clockwork Canary has followed up with another attack on the Darcy name. My brother Simon recently suffered a professional setback, a high-profile project damned by corruption." She snagged an issue—*yes!*—and scanned the front page. "Oh, bother."

"Something about Simon?"

"No, something about the race for the jubilee prize. 'According to Mr. P. B. Waddington, spokesperson for the Jubilee Science Committee,'" she read, "'inquiries pertaining to specifics on the contest have been rolling in. Waddington estimates at least two hundred professionals are now in pursuit of a lost or legendary invention of historical significance.'"

She glanced at Tucker, who was reading over her shoulder, and thoughts of the race derailed. Were he to lean a smidgen closer, he could suckle her earlobe, just as he had done last night, just before she'd seen sensual stars. Her inner thighs tingled at the memory of him plunging deep. . . .

"You okay?" he asked. "Your cheeks are flushed."

Crikey. "I was just thinking . . . wondering . . ." She cleared her throat. "What do you suppose Mr. Waddington means by 'professionals'?"

"Men who specialize in artifacts, maybe? Archaeologists? Professors of antiquities? Treasure hunters?"

"Two hundred," she said, forcing images of Tucker's naked body from her mind. "And within the first week. The deadline is five months away. Imagine how many people could join in the quest by then."

"But how many of those people will actually locate a lost or legendary invention? Not many, I'd wager. Furthermore the risk of not making the cut is damned high. What constitutes 'significant'? How does a buried abacus from 2600 B.C. stack up against legendary flexible glass lost under Roman emperor Caesar's reign? Who determines the level of brilliance, the value to mankind?"

"The Jubilee Science Committee, I suppose."

"Whoever they are."

Amelia ignored the doubt welling in the back of her

mind and traded the newspaper for another edition. "Are you preparing me for failure?" she asked in a soft voice.

Tucker cupped the back of her neck, his thumb stroking as if to ease the tension thrumming through her body. Instead, sensual shivers stole down her spine. "Just pointing out," he said reasonably, "that although the ornithopter might be judged significant and impressive, another invention could overshadow the magnitude of the discovery."

The way Briscoe Darcy's time machine overshadowed anything and everything invented by Papa. She shook off the somber thought. "I feel confident that between Jules, Simon, and myself, one of us will win that prize. I feel it in my bones."

"What inventions are your brothers tracking?"

"I don't know. They didn't say. But I'm sure they're something spectacular." She blinked at the headline midway down the front page of yesterday's issue. "What the devil?"

Tucker moved in and together, in glorious, stimulating silence, they read.

EXCLUSIVE SCOOP—THE CLOCKWORK CANARY TO SING DARCY'S EXPLOITS!

The *Informer*'s star reporter has taken a sabbatical in order to chronicle the exploits of the Honorable Simon Darcy, London's most controversial civil engineer (and relation of the infamous TIME VOYAGER), as he joins the Race for Royal Rejuvenation—now known as the Triple R Tourney! The Clockwork Canary will chronicle a firsthand account of Mr. Darcy's adventures, to be published in serial form upon completion of the expedition. Prepare to be dazzled by tales of risqué romance, high drama, and nail-biting intrigue! Will Mr. Darcy dazzle and deliver like his notorious cousin? Or, like his unfortunate father, will his dreams go up in smoke?

Amelia's hands shook—the whole paper shook—as that last line burned through her blood like a lit fuse.

"Let go of the paper before you rip it to shreds, darlin'." Tucker relieved her of the infernal *Informer*, then, after returning the newspaper to its proper place, steered Amelia toward the nearby exit. "Time to be on our way."

She trembled with frustration and rage as Tucker escorted her outside onto the bustling sidewalk. "How could Simon . . . Why ever would he agree . . . The *Canary*, of all people!"

"Maybe he was offered a substantial amount of money. I know I was, and that was just for an interview. This is for serialization. Could amount to a windfall."

"Surely Simon's not that desperate."

"If he's anything like you, the money's not for him but for the family. Here's another angle: This high-profile exposé could garner favorable attention and return respect to the Darcy name. Sounds to me like your brother's capitalizing on the situation. Stacking the odds in the family's favor."

She sighed. "Simon is rather enterprising."

"See there. No cause to fret." Changing subjects, he signaled an automocab whilst listing several popular restaurants. "You mentioned wanting to experience everything. Let's start with French cuisine and take it from there. I swan, I could eat an entire cow."

Amelia's lip twitched, and her mood lifted. The mention of something as ordinary as food helped to put her bizarre circumstance in perspective. Since they'd skipped a midday meal and were well into the evening, nourishment was indeed in order. In addition to settling her swirling stomach, sustenance might help to clear her thoughts. Her brain was jammed with the sketches and notes of a Renaissance genius, swimming with the story her father had repeatedly shared with her regarding their own innovative kin and his dimension-breaking launch from the Crystal Palace.

Although only once had he mentioned Briscoe's cryptic note. A note he'd given to Papa on that historic day. A note Papa had hidden away, then later destroyed. Indeed, Amelia had no proof that that note had ever truly existed. But why would her father lie? His distress had been all too genuine after he'd told Amelia about the contents — a secret he'd kept for twenty-some years. She'd always supposed that he had been bursting to share the revelation with someone, and she'd always felt honored it was her. He'd entrusted her with the secret and now she was set to betray his trust. Although not wholly, she reminded herself, and for very good reason. When she'd learned about the jubilee race, she'd taken it as a sign. Briscoe had intended for her father to benefit from his discovery. And he would.

Whilst Tucker signaled yet again for transport — goodness, the traffic was oppressive — Amelia shook off the enormity of her quest and absorbed her surroundings. Whereas the library had been achingly quiet, the streets and sidewalks buzzed with activity. Illuminated dirigibles sparkled in the sky amidst the twinkling stars. Music floated from a nearby café, and the tantalizing aroma of freshly baked goods tempted and teased. Relaxing into the whimsy of Paris, Amelia leaned into Tucker, her pulse racing when he slipped his arm around her waist and squeezed. She smiled up into his intoxicating eyes. "Whereas you crave steak, Mr. Peckinposh, I crave Parisian pastries. What say you?"

"I say I know just the place."

CHAPTER 17

Tucker couldn't pinpoint the moment he'd lost his heart to Miss Amelia Darcy. He'd fallen brains over boots somewhere between the library and the cruise along the Seine. Her inquisitive mind and independent nature would have been a deterrent for most men, but they stoked his desire something fierce. He got an iron-hard erection when she mused on da Vinci, mechanics, and anything having to do with aviation. Her loyalty to her family and falcon cinched his heart. He cursed the moment she'd almost flown her kitecycle into the *Maverick* and at the same time considered that moment a blessing. On the one hand, she'd complicated his life even more and twisted him up to the point of compromising his judgment. On the other . . . Amelia reminded him of everything good and pure, passionate and constructive.

After the tainted fiasco in his homeland and more than a year in exile, he'd grown damned cynical. He'd spent the majority of his days risking his life in the name of justice. Then, based on the word of a vengeful, powerful official, the system had failed him. His gut clenched and burned every time he thought about the goddamned betrayal. Years of honorable work overshadowed by one unfortunate affair. His reputation tainted, his livelihood ripped away, all because of a manipulative, twisted woman and her obsessive, twisted pa. If it weren't for StarMan and the rest of his crew, Tuck would've swung.

Six feet under American soil or three thousand miles across the Atlantic?

The choice had been instant, if not simple. Long-term agenda: Wrangle back his freedom and reunite with his sister. Short-term: Provide a comfortable and profitable existence for the men who'd saved his life by risking prosecution. Until Tuck cleared his name (one way or another), Star-Man, Eli, Doc, Axel, and Birdman were also banned from America—fugitives from the law, alienated from family and friends. Tuck was saddled with legal issues and moral obligations. Loving Amelia was bad all the way around for everyone concerned.

Unfortunately his brain was at war with the rest of his body.

"What troubles you, Mr. Peckinposh?"

They'd been playing this game all night, maintaining the Fantasy Factory ruse. Mr. and Mrs. Peckinposh. Tuck liked the thought of Amelia being his and his alone a little too much. "Bothers me that we're calling it a night with so much left undone," he lied.

"We dined in a luxurious restaurant and indulged in delicious pastries whilst floating along the Seine. I have never experienced such grand cuisine or glorious sights. What more could there be at this late hour?"

Throughout the evening, whether it was by comment or expression, Amelia's innocence had hog-tied his senses and deepened his tender regard. He'd lost count of the times he'd tempered the urge to pull her into his arms for a kiss, settling on holding her hand or caressing her cheek or gently embracing her waist. "Music. Dancing. Theater. You haven't experienced Paris in full until you've sampled—"

"Culture." She shook her head. "I fear I wouldn't know what to . . . how to . . . it's not something I've been exposed to."

"All the more reason to explore." Selfishly, he wanted to hurry her back to their hotel and behind closed doors. He ached to hold and caress her, to seduce her with sweet words and a kiss that would deepen and take them to another plane. But he was also sensitive to her almost desperate need to live life to the fullest. *What if there's no tomorrow?* Not that he aimed to allow any harm to befall her, but he sure as hell didn't want her leaving Paris with regrets. What if this was her one and only journey to France? "Thought you wanted to broaden your horizons, Flygirl."

"I do." She stopped and turned, looking up at him with her pretty painted face, the sparkles on her cheeks almost as tempting as smudges of grease. "I want to make the most of every moment. With you."

His heart pounded, an exhilarating and excruciating slug-slow thud.

"I've never made love in Paris."

Thud. Thud. "Neither have I." He'd bedded Chantel, but he'd done so with lust and friendly affection. Never love.

Amelia placed her hand on his chest, over his pounding heart, her mesmerizing blue eyes glittering with desire. "Then what are we waiting for, Mr. Peckinposh?"

"Hell if I know, Mrs. Peckinposh."

Amelia had never stayed in a hotel, certainly not one as spectacular as Le Meurice. She'd seen the exterior when they'd swung by earlier to drop off their overnight bags. Impressive architecture, multiple stories. She knew it was grand, but she was not prepared for opulence. The interior was breathtaking. Indeed, she found it impossible not to gawk. Patterned marble floors, white marble columns accentuated with gilded leaves, elegant furnishings, vaulted ceilings. Frescoes. She gaped up at the chandeliers, dripping with crystal and gold, and let out a breathy whistle.

"Do you really think show people such as the Peckinposhes would stay in such an extravagant hotel?" she whispered.

"They would if they experienced a recent windfall." Tucker leaned in, his warm breath tickling her ear. "And if this were their honeymoon."

She jerked around, bumping his nose. "You told the hotel clerk we were newly wed?"

"Best way to fortify a lie is to stick close to the truth. Newly acquainted, newly lovers, newly wed."

Sensible, she supposed, but troubling. They'd been posing as a married couple all day and she hadn't been bothered one whit. She'd simply played along, enjoying the freedom the conventional union allowed. However, once they'd left the library, the ruse had grown more personal. An intimate dinner followed by the moonlight cruise along the Seine. Heated looks, discreet touches, stolen kisses.

Initially they'd adopted the identities of Mr. and Mrs. Peckinpoh in order to move freely about Paris without incident. Yet as the evening progressed, Amelia's ability to discern reality from fantasy faltered. She knew they were not, in truth, married. She knew, deep down, that Tucker was not madly in love. But he *did* desire her, and that desire, coupled with the romantic dinner and cruise and his constant tender and possessive caresses, wreaked havoc on logical thought. By the time they'd docked she'd been mad with want, gloriously seduced. Still, she'd managed to grasp hold of the faraway fact that she would be making *illicit* love. En route to the hotel, she wrestled the situation into perspective; it was all part of her intention to experience life to the fullest. Scandalous, no-strings-attached sex with her aeronautical hero. A thrill to cherish as she moved forward in life, alone, in pursuit of her lifelong dream.

Then Tucker mentioned the word *honeymoon* and her dream developed a wrinkle.

Suddenly, for the first time ever, Amelia envisioned herself as a bride. Not just any bride, but *his* bride. Tucker Gentry, her Sky Cowboy. Former air marshal, current outlaw. A renegade air courier with questionable ethics and a scandalous reputation with women. A man who'd made it clear he couldn't offer marriage. Leave it to her to crave the unattainable.

Amelia's cheeks flushed as Tucker escorted her past the smiling clerk and valet. Her pulse skipped and raced as they moved through the grand hotel—*hotel!*—and closer to their room. Their room! Yes, they'd spent the last couple of nights in Tucker's cabin, but this felt different—both scandalous and romantic and like something out of a young maiden's dream. Was this how a real bride felt? Her stomach fluttering with anticipation? Her heart skipping with joy? Her intimate parts tingling at the thought of seeing her husband naked? No longer an innocent, Amelia knew precisely what to expect. Indeed, she could scarcely wait to feel Tucker's hands upon her bare skin, his mouth, his tongue, his . . . *Blast.*

She tried like the devil to tame her scandalous thoughts. When the gilded doors of the passenger lift opened, she focused on the regal decor of the sixth floor. Even the softly lit hallway was stunning. They walked in silence, and Amelia held her breath as Tucker slipped the key into the door (their door!). Once inside, he flicked a switch. Electricity! A soft amber glow illuminated the spacious room.

Elegant decadence.

A ridiculous giggle bubbled in her throat. Although her mother would be mortified that Amelia was anticipating a night of sin, she would certainly approve of the exquisite surroundings. Indeed, if Anne Darcy knew Tucker could afford such luxury, perhaps she would encourage a match with the American aviator. "Blooming hell."

"That your way of saying you like it?"

She took in the large room, the floor-to-ceiling windows, the Louis XVI furnishings. The bed, all satin and silk and begging to be rumpled. Or wait. Maybe that was her. "Crikey."

He grinned, then swept off Peckinposh's silly bowler and flung it on a blue-and-cream brocade chair. "Been anxious to rid myself of this frippery for hours." He shrugged out of the fancy coat and unbuckled his shoulder holster, placing his Remington Blaster on the elegant nightstand. Then he slid off several rings and the extravagant wrist cuffs.

All the while, Amelia struggled with the fastenings of her coat.

Tucker noticed her fumbling and moved in. "You okay?"

Trembling fingers, wobbly knees. Her insides clenched and fluttered, and trepidation stole down her spine. "Spectacular." She'd been dizzy with desire all night. Now she felt skittish. Just because of that bed. That glorious, sumptuous, insanely romantic bed.

"Let me help." He kissed her then, obliterating thought, igniting passion.

Amelia responded with fervor. His sensual charisma entranced and inflamed. One look, one touch, one kiss. Somehow she wrenched off her coat without breaking the kiss and feverishly attacked his ensemble. In the recesses of her mind it occurred to her that she should take care—no ripping of fabric, no popping of buttons—as these clothes were rented.

Restraint was ever so difficult.

"Slow down, darlin'."

"Don't want slow."

Yet the blasted man softened his kisses and tempered his touch. She could feel his fingers nimbly loosening her— *Cherry's*—corset whilst she fumbled with buttons of his— *Digger's*—trousers. Astonishing how the kiss survived, unbroken, amidst the awkward disrobing. Not that they were completely nude, but they were indeed gloriously disheveled. She could feel the heat of his skin, the bunching of his muscles, as her hands skimmed over his rippled abdomen, across his sculpted chest. She thought about the incredible tattoo across his strong back and nearly came apart. Never would she have imagined inked art on flesh to be an aphrodisiac.

When at last they broke away, the heated passion endured, and soon after they were naked and Tucker was carrying her toward—*blast*—that bed. Something about that bed terrified her. "Wait."

"What?" Shifting her in his arms, he swept away the lacy bedcover and plush pillows.

She eyed a marble table, desperate for a less conventional union. More lustful than romantic. "Were you to clear that table—"

"Not now."

He laid her gently on the massive mattress, his gaze intent. What was he thinking? Feeling? His expression, fierce yet tender, caused her chest to ache. If he couldn't promise forever, why was he looking at her as if she were his one and only? Did he seduce all women in this manner? "I prefer the lights off."

"I prefer them on." He moved over her. Conventional. Romantic. Smoothing her pink curls—*pink!*—from her face, he kissed her forehead, then her cheeks, then lingered on her mouth. So sweet. So tender.

She panicked. "You promised to expose me to various sexual delights. Scandalous delights." She thought about their morning romp in the storage room. Her cheeks burned, but she persevered. "Is there not another position—"

"Many. But I prefer this one."

"This morning—"

"Was for you. This is for me."

She gasped as he kissed a path down her neck, suckled her breasts, then blazed a trail over her ribs, belly, and, "Oh!"

Heaven, moon, and stars.

He was kissing her *there*. His palms urging her thighs apart. Kissing her intimate juncture in the most scandalous way. His tongue flicked.

"Ah!"

"Relax, honey."

How absurd. One could hardly relax whilst preparing to

launch to the moon. Her muscles quivered as he continued his wicked assault. *Can't breathe.* His finger eased inside and she imploded.

Crikey!

Before she could catch her breath, Tucker shifted and suddenly he was inside of her. Rocking gently. Slow. Deep. Her senses danced with the feel of him, the scent of him. Then, as she moaned and clutched his shoulders, begging yet again for release, he increased the rhythm, the intensity. She felt something beyond the mind-blowing physical sensations—bone-deep affection, besotted love—and she knew she would never feel this way again. There would never be any man but Tucker, her Sky Cowboy, the man she couldn't have. The sense of loss slammed into her just as they peaked and shattered together.

She trembled in the aftermath, thoughts whirling.

Weight braced on his forearms, Tucker dropped his forehead to hers. "Amelia—"

A knock on the door stopped him short.

Conscious of their ruse and her compromising position, Amelia felt heat suffuse her face. "Who could that be?"

"Just a minute," he called over his shoulder. He nabbed his Blaster and rolled out of bed. "Stay here," he told Amelia.

As if she'd move. She was naked and most certainly flushed from their dalliance. Why had he taken his gun? Did he anticipate Dunkirk or ALE? Maybe Mr. O'Donnell had come to remind him she was bad luck. She could scarcely think straight, her mind and body deliciously discombobulated in the aftermath of their lovemaking. Cheeks burning, Amelia pulled the sheets over her shoulders and turned her face to the wall. She contemplated slipping over the side of the bed and crawling toward her clothes, but the room was fairly well lit. So, as Tucker suggested, she stayed as she was.

And ruminated on this most perplexing and god-awful situation.

Deep in thought, she barely registered the door snicking closed.

"Champagne for the newlyweds," Tucker said.

Amelia looked over her shoulder and saw him, haphazardly dressed in trousers and a gaping shirt, carrying two long-stemmed glasses and a silver bucket stocked with ice and a corked bottle. He looked rumpled and to-die-for gorgeous. She cursed her smitten heart. "You ordered champagne?"

"Compliments of management." He set the bucket on the bedside table along with the glasses. Then he eased his Blaster from the back of his waistband and returned the gun to his holster.

She supposed that, given his profession—past and present—he always kept a weapon at the ready. She flashed on the penny dreadfuls she'd read over the years, compelling tales about Tucker's adventures as an air marshal. Her pulse skipped with a moment of hero worship. A courageous, industrious law official who'd wrangled the most dangerous of criminals. A superior aviator who'd stunned the masses with his death-defying abductions. Never in a million years would she have imagined herself in bed with Tucker Gentry, *in love* with Tucker Gentry. *Too good to be true*, her mind whispered. Impossible. Unattainable. Like so many of her papa's inventions, she saw this fantastic venture blowing up in her face.

The man of her wildest and improbable dreams peeled off his shirt whilst gesturing to the champagne. "Should we indulge now?" His tender gaze slid to her mouth. "Or later?"

"Now," she croaked. Instead of delighting at the hint of more magical kisses, she vibrated with an urgent need to vanquish her romantic delusions. Whilst Tucker uncorked the bottle, Amelia scrambled from beneath the sheets and nabbed her discarded pink blouse.

"What are you doing?"

"You didn't intend to drink in bed, did you?"

He quirked a gentle smile, shucking his trousers whilst she pulled on her blouse. "Come here, Amelia."

Sighing, she crawled back into that blasted bed. At least she was no longer naked. Tucker, on the other hand . . . Though his legs and man parts were hidden beneath the sheets, she had a full and splendid view of his muscled torso, his gorgeous face, his rumpled hair. She swallowed another sigh as he passed her a glass of bubbling champagne. Another first, although she'd sampled wine. Were they not the same?

He clinked his glass to hers. "Here's to locating the ornithopter."

The fact that he hadn't said something more intimate, like, "Here's to us," only intensified her desperation to quell her new and idiotic romantic illusions. There was no "us" beyond finding da Vinci's ornithopter and delivering it to the jubilee committee. After that she would be on her own, and he would be—

"Let's talk about what just happened."

Amelia blinked. Was he privy to her heart? Had he felt her falling in love? Had he read it in her eyes? Or was he referring to his own amorous display? Was this where he confessed that he looked at every woman he wanted to seduce into a stupor with that "you're my one-and-only" intensity? Was this where he reminded her that he couldn't promise forever? That their relationship was temporary? Her heart ached and her temper flared. Did he think her unworldly? Gullible? She gulped champagne, which tasted nothing like wine, scrambling for reasons—any reason—to dislike this man.

"Are you a New Worlder?" she blurted.

"Excuse me?"

"You cautioned me about bringing up political and religious views whilst in a skytown, but now we're alone and I'm desperate to know."

He sipped champagne, then regarded her with a raised brow. "Why?"

"Humor me," she said by way of a straight answer.

"I am not a New Worlder."

That should have snuffed her attraction. It didn't. She drank more champagne. "Old Worlder, then. I confess, given your aggressive and open views on advanced technology, I'm surprised."

"Not an Old Worlder."

She gaped. "Flatliner?" Even though she was disgusted, her inner self whooped with relief. An opportunist. Someone who cared only for himself with no thought for the future of mankind. She would never consider marrying a Flatliner. Her liberal and utopian views wouldn't stand for it. She finished off her champagne, waiting for her affections to die a swift death. Why did they linger? Stupefied, she held out her glass for a refill.

Tucker complied, though his expression clearly advised that she take this one slowly.

She downed the first quarter, hiccuped. "Excuse me." Mind whirling, she shook her head. "This makes no sense. You risked your life making America a safer place. Clearly you care or did care about humanity. Or did you merely combat injustice to make a name for yourself? Indeed, you have achieved great fame, first as an air marshal, then as an outlaw. Mr. O'Donnell mentioned that you're a hardheaded bastard when it comes to money."

"Axel talks too much."

"Are you truly motivated by money? If so . . ." She flashed on the newspaper articles from more than a year back. The scandal that had spurred Tucker to flee his own country. She hadn't believed him guilty, but *what if*? Were she looking to quash her tender feelings, believing the worst would do it.

"If so, then maybe I am guilty as accused of theft and murder." He drained his glass, then set it aside. "A couple of days ago you thought me incapable of, as you put it, such an atrocity."

She still did. Even though her head spun, her gut stood strong. Tucker Gentry wouldn't seduce a woman for nefarious reasons. He certainly wouldn't resort to murder when things turned bad. Regardless of the evidence, Amelia believed him innocent. Learning he was a Flatliner had knocked her off balance. Knowing his abominable political stance, however, had not shaken her infatuation. She still craved his company and affection. Still fantasized about being his one and only. Of all the rotten luck. She swigged deeply, hoping to numb her addled thoughts. Instead her mind spun with scenarios, mostly bad. "Blast." She palmed her forehead, fighting a dizzy spell.

Tucker relieved her of the glass, then rolled in and pulled her down into a spooning position.

She would've protested, except the room was spinning and his arms stabilized her somewhat. "I feel strange."

"You're not much of a drinker, honey."

"I drank plenty."

"That's what I mean."

She could feel herself drifting, a surreal tingly sensation that caused her to smile into the pillow in spite of her troubled mood. In the next breath, she tried to remember what had vexed her so.

Tucker tightened his hold, spoke close to her ear. "Amelia."

"Mmm?"

"Why so desperate to know my political stance?"

She snuggled deeper into his embrace, giving over to a soft, sweet haze. "Because I don't want to love you."

Chapter 18

Tuck didn't sleep a damned wink. He tossed and turned all night, Amelia's words ringing in his ears. *I don't want to love you.* Hell, it was the last thing he wanted, too. Bad enough that he loved her. He'd recognized the fact earlier in the evening, but then when he'd made love to her in the honeymoon suite, in a bed intended for man and wife, his heart nearly burst with marrow-deep, long-lasting affection.

Having her snuggled in his arms had intensified the need to wake with her every morning. When she'd roused, grumpy and distant, all he could think about was how vexing and cute she was. All he wanted was to toss her on the bed and kiss the holy discontent out of her. All he craved was a lifetime of sass.

Of all the impossible situations. Of all the women he'd encountered in his life . . . why Amelia? Why now?

Tuck had spent the short return flight from Paris to the skytown contemplating the reality of his circumstance. He needed that ornithopter, if it did indeed exist, or a mighty hefty fortune in order to bargain for a life that included his sister and cleared his men. Even without the artifact or jubilee prize, he was well on his way. Working for another year or so as an international air courier should do it. The riskier the cargo, the higher the payday, the sooner he'd reach his goal. That entailed circumventing ALE and sky pirates. He couldn't keep Amelia on the *Maverick* day to day and submit her to that sort of danger. He couldn't offer her a stable, respectable life on the ground either. So, what?

Ask her to wait for him until . . . when? What if it took longer than a year? What if there were complications? What if he got himself killed?

Banking on his accuser's obsession with antiquities, Tuck could revise his situation lickety-split with that priceless ornithopter, but that meant convincing Amelia to give it over. He'd been stewing on a solution that would benefit them both. He could afford to pay her a pretty pound up front and would continue to feed her bank account in order to provide for her family, but he worried that she cared more about aggrandizing her father's reputation and the family's tattered name than affording them a comfortable future. Money he could offer. Glory? Short of helping her deliver da Vinci's invention to the British Science Museum and somehow ensuring that she won the jubilee prize, how the hell could he bring glory and respectability to the eccentric and infamous Darcys? One thing was for sure and certain: He did *not* want to hurt Amelia.

Even in his darkest times, Tuck tended to be an optimist, but that adorable hellion had his senses twisted like a busted compass. As a result, he felt a mite lost. He'd intended to come clean about his tender feelings last night, initiating a frank, mature discussion, hoping to get his bearings. She'd blindsided him with politics. What the hell? They'd just shared a profound mating of body and soul and she wanted to argue worldviews? Then she'd uttered those words, *I don't want to love you*, and he'd understood. She was trying to drive a wedge between them.

While returning their costumes to the Fantasy Factory, Tuck considered the advantage of that wedge. The greater the gap, the less risk of hurting her feelings. Logically speaking, bargaining for possession of the ornithopter would be simpler on a purely business level. If he was smart he'd encourage her disdain by perpetuating the misconception that he was a Flatliner—clearly a sore spot with that woman. Were he looking to obliterate her tender feelings, professing disinterest in the future of mankind would do it. Damn, it vexed that she'd distance herself from someone purely based on political stance. Tuck didn't cotton to racial, religious, or political intolerance. She considered herself a New Worlder, a utopian, someone intent on steering humanity away from the wars and atrocities that, if they continued unchecked, would ravage the globe for decades, reaching a tumultuous boiling point in 1969. The Holocaust. Hiroshima. Race riots and the assassination of a civil-rights activist clergyman. Cautionary tales spouted by the time-traveling Peace Rebels. Tales meant to instill fear, his pa had said. Fanatical alien Bible-thumpers, he'd called them.

Tuck reserved judgment. He always reserved judgment.

Would Amelia exhibit tolerance when she learned his true stance on politics?

Just one question that had rattled in his brain throughout the night.

"Thank you for treating me to an exhilarating visit to Paris," Amelia said as they exited the Fantasy Factory in their own clothes. "I have to believe our time at the Bibliothèque Nationale was well spent. I just know once we reach"—she peered over her shoulder as they moved down the hall—"our . . . destination, something we read or something we gleaned from previous studies will, as you said, click with something we see in da . . . the genius's workshop. Between the two of us, we'll solve the mystery," she said as she climbed the ladder ahead of him. "Who better than avid devotees of da . . . the genius. Fate set our paths on the same course."

"To my recollection," Tuck said as they hit the deck, "it was your reckless flying that set us on the same path."

She whirled and zapped him with those dazzling blue eyes. A sensual thrill shot through him like a charged bullet. *Pathetic.* "Just wanted to get your attention."

She furrowed her brow.

He nabbed her wrist and pulled her out of the stream of

foot traffic. Six in the morning and the skytown was crowded
with the night owls who were just now preparing to leave.
"You woke before dawn," he said in a low voice, "and
launched into the day full-speed. You've been jawing non-
stop about da—"

"Shh!"

He removed her hand from his mouth, although, damn,
he would've enjoyed kissing her palm, her wrist. . . . "The
genius," he substituted for the sake of secrecy. "Not that I'm
opposed to the subject. Nor am I averse to listening to your
rants regarding the Clockwork Canary, nor your grievances
regarding your ma. I am, however, offended, Amelia, by
your obvious determination to ignore our delicate circumstance." Christ in heaven. Had he actually *said* that?

Her cheeks flushed. "Whatever are you referring to, Mr.
Gentry?"

"Don't play coy, Miss Darcy. It doesn't suit you."

She said nothing.

He pressed. "You care for me."

"No, I don't."

"You're falling in love. You admitted as much last night."

"I was weary with exhaustion, tipsy on champagne."

He grasped her hand, stopping her unconscious retreat.
"I care for you, too, Amelia. More than I should. Something
about you." He could name a dozen things. "But I'm not in
the position—"

"I know. You can't offer forever. Trust me, I'm grateful. I
have plans, Mr. Gentry. Big plans. I've always dreamed of
owning and piloting my own airship. To sail the skies, to
experience breathtaking sights and adventures. I've wanted
these things far longer than I've wanted you." She glanced
away. Not that she'd been looking him in the eyes to begin
with. "That is to say . . . I knew from the outset that this—
we—were temporary. I may have led a sheltered life, but I
am well-read and my views are—"

"Liberal."

"Exactly. Forward-thinkers—"

"Mods."

"—believe in free love. Marriage is for ... squares. Why would I want to give up my independence, my dreams and goals in the name of an official declaration of love? A ceremony and a piece of paper. How shallow and old-fashioned."

Did she really believe that? "The right man wouldn't ask you to give up your dreams."

Her head whipped around, and for the first time this day, she met his gaze full-on. "I'll keep that in mind, Mr. Gentry. Now. Shall we discuss your terms regarding transporting me to ... our destination and then delivering myself and the ... significant find to London?"

Oh, she was slick. And scared. What burned between them frightened the hell out of her. Balm for his ego. He narrowed his eyes, smiled. "I'll get back to you on that."

"Fine." She pivoted on her clunky boot heels and stalked toward where they'd left the air dinghy. Flygirl was back— her leather flight pants and skirted vest, her long hair braided and coiled. All that remained of Cherry Peckinposh was the pink-tinted hair. Guaranteed to wash away in three days, so she'd been told.

Tuck followed closely as Amelia brushed by several men, turning heads in her wake. She seemed oblivious. Tuck wasn't. He couldn't attribute the lingering looks to her pink hair, because the truth of it was, Amelia Darcy, whether in boyish britches or frilly cinched gowns, was damned stunning—a fresh-faced beauty with a curvaceous figure. A woman who exuded a stimulating combination of confidence and naïveté. To think she'd been a recent captive of Dunkirk's, a dangerous man who could be anywhere just now. Even here.

A protective and possessive streak bolted through Tuck, quickening his step. Just as he caught up to Amelia, she veered off. *What the hell?* Then he realized she was hurrying toward the sound of music.

"What is it? Who is it?" she asked without looking at him.

"Acid rock. Joplin. Wait." But she'd rushed ahead of him and into the dimly lit tavern. Three musicians backed a gritty-voiced female. "Take another little piece of my heart, yeah, sweetie," she wailed. He'd heard "now, baby," "yeah, honey," and several other variations of the lyrics over the years.

The longer the twentieth-century Peace Rebels dwelled outside of their time, the more they shared of their culture. Homesick, perhaps. Needing to cling to their reality to sustain their sanity, maybe. Tuck had always wondered about the mental and emotional state of the original Peace Rebels. Abandoning family and friends and the technological conveniences of their time—forever. Although they'd been convinced that, in their time, the end of the world was fast approaching. Events such as a cold war, a missile crisis, Vietnam, and nuclear reactors advancing the globe toward annihilation.

Hogwash, Tuck's pa had said when, as a very young boy, Tuck had run home, confused and worried due to stories he'd heard at school or in the town square—preachings of the Peace Rebels. *Those tales ain't nothin' but scare tactics, son*, Rebis Gentry had said. *One of the easiest ways to convert people to your way of thinkin' is by scarin' the bejesus out of 'em. How do we know they're who they say they are? So what if they can devise mind-boggling whatchamacallits and thingamabobs? So what if they have superior knowledge when it comes to science and medicine? They could be from Mars for all we know.* Then he'd ruffle Tuck's hair and smile. *Live for today, son. Not in fear of tomorrow.*

Hence Tuck's worldview had been instilled early on.

As if entranced, Amelia sat at a table near the stage, eyes wide as the singer belted out the passionate tune.

Draped in leather, sequins, and layers of love beads, Gia Joplin (as the sign on the tripod announced) swayed back and forth, rocked forward and back, her long, wild hair bouncing around her head like a wiry halo. "Oh, come on. Come on. Come on . . ."

"What do you want?"

Tuck looked over his shoulder. A barmaid dressed in a gauzy flowery gown. More love beads. "Got coffee?"

She smirked. "Considering this is a coffeehouse, what do you think, cowboy?"

Tuck grinned. "Two coffees."

"What fixings?" she asked. "Whiskey? Scotch?"

"Black."

"Side of weed?"

"No, thanks."

"Square," she mumbled, then sashayed away.

The second time today he'd heard that Mod term. Both times directed at him. Made him feel old and conventional, which he was not. Although there was a time he wouldn't have refused a toke. Especially if it meant sharing a joint with someone who possessed insight into one of his cases. Same as sharing a quart bottle of whiskey when moving in this circle. Tuck had been in hundreds of coffeehouses over the years. Typically they appealed to a more eclectic crowd. The artsy, liberal-thinking sort. Sure enough, the scattered few still in attendance looked on the younger side of thirty and dressed in a colorful, multiage fashion known as Mod-Vic, a bold fashion adopted widely by rebellious youth and Freaks.

Just as Gia Joplin and her ear-blistering trio screeched their last note, Tuck's gaze landed on a small group of people emerging from another room. Freaks. Tuck couldn't care less except—*shit fire*—Doc was amongst them, and he'd forgone his blue-tinted specs. If Amelia saw him, saw his surgically altered, eerie white irises, she'd know for sure and certain that he was born of two worlds. Knowledge Doc preferred to withhold from the rest of the *Maverick*'s crew. *Damn.*

"I've never heard music performed in such a manner," Amelia said, watching as Gia Joplin swigged liquor from a bottle while her band dismantled their equipment. "There was a primal quality to it. Stirring." She looked over her shoulder at Tuck. "Do you not think?"

He thought plenty. Probably too much. "Groovy." He grasped her elbow. "Let's get out of here."

"But you ordered drinks."

He slapped a couple of bills on the sticky table. "We need to get back to the ship." Doc and his Freak friends moved to the smoky bar. If Tuck stayed between them and Amelia and hustled her out, they could avoid confrontation.

"Why so irritable?"

"That music gave me a headache."

Amelia rolled her eyes as he hastened her out of her chair. "I suppose you prefer something more conventional. Stephen Foster? Beethoven? Shall I put in a request for 'Oh! Susanna'?"

"You're a pain in my ass this morning, Flygirl."

"Then the day is off to a glorious start." She sniffed as he guided her through a haze of smoke. "Odd-smelling tobacco."

"Weed."

"What?"

"Hemp. Cannabis. Marijuana."

"Oh. *Oh*. I've heard Mods and Freaks are most fond of . . . what do they call them? Joints?" They were almost to the door when she broke his hold. "Blast. I left my walking stick at the table."

She turned back, catching Tuck unaware, and though he moved fast, it wasn't fast enough.

"My, aren't they a bold and colorful group? And I thought Cherry and Digger were flamboyant." Amelia squinted through the haze. "I know that style. ModVic. Are they Freaks?" she whispered. "Goodness, is that—"

Tucker caught her by the waist and whisked her out the coffeehouse door quicker than a flea hoppin' out of danger. She'd noticed Doc, but he hadn't noticed them. At least, Tuck didn't think so.

Once outside, Amelia wiggled out of his hold. "What is wrong with you?"

"I'll explain later."

"But I saw Doc Blue. Shouldn't we say hello? Won't he think we're rude?"

"He wouldn't appreciate the intrusion."

"But—"

"Dammit, Amelia."

"But—"

"Do you like Doc?"

"Yes, of course. Very much."

Tuck smothered a spark of jealousy. "Then we're not going back and you're not going to tell him you saw him here. Unless you *want* to make him uncomfortable."

She blew out a huffy breath. "You are most infuriating this morning, Mr. Gentry."

"Then my day is shaping up." He grasped her elbow but she dug in her heels. "What now?"

"My walking stick. It was a gift from Eli and I refuse to leave it behind."

"Why did you bring it? Your wound is healed."

"It also serves as a weapon. I thought I should be prepared should we run into trouble."

"If we run into trouble you have me."

She crossed her arms and raised a defiant brow.

Tuck wanted to throttle her. "I'll get the damned cane." He maneuvered her into an alcove. "Don't move, and don't talk to strangers."

"You're being ridiculous."

"Do you want that walking stick?"

Smirking, she gave him a two-finger salute.

Tuck wrenched off his Stetson. "Hold this." He'd be less

conspicuous without his signature hat. He'd breeze in and out. If Doc did spot him, at least it would be without Amelia.

If only Doc would come clean about his heritage. Granted, the gentle-hearted Freak had good reason to distrust the intolerant portion of Vic society. The man's parents had been ostracized and then later killed in a suspicious house fire. His brother—younger by just one year—had rebelled, severing ties with Doc, dabbling in a life of crime, and ultimately going underground. Unjust fear and prejudice had ripped Doc's family from his life, rendering the young man suspicious and reclusive. Tuck understood caution. What baffled him was Doc's unwillingness to trust the men he'd lived and worked with on the *Maverick* for more than two years. Although Tuck had promised to keep Doc's secret, that vow was beginning to chafe. He'd promised Amelia an explanation, but damn, that put him in the position of betraying Doc's trust as well as slighting his crew. Didn't they deserve to know first?

"Dammit." Tuck kept his head down and steered clear of the bar. He couldn't, however, avoid hearing the heated conversation coming from Doc's friends. Something about a protest. *Well, hell.* Doc had mentioned a brewing rebellion among Freaks, but he hadn't mentioned being a part of that cause. Given Doc's pacifist mind-set, more likely he was exploring this avenue as yet another way to connect with his brother—a man he hadn't heard from in more than three years. Tuck wished he could say it wasn't his business, but if Doc somehow brought trouble to the *Maverick* . . .

He snagged the retracted brass cane from the table and glanced toward the bar. Only Doc was no longer with the plotting Freaks. The supernaturally gifted doctor was immersed in a conversation with a lone person. A woman, he assumed from a glimpse of stocking and skirt. Hidden in the shadows, Tuck couldn't make out whether she was Vic or Freak. Whoever she was, Doc was agitated. Given the younger man's normally docile character, Tuck's first impulse was to step in, but he resisted, knowing Doc wouldn't appreciate the intrusion amongst his own kind. Still, Tuck wouldn't be forgetting this.

He slipped outside, a bad feeling churning in his gut. Anxious to distance Amelia from brewing trouble, he handed her the walking stick, then finessed her toward the air dinghy. He hoped to hell the *Maverick* was up and running and in good order. The sooner they were on their way to Italy, the better. Skimming the clouds always cleared his head. Right now his brain was jammed tight with a dozen puzzles. Amelia. The ornithopter. Doc. To name three.

As they neared the first swinging gangway, Amelia glanced over, her brow scrunched in concern. "You okay?"

Hearing one of his phrases laced with her British accent, he almost smiled. "Spectacular."

CHAPTER 19

An emergency meeting.

Bingham had been at Wickford, locked in his bedchamber, indulging in a rather sadistic fetish with a beautiful but unemotional automaton, when he'd received a coded Teletype from Aquarius summoning him to London.

Three hours later, he sat in a dimly lit room surrounded by the secret society's members. Keen minds. Forward-thinkers. Yet they lacked his genius. His ruthlessness. They thought themselves bold because they plotted to assassinate the queen. He thought them pretentious knobs. Visually and conceptually, they blended. Self-important New Worlders with a noble cause.

Delving for patience, Bingham pretended concern whilst Saturn explained that a valuable inside source was no longer willing to cooperate. Faces and voices blurred—a panicked muddle.

"How can we proceed with our plans if we are uninformed?"

"The Golden Jubilee is several months away. Surely the day's scheduled events will change between now and then."

"Did you offer our man more money?"

"Of course. Unfortunately fear overrides greed in this matter."

"Meaning?"

"Apparently his conscience got the better of him," Saturn said. "He's been haunted by nightmares where he is accused of treason and imprisoned in the Tower. Or worse."

Bingham suppressed a disgusted snort. *Coward.*

"Any chance his guilty conscience will prod him into confessing his sins to an associate or the queen's adviser?"

"And bring his nightmare to life? I think not."

"Yet the possibility exists, in which case an investigation would lead to us."

"I am his only contact," Saturn said. "If anyone should worry, it is I."

"Who's to say you won't buckle under pressure and reveal our society and plot?"

"You dare to question my allegiance!"

Bingham closed his eyes as a heated argument ensued. Eight titled men hurling insults and exaggerated scenarios. How easily they were deterred. How easily frightened. *How revolting.* This past week had been fraught with incompetence and disappointment. Concetta. His Mod trackers. Dunkirk. Anger and frustration fueled his ruthless mindset. Ah, yes. Some things he could control. He opened his eyes. "Eliminate the source."

He hadn't shouted, yet his words cut through the chaos. Silence.

Saturn angled his head. "Say again, Mars?"

Bingham sighed as if his suggestion burdened his soul. "Think of all who will benefit should we succeed in silencing the woman who insists on halting progress. Think of the future. Of your fellow man. Beastly business, I confess. But it is our duty to proceed." He nearly choked on his feigned sincerity. "Eliminate the weak link. The cowardly inside source who could ultimately destroy us and, in turn, mankind." He waited a dramatic beat, then added, "Meanwhile, let us recruit a new source. Someone more . . . reliable."

More silence.

Knowing the power of patience, Bingham waited.

"How would we go about ... eliminating the problem?"

They all looked to Bingham. Not wanting to reveal the full force of his devious side, he remained cryptic. "I know someone."

"Do you trust this person?"

"Implicitly." Bingham, or Mars, as they called him, looked to Saturn. "Write down the source's name and I shall ensure our anonymity and cause." He looked to the other seven, as if he truly valued their opinions. "Are we in accord, gentlemen?"

Venus, the spineless worm who fed off the boldness of others, raised his goblet. "To Aquarius."

After a few traded glances, all repeated the toast. "To Aquarius!"

Bingham drank deeply, then stood and procured the unofficial death warrant from Saturn. "If you'll excuse me, gentlemen."

He left the room, anxious to distance himself from men who considered themselves his allies. He considered them pawns, but extremely valuable. Hence he would protect them to the best of his ability, in the name of Aquarius. In the name of his own selfish goals.

Speaking of ... Since he'd been summoned to the British Science Museum, he'd scheduled a meeting with Mr. P. B. Waddington of the Jubilee Science Committee. The man's office was in this very building, albeit three flights up, but since Bingham wished to keep their relationship quiet he'd arranged to meet the exhibitions and displays manager in Kensington Gardens. A chance meeting in a public area. Since he had an hour to kill, he ducked into a private club to make a discreet telephone call regarding the elimination. Thereafter he indulged in a smoke and a brandy whilst perusing the London newspapers and eavesdropping on a conversation regarding commercial flight. He left the club congratulating himself on investing in a profitable air transport company six months prior. He fairly rubbed his hands together in wicked delight. "Fearless and forward-thinking. The gateway to success."

The winter air was frigid, the skies hazy and gray, thick with smoke from the city's numerous steam stacks, yet nothing blighted the verdant hills and dales and stately trees of Kensington Gardens. Strolling well-kept footpaths, Bingham bristled each time he spied a horse-drawn carriage. The queen had prohibited steam- and petrol-fueled cabs—even private automocoaches—from any of the parks. With luck, it would not be thus by summer. There was a fortune to be made on noiseless electric recreational coaches. Just one of the inventions he hoped to develop and introduce into society.

Mind racing, he nodded in greeting at the fashionably attired pedestrians he passed along the way, his adrenaline spiking as he neared the Albert Memorial. It seemed fitting to meet a key employee of the science museum in the shadow of the prince consort, a progressive thinker who had championed technology. Were Prince Albert alive today, Bingham had no doubt the British Empire would be embracing instead of shunning twentieth-century technology.

Bingham approached the monument precisely on time. Anxious for an updated report on the global race, he hoped Waddington was equally punctual. Indeed the man waited on the designated park bench nearby. Bingham smoothed his greatcoat and eased down on the bench next to his scholarly-looking associate. "Beautiful day," he said by way of a formal greeting.

"Indeed."

"How fares the Triple R Tourney?"

Waddington dipped into the inside pocket of his frock coat. "I have a list of participants. Some mentioned the invention they are seeking. Some did not. Do you know one man bragged he would return with Noah's Ark? Extraordinary." He discreetly passed Bingham three sheets of typed notes. "We have almost two hundred official documentations. Then, of course, there are those who merely inquired but did not commit."

Like Jules Darcy. In an earlier meeting Waddington had mentioned the eldest brother as one of the first to call. The science fiction writer had asked specifics and offered nothing in return. Always in the shadows, that man. Bingham had learned easily enough that the other Darcy siblings had joined the race, although, skimming the list, he saw neither had officially registered. What did catch his eye were at least two scores of competitors citing the Briscoe Bus's clockwork propulsion engine as their target invention. The bus itself had been destroyed soon after arriving in this century; however, it was rumored that a rogue Peace Rebel had absconded with and hidden away the precious time-traveling engine. That engine alone would be enough to advance Bingham's personal agenda.

He smiled.

Waddington nodded. "As I said. Extraordinary."

"You'll alert me the moment any participant contributes a significant invention for the committee's approval."

"Before or after we examine and authenticate the item?"

"Upon delivery. Mr. Waddington," he said, prompting the man to shift and meet his gaze. "Given my position as benefactor and as a loyal servant of Her Majesty, Queen Victoria, surely you can understand why I would want to be involved in the entire process regarding authentication and merit."

The man blinked, his voice quiet but animated. "But of course, of *course*."

Just then Bingham's telepager vibrated in his inner vest pocket. Someone had important news. He returned the list to Waddington. "You have my contact information." When the man nodded, Bingham stood. "Thank you for meeting with me." He forced an easy and amiable smile. "Good day to you, sir."

Without looking back, Bingham circled the monument, then set off down a deserted footpath. He pulled the wireless telepager from his pocket. An ingenious contraption he'd purchased on the black market and spent weeks customizing. There were still glitches and bugs, but the communications device worked more often than not. He flipped open the brass cover and stared at the incoming code. The first digit indicated that the message was from an informant. The next segment—the phone number to call for details. The final portion of the code relayed the reason for the page.

Bloody hell, yes! A Freak informant had knowledge of Miss Darcy's whereabouts.

Bingham snapped shut the cover and set off at a brisk pace. His day was looking up, and Captain Dunkirk, the insolent bastard, was about to earn his money.

CHAPTER 20

Upon boarding the *Maverick*, Amelia had been greeted by a very vocal and seemingly happy Leo. The falcon had flown out of the surrounding woods and swooped in, eager for her attention. Whilst she was stroking her friend's feathers, Tucker had brushed past her, motioning to StarMan and Axel and demanding a report regarding the airship's condition.

Considering he'd just returned from a recreational visit to Paris, she sensed that his terse mood took his men by surprise. Not Amelia. The tension between them had been building all morning. He'd admitted to caring about her, which had rattled her far more than she'd let on.

What confused her most was that he had once again made it clear that he could offer no more than a momentary dalliance, yet he seemed irritated that, as of this morning, she'd initiated a physical and emotional retreat. For all his intelligence did he not recognize forward, logical thinking? Because of her liquor-induced ramblings, she'd intimated she was falling in love. Never mind that she had already fallen deeply and madly. Did he not see the wisdom in ending a casual affair that now involved caring and fervent affection? Did he *want* to crush her heart?

Crikey.

How arrogant she'd been. How ignorant of true love. Foolishly she'd believed she could keep company with a man she'd worshiped for years and then walk away at a moment's notice with an unscathed heart. She'd realized her folly in that honeymoon bed. After a restless night, she'd awoken with one clear thought: *Preserve your integrity and heart by establishing a professional relationship. No romping. Just business.*

Unfortunately, he'd stalled when she'd suggested they strike an agreement regarding his transport and courier services. Heart-pounding intimacy still sizzled between them, even though she'd erected a mental wall, even though she'd embraced each and every reason to find fault or to pick a fight with the man. She'd just have to push harder, stand stronger. *I no longer wish to explore the sensual universe with you. Thank you most kindly. Moving on.*

The tricky part was that she could not alienate Tucker entirely. She needed him. She needed the *Maverick. Focus, Amelia, focus.* Mount Ceceri. The workshop. The ornithopter. She had to win the jubilee prize for the sake of her family. In the name of her father.

Amelia jerked straight and Leo flew away, watching over her from Birdman Chang's iron-grilled crow's nest. She knew the falcon sensed her agitation as she reviewed her agenda and focused on a timeline. Had it been only ten days since Papa had passed? Less than two weeks, and yet she'd savored an adventure of a lifetime and the attentions of a famous outlaw?

Flushed with guilt, Amelia stalked past Tucker, StarMan, and Axel. She circumvented Eli, merely nodding at his "Welcome back, miss." Nearly tumbling down the ladder in her haste to get to the lower deck. The kitecycle. Never had she been so determined to conquer the impossible. She had to resurrect Bess.

"Her hair's pink."

Tuck ignored Axel's observation as Amelia stormed past. "So the blasterbeefs are in top form?"

"For now. Can't say what'll happen once we take off. What with a woman aboard and all."

"Don't start."

"She seems upset," StarMan said. "Maybe you should—"

"Butt out."

Axel whistled. "Talk about rotten luck."

Tuck raised an inquiring brow while trading his Stetson for a flight cap.

"You're sweet on Miss Crazy Pants."

"One more derogatory remark about Miss Darcy, Axel, and I'll knock you on your ass."

"If that don't beat all." The thick-necked engineer plucked a fat stogie from his pocket and clamped it between his teeth. "Of all the women in all the world," he muttered while scuffling toward the engines.

"Want to talk about it?" StarMan asked.

"About as much as I want to roll around bare-assed in a nest of red ants." Tuck rounded the thermoplastic shield of the cockpit, inspected the wheel and controls. He noted a few upgrades and repairs. Axel was no slouch, but Gaston's mechanics were exceptional. "Have Eli saddle Peg. I'll ride out and thank the duke for his hospitality while we're waiting for Birdman and Doc to return."

"The Duke of Anjou left last night on unexpected business. Asked me to bid you farewell and good luck."

"Something we could all use, if you ask Axel."

"Not that I'm buying into that particular superstition, but you have to admit we experienced an unusual amount of malfunctions and crises last time we flew with Miss Darcy."

Tuck shot him a look.

"Right. I'll have Eli ready the bally. Birdman boarded about an hour ago. He's below nursing a *baijiu* binge. Soon as Doc joins us we can cast off." StarMan moved to his custom-made station. Charts, maps, an iron-based globe, and a navigational and astronomical sextant were just a few of the items crowding the rear of the cockpit. He rooted himself, then looked to Tuck. "Where in Italy?"

Sensible question, especially for his chief navigator. In order to plot a course he needed a destination. "Tuscany."

"Can you be more specific?"

"Not at the moment." Tuck had been stewing on Amelia's invention of historical significance ever since she'd confided in him about the secret room. What was the connection between Briscoe Darcy's time machine and Leonardo da Vinci's ornithopter, if any? Why had Darcy left the miracle invention hidden where he'd found it? Why tell Amelia's pa about the secret vault, and why did Lord Ashford keep it a secret all those years? One thing was for sure and certain: Amelia knew more than she was letting on. He sensed something big. Something dangerous. Until he knew more, he figured it was best to keep his crew in the dark. The more they knew, the greater the risk of a leak. Given the money and notoriety at stake, this could be the discovery of a lifetime. Not that he didn't trust his crew, but—

"Sorry I'm late. Lost track of time. You know how it is in a skytown." Doc Blue adjusted his goggles and sleeved sweat from his brow. "Axel said we're clear for takeoff." He gestured to the globe. "Still heading for Italy?"

Tuck nodded.

"Miss Darcy clue you in on what we're after?"

"Why?"

Doc jammed his fingers through his spiky white hair. "Just curious, is all. I mean, we were pondering on the matter, you and me," he said to Tuck, "and I . . . I was just curious." After an awkward moment, he jerked a thumb over his shoulder. "I'll help Eli with the bally."

The anxious man trotted off nearly as fast as he'd blown in.

StarMan raised a brow. "What's going on with Doc?"

"That's what I'd like to know." Tuck couldn't shake the feeling that he'd been up to no good with his fellow Freaks. Nor could he dismiss Doc's nervous interest in their destination. Given his usually calm demeanor, his anxious behavior was damned suspicious.

"Maybe he finally danced the mattress jig." StarMan shook his head and returned his attention to the map. "Only Doc would get all flustered and self-conscious about bedding a woman."

Tuck didn't think that was it, but what the hell did he know? Maybe Doc had finally let his guard down, relaxed and indulged with one of his own kind. The woman in the shadows—maybe she'd been his first lover. He didn't want to suspect Doc Blue of ill intent. No, he did not.

Tuck heard the blasterbeefs firing up, saw the bally inflating via the steam engine. Soon they'd be in the air, and maybe his goddamned head would clear.

"You want the fastest or safest course?" StarMan asked.

"I want a long way 'round." Tuck moved in, placed his palms on the map, and studied the terrain alongside his friend. "If Dunkirk or anyone else is tailing us, I don't want to broadcast our destination."

"We could lose them in the Alps."

"Make it so." The long way around would also buy Tuck more time with Amelia. One way or another they were going to discuss what burned between them. They were sure as hell going to have a frank and detailed discussion about the Time Voyager and the ornithopter. He aimed on giving her the space she claimed she wanted. For now. Meanwhile he'd work out matters in his mind and determine a course of action. He'd outsmarted some of the most brilliant criminal minds in America, for chrissake. He could sure as hell handle Flygirl.

"You've been at the wheel for hours."

Tuck ignored StarMan, even though he hovered.

"You're two hours into my watch," he persisted.

"I'm good."

"Doc's got your supper waiting below."

"Not hungry."

"That's what Miss Darcy said."

Tuck glanced over his shoulder. "She still at it?"

"Even Eli, who typically minds his own affairs, voiced concern. She's been sequestered in that workroom since we launched from Château de Malmaison. Intent on repairing that dig. Unnaturally intent."

Tuck heard his friend's thinking loud and clear: He wanted Tuck to intercede. It had been the very action he'd been avoiding. He'd aimed at giving her time and space. Was certain she'd grow bored and come up for air. She'd pester him about something, like better supplies, or ask him to make good on his promise regarding Doc. She'd pick his brain about the blasterbeefs, or Peg, or question him about the estimated time of arrival in Italy. But here they were, hours later and sailing over southern France, and she hadn't done any one of those things.

Nor, for all of his deep thinking, had Tuck formulated a clear plan regarding their circumstance. If only he'd kept things professional. He'd been a fool to think he could engage in a sexual relationship with that woman without risking his heart. He'd known before he'd even kissed Amelia that she was different. She'd lassoed his interest when she'd tried pulling that kitecycle out of a nosedive, stirred his blood when she'd pointed a gun at Axel in defense of her bird. The warning signs had been plentiful; he'd just ignored them. He wanted Amelia, but he also wanted his life back. He needed that ornithopter, but so did she. The future of his family (including his crew) was at stake. So was hers. "What a mess."

"You'll sort it out." StarMan nudged him aside. "Meanwhile, go tend to Miss Darcy. Her self-imposed confinement is making the crew twitchy. Me included."

Tuck rolled his tense shoulders, glanced up through the shield, and saw Birdman in his crow's nest with Leo perched alongside, both looking down at him. He clearly read the minds of both man and bird. *Go to her.*

He looked toward the bow and caught Eli giving him the

evil eye before returning to whatever gadget he was tinkering with. Axel was busy polishing the blasterbeefs even though they gleamed. "What the hell's Ax got to be nervous about? Thought he'd be thrilled by Amelia's absence. Less chance of chaos."

"He thinks trouble's brewing."

At that moment, Axel shot him a look of the damned.

"Oh, for chrissake." Tuck swept off his flight cap and goggles, shoved them in a cubby on the console, then tugged off his gloves. "I'll be back."

"No hurry. Sun's setting. When night falls I'm doubling back. All's clear."

"For now." Tuck strode toward the stern, deep in thought. He couldn't shake the sense of foreboding that had dogged him since morning. Since the skytown. He hated fanning Axel's unfounded fears, but he felt it too: Trouble was brewing.

Just as he neared the ladder he caught sight of Peg, who'd been given free range of the deck for the past couple of hours. His heart swelled when the black steed left the rail he'd been staring over and walked toward Tuck, his mane and tail ruffling in the wind, soft black muzzle twitching. Tuck figured he wanted a licorice treat or his ears scratched. At the very least, an affectionate nuzzle. Instead, Peg nosed his shoulder, giving him a good hard shove toward the ladder.

"You, too, huh? Don't worry. I'm going."

Moments later Tuck stood two decks below, staring at the closed door of the workroom. He knocked.

"Go away."

Her voice was choked and quiet. Concern slithered under his skin. He knocked again. No answer. Tried the handle. Locked. "Amelia, it's Tuck. Open the door."

Silence.

Hitching back his coat, he reached in his vest pocket for a skeleton key. The key tripped the lock and Tuck entered the vast room, shutting the door softly behind him. *Whoa.*

Somehow, some way, she'd constructed new wings. That had meant building the frames, then measuring, cutting, and mounting the strong canvas. The wing span was greater than what he remembered of the original kitecycle. Impressive design, reminiscent of a da Vinci, even though he wasn't sure the dimensions would coincide with the tandem bicycle's chassis.

On the far side of one wing, he spotted Amelia sitting on the planked floor, cross-legged, hunched over, and, Christ almighty, sobbing. Though she barely made a sound, her small shoulders shook and she rocked back and forth. As he neared, he made out choked sobs and wheezes that tore at his heart.

Kneeling in front of her, he gently smoothed tangled pink curls from her tearstained face. "Amelia, honey, what's wrong?"

"I broke it."

"Broke what?"

"My screwdriver."

She was breaking down over a broken tool?

"The frame of the velocipede is horribly bent," she choked out. "I was trying to . . ." *Sniffle*. ". . . and then I . . ." *Wheeze*. ". . . when it . . . and then I . . . See?" Bawling loudly now, she offered up the mangled tool. "How am I supposed to . . . How can I finish . . . with this?"

Torn between amusement and perplexity, Tuck inspected the damage. The steel rod had broken plumb off of the wooden handle. The handle itself was in two splintered pieces. No way in hell could he fix it. "I'll get you another."

"But this was Papa's. He gave it to me. Gave me the whole set. I promised I'd take care," she sobbed, "but then I got frustrated and now he's broken."

He?

Oh, Christ. This wasn't about the damned screwdriver. "Amelia—"

"I should have been there. He'd been so obsessed with *Apollo*. Trying to outdo Briscoe, I think. Or maybe ... maybe he wanted to fly me to the moon. He got distracted sometimes. Scatterbrained. But usually I was there to help. Only I wasn't. I was ... I was ..." She doubled over, racked with grief.

Hell's fire. This girl blamed herself for her pa's death. Heart in throat, Tuck pulled Amelia into his arms. He leaned against the wall with her cradled in his lap. He shushed and rocked gently. Stroked her wet cheeks as she gripped his coat and soaked his shirtfront with tears.

"I'm sorry. I can't ..." *Sob*. "... can't stop ..." *Hiccup*. "... crying."

He thought about her nightmares, how she cried in her sleep but suppressed her grief by day.

"I can't remember the last time I cried."

"Long time coming, darlin'. Let it out. You'll feel better."

"I don't want to feel better. I don't want to heal and move on. I want to go back. I want one more day. No, fifty more years! I want to watch him fiddle with his toaster contraption. Do you know how many pieces of soggy or crispy charred bread popped out of that thing? But we always slathered it with jam and ate it. *Always*. I want burned bread. I want to help him test the wireless telecommunicator he'd been tinkering with for four years." She swiped her sleeve under her running nose, then held her thumb and index finger an inch apart. "He was *this* close to perfecting a palm-size telecommunicator. Do you know how famous he would have been if he could've marketed that?"

"And rich," Tuck said, wanting to support her elevated view of her pa.

"Stinking rich! But he could not focus on one thing long enough to perfect it. He had all these ideas"—she rapped her knuckles to her temple—"jumping and swelling in his brain. Imagine how that would *feel*? So you have to purge them, and because you are impatient things go wrong. Except I was usually there to help. I couldn't always make things right, but I could keep him safe."

She locked eyes with Tuck then, and his damned heart shredded and bled. "His obsession of the moment was *Apollo 02*," she said in a cross between a crazy and reverent whisper. "Have you ever seen a rocket ship?"

"Only in sketches."

"It was a magnificent thing, but Papa had been studying and experimenting with different fuels. I asked him to hold off until I got back. I wanted to be there in case he got, you know, distracted. He said he would, but he did not. I should've been there, but I was not." She choked and sniffled and raised her voice. "I was petty and selfish and now he's gone!"

Tuck held her close as she wept against his chest. "I'd bring him back if I could, Amelia."

"But you can't."

"No, I can't. And neither can you."

"I miss him, Tucker."

"I know, honey." Her words dried up, but the tears flowed. Tuck held tight, offering his presence, his calm. He didn't know what else to do. Hell, he'd thought he could handle Flygirl, but he'd never handled anything like this. Her tears, her guilt tore at his very soul.

After a spell the sobs eased and she relaxed in his arms. Exhausted, no doubt, between the hours of physical labor and the emotional breakdown. He stroked her back, kissed the top of her head. "Amelia—"

"I guess I will borrow a screwdriver, if you don't mind." She pushed out of his lap, looking tortured and limp from exertion. Eyes red and swollen, she sleeved tears from her cheeks while turning away and weaving toward the chassis.

Embarrassed and disoriented.

Tuck pushed to his feet and swept her into his arms.

She didn't fuss. Just rested her head on his shoulder and

held tight as he whisked her toward his cabin. As he neared, he spied Doc coming out of his room. *What in Sam Hill?*

"Looking for me?" he asked in a dark tone.

"No, I . . . Well, yeah. Sort of." Doc adjusted his wrap-around specs and leaned in. "What's wrong with Miss Darcy? Should I get my bag?"

"She'll be fine." He felt her grip tighten, sensed her humiliation. "What did you want?" Tuck asked as he sidestepped Doc. *What the hell were you doing in my cabin?*

"You missed supper and so did Miss Darcy. Thought you might want something later. Brought a tray, is all."

Tuck nodded and cursed his sudden suspicious streak. Doc often served him food in his cabin. He'd served Amelia too. "Thanks. Do me a favor. Go topside and spread the word that Miss Darcy's fine. Just tired. We'll be up later."

Doc nodded and left.

Tuck carried Amelia into his cabin and laid her on the bed. Unable to help himself, he glanced toward the table, primed to catch Doc in a lie. The food tray was there. Relieved, Tuck turned back to Amelia and stripped her to her chemise.

She didn't say a word.

He took off his coat and boots and crawled under the covers, pulling her against his body.

Not a peep.

He tried again. "Amelia . . ."

"Yes?"

Thank God. "Your father's death, the explosion, it was a tragic accident. Not your fault."

"If I'd been there—"

"Maybe you would've died, too."

She didn't comment, and he figured she'd never thought of it that way. "Sometimes bad things happen to good people. No rhyme or reason." He thought about his own parents. A random stagecoach robbery. Every day he thanked God that his baby sister hadn't been with them on that trip.

"Not fair."

"No, it's not."

"He wasn't a kook," she said, sounding weary.

"Bet your pa was a right interesting character." Tuck kissed her temple. "Like you."

"He was a great man. If people only knew. He could've been famous, like Briscoe, but he cared more about mankind than about himself."

Tuck didn't know what she meant by that. *Famous like Briscoe? Cared more about mankind?* Was she referring to something having to do with time travel? Was that something connected to da Vinci's secret chamber? Was that why Ashford had been adamant about withholding that knowledge from the world? Because whatever was in that chamber posed a ruinous danger to mankind?

Nothing like working a puzzle without all the pieces, but Tuck hesitated to ask Amelia to elaborate. Sensitive to her weary state, he allowed her to take the lead.

"Papa deserves some glory," Amelia said, her voice growing more ragged with every word. "I have to make this right."

"We'll make it right."

"We?"

Tuck held her close, feeling as if he were drifting through space, no control, no direction, no grip on the future or his life. The eternal optimist, he had faith that at some point all of the pieces would fall into place, and when they did he'd do his damnedest to spin this fiasco in their favor. "We."

CHAPTER 21

Astonishing how a good cry could cleanse one's soul. Amelia wondered whether her mother experienced such relief after a tearful vent. Although, if so, why was Anne Darcy always so miserable? Amelia felt . . . exhausted yet serene. Sad, but not depressed. Above all, ready to attack the new day with a positive mind-set. Granted, deep down she still harbored guilt concerning her father's demise. She didn't suppose that would ever go away, but she had put those destructive feelings into perspective.

Thanks to Tucker.

Remarkable how he'd gently coaxed her into baring her soul regarding that awful day. She'd been so weary and he'd been so strong. Later she'd melded against his body, reveling in his warmth. A chaste bonding. He'd been fully clothed. They'd slept that way through the night, tightly spooned except for the time he'd left her to cover his watch. She'd slept more soundly than she had in days, barely stirring when he'd returned in the wee hours, once again pulling her into his arms. Somewhere around dawn, he'd gently kissed her cheek and rolled out of bed, telling her to sleep in. Amazingly, she had.

We.

That one word kept floating though her mind. Calming. Reassuring.

We.

She didn't know how, couldn't imagine how, but she accepted Tucker's word on faith. Somehow they would conquer this quest together. Somehow they would make things right.

We.

Fresh from a bath and wrapped cozily in her dressing gown, Amelia padded to the concave windows of the man's cabin and watched the scattered clouds and distant landscape as the airship flew toward Italy. She smiled as she caught a glimpse of Leo soaring below and only wished that Peg could fly at will any time of the day rather than being confined to the cloak of night. She wondered whether the horse longed for the vast open skies over that ranch Tucker had owned in Wyoming territory. According to that candid interview in the *Informer*, Tucker had sold the ranch after he'd been arrested. To assist in covering the cost of legal bills, Amelia assumed. Or perhaps he'd been thinking ahead, stashing away the cash for a fast getaway. She'd been too consumed with her own problems and agenda to ask about the details regarding his flight from America and the life he'd left behind—details not covered within the penny dreadfuls. "I shall address that oversight today."

Amelia stood on her tiptoes and tried to see the ground directly below, but all she saw was white. Impossible to orient herself, although from the sudden drop in temperature she assumed they were nearing the Swiss Alps.

Shivering against a chill, she padded across the room and opened her leather valise, so much more sensible than Cherry Peckinposh's zebra satchel. She rooted through her sparse supply of clothing, less colorful than Cherry's wardrobe and not so frilly, yet far from conventional, according to her mother.

Amelia hurriedly dressed—boyish wool trousers, a white chemise topped with a wine-colored peasant blouse, a brocade waistcoat, and a green velvet mantle with dolman sleeves. She pulled on thick socks and her comfortable chunky-heeled boots and regarded herself in the reflecting glass. Instead of wasting time braiding and coiling her hair, she simply swept back the sides, securing them away from her face with decorative combs. The rest of her hair flowed unchecked to her waist, a wild mass of pink-tinted curls. She grinned. The overall look bordered on ModVic. "Mother would think you ridiculous," she said to herself, then frowned.

Why did she keep thinking about her mother?

Perhaps it was some sort of intuition. What if something had gone amiss at Ashford, or—horrors—with Simon or Jules? She could not bear it if she lost another . . . "Stop." She palmed her flushed cheek and cursed herself for a ninny. What nonsense. Her brothers were perfectly fine. Her mother was perfectly fine. She would send a Teletype at the first opportunity, just to make certain.

Her heart settled back in her chest, and Amelia turned in search of her leather duster. If she combined it with the mantle, surely she'd be warm enough in the frigid winds.

Someone knocked.

"Come in."

The door swung open and there stood Doc Blue. He held a tray of food. "Breakfast," he announced, hurrying inside and setting the fruit and breads on the table before turning quickly back for the door. "Enjoy."

"Doc."

He stopped on the threshold, but didn't turn. "Yes?"

Amelia stared at his back, chewed her lower lip, pondering how to approach this delicate subject. She'd been curious about the man from the first moment she'd met him. His attractive yet odd features, the strange tattoos on his hands, the same hands that had felt so warm and tingly upon her wounded thigh—as if they emanated some sort of energy. She thought about how fast that awful wound had healed. How he was never without his goggles or spectacles, both shaded a deep blue. Although she was pretty sure he hadn't been wearing spectacles in that skytown coffeehouse— not that she'd specifically seen his eyes. What she had seen was Doc conversing freely and easily with a small group of radical-looking Freaks. "Could I speak with you in private?"

One foot out the door, his hand gripping the doorframe, he barely glanced over his shoulder. "Are you feeling ill? I should get my bag."

"Something is paining me, I confess. But there is no need for your medical bag. Do come in."

He moved back inside, averted his gaze.

She shut the door and faced him. "When I first boarded this dig, I thought you compassionate and kind. Indeed, you were the friendliest amongst the crew. Now ... *now* you seem to loathe my company."

"Not true."

"Yet you keep glancing at the door, anxious for escape."

"Marshal wouldn't approve—"

"He'd understand."

"I'm not here in a professional capacity. It's inappropriate for us to be alone behind closed doors, Miss Darcy."

"I'm not the conventional sort, Doc Blue." She dug in her chunky heels. "Is it because you saw me in the skytown?"

"What?"

"The coffeehouse. You saw me and I saw you. With Freaks."

He stiffened.

She reached for his spectacles, holding her breath when he stilled her hands. He didn't push her away, verbally or physically, so she persevered. She pushed his wraparound specs to his forehead. "Open your eyes, Doc Blue."

"You will not like what you see."

"Do not assume."

She braced, but she was unprepared. "I ... I had anticipated kaleidoscope eyes."

"They were upon birth. Altered by surgery. My parents thought they were doing the right and kind thing. They wanted to give me a chance at a normal life. They'd planned to move to a remote town where no one knew they were

Vic and Mod. Where no one would suspect I was a Freak. But the surgery was botched, and the kaleidoscope of colors burst and blended into all colors—white." He swallowed hard whilst gazing down at her with his eerie eyes. No irises, just small black pupils in the middle of all that brilliant white. "Go on. Say it. I'm hideous."

"Do you think Leo with his iron beak and talons hideous? I do not. He is simply different. No shame in being different."

"Easy for you to say. You are not a Freak."

"But I am an outcast of sorts. The Darcy name is tainted. There are those who shun me merely because I am related to Briscoe Darcy. There are those who call me eccentric and my father batty, all because we embrace and explore modern marvels."

"You mean Old Worlders."

"Mostly. People who wish the Peace Rebels had never breached our time. People who fear technology and change simply because it is different."

"Your circumstance is unfortunate, but trust me, it does not compare."

"Maybe not. But it doesn't mean I don't empathize."

Doc Blue worked his jaw. "Marshal promised he wouldn't tell."

"He didn't. I surmised."

"Be obliged if you kept my secret to yourself, Miss Darcy," he said, his voice low. "On the *Maverick* I'm just the physician and cook, just another misfit taken in by Marshal Gentry."

That bit of information solidified her faith in Tucker's good character. The man seemed incapable of turning his back on anyone in need. Including herself. Apparently his heart was as vast as the sky. Acknowledging a sentimental ache in her chest, Amelia focused on Doc. "Surely you've confided in the rest of the crew."

"I have not."

"Why would you keep this quiet?"

"Why would I announce it? I don't simply look different. I *am* different. Freaks possess preternatural abilities. Mine is accelerated healing. There are people, governments, who would vie for my talents, and I fear my skills would not always be used for the best. I have no wish to be used."

Amelia swallowed. How awful that one should have to suppress a wondrous gift. "I understand, but . . . I am astounded that you would not trust the crew. StarMan? Eli? They are your friends, are they not? Surely they would understand your concerns, accept you for who you are. Your silence aside, how is it that they have not put two and two together as I did?"

"I think they suspect—all but Axel, who lives in denial of everything different—but they do not ask and I do not tell. Pretending is . . . easier. Safer."

"But—"

"Do not profess to know what's best for me simply because you empathize, Miss Darcy."

"I did not mean to offend. I simply think it's a shame that you cannot live your life freely without fear of being shunned or exploited because of your race."

"Yes, well, the world is flawed." Tight-jawed, he shielded his eyes once again with the tinted specs.

She was torn between feeling sorry for him and wanting to boot him in the arse. "One cannot make positive changes toward the future if one does not speak up and act out. Pretending may be easier and safer, but certainly does nothing to advance a utopian society."

His pale face pinched. "I have to go."

"Wait—"

"I would be most grateful if you'd respect my wishes and honor my secret," he repeated in a gruff tone as he reached for the door.

"Of course, but—"

"Good day, Miss Darcy."

Stunned and perplexed, she blinked in his wake. She had thought that if he believed her to be supportive and accepting of his altered race, he would relax and count her as a confidante and friend. Instead she'd somehow severed whatever goodwill existed between them. Perhaps Tucker could help her to understand.

Anxious to see him and to attack the day, Amelia donned heavy outerwear, anticipating the freezing temperatures of the Alps. As an afterthought she slipped Papa's stun gun in one pocket and Eli's retracted cane in the other. Just in case. Were they to be boarded by Dunkirk or ALE, she would not be taken or delayed without a fight. This Darcy would prevail.

CHAPTER 22

"The retracting mechanisms on the masts iced over, Marshal."

"Unfreeze them."

"I did. Five minutes later, they iced over again."

Tuck, who'd been at the wheel for two hours, noted a rise in temperature in the shielded cockpit as his men crowded in, bundled up and bent out of shape. You'd think they'd never flown through the mountains in the dead of winter. "I'm sure you'll think of something, Eli."

"You think you have problems," Birdman said, "try climbing the shrouds in subzero weather. Or sitting in my iron nest. My caboose near 'bout froze to the grille."

"Never mind your scrawny ass," Axel grumbled, then held up his meaty paws. "What about my fingers? How am I supposed to maintain machinery when my digits are frozen stiff?"

"You could trade your leather gauntlets for fur-lined gloves," StarMan said reasonably.

"Yeah, well, you could plot a less hostile course next time," Axel said, his breath coming out in white puffs.

"Not to complain," Eli said, clapping the flaps of his aviator cap over his big ears, "but why are we serpentining through the Alps when we could have flown on to the south of France and over the Mediterranean Sea?"

"Or even a straight shot from Geneva to Genoa and on to Florence," Birdman said, shifting back and forth to keep his blood pumping. "You did say Tuscany, right, Marshal?"

"I did. But given our hot cargo—"

"Meaning Miss Craz . . . er, Darcy," Axel said.

"—and the fact that we're in pursuit of a historical invention of monumental value—"

"Whatever that is," Birdman said.

"—I preferred a less direct route." Tuck consulted his astronomical compendium while the crew absorbed his meaning. Because of the run-in with Dunkirk, they knew Amelia had knowledge that would lead her to a treasure. They read the *Informer* and various other newspapers and therefore knew about the Triple R Tourney.

"You're trying to lose Captain Dunkirk or anyone like him who may be tracking us," Eli said. "Makes sense, I guess."

Birdman hopped faster. "Best be worth a case of frostbite."

"What is our cut, anyway?" Axel asked point-blank.

Tuck had pretty much decided how he wanted to handle this transaction, but he'd yet to broach it with Amelia. It was all in the timing. "Working out the details, boys, but I promise it'll be worthwhile."

Just then footsteps and an ecstatic "Remarkable!" turned everyone's head.

Tuck pushed his goggles to his forehead for a crystal-clear view. *Amelia.* Bundled up and wide-eyed with wonder. Spinning around to get a hundred-and-eighty-degree view of the snow-covered peaks. He sensed the same awe she'd expressed flying over the English Channel. Didn't surprise him one bit when she turned and smiled at him and his damned heart skipped.

"Have you ever seen anything so incredible?" she asked them all. "So majestic? So terrifyingly dangerous? And what about all that snow?" She spread her arms wide and breathed deeply. "How invigorating!"

"I'm shiverin' like a lizard lookin' for a hot rock," Axel grumbled, "and she's invigorated."

Tuck grinned. "Why don't you boys head below. See if

Doc'll wrestle you up some hot cider?" He hadn't had a private moment with Doc Blue since the skytown near-miss. Then again, Tuck had been preoccupied with Amelia, and Doc had been plain preoccupied.

"Could do with getting out of this wind for a while," Eli said.

Birdman rubbed his ass. "Maybe hot cider will warm my numb caboose."

"Supposed to drink it, not soak in it," Axel said as the three men moved away from the cockpit.

Amelia moved in and blinked in their wake. "Was it something I said?"

"Think I'll join the men." StarMan dipped his head in greeting—"Morning, Miss Darcy"—then strode after the crew.

She frowned. "I interrupted something."

"Just a boodle of bellyaching."

"About me?"

"About the weather."

"It is quite brisk." She adjusted her goggles, tugged down her cap. "Thank goodness for fur and fleece."

Damn, she was pretty. Even trussed up like an Eskimo, Flygirl ignited randy thoughts. Instead of pinning her against the chart podium and exploring her curvy landscape, Tuck offered his hand. When she took it he pulled her into the cockpit and placed her gloved hands on the ship's wheel, just where his had been. He pointed out various controls and functions. She absorbed his words, intently focused, interrupting only twice to ask for clarification.

He tried not to notice how good she smelled, or how fetching she looked with her long curls tumbling to her waist. "Don't stray too close to the peaks," he said. "Hold steady."

Standing flush to her back, Tuck looked over her shoulder, delighting in her exuberant expression as she piloted his airship through the Alps.

I've always dreamed of owning and piloting my own airship.

She'd fired off those words when telling him about her big plans and venting about the shackles of marriage. He admired her passion, but damn, it worried him to think about her living that dream alone. Later, when she'd broken down and confessed her guilt regarding her pa, he'd tucked away her every wish and memory. He'd learned more about Amelia Darcy during that short breakdown than he knew about women he'd been acquainted with for months. He knew that he liked her, admired her, and wanted her in his life.

After last night, he wasn't sure how'd she'd feel today. Although he'd taken it as a good sign that she'd slept restfully through the night. No nightmares. No tears. Just now her mood seemed bright, her world balanced as she gripped the ship's wheel. "How's she feel?"

"Big. Powerful. The controls—indeed, the entire construction—is far more advanced than the *Flying Cloud*. The clipper ship Papa altered three years back," she clarified. "Simon confiscated her for his quest. I wonder how he's faring. The *Flying Cloud*, like Bess, was prone to malfunctions."

"Simon's an engineer, right? He'll manage."

"He did mention upgrades. I just wish . . . Do you perchance have a Teletype and printer aboard?"

"You want to contact Simon?"

"The *Flying Cloud* lacks any sort of telecommunication device. Or at least it did before Simon seized it. No, I wish to contact Mother. I want to make sure she is faring well and to ask whether she has heard from either Simon or Jules. I just . . . I need some sort of reassurance regarding my family."

He understood more than she knew. Lack of contact with his sister was a constant source of frustration. "The *Maverick*'s equipped with ship-to-shore and ship-to-ship, but I'm not keen on transmitting signals. Could alert anyone listening to our presence."

"Like Captain Dunkirk?"

"Maybe. I definitely sense trouble's coming, just not sure from what direction."

Amelia relaxed against him. "We'll handle it."

Christ, yes, he'd made up his mind on that one thing, at least. *We.* The two of them. *Together.* Wrapping his hands over hers, he nuzzled her ear. "Yes, we will."

"Forgive the intrusion." StarMan stepped in and offered two steaming mugs. "Thought you might like some hot cider." He jerked his head as if to prod them out of the cockpit. "My watch."

Tuck wasn't sure whether his navigator was nervous about Amelia piloting the *Maverick* or if he simply wanted to afford them time alone. He had to admit the route was tricky, but so far she'd exhibited sound judgment.

Amelia relinquished the wheel with a gracious smile and accepted a mug. "How thoughtful. Thank you, StarMan."

The man nodded, and Tuck knew she'd just won points with his navigator.

"Perfect timing." She looked up at Tuck. "May we talk?"

"Let's go below, where it's warmer."

"I prefer to stay topside, if you don't mind. The scenery is spectacular."

Hand settled at the small of her back, Tuck escorted Amelia toward the stern, where the wind was less fierce. He helped her perch on a barrel, then moved in beside her. Together they sipped cider and looked out at the vast and varied landscape. She was right—the view was spectacular: sparkling white slopes, rugged gorges and icy glaciers, lush green valleys and sky blue lakes. He'd been focused on navigating this boat through the craggy passes and watching for spontaneous storm clouds. Appreciating the scenery hadn't entered his mind. He'd taken the Alps for granted, just like the English Channel. A man who'd traveled extensively and experienced numerous adventures, Tuck was usually impressed by very little.

He was most definitely impressed with Amelia.

"About last night," she said, breaking their companionable silence.

"You already apologized and you already thanked me. Both were unnecessary."

"I disagree, but will not argue the point." She sipped cider, then fidgeted, looking uncomfortable as a camel in the Klondike. "I want you to know that . . . I'm slowly coming to terms. Which is a goodly distance from refusing to believe Papa's really gone, but also a long way from being all right with it."

"I understand."

"Because you're someone who tragically lost both of his parents, I believe you do." She held his gaze, though her cheeks burned red. "I just wanted to thank you again for being so . . . kind."

Tuck ached to pull her into his arms, to kiss her deeply and soundly, making her flush and tremble head to toe, but he'd vowed to respect her need to sever their intimate relationship. Restraint was damned hard, especially when he saw mutual desire sparking in those pretty blue eyes. Typically a man of his word, he hoped to hell she broke before he did.

"I do not recall ever losing control like that. Both mortifying and . . . oddly freeing. I wish I could do something to repay your kindness."

"You did, honey. You slept restfully through the night. Gave me peace of mind."

"Yes, well . . ." She cleared her throat. "I'm about to aggravate that well-being."

"Thanks for the warning." He drained his cider, set the mug aside, then leaned back against the gunwale, arms crossed. "Shoot."

"I spoke with Doc this morning. I think . . . no, I'm quite certain he's angry with me."

"Let me guess. You mentioned you saw him at the sky-town, mingling with Freaks." Even though he'd warned her against it. Somehow he wasn't surprised.

"I went a bit further than that. I acted on a suspicion and verified that Doc is indeed a Freak himself."

Tuck raised a brow. She'd not only figured out Doc's secret; she'd called him on it. He couldn't decide whether he was impressed or concerned.

"I know you know," she said in a soft voice. "I know you're the only one aboard who does. Except for me. Although Doc thinks that most everyone suspects."

"Except Axel."

"Mr. O'Donnell and his absurd phobias aside, I strongly believe that the rest of the crew would accept Doc for who he is."

"They would. Do you?"

She pushed her goggles to her forehead and regarded him with a perplexed expression. "But of course."

"You're not scared of him?"

"Just because he's not wholly of this time? No."

"Have you seen his eyes?"

"I admit they are a bit disconcerting, but hardly something that would send me running in fear or repulsion. As I said to Doc, there is no shame in being different."

He appreciated her stand, but sensed her opinion was hindered by her youth and sheltered upbringing. "Not quite as simple as that, darlin'."

"So Doc said. Indeed, he became quite agitated when I pointed out that it is difficult to change the views of the prejudiced by remaining silent, or in his case, hidden."

He thought about the brewing rebellion amongst Freaks and the overall social unrest. Thought about the original preaching of the Peace Rebels—"Make love, not war"—and how their utopian mind-set had eventually backfired and sparked the Peace War. He thought about sharing his personal political views, but decided to focus this particular discussion on Doc.

"Don't get me wrong, Amelia. I wish Doc would come clean with the crew. If for no other reason than to relieve him of keeping up pretenses, at least while in our company. We've been together a long time. We all have baggage. Every man on this crew has been persecuted in some way because of his race or beliefs. Even Axel, believe it or not. I won't go into detail, because each man's story is his own. But I will give you some insight into Doc's plight, because he's a rare breed, and like most people where Freaks are concerned, I think you're operating under misconceptions or lack of knowledge."

"Because I'd never seen or met a Freak until this week?"

"Because they are an anomaly."

"Yet you are an expert on their race?"

"Far from it. But I have been around longer than you and know more than you. I've been Doc's confidant for five years, and I've had a fair amount of interaction with random Freaks due to my past and present professions. You probably know the basics, but hear me out."

She blew out a breath. "I apologize for my sarcasm. Of course you would be more knowledgeable, given your background. Please do enlighten me."

"Humoring me, Miss Darcy?"

"Not my style, Mr. Gentry." Her lush mouth twitched. "Well, perhaps sometimes. But not just now."

He smiled, then turned his face to the mountains. It was that or kiss her senseless. The frigid temperature did nothing to cool his burning passion. "Right. The facts." He started with what most everyone on the planet knew, whether from reading or gossip. "Freaks are the offspring of twentieth-century Mods and nineteenth-century Vics. They're products of two dimensions, the oldest of their altered race only thirty years old. The one common physical abnormality is their multicolored eyes and the kaleidoscope effect when you look into them. Some say this was a direct result of time travel, what one saw while jumping dimensions."

"Streaks of colors whirling and rushing past as you hurtle through a tunnel or wormhole. Like being propelled into a massive kaleidoscope, the Peace Rebels said."

Tuck resisted the urge to veer off on the subject of time travel—or, more specifically, the Time Voyager's connection to the da Vinci ornithopter. Another discussion for another time. "The most compelling shared trait of Freaks is that they're all born with a supernatural gift. A lesser-known fact: that gift evolves with age. No one, including their own kind, has a firm grip on what they're fully capable of. At twenty-one Doc can cure wounds at an accelerated rate. At forty, will he be able to cure deadly plagues? Will his gift diminish at some point or become unmanageable? Unpredictable? No Freak healer has gone before him, so no one knows."

"Hence he lives on pins and needles daily," Amelia said. "What of the Freaks who read immediate thoughts? What if their skill progresses to a point where they can read one's future intent?"

"You see the moral dilemma."

"Indeed."

"And those are just two of several reported 'gifts.' Talents vary, and many have yet to hone and master their skills. Freaks are a minority, yet their gifts make them powerful and potentially dangerous. Hence most people fear them. Freaks are shunned or they're exploited. Between their bizarre eyes, otherworldly skills, and progressive natures, they are not welcome among polite society. Many are denied the opportunity to excel in the professional field of their choice, and all are denied citizenship. British law also prohibits marriage between Freaks and Vics."

Amelia frowned. "I was unaware."

"Most people are. On top of all this, Doc has personal

issues that make him extra cautious. His parents were persecuted and, though it was never proven, killed for bringing two Freaks into this world."

"Two?"

Tuck nodded. "Doc has a younger brother, Jasper. After their parents were killed he went on a bit of a rampage. He's been in hiding for years. Given his altered race, Jasper's punishment, if he is discovered by radical Old Worlders, would be more extreme than his crimes merit. Doc's riddled with guilt," Tuck went on, "thinking he could have somehow prevented Jasper from going rogue. I know Doc wants to save Jasper, but thing is, that boy don't want to be saved."

Amelia palmed her forehead. "I had no idea Doc's life was so complicated. No wonder he took offense to my views."

"He'll get over it. Doc's a gentle soul. Easygoing. Usually." Of late he'd been jumpy as a bit-up bull in fly time.

"I can't imagine living under that kind of pressure. Between being estranged from his brother and being damned because of his race . . ." Empathy burned through her blood.

Tucker cut her a warning glance. "Don't pity him, darlin'. He won't like it."

"Of course not. That would be like expressing sympathy regarding Jules's limp."

"Your brother has a bum leg?"

"War injury." She sat up straighter, pride shining in her eyes. "He's a decorated hero. Not that I know details, and not that he'll talk about it. But it's rumored he acted most courageously in a very important matter to the Crown. Unfortunately, his legs were mangled in the process. His recovery was quite astonishing, though hard-won. Now, to Mother's horror, he lives in London, indulging in decadent vices and writing science fiction books."

Sounded to him like Jules Darcy had demons, but instead he focused on the man's present profession. "A visionary." Like all of the Darcys.

She furrowed her brow. "I wonder whether Doc could heal Jules's leg. Although I suppose it would be intrusive to ask, considering he wants to keep his gift a secret."

Tuck suspected Amelia loved and admired her brothers deeply. That she'd refrain from tapping Doc's special skill in deference to his desire for anonymity spoke volumes of her character.

"At any rate, I am not sure Jules would succumb to Doc's touch. Not because he is a Freak, but because he is a physician. He swears he's been poked and prodded enough for two lifetimes."

"Something tells me I'd like your brothers."

"You would. Did I mention they are twins? Different, yet alike. Innovative. Reckless. Confident. Much like you. Unfortunately, it would be unwise for you to meet them. If they knew about . . . us . . . I fear they would kill you. Or march you to the altar at gunpoint. Which is, of course, something we both wish to avoid."

He didn't comment, and she scrambled to safer ground. "Regarding Doc Blue, I will honor his secret. Although . . ."

"What?"

"It seems sinful to withhold the gift of accelerated healing from the world. He could ease so much suffering."

"Something he wrestles with every day, trust me. But there's also the risk of being coerced or manipulated into using that gift for ill means. Living in the shadows has advantages. Doc uses his gift at his own will and discretion."

"And with good intent. Unlike the Stormerator."

Tuck angled his head. "What do you know about the Stormerator?"

"Only what I overheard Mr. O'Donnell and Mr. Chang discussing. Captain Dunkirk's secret weapon. A Freak who generates tornadoes, blizzards, and lightning storms, enabling the air pirate to discombobulate, disable, and escape his quarry. At first I thought they were sharing a tall tale, but then I thought about the night you rescued me. The Stormerator generated the rainstorm that extinguished the airship's fires, correct?"

"That would be my guess."

"A most curious gift. Surely one that would be better used by providing rain for farmers suffering a drought."

"Spoken like a true utopian."

She gave a righteous sniff. "What, pray tell, is wrong with yearning for a world where all live harmoniously?"

"Nothin', darlin'." He cut her a glance brimming with cynicism born of life experience. "But it *is* unrealistic."

Incensed, she scrambled off the barrel. "How can you be so jaded? Oh, wait. That's right. You, sir, are a Flatliner." Fists clenched, she paced back and forth. "The only future you are concerned with is your own. Only . . . only that isn't true." She studied the toes of her boots while wearing a path on his deck. "Doc mentioned that you took in misfits. You mentioned that everyone on the crew was persecuted at some point. So . . . you must have taken them in. Given them a job, purpose. Provided them with sanctuary as well as camaraderie." She stopped in her tracks. "You are not a Flatliner."

"No, I'm not."

"What are you?"

"Why does it matter?"

She stared.

Exasperated, Tuck grasped her forearms. "I'm open-minded, Amelia. I understand the views and concerns of Old Worlders and New Worlders. Of Mods, Vics, and Freaks. Of Indians, Africans, Orientals, and every other ethnicity I've come across. I don't cotton to one religion or one political affiliation. I tailor my actions according to specific circumstances. Take life as it comes. Accept people as they are. When they disappoint, as they often do, I put it in perspective and adjust."

He tightened his grip and stared hard into those intense blue eyes. "I don't give a good damn whether you're an Old or New Worlder. What I care about is intent. Good or bad. Determined or lazy. Generous or stingy. Your utopian mind-set grates, but I respect it. I respect you. Now that I've bared my moderate stance, can you say the same about me?"

She blinked, then pulled away, as if distance would clear her thoughts. "I don't know. I've . . . I've never met anyone like you, Tucker Gentry."

"Which makes me unique in your eyes." He grinned, hoping to alleviate the tension. "Admit it. I intrigue you."

She pursed her lips. "Arrogant *and* perplexing."

"Independent and adventurous. Like you. We're good together, Amelia. In more ways than one."

It occurred to him that he'd never been inclined to spend the rest of his days with one woman because he'd never met a woman who would accept and nurture his love of flying, his addiction to adventure, and his preoccupation with technology. With Amelia he could live full-out and guilt-free. Then there was the matter of the affection and possessiveness building steam by the day. He'd been her first. He damn well wanted to be her only.

"Stop looking at me like that," she said.

"Like what?"

"Like you want to . . . you know. Kiss me."

"I do want to kiss you. I want to make love to you, show you the stars. I want to explore the skies with you, grow old with you."

Her eyebrows shot up. "What . . . what madness is this?"

"The kind that involves forever. A life as man and wife. I just have to figure out how to make that happen."

She opened her mouth, closed it. Clenched her fists, frowned. "Was that your idea of a proposal?"

"No, it was not. Just letting you know my intention."

"How awful! Has the thin air addled your mind? I insist you retract that sentiment at once."

"Can't do it, darlin'." Before now he'd considered only

the negative aspects of an official union. He'd operated under the assumption that Amelia would be better off without him. Somewhere along the way he'd changed his mind. He just hadn't known it until the words had tumbled out of their own accord. His plan had altered. Clear his name, free his men, reunite with his sister, and marry Amelia Darcy.

Eyes narrowed, the hellion who'd lassoed his heart marched up and punched his chest.

"What the hell?" Most women would've smiled or swooned at the prospect of hitching their wagon to his post. He knew she had a dim view of marriage, but damn.

"You lied to me."

"How so?"

"You said you couldn't offer forever."

"You're right. I lied. I can. After I clear a few obstacles."

"This is absurd! You barely know me. Why would you . . . Is it because you feel guilty for being my first? Or . . . or because you're worried about my brothers hunting you down? No, no, that wouldn't be it. You handled the James brothers. I'm certain you think you could handle the Darcy twins." She resumed her pacing, chewing the thumb of her glove, deep in thought.

Tuck couldn't decide whether he was amused or insulted. She admired him, desired him, maybe even loved him. Why the hell wouldn't she want to marry him? "I can alleviate your family's financial woes. Provide for your mother. For you. As soon as I clear my name—"

"Is this about the ornithopter?" She stopped in front of him and glared. "About the Triple R fortune? Am I merely a ticket to freedom? You promised you wouldn't steal the invention from me, but if we were married, it would be yours by law."

Tuck's mood turned dark. He was definitely insulted. "Now you're being ridiculous."

"Am I? Tell me you don't want da Vinci's ornithopter."

He couldn't. That artifact would afford him the return of everything he'd lost, but it wasn't the reason he wanted to marry her. "Let me explain."

She swung out and clipped his jaw.

Tuck cursed, resisting the urge to grab her when she marched away in a huff. He was pissed. Not because she'd hit him, but because she'd just insinuated that he cared more about his freedom than about her. Not true. He wanted both. She'd also implied that she cared more about glory than about him, when she could damn well have both. *If* she wanted. Tuck had never considered himself insecure, but his thoughts took a powerfully ugly turn.

Had Amelia manipulated him, the way she'd intended to manipulate Dunkirk? Was he nothing more than a convenient courier? Someone to help her crack the mystery of the secret chamber and to transport her and the ornithopter to London? Part of him didn't believe her capable of such cold-hearted calculation. Then again, she'd misled him more than once, and she hadn't been entirely forthright about the information relayed to her father by Briscoe Darcy. Had Briscoe shared his secret via a journal? A letter? Word of mouth? What was the full story? Amelia kept harping on that ornithopter. Did the ornithopter even exist, or was that her coded misnomer for *time machine*? Or maybe the ornithopter was in fact a da Vinci prototype *of* a time machine. The man had been a genius. He'd explored fantastical theories. Why not time travel? Tuck's mind whirled with scenarios, and the more he thought about Amelia's caginess, the greater his fury.

The last time he'd misjudged a woman, he'd ended up being accused of theft and murder.

Tuck spied Peg near the stern, looking up at the sky, pawing at the deck. His stallion wanted the hell out of here and so did he. He checked in with StarMan before setting off to fetch the horse's wings. "Taking Peg for a flight."

"In broad daylight?"

"We'll take our chances."

"Marshal—"

"Stay the course. I'll rejoin you before nightfall." He needed to clear his head, shake off his anger. Shelve his emotions and attack the problem analytically.

"If a storm approaches—"

"Protect Miss Darcy at all costs." Tuck's gut kicked "There's more at stake than a fortune."

Possibly the future of mankind.

Most definitely his heart.

CHAPTER 23

Never in a million years would she have believed it, but Amelia was desperate to get out of the air. More specifically, off of this ship. After the mind-blowing altercation with Tucker, she'd stormed below and locked herself away with Bess. She needed time alone to fume, to settle, to sort her muddled emotions. In one morning she'd gone from thinking the world of Tucker Gentry to thinking the worst.

She supposed she could deal with the fact that the man's political views shifted with the wind, depending upon who or what impressed him most genuinely at the time. Although his realistic—therefore, in her eyes, *cynical*—approach would most certainly *grate*, as he had put it, she had to respect his passionate determination to walk his own path. Indeed his tolerance was to be commended, as was his knowledge of world affairs. He'd simply caught her off guard.

But *then* he'd knocked her arse over teakettle by alluding to marriage. He'd offered up her altered dream on a platter. Had she thought his intentions sincere, she would have been over the moon. Given the circumstances, she was highly skeptical. Since their first intimate moment, he'd been adamant regarding his inability—or perhaps unwillingness—to commit to forever. Why the sudden turnaround? Why her? The man was a dime-novel hero even with his outlaw status. He could have any woman at any time, and from what she'd read he enjoyed the variety and relished his bachelor status. Beholden to no one. Free to live the life of his choosing.

Only *this* life, his present life, was not of his choosing. It had been forced upon him by the American judge who'd accused him of seducing and murdering his daughter.

A man can buy anything with enough money. Including freedom.

Axel O'Donnell's words rang in her ears, poisoned her thoughts. She couldn't get the notion out of her head. She fixated on things she knew, and a scenario played out based on facts and assumptions.

Tucker wanted to buy back his freedom and good name. He wanted to return to America, to his former occupation. He was one of the best—easily the most famous—air marshals of their time. How could she blame him for wanting to return to what he loved, what he excelled at? How could she judge him for wanting to mend his tattered reputation when that was exactly what she wanted to do for Papa? Yet she *did* condemn his intent, because it meant using her and putting their goals at odds and her heart through the wringer.

Stunned and hurt, Amelia had paced the workroom for twenty minutes, dredging up all the reasons she should despise Tucker, yet for all her fury, she commiserated with his plight and—*bloody hell*—she still lusted after the man. She hated that she loved him, but there it was. Such a mess. Such a bloody awful, confusing debacle.

Twenty minutes alone, pacing, fuming, musing, and she still didn't know what to do. It wasn't like she could simply jump ship. She could always pinch a Pogo Pack and rocket to the ground. Then what? Trudge through the frozen tundra until she came upon a town? Hire passage to Tuscany? How would she get the ornithopter to London? How big was it, anyway? Could she *fly* it to London? Talk about making an entrance.

Her mind raced and circled, leaving her dizzy and clueless. She needed to do something constructive. To seize control. Perhaps then she could think calmly and rationally. Perhaps then she'd be clear on what to do, because what she *wanted* to do was to spend forever with her aeronautical hero, even though he'd slipped off his proverbial pedestal. Unfortunately that would mean forsaking her father and family, and that was unthinkable.

Highly distressed, Amelia palmed her aching chest. Her heart cracked even more when she caught sight of Bess's bent chassis. She couldn't even fix the kitecycle. How could she mend the mess she'd made with Tucker?

That thought propelled her out the door and back to his cabin. He wasn't there. She procured the money she'd hidden in her valise, stuffed it in her inner pocket, then hurried topside, hoping to find the cause of her angst at the wheel. Instead she found StarMan. "Where's Mr. Gentry?"

"Took Peg for a ride."

Puzzled, she indicated the sky, the bright blue, clear-as-glass sky. "Out there?"

StarMan nodded.

"In broad daylight?"

Another nod.

"But what if someone sees them?"

"He'll handle it."

"How?"

"Can't say."

Can't or won't? she wanted to ask, but didn't. What was the point?

"He'll be back before nightfall," StarMan said, as if that was supposed to ease her anxiety.

It didn't.

Nerves taut, she pushed Tucker from her mind and focused on her own agenda. "Where are we, pray tell? More precisely, where is the nearest town?"

"Nearest or most substantial?"

She thought about what she needed: a chassis and a Teletype. Surely she didn't need a thriving metropolis for such basic conveniences. Even a secondhand chassis, if in good condition, and a telegraph would do. "The nearest."

"Gressoney-La-Trinité. A village at the base of Monterosa. Few kilometers south of here."

"Outstanding. Mr. O'Donnell can take me in the air dinghy."

That whipped the navigator's head around. "You want to leave the *Maverick*?"

"It is crucial."

"Marshal won't like it."

"I don't give a fig."

"But—"

"Am I a prisoner?"

"No, but—"

"Very well, then. I have business in town. Don't fret. I shall return before nightfall."

StarMan frowned. "It's not safe. That is to say, you're not safe. Captain Dunkirk—"

"That is why I'm enlisting Mr. O'Donnell. He'll protect me. He may not like me, but he worships Tucker and hates Dunkirk. He's also big, mean, and handy with that Blaster thingie."

"I cannot sanction this, Miss Darcy."

"I'm not asking you to, StarMan. Where's Mr. O'Donnell?"

"Starboard blasterbeef. Good luck getting him to do you any favors. In case you haven't noticed—"

"I've noticed." The chief engineer wanted her off this ship and out of their lives, and that was exactly the approach she'd take to get her way. Five minutes later they launched for Gressoney-La-Trinité.

"Remember your promise," Axel said as he engaged the air dinghy's steam-powered balloon. "In and out. I'll purchase the velocipede. You Teletype your ma. Back on the *Maverick* before the marshal knows we're gone."

"Agreed." Amelia scanned the area, then consulted her astronomical compendium to orient herself.

"I know where I'm going," Axel groused after shooting her golden sundial-compass the evil eye. "Ain't nothin' worse than a backseat navigator."

She rolled her eyes, then flipped shut the antiquated compendium and stashed it in an inner pocket, close to her heart. Just one of the many "prized possessions" Papa had gifted to her over the years. A family heirloom, he'd said. For that reason, she'd resisted purchasing a newer, more complex model. Feeling nostalgic and just a bit sad, Amelia adjusted her scarves and hunkered down against the frigid wind. She tried to focus on the incredible scenery, but failed. She summoned memories of da Vinci's codex and Briscoe Darcy's message to Papa, but all thoughts led back to Tucker.

She peered through her goggles across the small transport, eyeing the burly, broad-shouldered man she'd chosen as her temporary protector. He'd donned fur-rimmed goggles and fur-lined gloves, a fleece-lined aviator cap, and a brown leather greatcoat. She'd watched as he'd slid a Remington Blaster into his shoulder holster and some sort of derringer into his ankle holster, and slapped a stun cuff on his wrist. His signature cigar was clamped between his teeth, and a fierce scowl darkened his brutish face. A menacing figure indeed. She wondered about his particular baggage. Who had persecuted this man, and why?

"You're starin'."

"Just wondering about your past."

"Well, don't."

"How long have you known Tucker?"

"A long time."

"Where did you meet him?"

"Back in America."

She suppressed a frustrated growl. "Have you always been an engineer or did you develop the skills after Tucker, um, enlisted you?"

"Don't cotton to people pokin' around my past."

God forbid she alienate the man even more. What if he abandoned her in the village? She supposed that was possible either way, except Tucker wouldn't like it. She switched tactics. "I read somewhere that you and the crew forfeited your freedom in order to rescue Tucker from the gallows."

"So?"

"Why would you do that?"

"Because he was wrongly accused."

"Even so, to risk your own necks, give up your homeland?"

"Small price to pay."

"For what?"

He cut her a glance. "That's personal. Let's just say we all owe the marshal, and we'd follow him into hell if need be. Great Britain, Europe . . ." He shrugged. "Ain't home, but it ain't hell."

"Nevertheless, he wants to go back to America. Wants to resurrect his famous career."

The big man snorted.

"No?"

"Marshal couldn't give two nuts about fame. He just happened to be exceptional at his job. His exploits and charisma make for good press, is all."

"But he does wish to return."

"You bet."

Her stomach clenched. "To clear his name."

"That's one reason."

"To reclaim his job as air marshal?" she surmised.

"Can't say that's a prime motivator. The law system failed him. He's a mite vexed about that. Besides, he could track criminals anywhere."

"Instead he's working as an air courier. Transporting valuable, sometimes illegal cargo."

"More money to be made, faster."

Back to money. She hugged herself against the cold and the chilling thought that Tucker's marriage talk was based on finance. "Back in France, you implied that Tucker needed volumes of money to buy back his freedom."

"So?"

"So, how would that work exactly? Would he bribe someone to eliminate the so-called evidence? Pay his accuser to drop the charges? Isn't that illegal? Immoral? What if they refused? Or what if he got caught? Wouldn't he be in twice the trouble?"

"Crazy *and* nosy. Hell's fire."

"I'm simply trying to understand his motivation. Hardly anyone—well, in England, at least—believes Tucker guilty of that odious crime. He could continue on as he is, as an air courier, making a good living. Why risk going back?"

"Not that it's any of your business, but will you shut up if I tell you?"

She fairly tipped over the side of the boat in surprise. She honestly hadn't expected Axel to be forthcoming. She thought she'd have to guess. "Quench my curiosity and I shall be as quiet as a church mouse."

"Swear?"

She raised her right palm and nodded.

He slipped his gnawed but unlit cigar into his pocket, checked his astronomical compendium, and adjusted the steam. "First of all," he said, as they started their descent, "the marshal's innocent. He didn't steal those paintings from Judge Titan's personal collection. The judge's daughter, Ida, did. Sold 'em off and stashed the cash somewhere, thinking it was a nest egg for her and the marshal. Thought she'd get him to marry her, thought they'd run off together, live on some exotic island. The woman was a loon, 'cept Tuck didn't realize how far gone she was till she was, well, *gone*. When he refused to play along with her plans, that crazy girl threatened to shoot him—with his own gun, no less—only it backfired. Literally."

"What do you mean, *literally*?"

"That six-shooter was in fact a seven-shooter. A customized piece especially made for an instance where someone got the drop on ya and stole your gun. Unless you tripped the secret mechanism, the bullet fired out the back, not the front of the barrel. Ida didn't know about the secret mechanism."

Amelia gaped. "So she meant to shoot Tucker and killed herself instead? How awful!"

"Way I see it, she got what she deserved, not that the marshal would agree. It's a sordid affair," Axel said, "and I ain't gettin' into it with you. Just know that Judge Titan, a vindictive, sick bastard, turned everything around, vilifying the marshal instead of admitting he'd driven his daughter loco with his domineering, obsessive ways."

"I don't understand."

"And I ain't explainin'."

Amelia palmed her forehead. Axel had just revealed more details than she'd ever read, yet she felt more confused.

"Ask the marshal if you want the inside scoop. I'm just tellin' you why he wants to go back. Everything went down fast and wrong, and before we knew it the marshal was set to swing. The boys and I acted, and let me tell you, losing that air posse wasn't easy. No time for second thoughts, no time to settle affairs. It was flee or fry."

"Hence you ended up on the other side of the Atlantic. Out of U.S. jurisdiction."

"Ain't a bad life, but some of us have folks back in the States, and the marshal won't rest until we're free to come and go in America as we please. Mostly, though, Tuck wants to go back for Lily. Only gal he ever really loved."

Amelia's heart stopped; her bones jarred. Axel's bombshell hit her at the same time the dinghy touched down. Only it wasn't the softest landing and they slid. She held tight as the dinghy skated down a slope and Axel struggled for control. They twirled once, twice. She was too stunned to be scared. Too confused to scream as they hit a snowbank and went flying. She landed flat on her back, staring up at the lovely blue sky through the snowy branches of an ever-green tree and seeing stars. She fought a wave of dizziness as her heart hammered against her ribs. As Axel's words clanged in her head.

Tuck wants to go back for Lily. Only gal he ever really loved.

Between the crash and the bombshell, she could scarcely breathe.

"You all right?" Axel loomed over her, looking worried. "You didn't break anything, did you? Don't see any blood. Damn. Ain't never had that happen before."

"I'm fine."

"Then why ain't you movin'?"

"Knocked the wind out of me." Pulled the world from beneath her. She wanted to ask about Lily. Who was she? Where was she? Was she even real, or had Axel made her up in order to ruffle Amelia's feathers? Since he'd never liked her, Amelia could well imagine him delighting in crushing her heart. Anyone who had eyes had seen the af-fection she felt for Tucker. Then again . . .

What if Axel spoke the truth? What if Lily was real? Although how could Axel be certain Tucker still loved this woman, or that she loved him? He'd been on the run for a year. Things changed. People changed. Amelia's heart cracked even as she tried to reason through the existence of a mysterious woman who had, at least at one time, owned Tucker's affections.

"Miss Darcy?"

Gathering her wits and calm, Amelia gave a curt nod. "I'm fine."

"So you said. Gimme your hand."

She did, and he tugged her to her feet. "Is the dinghy all right?" she asked in a raspy voice.

"What? Oh." He turned to check the capsized boat and collapsed balloon.

Feeling a bit woozy, Amelia plucked a twig from her hair and pushed Tucker and the mysterious Lily out of her aching head. Were it not for her pesky pride, she'd sit Axel down here and now and question him at length about Lily. Unfortunately, their prickly relationship hindered intimate queries and confidences. Instead, she shelved her curiosity and raised barriers around her heart. Just in case.

"Dinghy's good," Axel said. "Snowbank cushioned the impact." He righted the dig, shook his head. "Don't know why she slid like that. Must've hit a patch of ice. Sorry about that."

"No worries," she said, still half-dazed, but wanting to press on. "Which way to the village?"

She heard Axel's boots crunching in the snow as he moved in beside her. "It's right in front of you. Just beyond those trees. Plain as day."

Focusing on her immediate agenda instead of the past and future, Amelia headed on shaky legs toward the small Italian town.

Axel fell in alongside her. "You sure you're okay?"

"Spectacular."

CHAPTER 24

Amelia wasn't sure how long she'd been in the lobby of the quaint chalet lodge. There'd been a bit of a language barrier. She didn't speak Italian and the clerk's English was broken. They'd finally settled on a reasonable price and she'd been escorted into the cramped office, where she'd sent off a brief but heartfelt Teletype to her mother.

> *Letting you know I am fit and fine and in pursuit of the prize. How are you? How fares Ashford? Have you heard from Jules or Simon? Please respond as soon as possible. I am in transit.*
>
> *Your daughter,*
> *Amelia*

While waiting for a reply, she sat in a chair by the fire. She imagined Ashford, envisioned each room of the house she'd grown up in. Imagined the sound of the bell announcing an incoming Teletype. Imagined her mother, anxious for news, waddling to the library and sliding over the polished floor in her haste to get to the communications device installed by Papa. Or perhaps Mother was away on an errand or a social call. Perhaps Eliza was reading the Teletype. She imagined the housekeeper rushing the note to her husband, Harry, and coaxing him to deliver it to Anne Darcy posthaste.

Crikey.

Suddenly homesick on top of everything else, Amelia focused on her present surroundings. The chalet was cozy, the fire toasty. The cup of hot chocolate the clerk brought tasted divine and warmed her throat and stomach. Odd that she still felt chilled.

She hugged herself, tumbling deeper into her scrambled thoughts revolving around Tucker and Ida, Tucker and Lily, and the fact that he'd all but proposed marriage to Amelia. That Tucker would marry her to secure a fortune in order to return to another woman went against every noble notion she had of the man. There had to be more to the story. If this Lily had indeed been a major love interest in the Sky Cowboy's life, why had Amelia never read about her in the romanticized dreadfuls? The more she tried to puzzle through the mystery, the more her head hurt.

"Signorina?"

Amelia jerked as someone touched her shoulder. Had she nodded off? Feeling hazy, she blinked up at the clerk, who handed her a note. She thanked the man, then squinted at the type.

Relieved to hear from you. Was worried. Lonely, but Ashford thrives. For now. Brothers are in pursuit as well. Heard from Simon. I lied and said you were safe at home. Have not heard from Jules, but you know Jules. In my heart I know you will redeem your father's name. For that I am glad and grateful. Safe travels and good luck.

Your loving mother

Amelia's throat tightened. Her mother had been worried? About her? In one short Teletype Anne Darcy had intimated notions that Amelia had longed for all her life: her mother's approval and the knowledge that the woman truly cared about her husband. Plus she'd signed off using the word *love*. Amelia hadn't thought that word existed in her mother's vocabulary. Maybe Jules was right: Maybe their mother ran deeper than Amelia gave her credit for. Maybe she'd been too blinded by Papa's glorious charisma and glowing affection to see through Anne's intrusive and manipulative veneer.

Another conundrum.

All Amelia knew for certain was that she was more determined than ever to make things right for the Darcys.

That meant getting back to the *Maverick* and on to Mount Ceceri. It meant striking a deal with Tucker.

Head throbbing, she tucked away the note, returned the mug to the clerk, and quietly thanked him for his help. He said something in return, only the words didn't register. Feeling ill, she simply smiled and made her way back onto the pebbled street. She shivered whilst pulling on her gloves. The sun was shining, the temperature milder than when they'd been flying high, but her coat felt damp and the wind cut through her bones.

Amelia stamped her feet, two blocks of ice that refused to warm. She looked left and right, eyed a few pedestrians and one scraggly cat. Gressoney-La-Trinité was relatively small. Definitely quiet. Since Axel wasn't waiting, she wandered to the shop he'd pointed out earlier. She didn't see him in there either. Again, the clerk spoke broken English, but she ascertained that Axel had indeed purchased a bicycle. Maybe she'd misunderstood him. Maybe she was supposed to meet him at the dinghy.

Feeling as though something were off, she kept her head down and hastened toward the patch where they'd landed. That was when she saw a monster of a man utilizing a vicious stranglehold on Axel. She couldn't believe someone had gotten the better of the burly engineer. Then she noticed the bright red bone-shaker bicycle lying on its side, front wheel spinning. He must've been pushing it toward the dinghy when the scraggly-haired brute jumped him from behind. She saw no weapons, even though Axel carried many. Had his stun cuff malfunctioned?

Stun.

Amelia dipped into her coat pocket and palmed Papa's stun gun. She'd never shot a man. Then again, maybe she wouldn't have to. Adrenaline pumping, she steadied the gun with both hands and aimed at the man dressed in an odd combination of leather armor and animal pelts. She advanced, knees quaking. "Release him. Now!"

Monster Man spared her a look and her breath caught at the menacing sight. Pocked skin and a fleshy nose. A brass magnifying loupe was strapped over one eye, while the other red-rimmed eye drooped, reminding her of a hound dog. He paid her no mind, as if she were no more of a threat than a bothersome gnat. Instead he tightened his hold on Axel. That was when she caught a glimpse of hinges, screws, and metal. Was the brute's arm made of steel? And, good Lord, it wasn't a hand exactly, but more like a vise-claw!

"Get. Out. Of. *Heeeere*." Axel choked and wheezed, and though he clutched at the man's arms and bucked like a wild horse, he could not break free.

She willed her hands not to tremble, her courage not to waver as she took another step forward. Sweat beaded her upper lip. "I'll shoot!"

Axel's face turned purple; his legs wobbled.

Amelia aimed for the biggest target. She couldn't bring herself to shoot a man—any man—in the back, so she lowered her aim and pulled the trigger. A bolt of electricity surged and zapped Monster Man in the backside.

His arms flailed as he roared in pain.

Axel keeled over face-first, while Monster Man dropped to his knees, arse smoking.

Amelia nearly sagged with relief. Papa's gun had worked! Just enough to jar the man. Just enough for Axel to break free.

"Damned . . . Dogface." Gasping for air, Axel pushed to

his knees and reached under his coat for his Blaster, only Monster Man/Dogface recovered more quickly. He pounced and suddenly they were rolling in the snow, throwing punches. Weakened from lack of air, within seconds Axel was once again pinned under that steel claw. "Shoot. Him."

She tried, but this time the gun jammed. Once. Twice. She threw it at the monster's head. It hit with a clang and bounced off. Was his skull metal too?

"Hit. Him."

She looked for a rock, then remembered the retracting cane. She pulled it from her pocket, thumbed the button— *snick, snick, snick*—and swung with all her might, cracking the brass rod hard across the attacker's shoulders.

He whirled and grabbed the cane with his good hand, shoving it away with a force that sent her flying.

Axel made some sickly sound and, though bleary-eyed, Amelia scrambled to her feet. She remembered Doc's advice regarding the use of the cane as a weapon. *Conk and stab.* Fearing Axel was moments from death, she burst forward, the skinny tip poised, and plunged.

Another roar and a whirl. He reached back and pulled the rod from his side, then turned on Amelia, eyes blazing.

"Run," Axel choked out.

She could not. She'd frozen in fear. She'd shot, conked, and stabbed Monster Man/Dogface and now he was going to kill her. He lumbered forward, his hinged claw snapping like a grotesque lobster as he reached for her. She couldn't breathe and he'd yet to touch her. She heard a whoosh, then thunderous hooves, saw Axel struggling for his Blaster, heard a shot, then—God in heaven—saw blood spurting and gushing from the man's head. Droopy eyes wide, he faltered and reeled.

So much blood.

The edges of Amelia's vision blurred and her knees gave way just as Tucker vaulted off Peg's back and scooped her into his arms.

CHAPTER 25

"What's wrong with her, Doc?"

"Concussion maybe. She's got a large bump on the back of her head."

"According to Ax's account," Tuck said, "she could've gotten that when she was thrown from the dinghy or knocked flat by Dogface Flannigan." He'd witnessed the latter through his spyglass as he swooped down from the sky. It had sickened him, and filled him with murderous rage.

"Plus she has a fever. Maybe she caught a chill."

"Her clothes are damp."

"Get her out of them. Keep her warm. Even if she complains about being hot."

Tuck unwrapped her scarves and unlaced her boots. After making sure Axel could manage the dinghy on his own, he'd lifted an unconscious Amelia onto Peg and flown her back to the *Maverick*. Eli had taken Peg in hand, and Tuck had carried Amelia to his cabin. Lying in the middle of his big bed, she'd never looked so small or fragile.

Doc hovered, looking nearly as anxious as Axel when he'd confessed he'd been caught unaware. *She saved my life*, Axel had said. If he said it once, he said it five times.

"Also," Doc said, "I wouldn't rule out shock. Between the tussle and you shootin' Dogface dead in front of her . . . that's a lot to handle."

Tuck palmed her feverish brow. "Make her better. Now."

"I don't want to use my gift until I'm sure and certain of all her ailments, Marshal. Accelerated healing drains me.

You know that. How severe is the concussion? Did she sustain a neck injury as well? Any internal bleeding? I don't want to waste immediate energy, only to miss something important."

"What can I do?"

"Like I said, keep her warm. Try to rouse her. Get her talking and keep her talking. Call for me when she's alert or if she takes a bad turn."

"Thanks, Doc." Tuck peeled off her duster, expecting the younger man to take his leave.

"Maybe we should turn back."

"What?"

"We've had nothing but misfortune since taking on Miss Darcy and her expedition."

"You falling in with Axel, Doc? Thinking Miss Darcy's bad luck?"

"No. No, of course not. But what if the treasure she seeks is to blame? What if it's cursed? Bad for her. Bad for us."

"It's not cursed."

"You know what the treasure is?"

Tuck paused in the middle of finessing Amelia out of a waistcoat. The layers were endless. "An invention of historical significance." He'd never known Doc to be so intrusive. It felt wrong. Bad.

"Something to do with a time machine?"

"Why would you ask, Doc?"

The man jammed his fingers through his spiky white hair. "We touched on the theory. When you were going through her things. Right after Captain Dunkirk kidnapped her. Remember?"

"I remember."

"Just saying . . . Just wondering . . . what we are getting into."

"Nothing we can't handle."

The frazzled man nabbed his medical bag. "I should see to Axel. Shout when there's a change."

Tuck spared Doc a look as he blew out of the cabin. *What's goin' on with you, kid?* Amelia moaned and all his thoughts turned to her. "Wake up, honey." He continued to strip off her clothes. Her chemise was bone-dry, so he stopped there and pulled the covers to her chin. "Amelia."

Her eyes fluttered open.

Thank you, Jesus.

She looked at him through glazed blue eyes. "What would you do for love?" she asked in a dreamy voice.

His heart lodged in his throat. "Just about anything, I expect." He'd sure as hell killed Dogface without regret.

She traced her fingers along his jaw, quirked a sad smile. "Me too. Thirty percent."

"What?"

"Our deal. Help me deliver the ornithopter. If we win the prize ... Thirty percent to you. That should ... should be enough to buy Lily."

The mention of his sister caught him off guard. "How do you know about Lily?"

"Axel told me. You love her. You don't have to marry me to be with her. I don't ... don't want to share you, so ... Good-bye." Her fingers fell away. Her lashes fluttered closed.

"Amelia."

Someone knocked.

Tuck checked her breathing. Deep. Steady. She'd fallen back under. *Dammit.* He swung off the bed and opened the door.

Axel loomed on the threshold looking like he'd been to hell and back. Bruised and bloodied face, scratched and discolored neck. "Why aren't you with Doc?"

"Told him I'd be back. I needed to see ..." He peeked around Tuck's shoulder. "Doc said she'll be okay, but I needed to see for myself. She still out?"

Tuck moved partially into the hall and lowered his voice. "She woke long enough to mumble something about me loving Lily and her not wanting to stand in the way. Offered me a boodle of money, then said good-bye. She wasn't entirely coherent. What the hell did you tell her, Ax?"

The big man frowned. "Just that ... Oh, hell. Don't think I mentioned Lily's your sister."

Tuck listened as Axel recounted the discussion he'd had with Amelia. He could only imagine what was going through her mind due to his engineer's fragmented story. Not that it had been his place to relate Tuck's business in the first place. "Anyone ever tell you that you talk too much?"

"I shouldn't have taken her to the village. I thought ... in and out. What were the chances Dogface Flannigan would be lyin' low in northern Italy? Damn slim to total zero, right?"

"Did he tell you he'd been hiding out? Maybe he'd been trackin' us all along. Revenge against us for turning him in to Scotland Yard. Or, hell, maybe he got wind of Amelia and her treasure. Maybe, like Dunkirk, he wanted it for himself. Saw his chance to kidnap her when you two took off on your own."

"He didn't say nothin'. Just jumped me. I'm thinkin' the attack was inspired by revenge, pure and simple. Dogface was on the run, and what better place to hide than the Alps? Just my recent bad luck, he spied me alone in the village and figured he'd send you a message by way of my dead carcass." Axel stole another look into the room. "She saved my life." He sounded amazed and chagrined and looked damned miserable. "Sorry, Marshal."

Tuck dragged a hand through his hair, absorbing his own measure of blame. "If I hadn't lost my temper and patience, I would've been aboard, where I should've been. I would've interceded before you two ever left the *Maverick*. You're not the only one guilty of poor judgment. Cut yourself some slack and have Doc tend those wounds."

Axel nodded. "Tell Miss Darcy I said thank you."

"You can tell her yourself when you're both on the mend." Tuck shut the door between them, figuring that from here on out Axel would be treating Amelia with the respect she'd deserved in the first place. Tuck had known from the moment he'd watched her go down with that kitecycle that she had guts. But he hadn't realized the extent of her courage and ingenuity until she'd gone up against Dogface in defense of Axel. Hell, she didn't even like the gruff engineer.

"Hot."

He turned and saw the lionhearted hellion kicking off layers of covers. "Oh, no, you don't."

"Hot," she repeated when he tugged the blankets back up.

"Feverish. I need you to stay bundled and warm and I need you to wake up, Amelia." He gave her a shake. "Talk to me, dammit. Open your eyes." She did and he smiled. "Thirsty?"

She nodded.

He poured water from a pitcher and held the glass to her lips. She wrapped her warm hands over his and drank deeply. When she eased back against the pillow he asked, "Better?"

She nodded yes, then shook her head no. Tears sprang to her eyes. "I've never killed a man."

What the . . . "Amelia, look at me. Listen. You didn't kill Dogface Flannigan."

"Shot him."

"Stunned him."

"Stabbed him."

"Injured him." He gripped her shoulders. "You've got it addled in your mind, honey. Focus."

She licked her lips, breathed. "Mr. O'Donnell. No. He reached for his Blaster, but the shot came before." Clutching the blanket to her chest, she regarded him with confusion. "You?"

"I took Peg out to clear my mind. StarMan contacted me

on a device we picked up on the black market. Something called a telecommunicator. We have four, although none of them work properly. At best, it's an emergency signal. A cry for aid. I assumed the *Maverick* was under attack. Upon return I learned you'd left the ship with Axel. I came after and . . ."

"You slayed the monster."

"I saw him attack you and followed instinct."

She shivered. "The blood."

"You need to put that out of your mind. Dogface was a smuggler, a coldhearted murderer who escaped persecution due to deep pockets and corruption. He had a fierce bone to pick with me and the crew. He would have killed Axel. He would have killed you." He cradled her flushed face. "Do you understand?"

She nodded.

"Are you with me?"

"What?"

"You have a possible concussion and a definite fever. I need you to stay with me. Stay alert."

Another nod.

The relief was almighty. "I'll call Doc."

She grasped his arm with a feeble hand. "Please don't."

"Why not?"

"I just . . . I need a moment. With you."

The insecurity in her gaze shredded his soul. "You can have a lifetime with me, Flygirl."

"Don't lie."

"Lily is my sister."

"What?"

"My one and only sibling. My little sister. I'm very protective of her and worked hard to shelter her from the press. Yes, I love her. Yes, I want to go back for her. But I also want to be with you." He looked hard and deeply into her disoriented gaze. "You believe in utopia, Amelia. Believe in me."

"I want to."

"Then do it." He pulled her into his arms. "Say it."

She clung to him and sighed. "I believe."

"Hold tight to that notion, no matter what." He stroked her back, his mind racing ahead. "About your offer . . ."

"What offer?"

A disoriented rambling then, and for the best, since he wasn't sure thirty percent would do it. Plus, he still didn't know for certain what he was dealing with regarding the "invention." "Never mind." He stroked matted curls from her damp forehead, held her close. "Still with me?"

"I'm here," she said in a scratchy voice. "Dizzy but present."

"Coherent. That's good. I need you strong in body and spirit, Amelia. We're less than a day from Tuscany, and I've got a bad feeling about Dunkirk. He's not one to forgive or give up. Let's just get the damned ornithopter and we'll sort things out after. Sound good?"

"Sounds logical." She offered her hand in agreement.

Instead of grasping her palm he placed it over his pounding heart. "I can think of better ways to seal the deal, darlin'." He kissed her then, sweetly, softly. To hell with denying the physical attraction burning between them. She kissed him back and his heart did a jig. Bursting with affection and relief, Tuck eased her back on the pillows. "Can I call for Doc?"

She nodded. "The sooner, the better." Shivering now, she snuggled deeper beneath the covers. "I'm most anxious to . . . sort things out."

Tuck moved to call Doc Blue, pausing to unleash a heartfelt plea. "For chrissake, Flygirl, don't ever scare me like that again."

She quirked a shaky smile. "I shall strive to bore you instead."

He laughed at that. "As if you could."

CHAPTER 26

The *London Informer*
January 16, 1887

ROYAL REJUVENATION
OR ROYAL MISTAKE?

According to an inside source, Her Majesty, Queen
Victoria, has embraced the Triple R Tourney spon-
sored by an anonymous benefactor via the British
Science Museum. Celebrating inventions of historical
significance not only honors Prince Albert's passion
for science, but maintains the queen's conviction to
focus on past accomplishments rather than encourage the pursuit and development of anachronistic
marvels beyond our natural scope. Old Worlders celebrate any cause for the reclusive queen's enthusiasm
and therefore rejoice in the mounting excitement of
the Triple R. Outspoken New Worlders continue to
condemn the suppression of technological knowledge
and ideological preachings of the twentieth-century
Peace Rebels. Rumblings of an underground rebellion have jubilee coordinators on their proverbial toes,
although they have assured our source that the threat
of violence will not dampen the festivities. Voice your
opinion to the editor. The Triple R Tourney—Royal
Rejuvenation or Royal Mistake?

Bingham smiled as he skimmed similar articles in the *London Daily* and *Victorian Times*. Civil unrest benefited his personal cause. He welcomed it. Encouraged it. *An uprising*. His mind churned with a dozen different ways to profit from a rebellion. Meanwhile his own inside source had assured him that he would be notified promptly of any changes in the scheduled jubilee celebration. As of yesterday, his covert activities were beginning to pay off.

The members of Aquarius were mollified, and plans for the assassination were in motion.

He'd heard from a Mod tracker who had a new lead on the location of Professor Maximus Merriweather.

Wilhelmina Goodenough had joined Simon Darcy on his quest, and Captain Dunkirk had a jump on Amelia Darcy, thanks to information leaked to a Freak informant from one of Gentry's own men. The elder brother, Jules, was the only Darcy to escape Bingham's web just now. With so many new and positive developments, he scarcely cared. Not that he intended to give up the hunt. One of his contacts would come through and he'd soon have a tail on the science fiction writer as well. By hook or by crook, he'd have possession of a time machine, or at least the designs allowing him to build his own.

"You're looking quite smug," his mother said whilst breezing into the room.

"I confess I am in a brilliant mood."

"I revel in your happiness, dear, and thus regret being the harbinger of troubling news."

Bingham carefully folded and stacked the newspapers on his desk, confident that little could spoil this most promising day. "Do tell."

Shoulders hunched, eyes bright, she wrung her hands—a rare and nervous gesture. "Constable Newberry is here and wishes to speak with you regarding the death of Lord Ashford."

CHAPTER 27

Amelia woke from oblivion, smiling when she realized she was cocooned in Tucker's embrace. Her face snuggled against his bare chest, she breathed deeply. Soap mixed with the lingering scents of bay rum and leather. *Heaven.* She shifted gently and lifted her gaze, surprised that he was wide-awake. "Why are you here?"

"Good morning to you too, Flygirl."

She flushed under his teasing expression. "I just meant . . . shouldn't you be topside?" Sunbeams slanted through the partially cracked drapes of the stern windows, announcing a new day. "Isn't it your watch?"

"The crew insisted I relinquish my shift in order to watch over you."

Thoughtful, she supposed, but bothersome. "Yet again I have proven a disruption and an inconvenience. And poor Mr. O'Donnell. If not for me—"

"If not for you, he'd be dead. He's the first to admit it and means to thank you."

She furrowed her brow. "Really?"

"Amelia, honey, there aren't many women who'd go head-to-head with a miscreant like Dogface. Ax still thinks you're crazy, but crazy like a fox."

"As in sneaky?"

"As in unpredictable. Sly. Fearless."

She snorted. "I froze when he told me to run. I was plenty scared."

"You did your share of damage. Trust me. And in defense of a man who treated you with disdain from day one."

"Mr. O'Donnell is a frustrating man, to be certain, but he didn't deserve to die. As for Dogface Flannigan ..." She shook off his gruesome last breath. "Given his odious past and horrid inclinations, I am striving to dismiss him from my mind."

"Good."

"The world is a better place."

"Yes, it is."

"One step closer to utopia."

"A fervent believer," Tucker said with a lopsided smile. "Smacks of trouble, yet I love you for it."

She stared at him, heart pounding, skin burning. Surely he didn't mean ... No. He mentioned the word *love* casually, in passing, pertaining to her passion, not her person. Not the same as saying, *I love you.* That would be, well, awful. Glorious and awful.

He pushed up to his elbow. "What's wrong?"

"Nothing."

"You look funny."

She smoothed a hand over her tangled hair. "It's the pink."

"I love the pink."

"Stop saying that."

"What?"

The man was oblivious. Clueless. Yet if he mentioned the word *love* one more time, she'd have to conk him. It made her stomach flutter and her head swim. Marriage was one thing, love another. She couldn't wrap her brain around either. Yes, she believed in utopia. Yes, she believed in Tucker. But with her wits fully about her, she didn't quite believe in her own utopia *with* Tucker. A happily-ever-after seemed too surreal. Too good to be true. As it was, she was already in pursuit of a happily-ever-after for her family. Fame and fortune? Love and wedded bliss? Surely God would not deem her worthy of *two* grand prizes. What if she had to choose? "Can we change the subject?" she asked, pushing upright.

"The subject of your hair?"

"Never mind."

He crossed his muscled arms over his magnificent chest, angled his head, and studied her hard. "You okay?"

"Spectacular."

"No aches or pains? No dizziness?"

She blinked, thinking back on how horrid she'd felt the day before. "Now that you mention it . . . No chills. No headache. No nausea." The last time she'd taken truly ill, she'd been down for four days. She smiled. "What an astonishing recovery!"

She remembered then that Doc had returned and laid his hands upon her, generating blessed warmth and tingly vibrations that surged beneath the skin and ran hot in her blood. Soon after she'd fallen into a deep sleep. No dreams of Papa or troubling explosions. No nightmares involving Monster Man/Dogface. Just blissful, healing darkness. "Doc Blue's gift . . . When I think of what he could do for others—"

"Don't start, darlin'. Doc needs to make his own choices. Follow his own path."

"I know, I just . . ." She shook her head. "His circumstance is most troubling."

"He seems to be wrestling with it these days, more than usual. I need to talk to him about that." Tucker kissed her forehead, then rolled out of bed.

"Now?" Amelia gawked at his naked body as he strolled toward the electric water heater. Every muscle rippled, and that fantastical tattoo seduced her more soundly than a shiny new aerostat. When he regarded her over his broad shoulder, hair rumpled, eyes twinkling, her vow to sever their physical relationship went up in smoke.

As if reading her thoughts, he quirked an ornery brow. "Ask."

A sensual thrill shot to her core. "Come here."

He turned and she got a look at him full-on. "That wasn't askin' so much as tellin'."

She eyed his jutting erection, then yanked her chemise over her head, giving him a prime view of her full breasts and pebbled buds.

"Good enough." He closed the distance between them, pressing her back on the bed and kissing her dizzy. "We're closing in on our destination, darlin'. Don't have time for slow."

"Don't want slow," she rasped, wrapping her legs around his thighs and grasping his spectacular rear.

"And there's a matter of restraint. I've been hard for you since—"

"Tucker."

"What?"

"Shut up and give me a fast and furious ride to the stars."

Smiling, he slid deep. "Hold tight, Flygirl."

"You too, Cowboy."

Thirty minutes later, dressed and flushed from their frenzied lovemaking and hurried ablutions, Amelia and Tucker stepped into the hall.

"We should be over Florence by now," Tucker said. "I asked StarMan to circle and blend with local air traffic until we joined him topside."

"I fail to see how the *Maverick* could blend. She's magnificent."

"Much obliged, but her magnificence lies in her workings, not her shell. We're not flying a distinctive flag, the blasterbeefs are cloaked, and we lowered the masts and hoisted the bally. No fancy maneuvers. Just an ordinary air transport on ordinary business."

"No offense, but I don't think any of that would fool Captain Dunkirk."

"It would not. But he'd be daft to attack in broad daylight over a major city where Italia ALE could easily intercede."

Amelia smiled. "True. But what about the open skies between here and Mount Ceceri?"

"This is as far as the *Maverick* goes. Wait," he said when she reached for the ladder. "I want to show you something."

Her pulse kicked as he guided her to the lower deck. She didn't remember much about yesterday's rescue via horseback. "Is it Peg? Is he all right?"

"Peg's fine." Tucker stopped in front of the workroom and opened the door. "This is about Bess."

Heart in her throat, Amelia moved into the room. Her breath stalled and her mind whirled. "How . . . Who . . ." Words failed her as she took in the wondrous sight. Papa's kitecycle. Whole, but different. *Better.* She moved closer and inspected the bright red bone-shaker converted and fitted with dual engines and augmented wings.

"Axel helped me build this additional outboard. Similar to a streamlined blasterbeef. You won't need a second pedaler anymore. Although if you need room for a passenger . . ." He thumbed a control on an added dash just below the handlebars. The section between the driver's saddle and main rear engine expanded. He popped a switch and a cushioned seat unfolded.

"Oh, my." Matching footrests had appeared as well. Just when she thought she had the contraption figured out, she spotted a new variance.

"We adjusted the wingspan and design. Not that there was anything wrong with your construction except—"

"This design minimizes drag and optimizes the ability to soar long distances." Her throat tightened as she ran her hand over the canvas and peered beneath and between. "The frame—"

"Aluminum. Eli's idea. The overall construction is similar to what I designed for Peg, although Eli incorporated his own twist." He smiled and waggled his brows. "Step back."

Eyes wide, Amelia held her breath as Tucker flicked another switch on the dash.

Snick, snick, snick. Thump, thump.

The wings retracted and folded into two cylinders on either side of the chassis.

"Now Bess doubles as a land velocipede." He shook his head. "I swan, that man's a genius."

Amelia burst into tears.

"Oh, Christ." Tucker rushed over and pulled her into his arms. "We tried to maintain the integrity of your pa's design, honey. What we'd seen of it, anyway. No gondola. Open-air, just like you wanted."

"It's ... I ..."

"You hate it."

"I ..."—*sniffle*—"love it."

"Then why are you bawlin'?"

For years she'd been dry-eyed. Calm. In control. Buttoned up. Buttoned down. Never had she been so emotional. Given her mother's ever-dramatic state, her papa's scatterbrained nature, and with her brothers constantly away, someone had to be the rock at home. She was out of her element, out of sorts, and amazingly touched by the kindness of veritable strangers. "I ... I can't afford to pay for the supplies and labor."

"What?" Tucker nudged her chin up and forced her to meet his gaze. "Amelia. Honey. You don't have to pay. It's a gift. A thank-you from Axel for saving his life. A work of art from Eli. First off, Eli lives for a challenge. Second, he likes you. As for me, I—"

She clapped her hands over his mouth. "Don't say it. Don't speak. Not if it's what I think ..." Her heart pounded. "I'm not ready."

"Mohmay."

"What?"

He removed her hands from his mouth. "I said okay."

Unable to read his mood from his expression, she

stepped back and swiped her sleeve across her wet cheeks. She glanced at the kitecycle. "She's not Bess anymore."

"Amelia—"

"She's better. The next generation. Bess Two." She smiled and Tucker smiled back. "I don't know what to say."

"'Thank you' would be appropriate."

She moved back into his arms and hugged tight. "Thank you, Mr. Gentry."

He kissed the top of her head. "You're welcome, Miss Darcy."

She bounced back on her heels and clasped her hands to her racing heart. "I must thank Eli and Axel straightaway. Oh, I cannot wait to try her out!"

"No time like the present."

"I thought you were anxious to proceed with our mission."

"I am." He grinned and gestured to the kitecycle. "Bess Two is our transport to Mount Ceceri."

CHAPTER 28

"You sure about this, Marshal?"

"He's sure," Amelia told Axel as she buckled the straps of her parachute pack.

"But we didn't perform a test run."

"Hence the parachute, should anything go wrong, not that it will. Do you not have faith in your work, Mr. O'Donnell?" she asked. "I do."

"You *do*?"

"I do." Amelia stood on her tiptoes and kissed the engineer's bruised cheek. "Thank you again for my thank-you. I am forever grateful."

Red-faced, Axel chomped on his unlit cigar and retreated a step. "Safe flight."

"Remember what I told you about the wings," Eli said.

Tucker nodded as he tugged on his gloves. "Will do."

"Remember what I showed you," Chang said to Amelia. He turned to Axel, reached up, and tapped his temple. The big man crumpled. "Like so."

She gasped. "Oh, my. Um, yes. To be honest, I am not sure one lesson in acupressure was sufficient. But, yes. I will remember what you showed me."

Tuck shook his head. "Ax is gonna be pissed when he wakes up, Birdman."

Eyes twinkling, his mischievous friend waved him off. "I can handle Ax."

"You have the coordinates?" StarMan asked Tuck.

"I do." StarMan was the only one he'd trusted with their specific destination. "You have your orders."

"I do."

They clasped hands, then parted. StarMan returned to the cockpit and Tuck mounted Bess Two. "Sure you want me to pilot?" he asked Amelia.

"I'm sure." She adjusted her flight cap and goggles. "One moment, please."

She stepped away and Doc stepped in. "We always work as a team," he said to Tuck.

"Nothing's changed in that regard. Miss Darcy and I are making the initial move, and you and the rest of the crew will follow through on my command. Teamwork."

"Yes, but . . ."

The man trailed off and Tuck frowned. "You ain't been right since that visit to the Parisian skytown," he said in a low voice. "If it's because Amelia knows . . ."

"Disconcerting," he admitted, "but no."

"Then what?"

"I have a bad feeling."

So did Tuck. It had been gnawing at his gut ever since he'd seen Doc and those rebel-talking Freaks in cahoots. "Something you wanna tell me?"

"No. I just . . . Doesn't seem right, you flyin' off with a defenseless woman."

Tuck laughed. "Nothin' defenseless about Amelia, kid."

Axel stirred and moaned.

"I should tend to Ax," Doc said.

"You do that," Tuck said, distracted by the sight of Amelia feeding his horse a licorice drop. She must've filched it from his stash.

"We'll return soon," she said to Peg, "and when we do I promise you a long and wondrous flight." Then she turned her attention to Leo, who'd perched on the stallion's shoulder. "As for you, my friend, you must stay here. With the

Maverick. With Peg. I have worries enough without fretting about your safety."

Leo screeched and she smoothed her hand over his feathers. "We'll sort this out," she told the falcon. "Tucker promised."

Her faith in him was unsettling. Sweet, but, in the words of Doc, disconcerting. Tuck still hadn't settled on the best way to approach his past and their future. He'd been pondering the matter all night and had decided da Vinci's supposed ornithopter was a wild card. He didn't know how to play his hand until he held all the cards. Did the ornithopter truly exist? Was it worthy of the jubilee prize? Would Judge Titan consider it appropriate compensation for his stolen collection of miniatures once owned by King Henry VIII? What if they found something even more valuable within that secret chamber? Indecision and anticipation made him twitchy as a prostitute in church. "We need to go, Flygirl."

She scrambled forth and mounted behind him, wrapped her arms around his middle, and squeezed. "Ready."

The kitecycle felt sleek but sturdy beneath him. Amelia felt good and right behind him. In theory they were sitting on a powerful, though compact dig. In theory—and based on his and his men's expertise—she'd work like a charm. If he were flying solo, he wouldn't have a second thought. He glanced over his shoulder. "You sure about this?"

"Show some sass, cowboy," she said close to his ear. "Da Vinci awaits."

God, he loved this woman, not that she'd let him tell her.

Eli initiated the mechanism that lowered the stern gunwale, then extended a short, wide gangway.

Tuck tripped several controls on the kitecycle, primed engines, and, just as he'd done with Peg hundreds of times, gained speed and launched off the *Maverick*'s makeshift runway.

Amelia screamed in his ear. "Go, go, go! *Yeeeeeees!*"

He smiled as Bess Two's wheels left the deck and the wings took flight. Took pride in the fact that she handled like a dream. Took joy in the knowledge that Amelia had to be thinking about her pa and his initial invention—resurrected, though revised. He steered the embellished kitecycle away from the *Maverick*, circumvented sporadic airships, keeping an eye out for the *Flying Shark* or any suspicious cloud formations. Nothing tweaked his suspicions. Still, he didn't aim on flying open skies for long. The plan was to hit the ground and motor to Mount Ceceri amidst local automocoaches. The plan was to blend. Thanks to StarMan's charted "shortcut," they'd make the master's hillside workshop in less than an hour.

Tuck checked the astronomical compendium attached to his wrist cuff and nosed Bess Two north. They buzzed over the crowded streets and ancient terra-cotta structures of Florence—churches, palaces, and museums that dated back to the Renaissance. Tuck made a mental note to return someday with Amelia, to show her the sights and wonders of a city that boasted the works of Michelangelo and Botticelli, as well as an entire museum devoted to Leonardo da Vinci.

His mind stuck on the Renaissance genius and his Tuscan workshop. How had that secret chamber remained secret all these centuries? How was it that Briscoe Darcy had been the only one to discover it?

The kitecycle dipped and rose due to an unexpected air pocket. Tuck compensated and leveled off, cursing his wandering mind. "You okay?" he shouted over his shoulder.

"Spectacular!" She rapped his shoulder. "Faster, Flyboy!"

The chilled wind roared in his ears, along with Amelia's laughter and the rumblings of the engines. The open-air ride was similar to soaring horseback on Peg, but the engines provided greater speed and far more noise. It had been a long time since he'd felt this sort of bald rush. Amelia's enthusiasm only intensified the thrill.

Tuck spied the edge of the city, the connecting roadways, and sporadic traffic. Utilizing his spyglass, he pinpointed landmarks and the remote field in which StarMan had suggested they land. "Hang on!"

"You're coming in too fast!" Amelia shouted. "Kill the engines!"

"We'll lose momentum too fast!"

"Glide! Like Peg! Like Leo!"

Right. What the hell did he know? When was the last time he'd flown and landed a mite dig like this? Never. The air dinghy was a whole different animal. Trusting Amelia's experience and instincts, he cut the engine. The silence nearly stopped his heart, and though the subsequent landing wasn't soft or by any means perfect, at least they didn't crash.

The wheels bounced—once, twice, three times. Tuck applied the brakes as they skimmed the lush grass.

"Retract the wings!" Amelia shouted.

They were still in goddamned motion, but he saw the wisdom in her direction. Coming up fast: a grove of cypress trees. If he veered off at this speed he risked damaging the wings. If he didn't veer off, he'd never make it between those trees.

"Tucker!"

Never engage or disengage the wings while in motion. Ignoring Eli's advice, he thumbed the control.

Snick, snick, snick. Thump, thump.

The wings retracted in the nick of time as they whizzed between two trees. Kitecycle unscathed, brakes fully engaged, Bess Two skidded to a stop.

Amelia dropped her forehead to his shoulder. "Bloody hell."

"Damn."

"That was—"

"Yeah."

They burst out laughing.

Amelia caught her breath first. "Know where we are? How to get where we're going?"

"I do."

"Good. You navigate." She dismounted and flashed him a blinding smile that melted his heart. "My turn to drive."

CHAPTER 29

"I do not mean to question your judgment—"

"Then don't." Bingham ignored his mother's scowl and continued packing. The two telepages he'd received during the unexpected visit by the police had determined this course of action. Anxious to be on his way, he'd dismissed his butler to see to his own affairs. If only his vexing mother would disappear.

"But Constable Newberry—"

"Is aware of my substantial collection of aerostats and automocoaches. As such, he assumed I store mass quantities of petrol on the grounds, and as a matter of public safety, asked me to exercise caution in its use. The shire is still reeling from the fallout of that buffoon Ashford's explosion. Concern is natural."

"Yes, but that was two weeks ago, and he was unusually curious about the kind of petrol you use. Though he rephrased his question, he inquired at least three times about rocket propellant."

"And I confessed to selling Reginald Darcy a meager amount from my meager supply. The transaction was aboveboard. A favor for a neighbor. It was not my place or responsibility to monitor his use of it."

"I got the distinct feeling that the constable felt you were somehow negligent. What if Darcy's devil of a daughter or shrew of a wife means to make you accountable? What if the police continue to snoop and learn—"

"I find this paranoid line of thinking tiresome, Mother. You're reading too much into Newberry's visit." Bingham snapped shut his valise and breezed out of his bedchamber, his bulldog of a mother unfortunately nipping at his heels.

"I am not so sure," she said, crowding him as they descended the grand staircase. "Regardless, do you not think he will find it suspicious that you disappeared directly after his inquiry?"

"I'm going away on business, as I often do."

"If only you weren't going out of the country."

Irritated with her constant nagging of late, Bingham stopped cold. "I would circumnavigate the globe in order to speak face-to-face with Professor Maximus Merriweather. As it happens, I need fly only to the Australian outback."

"What if your Mod tracker is wrong about his whereabouts?"

"What if he is right?"

"You risk much in pursuit of this time machine."

"I would, in fact, risk all." He raised a brow to emphasize his meaning. "Either you are with me or against me."

Her gray eyes sparked. "Is that a threat?"

"A warning."

She wrung her hands briefly, then clenched them at her sides. "I only wish to help," she said with a righteous sniff.

"When I want your advice, I'll ask for it." He kissed her on the cheek and smiled. "Good-bye, Mother. Don't contact me; I'll contact you."

Bingham hurried out the door and made haste for the aero-hangar. He consistently withheld details of his seamier actions from his mother in order to protect her as well as himself. Yet she insisted on prying, projecting, and advising. Damned annoying and potentially hazardous. He welcomed time away from her for multiple reasons.

As for Constable Newberry, that he'd linked Bingham to Ashford via the rocket propellant was a surprise. He'd not thought the local police technologically savvy. Regardless, unlike his mother, he did not fear further snooping in regard to the explosion. Ashford's death had been ruled an accident. The constable's visit had pertained to civil safety. Period. Bingham could not be blamed for that scatterbrained inventor's deathly bumble. He'd made sure of it.

Therefore he embarked on this journey with confidence.

He'd alerted his small crew to prepare *Mars-a-tron* for a long flight. What they didn't know, and what he'd withheld from his mother, was that he intended a short detour. First stop, Corsica, a small island in the Mediterranean Sea where he'd meet up with that vexing Scottish pirate. According to his most recent communication, Dunkirk had Amelia Darcy in sight and would soon take possession of her "hidden treasure."

Bingham's pulse raced as he spied his zeppelin, and he considered the most optimal of circumstances. If that treasure had anything to do with Briscoe Darcy's time machine, there would be no need to travel on to Australia in hopes of tapping Merriweather's genius. Bingham would be trekking into the future, compliments of the Time Voyager.

CHAPTER 30

North of Florence, south of Fiesole.

Those had been Tucker's general directions pertaining to the location of Mount Ceceri. After consulting her astronomical compendium to orient herself and quickly reviewing the augmented controls of the kitecycle, Amelia had set the wheels of her wondrous new dig in motion. Adrenaline surged, as she envisioned the climactic stage of their escapade.

Once they'd set upon a road dictated by StarMan, Tucker's directions became more specific. She'd easily and gleefully navigated the wide path populated by a curious combination of horse-drawn carts and carriages and various steam-belching and gear-grinding automocoaches. Papa would've been vastly intrigued by the foreign makes and models, though in her eyes, none compared to Loco-Bug. Or, for that matter, Bess Two. A vehicle that doubled as an airship and land velocipede?

Astonishing.

Though traffic was mild, Tucker soon directed her to a less traveled path. Rumbling along on this clear, sunny day, Amelia felt confident that they would reach their destination swiftly. She could scarcely contain her excitement.

While they roared along on her new kitecycle, Amelia's senses reeled as she absorbed the breathtaking Tuscan landscape. Leonardo da Vinci had gazed upon these same sights, breathed this very air. The master had lived, studied, and created in these hills. She could almost sense his presence. How would she feel when they entered the cave as described by Briscoe, when they discovered the secret chamber, when she laid eyes and hands on da Vinci's ornithopter? Dizzy with anticipation, she pedaled faster. Her actions revved the engines and garnered a squeeze from Tucker.

"Easy, Flygirl."

He didn't have to elaborate. She had eyes. The path was narrow, winding, and rocky. The greater their speed, the more perilous the journey. *Slow and steady wins the race.* Oh, how she wanted that ornithopter.

"We're coming up on the quarries," Tucker said.

For centuries precious stone used in the construction of monuments had been transported from here to Florence. Da Vinci had walked these quarries, these hills. And so had Briscoe Darcy.

Amelia's pulse flared. They were close. She let her mind wander back to the day Papa had shared the contents of his letter, including the landmarks Briscoe had mentioned. Obsessed, over the years she'd secretly studied maps and photographs. She had never been here, but amazingly she knew exactly where she was. She slowed the kitecycle to a crawl as she scanned the rocky hills and distant clearings. Oh, yes. So very close.

"Now would be a good time to share some specifics," Tuck said. "I've read there's a cave dedicated to the memory of da Vinci near the Cava Sarti quarry."

"The place we seek is not far from there," she shouted over the hiss and rumble of the engine. She glanced up, noting narrow, rocky paths and thick wooded areas of cypress, poplars, and oaks. "It would've been easier to fly to the top."

"But not safer. Don't forget about Dunkirk."

"It's been four days. If he wanted to retaliate, do you not think he would have done so by now?"

"If revenge were his sole motivator, yes. Remember his initial intent."

She grimaced whilst thinking back on his seduction dinner. "To plunder my booty."

"I was referring to your hidden treasure."

"So was I." She furrowed her brow and pondered his words. "Oh. *Oh*. I was not speaking of my virtue, but, yes, that too. The scoundrel. Frosts my blood just thinking about it."

"Burns my ass. Should've blown his damned ship to smithereens."

Her lip twitched. "You did try."

"Men like Colin Dunkirk don't give up easy," Tuck said over the escalating noise.

"But we haven't seen hide nor hair, and the weather is clear."

"High stakes call for high cunning."

"So he's cloaked? Tracking us? Following us?"

"Someone sure as hell is." He squeezed her thigh. "Step on it, Flygirl."

"You just told me to slow—" She glanced over her shoulder. *Bloody hell.* Someone—some*thing*—was following them and gaining fast. It looked like a frog, a mammoth rusty automaton toad with glowing red eyes and visible gears and a steam turbine. Spiked metal wheels ate up the dirt and gravel path as it bore down with a deafening croak. "Maybe it's a circus automaton, running late for a performance," she shouted whilst Tucker stoked the rear engine and she pedaled faster.

A shot rang out and splintered the bark of a tree to her right.

"Or road bandits," Tucker snapped whilst shielding Amelia and drawing his Blaster.

Crikey. Amelia veered off just as he fired. His bullet ricocheted off the frog with a loud metallic ping.

"Iron armor!"

"Where are they?"

"Right behind us!"

"No, I mean—"

"Inside the frog!"

More shots rang out and peppered the dirt in front of Bess Two.

"Either they're lousy shots or just trying to scare us into running off the road!" Tuck shouted as she serpentined up a hill. "Pull off. If I can draw them out—"

"No! What if they steal Bess? Or kill you and kidnap me? What if it's Dunkirk?"

"Not his—"

"Hang on!" Amelia hunkered low, triggered more steam, and pedaled fast and furious, hoping to lose them in a densely wooded area. "Duck!"

"Frog!"

"No, *duck*!"

Tucker bent over just as they sailed under a mass of low-lying branches. "Hell's fire!"

"Did I lose them?"

"Still there!" Wood splintered and exploded behind them. "Crashed plumb through that tree!"

Amelia gunned the kitecycle, her heart skipping as they burst through the shade of the woodland onto open ground. *Crikey*. Beyond, nothing but blue skies and a distant overview of Florence.

Pop! Pop!

"God*dammit*!"

Her heart nearly burst through her ribs. "Did they hit the engine?"

"No."

Oh, no. Oh, God. "You?"

He fired his Blaster three times by way of an answer.

Ping! Ping! Ping!

The frog barreled on.

Blooming hell! Imagining blood pouring from some bullet hole in Tucker, she fired up the miniblasterbeef.

"What are you doing?"

She steered Bess Two directly toward the edge of a sheer dropoff.

The great bird will take its first flight on the back of Monte Ceceri. . . . If da Vinci's associate could do it, so could she. Although she would strive not to crash.

"Amelia . . ."

Another flicked switch, then . . . *Thwap, thwap. Snick, snick, snick.*

The wings fully extended just as Bess Two rocketed off the ridge. They dropped, bounced twice—"No!"—then lifted and—"Yes!"—soared.

"Hell of a game of leapfrog," Tucker said as they swung around.

Amelia looked down.

Unable to veer away in time, the frog plunged over the side, tumbling over jutting rocks, landing dented and mangled in a field. Amelia refused to ponder whether or not the ruffians had croaked with the frog. They'd shot Tucker. All she cared about was attending to his wound lickety-split. "Hold on, Cowboy."

"Why?" he asked sounding somewhat amused. "Gonna attempt another wild stunt?"

"Does landing on a rocky plateau count?"

"Damn."

Tuck's shoulder hurt like hell, but not half as badly as his pride. Considering the rough terrain, Amelia's landing had been pretty damned amazing. She'd also managed an impressive motor chase up the hillside and through a copse of trees. And damn, it had taken some balls to race toward a cliff's edge without knowing for sure and certain the wings would engage in time. He was supposed to protect her, but *she'd* saved *him.*

Wings retracted now, he helped Amelia hide Bess Two in one of the many hillside caves, then proceeded to slip out of his bloodied coat. He eyed her as she wrenched off her parachute pack. "You're crazy. You know that?"

She quirked a shaky smile. "Like a fox."

"Mmm."

"I'm almost afraid to look."

"Pretty sure the bullet went straight through. Doc packed an emergency kit in Bess's right saddlebag."

"I'll get it." She scrambled to the kitecycle. "How could it go straight through and not hit me, seated flush as we were?"

"I leaned and angled to get a good shot." Grimacing, he peeled off his ruined shirt, rolled and prodded his damaged shoulder. Near as he could tell, no bullet.

"Do you really think they were road bandits?"

"These are hard times, Amelia. Thievery is common."

"It just seems everywhere I go, criminals follow. Dunkirk, Dogface, frog thugs."

"Makes you yearn for the serene seclusion of Ashford?" Had her constant exposure to danger and unpredictability soured her taste for adventure? His gut kicked with dread.

"I confess to a smidgen of homesickness, although I attach it to the people, not the place." She returned with the kit and met his gaze. "I wouldn't trade this adrenaline-charged journey for the world, although I do fret over the end."

Before he could comment, she looked to his wound and paled. Tuck quirked a grin. "Looks worse than it is, darlin'. We're gonna clean this, bandage it, and move the hell on."

"But—"

"I've suffered worse. Come on." He sat on the dirt floor near the cool stone wall.

She hunkered down in front of him, gaze averted. "Need to wipe away the blood and stem the flow." She ransacked her parachute pack and utilized the silky material.

"Don't faint on me, miss."

"Don't be ridiculous, sir." Yet sweat beaded her brow.

Tuck smiled as he watched her fuss over his wound. Brave in spite of her trepidations. "Should be some whiskey in Doc's kit. Pour it in and over the wound. Then use those strips of linen as bandages."

She nabbed the flask from the medical kit, uncorked the bottle, and sniffed. "Smells strong."

"I'm sure it is."

"Good." She took a swig, winced, and coughed. "Okay."

Before he could brace himself, she poured copious amounts over the open wound. "Jesus."

"Sorry."

"Get the back of my shoulder too." He clenched his teeth and hissed as the alcohol seared. "Christ."

"You told me—"

"I know. It's fine. Hand me that strip." *Damn.* He folded the cloth and pressed it hard against the front of his shoulder. "You're gonna have to do the same to the entrance wound, and use the rest of these strips to wrap around my shoulder and chest. Can you do that?"

She nodded, wide-eyed and worried.

Tuck grasped the back of her neck and pulled her in for a kiss, sweet and slow. The pain in his shoulder dulled, his heart pounded, and his thoughts whirled. Her lips, her tongue—more intoxicating than the whiskey on her breath. He'd meant to calm her and instead had stirred his own senses. Easing back, he grazed his thumb over her cheek. "All right?"

She swallowed, smiled. "Right as rain. And you?"

He shifted, winced. "That kiss was a welcome distraction."

She studied him a moment, then nabbed another bandage. "I know you're curious about the relationship between Briscoe Darcy and my father. Perhaps I can distract you further with their history. What I know of it, anyway."

Tuck's heart swelled at Amelia's show of faith. Hell, yes, he'd been hungry for details, but he'd vowed to himself he wouldn't pry, hoping all along that she'd instead offer the information. "Won't deny your pa's a source of fascination." He smiled as she tenderly and awkwardly bandaged his wound. "Like you."

Her own mouth lifted into a nervous smile. Gaze averted, she shared her tale while tending Tuck's shoulder. "Papa and Briscoe were distant cousins, so they knew of each other and had in fact spoken at family gatherings—back when the majority of the Darcys lived in England and when they still gathered. That said, Briscoe was twelve years my father's senior, so they did not have much in common."

"Except a passion for science."

"Except that." She cast him a glance. "I assume you know about the Grand Exhibition of 1851."

"Held in London at the Crystal Palace. A pet project of Prince Albert's intended to celebrate scientific and industrial technology and designs from all nations."

She nodded. "Millions of people, including several notable dignitaries, attended. Papa made several visits. He was eighteen summers old, impressionable and inspired by various scientific marvels. Imagine his surprise when his cousin showed up announcing his own grand and wondrous invention. A time machine. An engineering marvel that would breach dimensions."

"Must've caused quite a stir."

"Indeed. Briscoe, as I'm sure you've heard or read, was a confident, boastful man," she continued while knotting off one strip. "He made quite a scene, colorfully describing what he predicted as a mind-bending flight through time. Then he stunned the audience by announcing he would be traveling approximately one hundred years into the future. An entire century! Papa said many scoffed, comparing Briscoe to a snake-oil salesman, but Papa dared to believe. In a moment of hero worship, he rushed forward to wish Briscoe safe travels."

Anticipation nettled Tuck's skin as her voice grew hushed, her expression intense.

"Briscoe pressed a folded letter into his hand. 'I had hoped someone would prove worthy,' he said to Papa, 'and here you are. Family, no less. If I do not return, then something went wrong. Perfect the process and profit from my knowledge, cousin.' Minutes later, strapped into his time machine, Briscoe Darcy disappeared in a gust of wind and a burst of rainbow colors. At the time, everyone marked the moment as a magician's trick. An illusion."

Caught up in the story, Tuck couldn't help himself: He pried. "What was in the letter?"

"Directions leading to da Vinci's secret chamber."

"And the mention of a rare ornithopter."

"Yes."

"And?"

"And what?"

"There had to be more. Something pertinent to his time machine. Why else would Briscoe give your father the letter, deeming him worthy? Worthy of what? Mastering time travel? Amassing fame and fortune in the name of science?"

Anxious now, Amelia rocked back on her haunches. "Done! Wrapped tight as a mummy. How do you feel? Passable? Yes? We should go."

He grasped her wrist when she moved to stand. "Why did your pa never travel here, Amelia? Five years passed between Briscoe's departure and the arrival of the Peace Rebels. Why didn't he spend that time 'profiting' from Briscoe's knowledge and 'perfecting' the process?"

"Because he considered the information within the letter sacred. Because he kept expecting Briscoe to return."

"And when he didn't? When the Peace Rebels arrived in the Briscoe Bus, when they claimed Briscoe's time machine had been confiscated by the government and Briscoe himself apprehended and sequestered by a covert agency, why didn't that spur your pa into action? Even if only in an attempt to retrieve his cousin?"

She held his gaze, though her eye twitched. Annoyed? Anxious? He couldn't tell.

"Talk to me, Amelia."

"Because by that time Papa had a wife and sons, and mostly because he deemed it dangerous."

"To whom?"

"Mankind."

Tuck's brain raced along with his pulse. "There's something more in that chamber than that ornithopter."

"But the ornithopter is all we need! The ornithopter poses no threat, only salvation. For my family. For Lily. Name your percentage."

Her rising anxiety and an extreme dip in temperature prodded Tuck into action. He pulled on his bloodied shirt. "What's in that chamber, Amelia?"

A distant rumble catapulted her to her feet. "I don't know . . . specifically."

"Generally. I need to know what we're dealing with, honey."

"Something to do with time travel, dammit! Are you happy now?"

"So Briscoe Darcy wasn't a genius after all," Tuck noted aloud. "He stole or borrowed from da Vinci. Interesting, but not particularly pertinent to this moment." Heart hammering, he pulled Amelia into his arms. He looked into her eyes, telegraphing his sincerity. "To answer your question, no, I'm not happy. I'm concerned. Feel the frigid drop in temperature? Hear the wind kicking up? Trust me when I say I'm the least of your worries."

Her eyes grew wide. "The Stormerator? You think Captain Dunkirk's here?" She rushed out of the cave without an answer.

Tuck nabbed his coat, holstered the Blaster, and hurried after her into the open air, the frigid air. The sky had darkened with an incoming thunder buster. "Good chance that particular storm's a work of nature," Tuck said. "That rumbling, black cloud bank's massive and slow rolling. From what I've witnessed thus far, Dunkirk's mercenary Freak strikes fast and furious."

Amelia cast Tuck a panicked look. "What if it's a new trick up the Stormerator's sleeve?"

Good point. "We should hurry."

"Once we get the ornithopter—"

"I'll signal StarMan and the *Maverick* will be here lickety-split."

"We'll load up the ornithopter—"

"And be on our way."

She licked her lips and glanced at the sky. Motioning Tuck to follow, Amelia took off on foot. "Come on!"

CHAPTER 31

Astonishing how one decision could affect the entire world.

In spite of a brutal headwind, Amelia raced forward, contemplating fate and happenstance, and the possible ramifications of her actions. Was she about to open Pandora's box?

Tucker was right.

Briscoe had borrowed something that had been locked away for centuries by Leonardo da Vinci. That artifact, or knowledge, had enabled Briscoe to launch himself into the twentieth century, and it enabled men of the twentieth century to catapult back to the nineteenth century. That one decision, whether impulsive or calculated, had altered the course of natural history.

Papa's warnings about tampering with dimensions and time rang in her ears, along with wicked winds and distant cracks of lightning. "The ornithopter," she said to herself as she ran past two landmarks mentioned in Briscoe's letter. "That is all we will take. In and out. Here and gone." She hadn't come this far to give up. Papa's death would not be in vain, and her family would not succumb to ruin. As for the time-travel artifact ... "We won't touch it. We won't take it." She repeated that vow like a mantra.

"Amelia."

She turned and saw Tucker lagging behind, jaw clenched in dogged determination, complexion ashen. Blooming hell, she'd been running full-out and he'd been hot on her heels. Until now. "Your wound!" How could she have forgotten?

"I'm fine." He caught up in three long strides. "Just don't get out of my sight. How can I protect you if . . . Oh, Christ. Never mind." Irritated, though she wasn't sure why, he glanced around. "Sure you're going the right way?"

"Yes," she said, moving on at a slower pace. "I've studied maps. I recognize landmarks. I know where the cave is, the secret workshop. I just don't know how to access the secret chamber." She stopped at a stone marker. "Cava Sarti is that way." She turned in the opposite direction. "So our cave is just over here. I'm surprised we haven't spotted more tourists." In fact, she hadn't spied another soul. "I was under the impression that, given its history, Mount Ceceri was a popular destination."

"Typically is," Tucker said, glancing up at the ominous sky. "Weather scared everyone off, I suspect. Looks like a damned cyclone is gearing up."

Just then balls of hail rained down, assaulting them like icy minicannonballs.

"Crikey," Amelia complained. "Ouch!"

Tucker grasped her arm. "Take cover."

"No, wait! There!" Her heart pounded as she moved toward the last landmark. "The vine-covered wall. That's the entrance."

They both tore at the ancient twisted vines as balls of ice continued to pound.

"Nothing but stone!" Tucker yelled over the wind and hail.

"Keep looking!" It had to be here. Her fingers ached and her palms stung as sharp twigs and burrs poked and scratched. Then, without warning, a portion of the wall swung open and Amelia careened face-first into a dark, musty cave.

Tucker followed and pulled her to her feet. "You okay?"

"Spectacular." After the motor chase, the full-out run over rocky hillside, being assaulted by hail, and now this . . . every muscle ached. Her head throbbed and her hands stung. She couldn't imagine how Tucker felt, what with the gunshot wound. "What about you?"

"Ducky."

Amelia's lip quirked. The irritation she'd felt toward Tucker had evaporated the moment they'd made haste and fallen into this cave. This moment she burst with anticipation and wonder. She spun in a circle. "Can't see a thing."

"Hold on."

A beam of light burst forth.

Amelia gawked at the tubular device in Tucker's palm. "What is it?"

"An electric torch. Compliments of Mod technology. Bought it on the black market." He dipped back into his coat. "Here's one for you." He thumbed a switch and passed her the flameless torch.

She squinted into the lit end. Some sort of lens and bulb. "Astounding. I must know how it works."

"I love that you must know, and I'll be happy to explain. Some other time." He flashed the beam across the dirt floor and stone walls. "Workshop, huh?"

No shelves. No tools. No tables. No evidence of a workshop at all. "Long deserted, I suppose." She flashed her own torch about. "Not what I expected."

"Maybe this is the wrong cave."

"No."

"Maybe *this* is the secret chamber. Well hidden. Difficult access."

"Do you *see* an ornithopter?" she asked, unable to keep the sarcasm from her voice. "You know, a man-size, wing-flapping device?"

He didn't answer.

She turned to find him staring at one of the walls. "What is it?" she asked whilst he sleeved away dust and grime.

"Markings."

"Like hieroglyphics?" She moved in beside him and flashed her torch on the wall. "Oh."

"Yeah."

Sketches and writing. Calculations and codes. Definitely da Vinci.

"It's as if he used this wall like a blackboard."

Her skin prickled with excitement. "Can you make out any of the words?"

"Not really. They're pretty faded." He moved along the wall. "Fascinating. This one's almost three-dimensional. More of a carving than a sketch. See the strange indentation here? Looks familiar. A circle filled with clockwork and a cannon shooting . . . flowers?"

"What?" She fumbled her torch and caught it before it hit the ground, then crowded in next to Tucker. "Where?"

"Here."

She was too short to see it straight on, so he swung his arm around her waist and hoisted her up. She shone her torch next to his. "I don't believe it!"

"What?"

"My astronomical compendium!" She wiggled about, reaching under her coat into her inner vest pocket.

Tucker grunted.

"Your shoulder. Good heavens, put me down." The moment her feet touched down she whipped out her compendium. "Look!"

With both torches now shining on the back of the gold disk that served as both sundial and compass, Tucker whistled. "Perfect match. Where'd you get it?"

"Papa. Gave it to me for my tenth birthday. Said it was a family heirloom. You don't suppose Briscoe gave it to him, do you?"

"Your pa never mentioned?"

"No. Just said it was his most prized possession. But he said that about a lot of things. Like the top hat he gave me. He was sentimental that way." She flipped open the compendium. "You can see how old it is. How simple the workings are, but . . ." She flashed her light along the sketches and calculations on the cave walls. "It couldn't be this old, could it?"

"What if, along with the letter," Tucker said, borrowing the compendium, "Briscoe passed along the key to the secret chamber?"

Her lungs seized as he matched up the back of the compendium with the indented carving on the wall and pressed it in like a puzzle piece. "It couldn't be that simple," she rasped.

"Sometimes it is." The wall groaned, dust spit, and the section in front of them gave way.

Anxious and mesmerized, Amelia burst in and . . . *"Arrrrrrgh!"*

"What the hell?"

"Spiderwebs! In my face and my fingers! Are there spiders in my hair? Get them out! Get them off!"

"Hold still. Jesus." He laughed while sweeping away the silky, creepy webs.

"It's not funny!"

"After all you've been through today, you're terrified of a few teeny spiders? Well, at least I can save you from something. There. Gone. No cobwebs. No spiders. Well, one." *Stomp.* "None. All clear."

"I hate spiders."

"Obviously."

"Stop laughing."

"Yes, ma'am."

"Let's just roll the ornithopter out of here and . . . Where is it?" She flashed her torch around the chamber. The teeny, tiny chamber. "No ornithopter could fit in here."

"Unless it was a miniature model."

Amelia squeezed in beside Tucker. There, nestled in a recessed cubby about the height and width of her forearm, was a wooden model of an intricate ornithopter. Her heart danced even as it shattered. "I thought . . . I dreamed of flying it into London and making a grand entrance."

"It's magnificent."

"Magnificently small."

"Not the size of the instrument that matters. It's what you do with it."

"Good things come in small packages?"

"I was talking about the ornithopter."

"So was I." Smiling to herself, she leaned in as far as she could and shone light over the model. "It reminds me of one of his later sketches. Only . . . No, it's different. Look at the way the wings . . . Tucker?" He was no longer beside her. Panicked, she spun around. "Where are you? What are you . . ." He was standing at the opposing wall, back to her, studying . . . *Oh, no!* She rushed over. "Don't touch it! Don't look!"

"It's a codex."

"What?" She didn't want to look. She promised not to look, but she couldn't help herself. A book. Tucker was carefully turning the pages of an ancient book. Leonardo da Vinci had written several codices throughout his life. Their subjects ranged from botany to weaponry to mathematics and flight, to name a very few. Drawing and musings and . . . "That sketch. It's similar to—"

"Briscoe Darcy's time machine."

"The clockwork propulsion . . . Oh, Tucker."

"Fascinating."

"Don't read it. *Can* you read it? You said speaking and reading Italian were two different animals." She squinted at the cramped scrawl. "The writing's backward or upside down, or maybe both. I can't tell. Please say you can't tell." Amelia broke out in a full-body sweat. She eyed the skinny empty cubby in the wall. "Put it back."

"If I went back in time I could change things. Bring back Ida. Save Lily."

"Ida tried to manipulate you. Tried to *shoot* you. You're not to blame for her death, Tucker. And Lily?" Amelia palmed her forehead. "Lily's alive. You want to return to America for her, remember? I mean . . . You're talking crazy, Tucker. Is it your shoulder?" She shoved aside the lapel of his leather coat and shone the light on him. "You're bleeding through your bandages. Through your shirt! Blast! Put the codex back. We have to get you to Doc!"

"I'm not crazy, and I'm not delirious," he said, gaze fixed on the pages. "Not saying I want to use this information, but it damn well fuels the imagination. Christ almighty, Amelia, it's Leonardo da Vinci's codex on time travel. Aren't you curious?"

"No. Yes. Of course I'm curious. But I don't want to know. I don't want to be tempted. One Darcy already tampered with the natural march of time and look how *that* turned out. The Peace War. A globe divided into Old Worlders and New Worlders. Mods and Vics. Freaks—an altered race that has no rights."

Tucker raised a brow. "Thought you were a staunch New Worlder committed to saving the world from rack and ruin? Advanced knowledge could go a long way toward creating utopia."

His words slammed into her like an iron hammer, shaking her belief system. She licked her lips and searched her heart and mind. "I've decided flexibility in certain matters is wise and henceforth will determine my actions according to specific circumstances." Similar to his own belief. "And in this circumstance—"

"Let sleeping dogs lie." His lip twitched and he shot her a look that said they were in accord. "Grab the ornithopter."

Gloriously relieved, she watched as he slid the codex back into the stone cubby. She grabbed the ornithopter. "Let's get out of here." She zipped back out into the main cave, alarmed by the sounds of the mounting storm. "Make the wall close!"

"I need your compendium."

Ornithopter secured tenderly in one arm, she tossed him the ancient compass. "Listen."

"Don't hear anything."

"Exactly. The eye of the storm? It must be Dunkirk. Close the chamber. Hurry! He cannot know of the codex. If he wants the ornithopter—"

"No, goddammit. Wait—"

"I'll distract him. Close the bloody chamber!"

"Amelia!"

Committed to saving the world in her own way, she dashed outside . . . and into the arms of the Scottish Shark of the Skies.

CHAPTER 32

"*This* is the invention of historical significance?" Captain Colin Dunkirk frowned at the priceless model now in his unscrupulous possession. "Hardly seems worth the trouble, yeah?"

Tuck smiled up at the bastard who'd gotten the best of him and Amelia, trussing them good and tight to a cypress tree. "Then why bother?" His shoulder hurt like a mother. His jaw throbbed from being coldcocked with the butt of a blunderbuss, but by God, he refused to show vulnerability. Next to him, Amelia trembled with fury or fear. Probably both.

The pirate smiled back and hunkered down to eye level. "Let me list the reasons. One: I dinnae like ya, Gentry. Respect ya, but dinnae like ya. Two: Ya stole the lass away. I like the lass. A lot. Three: Ya set fire to me ship. Revenge is sweet. Four—and most important: Someone's paying me a substantial reward for this little treasure."

"Who?" Amelia blurted.

His smile broadened. "A mutual acquaintance, lass."

"Impossible."

"Possible. Surprised you'd consort with such a bastard." Dunkirk studied Amelia with an intensity that made Tucker want to rip off the man's head. "Come with me willingly, lass, and I'll spare ya."

The last thing Tuck wanted was for Dunkirk to take Amelia, but at least she'd be alive. No guarantee the rescue he'd initiated with StarMan would come in time. Rather than risk her life, and trusting, *believing* she'd somehow take care of herself, Tuck nudged her.

"I'm thinking about it," she said through clenched teeth.

She was? He hadn't expected that. He shot her a look.

She glared back.

"What's this?" Dunkirk asked with a grin. "Trouble in paradise?"

"Stuff it, Dunkirk," Amelia snapped.

The pirate laughed. "On second thought, not sure I have the time to tame ya, lass."

"As if you could," she groused.

Still laughing, Dunkirk stood and passed the precious artifact to his second in command. "I've secured the two of ya a discreet, though not fully safe distance from that cave, which is rigged to blow in"—he checked his pocket watch—"ten minutes. Giving you a fifty-fifty chance of survival, Gentry. Not near what you gave me and my crew. Thought about blowing the *Maverick* sky-high, but decided I'd rather own her. I'll attend to that as soon as I collect on the artifact."

"I don't know what your *employer* is offering you," Amelia said, "but that ornithopter is potentially worth half a million pounds. Maybe more."

"Not helping," Tuck said.

"Do you not read the newspapers?" she plowed on. "Are you unaware of the Triple R Tourney and the jubilee prize?"

"I'm aware," Dunkirk said, sobering. "I'm also a wanted man. Stroll into London in pursuit of that prize and I'll lose my head."

"Literally," Tuck said.

Amelia gave his boot an annoyed kick. She looked back to Dunkirk. "I'm not wanted. Let us go and let me deliver the invention. Whatever I win, I'll split with you. Fifty-fifty."

"Ya think to bargain with me, lass? Again?"

"Twenty-five-seventy-five. We can live with twenty-five percent."

"No, we can't," Tuck said.

She cast him a scathing look. "Yes, we can."

Dunkirk looked at Tuck with something akin to god-damned pity. "Oh, this is rich."

Tuck's senses flared when the pirate signaled his three cohorts back to the *Flying Shark*. Not that he could see the damned airship, given the dense fog. As long he had that weather-meddling Freak with him, Colin Dunkirk was fairly invincible.

"Ten-ninety," Amelia said, obstinate to the end.

"Ya make life interesting, Amelia Darcy." Dunkirk adjusted the clockwork mechanism. "Ten minutes." Then he triggered a toggle and disappeared into the mist.

Amelia squirmed against the ropes and cursed. "I despise that man."

"Yet you'd strike a deal with him?" Tuck asked while working the rope around his constrained wrists.

"I was trying to stall for time. Bargaining seemed smarter than stonewalling."

"Men like Dunkirk don't bargain. Thought you'd learned your lesson on that score."

"Is this really the time to lecture my methods?" she asked, sounding wounded and mad. "I was trying to save our skins."

Tuck's pride kicked. "Don't you trust me to do that?"

"Of course, but I . . . *Oh!* How I ever fell in love with you . . . I must be crazy, because you, sir, are an insufferable sod."

Tuck stilled. "What did you say?"

"I called you an insufferable sod, you infuriating bastard!"

"Before that." His heart pounded, overshadowing the eye-crossing pain in his shoulder. "You love me."

She froze. "No, I don't."

"You said you did."

"No, I didn't. I said . . . I said I *fell* in love with you, which is not the same thing."

"Exactly the same," he said, feeling light-headed.

"We're going to die and you're arguing semantics?"

"We're not going to die, although we might sustain serious injuries, depending on timing. We need to free ourselves from this tree."

"These ropes aren't budging, and I'm fairly certain the tree isn't going anywhere. Have a trick up your sleeve, Sky Cowboy?"

"No. But I've got a jackknife in my pocket. See if you can reach it." His vision blurred. "Dammit." He banged the back of his head against the trunk of the tree, fighting a wave of dizziness.

"What's wrong?" she asked while fidgeting and exploring his pocket.

"Woozy."

"You've lost a lot of blood. Don't pass out on me, Tucker Gentry. I don't want to die alone."

"Not gonna die. Too much to live for."

"Got it," she said. "If I can just angle . . . Don't move."

"No problem." He licked chapped lips and banged his head again. *Stay alert. Stay focused.* "Who'd you consort with before you consorted with me?"

"What?"

"Dunkirk said—"

"Oh, that. I don't know whom he could have meant. I've never consorted. Although there was Phin."

"Phin?"

"Phineas Bourdain," Amelia blurted, red-faced. "It was nothing. Just a kiss."

Jealousy cut through the haze of pain. "Does this Bourdain have a lot of money?"

"Not really. Besides, he's a good friend of Jules's. Fiercely loyal." She continued to saw at the ropes. Slowly. Awkwardly.

Tuck glanced at the timer, then at the sky. The fog had lifted. No sign of the *Flying Shark*, but no sign of the *Mav-*

erick either. He'd signaled StarMan via his telecommunicator at the same time he'd been shutting the door of the secret chamber. He'd hoped by now . . . unless the communication had failed. "Pass me the knife."

"You're too weak—"

"Dammit, woman."

"Fine." She shifted and managed to pass off the blade. "How much time do you think we have left?"

His heart broke at the fret in her tone. Was she thinking about the explosion that had taken her pa? "All the time in the world, Flygirl."

"Before the cave blows, I mean."

He worked the knife over the ropes enslaving Amelia. "Maybe five minutes." *What if there's no tomorrow? Christ.*

She fell silent for a second, as if contemplating her most dire concern. "The ornithopter," she said. "I want you to know I was trying to think of a way that it could benefit both of our causes. I thought we . . ."

"We?" Heart full, Tuck smiled. "Just so you know, my mind was travelin' that same road, honey."

"You are indeed, as I'd first believed, a noble man, Mr. Gentry," she said with a catch in her voice. "Had you a specific plan in mind?"

"I was going to make you a substantial monetary offer, plus a promise to look after you and your ma in exchange for the invention. With your brothers in the race, your family still has an almighty shot at glory. That ornithopter, magnificent though it is, stands a slim chance of winning the jubilee prize. On the other hand, Judge Titan collects rare antiquities. Even though Ida stole his priceless collection of miniature paintings, he blames me. He's a vengeful man, but he's also greedy and obsessive."

"You honestly think he'd clear your name in return for a da Vinci model."

"It was worth a shot."

"You love your sister very much."

"As you love your brothers."

Her voice grew contrite. "I suppose we could have indeed struck a compromise."

"That was my plan. Part of it, anyway." He felt one rope give way. With his hands tied behind his back and his senses fuzzy, the effort was tricky. He sure as hell didn't want to cut Amelia. He glanced at the timer, then at the sky again. *Fuck.*

"Tucker, I—"

"Hold still." His ears buzzed as he cut through another rope. "Try it now. Work your wrists, darlin'. Hurry." The buzz intensified to a roar.

"Free! I'm free!" She scrambled to her knees. "Give me the knife."

"Run."

"Give me the bloody knife, Tucker!"

Just then Doc Blue appeared in front of him, as if he'd fallen directly from the sky. Then Tuck smelled the rocket fuel, felt the heat. *Pogo Pack. "Maverick?"*

"ALE."

That didn't make sense.

"Would've been here sooner," he said. "Inclement weather."

"Cave's rigged to blow!" Amelia screamed as two air constables touched down. She sliced through one rope. "Help me!"

"Get her out of here, Doc."

"But—"

"That's an order."

Doc snatched Amelia away as the air constables moved in. He heard her scream. Heard a roar. An earsplitting explosion.

Then silence.

CHAPTER 33

Bingham adjusted his magnifying specs and tempered his disappointment as he inspected the compact, though intricate model of a da Vinci ornithopter for the third time. He had to be sure. Unfortunately, he was. "This isn't it."

Dunkirk, who'd been insolently lounging in the most comfortable chair in *Mars-a-tron*'s gondola, leaned forward with a sneer. "It's what she came oot of that cave with, and she was damned well averse to letting it go. I searched the cave for anything else. Empty. Ya told me to steal whatever Amelia Darcy was after, yeah? This is it. A da Vinci ornithopter. An invention of historical significance."

"But it is not significant to me."

"What the fook does that mean?"

Bingham straightened and slid the specialized specs to his forehead. "I don't want it." It did not apply to time travel. It was not even a full-scale working ornithopter. A prized artifact for a museum or a private collector, but nothing but a disappointment to him. "It will not advance my cause."

"Could be worth half a million."

"Ah. The jubilee prize." Bingham refrained from rolling his eyes. Dunkirk was ignorant of his role as anonymous benefactor of the Triple R Tourney, and he intended to keep it that way. He'd learned long ago that the best way to control his "employees" was by controlling what they did and did not know about him and his many ventures.

Bingham rocked back on his heels, anxious to be on his way. He had many irons in the fire, Professor Maximus Merriweather at this moment being the hottest. He gestured to the sixteenth-century model. "By all means."

Dunkirk stood. "You're offering me the invention instead of the payment we agreed upon?"

"The ornithopter is worth more than I offered you."

"*If* it wins the prize."

"Thought you were a gambling man, Captain Dunkirk."

"We had a deal."

"Indeed. You failed to deliver what I anticipated. I am not satisfied with your services and thus shall not pay." He flashed a lethal smile. "Take the ornithopter or leave it. This transaction is over." Bingham had toyed with killing the insolent pirate, but the man was a valuable minion—as long as he stayed in line. Cutting Dunkirk loose for a while, denying him lucrative "work," might inspire the man to treat Bingham with more respect in the future—when next Bingham needed him. The Scottish bastard eyed him up and down, then smiled. "I be takin' the ornithopter."

Bingham watched as the intimidating man gently scooped up his prize. "Oh, Dunkirk. You neglected to mention the status of Miss Darcy."

"Dead."

"Pity."

"Aye, it is," he said on his way out.

Bingham sensed true regret in the pirate's voice, when all Bingham mourned was the chance to dominate Miss Darcy in bed. Ah, well. At least her demise would please his mother.

He called for his captain. "Set a course for Australia." He would not dawdle and pine over Miss Darcy's less than thrilling discovery. He would seek the expertise of Merriweather, who had firsthand knowledge of the Briscoe Bus. As backup, he intended to contact Miss Goodenough.

Time to turn up the heat on Simon Darcy.

CHAPTER 34

"What do you mean, I'm being detained for another day?" Amelia paced the floor of the tiny room she'd been led to six hours prior. "I'm not the one who stole the ornithopter! Captain Dunkirk has it! I'm not the one who blew da Vinci's workshop to smithereens. Again, Dunkirk!"

"So you said, Miss Darcy. It has been looked into, but there have been no sightings of Captain Dunkirk or the *Flying Shark* in this area."

"That's because his airship's cloaked in a cloud or a cyclone or fog. He has this Stormerator. . . ."

Her visitor dragged a hand over his gaunt face and sighed.

She stopped in front of him. "Who are you again?"

"Agent Cyrus Toppins. I'm from the British consulate, and you, Miss Darcy, are in a bit of a pickle. Do please sit."

Miserable, she dropped into the stiff-backed chair across from the agent. "Do you know anything of Mr. Gentry? I was told he escaped serious harm from the explosion, but he had this gunshot wound and . . . I'm worried."

Doc Blue had been little more than a mirage. He'd appeared, rocketed her to safety, told her he was sorry, and promised to make things right. Then he was gone. Even though the air constables had been kind enough, their English was broken, and after she'd mentioned the theft of a da Vinci artifact and the fact that she was on queen's business, they had hustled her straightaway to their headquarters. They'd asked her the same questions over and over, answering none of hers in return. She'd stayed calm for the most part, but now . . . anxious tears filled her eyes. "Please, Agent Toppins, if you have news of my friend, I would be most grateful."

He placed his palms flat on the table between them, then nodded. "Gentry has received medical attention. He is mending rather quickly. Quite amazing."

"Doc Blue."

"Indeed, a man by that name did visit your friend. After a short discussion, Mr. Gentry punched the young physician in the nose, knocking him across the room."

"What? Why?"

"Neither would say."

She palmed her forehead, more distressed by the moment.

"Given the severity of the situation—theft and destruction of prominent Italian property—there's a good chance that Gentry will be extradited to America due to previous charges."

She bolted to her feet. "You can't let that happen! He's been wrongly accused, and he doesn't have the ornithopter to offer the judge in return for his release!"

"Do lower your voice, Miss Darcy, and please sit down," Toppins said. "No offense, but every time you open your mouth you dig a bigger hole for yourself and Mr. Gentry. You claimed to be on a mission for the queen—"

"I only meant—"

"A da Vinci artifact has been stolen, and who knows what other works of the master destroyed in that explosion."

She knew exactly what else had been destroyed: the codex on time travel. She couldn't say she was sorry. At least one good thing had come out of this debacle.

The agent leaned forward and looked her earnestly in the eyes. "You are at the heart of an international incident, Miss Darcy. You would be wise to speak to no one as I try my best to sort through the legal mayhem."

She nodded, not knowing what else to do. Soon after Agent Toppins left, she lowered her head to the table, forlorn. *Crikey*. What would her brothers do were they in her shoes?

"They wouldn't get themselves into a pickle like this in the first place," she said to herself.

Someone knocked on the door. "A visitor, Signorina Darcy."

Her pulse raced in hopes of seeing Tucker.

Axel O'Donnell walked through the door.

The constable held up his hand, intimating that they had five minutes.

The moment the door shut, she threw herself into the burly engineer's arms. "Oh, Axel." She held tight, breathing in the scent of grease, lemon oil, and petrol. The *Maverick*. "Is everyone okay?"

"Fine. We're fine." He cleared his throat and eased her back. "They treatin' you all right?"

She nodded and swiped her grimy sleeve across her wet cheeks.

He cleared his throat again and passed her a surprisingly pristine bandanna.

"Thank you." She blew her nose. "I'm in big trouble."

"So's Tuck, but he told me to tell you not to worry. He told me to tell you the adventure's only just begun. Which, considering what's gone on so far, troubles me a mite, but that's neither here nor there. Tuck said to tell you not to make waves. Stick to the truth, do what the British consulate tells you to, have faith in utopia, and everything will be right as rain."

She could scarcely breathe. Tucker was asking her to believe in *him*. She swallowed past a rusty cog in her throat.

"Why did he send you and not StarMan?" The soft-spoken, even-tempered navigator seemed the more likely diplomat.

"I asked the same thing. Tuck said he picked me because I talk too much." He quirked an awkward smile. "Tuck's powerful worried about you, Miss Crazy Pants. Can I tell him you're okay?"

"You can do more than that. Tell him I believe." She smiled. "He'll know what I mean."

The big man nodded, then glanced at his cuff watch. "I should go. Crew's waiting. We're taking mighty fine care of Leo, so don't worry about him. Eli retrieved Bess Two. Birdman said to tell you to gear up for another lesson in acupressure, and StarMan's making you some sort of navigational something or other."

Her heart swelled. "What about Doc? Toppins said Tucker hit him. Why would he do that?"

Axel frowned. "Because Doc ratted you out. He's lucky the marshal didn't do worse. If I get my hands on that skinny-ass traitor—"

"Wait. Whatever do you mean? Doc saved us. He was with ALE." Amelia furrowed her brow. "*Why* was he with ALE? Instead of aboard the *Maverick*?" It wasn't the first time she'd wondered, but no one here seemed obliged to answer her questions.

Axel glanced at the door. "Don't have much time."

"Then talk fast," Amelia said, motioning the engineer into the seat vacated by the British agent.

Axel sat and leaned across the table, gesturing Amelia to lean in as well. "Don't know all the specifics," he said in a low voice, "but Doc got himself mixed up with a bad Freak, a woman he met back in that Parisian skytown. Apparently Doc's brother's a criminal sort, livin' on the dodge. This woman told Doc that she knew the whereabouts of his brother—gave him a photograph that belonged to the man as proof of their association."

"Jasper," Amelia whispered, deep in thought.

"You know about Doc's brother?"

She faltered, not knowing how much Axel knew. Had it come to light that Doc and Jasper were Freaks themselves? If not, she didn't want to expose them. Regardless of the supposed betrayal, Amelia felt sorry for Doc Blue. "Only that Jasper exists and Doc feels guilty that they're estranged."

"Yeah, well, that guilt led Doc down a deceitful path. That Freak woman promised Doc she'd lead him to Jasper if Doc informed her of *your* whereabouts the moment you made your destination clear. Doc claims he balked, but she swore she wasn't after you. All she cared about was the treasure.

"Thinkin' no harm would come to you, once Doc learned the *Maverick* was headed toward Tuscany, he contacted the woman via the ship-to-shore Teletype in the marshal's cabin."

Amelia pressed a hand to her aching heart. "Oh, Doc."

Axel grunted. "Near as the marshal can figure, that Freak spy was in league with Dunkirk or Dunkirk's employer. Either way, Doc ratted you out, and you and the marshal almost died."

"But Doc must've had a change of heart, right?" Amelia asked, desperate to defend the good in the man.

"So he says."

"It *must* be true. How did ALE get involved? How—"

The door opened. "Time's up."

"Comin'." Axel reached into his coat pocket. "Never mind about Doc. Just remember this," he said to Amelia in a hushed voice. "Tuck said this is your invention of historical significance." He pressed her astronomical compendium into her hand. "See ya soon, Miss Darcy."

Soon after, she was alone once more, except she didn't *feel* alone. She could feel Tucker's love and the friendship of the crew. As for Doc ... Although she understood his motivation—sibling love was a powerful bond—she found it difficult to fully forgive his actions when those actions could well lead to Tucker's being extradited back to America. And what did it mean for the rest of the crew, the men who had aided in his initial escape? Dear Lord, was it possible they'd all hang?

Amelia pushed the sickening thought from her mind. She had to stay strong. For her family. For Tucker. She had to think positively.

Have faith in utopia and everything will be right as rain.

Worried, yet hopeful, Amelia stared down at the compendium in her hand. Even though his own fate swung in the balance, Tucker had been thinking of her. She didn't need the ornithopter. She could contribute to her family's financial future with the sixteenth-century compass once owned by, and maybe even developed by, Leonardo da Vinci. Tucker could have kept it and sold it in his quest to reunite with his sister.

He'd sent it back to her.

Heart aching, Amelia hugged herself and envisioned the night he'd shown her the stars as they flew on Peg's back. She hadn't wished on a star since she was a little girl, sitting in the meadows of Ashford and staring up at the sky as Papa taught her the constellations. This moment she closed her eyes and wished upon every star she could conjure in her mind's eye.

She wished for Tucker's freedom and safety. And then the same for his men. She wished for Tucker and his sister to be reunited, and for Doc and his brother to find some sort of peace. She wished good fortune for her mother, Jules, and Simon. She wished for a wondrous workshop in heaven for Papa, and lastly . . . she envisioned the brightest star, imagined herself in Tucker's arms, and wished for her heart's desire.

In essence, Amelia prayed for a miracle.

CHAPTER 35

"Stop fussing, Mother."

Anne Darcy rearranged her daughter's hair combs for the third time and smoothed the pleats of her cutaway skirt for the fourth. "If an audience with Her Majesty, the queen, does not call for fussing, I do not know what does."

Amelia suppressed a bout of stomach wrens. "It is not an audience so much as a royal inquiry. I'm in wretched trouble and could well be on my way to the Tower."

"Then you shall be the most fetching prisoner by far. Jesting," she said with an awkward smile.

Amelia cast her fashionably though conservatively dressed mother a suspicious glance. "I have never known you to jest."

"I have never been inside Windsor Castle." Seated next to Amelia on a cushioned bench in an ornate hall, the pudgy woman leaned close and whispered, "I am nervous. What if we say or do the wrong thing? Are you certain you do not want me to try to contact your brothers?"

"I am certain. Please, Mother. Simon and Jules are on a quest, and I don't want to be the cause for their failure. Someone has to restore respect to the Darcy name." Amelia had only heaped on more scandal.

Upon being escorted back to England by an ALE

cruiser, she had refrained from reading the newspapers, specifically the *Informer*. She was anxious and chagrined enough without reading about her "international incident," as reported by a sensational journalist. She had, however, asked her mother, who'd joined her in London, to peruse all of the city's papers for news on the Sky Cowboy. There had been none. Bothersome, that. Nor had she heard from Tucker himself, or any of the crew. Distressing. She worried that they had indeed been sent back to America. But, given his fame, wouldn't a sensational story like that make the news or a penny dreadful? She'd tossed and turned every night, pondering their fate, pining for Tucker—even worrying about his poor sister, Lily, a woman she knew nothing about, but still felt a kinship toward.

"Did you skim every newspaper this morning, Mother? Even the *City Beacon*?"

The woman nodded and fiddled with her decorative bonnet. "Every paper, Amelia. No mention of Mr. Gentry. No mention of you. As you know, I have scanned the news every day for the last three days, and even in the days before that, as I try to follow the latest on the Triple R Tourney. There has been no mention of the 'incident,' nor of you and Mr. Gentry. At. All." She lowered her voice to a conspirator's whisper. "I suspect a cover-up. You are an embarrassment to the British Empire, dear."

Amelia cringed. "Let us hope they do not strive to brush me under the royal rug."

Her mother patted her hand. "I meant no offense. I am, indeed, most impressed with your efforts, Amelia. I am"—*sniffle*—"proud."

She swallowed an emotional lump. "I confess you have been most supportive these past few days. I'm surprised and most touched."

"Yes, well, things have changed for the Darcys. We must adapt." She sniffed into a dainty handkerchief. "I miss your father."

Amelia blinked back tears and squeezed her mother's hand. "As do I."

Agent Toppins stepped into view and cleared his throat. "Forgive the intrusion, but Her Majesty, Queen Victoria, will see you now."

Both women stood.

Toppins, who'd been assigned to escort Amelia back to London, had been intervening on her behalf and acting as her official bodyguard for the past week. Today he'd escorted her and her mother to Windsor to learn her official fate. Ever formal, he nodded apologetically at Anne. "Miss Darcy only, please."

Amelia expected her mother to bluster. She'd been most keen on meeting Queen Victoria, not only as her ruler, but as a woman who shared her Old Worlder views. Instead of complaining, Anne smiled and squeezed Amelia's hand. "I'll wait here and . . . think good thoughts."

In a spontaneous show of affection, Amelia briefly embraced her mother, then, pulse tripping, followed Agent Toppins through a great many large rooms and halls. Never had she seen such opulent furnishings and decor. "Astonishing."

"Quite," Toppins said with a stiff nod. "Miss Darcy."

"Yes?"

"Remember what I told you about loose lips." He guided her through a small antechamber, opened a door, and . . .

"Crikey."

Toppins groaned, then disappeared.

"I mean . . ." Amelia performed a small awkward curtsy. "Beg your pardon, Your Majesty."

The queen was sitting on a small chair near the window, and a book lay open nearby. Amelia would have recognized the short, stocky, grandmotherly-looking woman anywhere. Her white hair was pulled into a severe bun. Her conservative gown: mourning black. Yet, unlike in most of the portraits Amelia had seen, the noble queen's expression was not dour, but sweet.

She waved Amelia into the warm and welcoming room. "Come in, child."

Amelia moved forward. Another curtsy. Was that wrong?

"So you are Miss Amelia Darcy. Distant relative of the Time Voyager. Sister to the civil engineer who thought to construct a futuristic monorail high above the streets of London. Daughter of the inventor who blew a hole in Kentshire." The older woman raised a brow. "And now you, a mere wisp of a girl, have created an international incident between Italy and the British Empire."

Amelia flushed hot. She wondered whether they would float her into the Tower through Traitors' Gate. Would she be imprisoned for life, or perhaps would they lop off her head? Was Tucker facing a similar fate this very moment? Her stomach churned with the possibility. For an instant, she understood the temptation of time travel. If only she could go back and confess her heart to Tucker.

I love you.

Why had she been so obstinate in the matter?

"Regarding this scandal," the queen said, "we are most displeased. However, I understand that this incident also involved the destruction of a codex containing perilous information." She smiled a little. "On this matter, we are pleased."

Amelia blinked. Was she referring to da Vinci's codex on time travel? Amelia had said nothing to ALE or the Italian officials, or even Agent Toppins regarding the existence, or onetime existence, of that codex. She had not seen the point.

"We would be even more pleased if Mr. da Vinci's rare ornithopter were returned to the Italian government."

Was that her punishment? Her penance? Her salvation? To reclaim the ornithopter?

"We are taking steps to ensure this. We are also inclined to attend to your tarnished reputation, Miss Darcy. Although we frown upon most of your family's escapades, we are most fond of your brother Jules. We do not wish him worries or hardship"—she pursed her lips—"or scandal. Given your frolicking with the Sky Cowboy and his crew, no respectable Englishman will have you. Thus, I have secured you a foreign husband."

For the first time since she entered this room, Amelia's legs threatened to give way. Stomach wrens fluttered until she was certain she would be sick. How could she marry another man when she was so hopelessly in love with Tucker Gentry? She started to speak, but then remembered Toppins's observation regarding her digging deeper holes every time she opened her mouth.

"Do not look so stricken," the queen commanded. "I wedded a foreigner. I assure you, I was blissfully happy. Of course, Albert was from Germany. I have no idea what you can expect from an American."

Amelia's heart pounded. "An American?"

"She speaks! I was beginning to worry you'd lost your wits, Miss Darcy. Mr. Gentry," she called, and Tucker magically appeared on the threshold of an adjoining room. "Do take this young woman and explain the bargain we have agreed upon." She fanned her face. "Good heavens, her mere presence is draining."

"Yes, Your Majesty. Ma'am," he said with a slight bow, excusing himself and crooking a finger at Amelia.

Adrenaline surging, she smiled at Queen Victoria and curtsied. "Ma'am." Then she backed out of the room and into Tucker's arms.

He shut the door and smiled. "You look beautiful, Flygirl."

Oblivious to her surroundings, she threw her arms around her aeronautical hero, her one and only Sky Cowboy, and kissed his cheeks, his jaw, his mouth.

"Missed you too, darlin'." Smiling into her eyes, he finessed her across the room to a more private corner, then proceeded to kiss her senseless.

Heaven.

No. Windsor.

Remembering her royal whereabouts, she eased back, embarrassed by her fervent display but smiling like an idiot. "You're alive. And well!"

"You were worried?"

"Yes," she said plainly. Heart pounding, she caressed his handsome face. "I hoped and wished . . . I imagined you coming back for me, but I never expected this. How? What?"

"Sit." He grasped her hand and pulled her down alongside him on a velvet settee. "I promised the queen I'd speak plainly and quickly with you and then we'd be on our way."

"I'm listening." She couldn't stop staring. He looked so dashing, dressed to the nines in an American frock suit. So handsome, even with the lingering bruise on his clean-shaven jaw. "Wait. How's your shoulder?"

"Good as new, thanks to Doc. Although . . ."

"He betrayed us," she said, acknowledging the sadness in Tucker's eyes. "Mr. O'Donnell told me. I've been pondering on this, and although Doc's actions were unwise, they are not unforgivable. I'm convinced he's a good man, Tucker."

"I know he's a good man, Amelia. But a troubled one. Doc needs to put his grievances with Vics to rest. Needs to banish his fears and prejudices. If he'd trusted my men with his true race and quandary, I guaran-damn-tee you, we would have worked as a team to learn his brother's whereabouts."

"Instead he trusted a stranger, simply because she was a Freak, one of his own kind," Amelia said.

"Betraying good folk, folk who lived, breathed, and fought beside him for more than two years, that ain't no way to right a wrong. Doc not only betrayed you, honey; he betrayed me and every man on the *Maverick*."

"But—"

"Ain't sayin' I don't understand his motivation. Sayin' he needs to grow some . . ." He dragged a hand down his clenched jaw. "Needs to show some sass."

"When push came to shove," Amelia pointed out, "Doc did stand by me, you, and the crew. He alerted ALE, and because of their timely arrival we're alive."

"The only reason I didn't kick his ass to the Klondike."

In spite of the betrayal, Amelia couldn't dredge up any anger. "So Doc's still with the *Maverick*? Still part of the crew?"

"Not presently. A mutual parting of the ways. At least for now. Meanwhile, I'm trying to focus blame on the person at the heart of this chaos. The person who turned Doc's head. Someone out there's paying a lot of money and twisting a lot of arms for certain information. It's all tied in somehow to whoever paid Dunkirk to seize the ornithopter. Only I suspect the person of interest was expecting something more grandiose than a miniature aerostat."

She scrunched her brow. "Like the codex? But why would someone suspect or assume I'd know the whereabouts of a codex on time travel?"

"You're a Darcy, hon."

She shook her head, trying to take it all in. "This person, he must be extremely wealthy, ruthless, and somewhat mad. I don't know anyone who fits this description."

Tucker smoothed a renegade curl from her flushed face. "Maybe it's enough that this person knows you, darlin'. We'll confer at greater length with Agent Toppins. Let it go for now."

"But—"

"We're wearing out our welcome," he said with a nod to the adjoining room.

Her brain jumped tracks. "How is it that you ended up here at the palace, and on such friendly terms?"

"I've spent the past week tap-dancing, calling in some favors and such. As it happens, I've made a couple of illegal 'runs' for several close friends of the queen. Dignitaries who vouched for me and secured an audience. She may be a staunch Old Worlder, but she's reasonable. In fact, she was quite pleasant."

"That's because you're so charming."

"I can be, when it suits my purpose." He smoothed his thumb over the back of her hand, inciting a delicious tingle. "I presented my case with an open heart and valiant intentions. Especially in regards to you."

Amelia licked her lips. "What is this deal she spoke of?"

"In return for making an honest woman out of you, Miss Darcy, and agreeing to recapture the ornithopter and bringing in Captain Dunkirk—the 'scourge of the English skies,' I believe she said—she will see that my name and reputation are exonerated in America, and has even arranged safe passage for Lily."

Amelia's pulse raced. "I'm pleased about your reputation and your sister."

"But not the rest?"

She averted her gaze, needing him to say more. Something . . . romantic. Even though she believed his intentions noble, somehow the wording of that deal vexed. "So by marrying me, you're gaining your freedom?"

"By marrying you, I'm gaining the wife of my dreams, a woman who'll share the wheel with me, soar the skies, experience adventures."

Her heart tripped and danced. "Was that a proposal, Mr. Gentry?"

"No, darlin', it was not." He shifted and knelt on one knee, and pressed a kiss to the back of her hand. "I love you, Amelia Darcy. A bone-deep love that will never waver or die. Will you marry me? Will you promise me forever?"

Simple. Heartfelt. Perfect. "I will."

"You won't regret this, darlin'."

She quirked a grin. "You might."

"Nothing like living dangerously."

Stars danced in her heart and mind. Her soul rocketed to the moon. "I love you, Cowboy."

Cupping the back of her neck, he kissed her softly, deeply. "The adventure begins."

Please read on for the next
exciting installment in the
Glorious Victorious Darcys series,

HIS CLOCKWORK CANARY

Available from Signet Eclipse in June 2013.

Since the day he'd been born (three and a half minutes later than his twin brother), Simon Darcy had been waging war with time. Either he had too much of it or not enough. Somehow his *timing* was always off. Bad timing had cost him much in his thirty-one years. Most recently, his father, Reginald Darcy, Lord of Ashford.

The proof was in his pocket.

Simon didn't need to read the abominable article — he had it memorized — yet he couldn't help unfolding the wretched newsprint and torturing himself once again. As if he deserved the misery. Which he did.

The London Informer
January 5, 1887

MAD INVENTOR DIES IN QUEST FOR GLORY

The Right Honorable Lord Ashford, lifelong resident of Kent, blew himself up yesterday whilst building a rocket ship destined for the moon. Ashford, a distant cousin of the infamous Time Voyager, Briscoe Darcy, was rumored to be obsessed with making his own mark on the world. Fortunately for the realm and unfortunately for his family, Ashford's inventions paled to that of Darcy, earning him ridicule instead of respect, wealth, or fame.

Simon's gut cramped as he obsessed on the article that had haunted him for days. For the billionth time, he cursed the Clockwork Canary, lead pressman for the *Informer*, as heartless. The insensitive print blurred before Simon's eyes as his blood burned. Instead of tossing the infernal sensationalized reporting of his father's death, he had ripped the article from the London scandal sheet, then folded and tucked the inflammatory announcement into an inner pocket of his waistcoat, next to his bloody tattered heart.

For all of his guilt and grief upon learning of his beloved, albeit eccentric, father's hideous demise, Simon had stuffed his emotions down deep. His mother and younger sister would be devastated. Especially his sister, Amelia, who shared their papa's fascination with flying and who'd lived and worked alongside the old man on Ashford—the family's country estate. For them, Simon would be a rock. As would his ever unflappable twin brother, Jules.

Simon had made the trip from his own home in London down to Kentshire posthaste. He'd remained stoic throughout the constable's investigation of the catastrophic accident as well as the poorly attended funeral. He'd even managed a calm demeanor whilst listening to the solicitor's reading of the will. Unlike his dramatic and panic-stricken mother. Although upon this occasion, he could not blame the intensity of her outburst.

The Darcys were penniless.

Even after sleeping on the shocking revelation, Simon couldn't shake the magnitude of his father's folly. His mind and heart warred with the knowledge, with the implication, and with the outcome. Because of Simon's ill timing and arrogance, his mother and sister were now destitute.

"Do not assume blame."

Simon breathed deep as his brother limped into the cramped confines of the family dining room. "Do not assume to know my mind."

"Has grief struck you addled, brother?" Dark brow raised, Jules sat and reached for the coffeepot. Like their father, the Darcy twins had always preferred a brewed coffee over blended teas.

Simon flashed back on one of his father's quirky inventions—an electric bean-grinding percolator—which might have proven useful except, as a staunch Old Worlder, their mother had refused to allow Ashford to be wired with electricity.

Destitute and living in the dark ages.

Riddled with emotions, he pocketed the blasted scandal sheet and met his twin's steady gaze. But of course Jules would know his mind. The older brother by mere minutes, he always seemed to have the jump on Simon. Even so far as guessing or knowing his thoughts. Simon was often privy to Jules's notions as well and sometimes they even had what their little sister referred to as "twin conversations." Whether spurred by intuition or some bizarre fashion of telepathy, they often finished each other's sentences. It drove Amelia mad.

"I could've been working alongside my mentor on England's touted engineering marvel, Tower Bridge," Simon said. "Instead I chose to pursue my own *brilliant* idea."

"You doubt the merit of a fuel-efficient public transportation system high above the congested streets of London?"

"No." His monorail system inspired by the Book of Mods would have eased ground traffic and air pollution caused by the rising population and number of steam-belching and petrol-guzzling automocoaches. It would have provided an affordable mass transit alternative to London's underground rail service.

It would have afforded Simon the recognition and respect he craved.

"I regret that I boasted prematurely about my project. Had I not bragged, Papa would not have invested the family's fortune." Sickened, Simon dragged his hands though his longish hair. "Bloody hell, Jules, what was the old fool thinking?"

"That he believed in you."

"Then when the project failed due to political corruption, I teletyped Papa posthaste." Simon rambled on, suddenly unable to contain his angst. "Railed against the injustice. Wallowed in self-pity. What was *I* thinking?"

"That he would damn the eyes of the narrow-minded and manipulative Old Worlders. That he'd side with you. Ease your misery." Jules looked away. "He was good at that. Building us up. Making us believe we were capable of whatever our hearts and minds desired."

For a moment, Simon set aside his own heavy remorse and focused on his brother, who had always been darker in coloring and nature than the more fair and frivolous Simon. Though presently residing in London, where he worked as an author of science fiction novels, Jules Darcy was retired military, a decorated war hero. Details revolving around the skirmish that had mangled his legs and left him with a permanent limp were classified. The period of rehabilitation had been extensive and also shrouded in secrecy. Even Simon was clueless as to those peculiar days of Jules's mysterious life. Although he was often privy to his brother's moods and inclinations, he'd never been able to read Jules's mind regarding the covert nature of his service to the Crown.

"Coffee's bitter," Jules said, setting aside his cup and reaching for the sugar bowl.

Everything had tasted bitter to Simon for days, but he

knew what his brother meant. "Eliza made the coffee. Be warned: She cooked as well."

Frowning, Jules glanced toward the sideboard and the steaming porcelain tureens. Though an excellent house-keeper, Eliza was famously ill equipped in the kitchen. "What happened to Concetta?"

The skilled though crotchety cook who had been in their mother's employ for months. "Mother dismissed her this morning. Said we could no longer afford her services."

"Did she not offer the woman a month's notice?"

"She did. Along with excellent references. But Concetta's prideful. She ranted in her native tongue, and though I do not know Italian, I understood the intention. She's leaving today."

"Damnation," Jules said.

In this instance, Simon knew the man's thoughts. Things were indeed dire if Anne Darcy, a conservative woman obsessed with old ways and upholding appearances, was dismissing servants. Another kick to Simon's smarting conscience.

Just then Eliza's husband, Harry, appeared with two folded newspapers in hand. "As requested," he said, handing the *Victorian Times* to Simon, then turning to Jules. "And the *London Daily* for you, sir." The older man glanced at the sideboard, winced, then lowered his voice. "I could fetch you some fresh bread and jam."

If anyone knew about the poor quality of his wife's cooking, it was Harry.

Simon quirked a smile he didn't feel. "We'll be fine, Harry. No worries." The man nodded and left, and Simon looked at his brother. "We'll have to sample something, you know. Otherwise we'll hurt Eliza's feelings."

"I know." Distracted, Jules seemed absorbed with the front page of the *Daily*.

Simon immediately turned to the headlines of the *Times*—a respectable broadsheet unlike the *Informer*.

The Victorian Times
January 10, 1887

ROYAL REJUVENATION—A GLOBAL RACE FOR FAME AND FORTUNE

In celebration of Queen Victoria's upcoming Golden Jubilee, an anonymous benefactor has pledged to award a colossal monetary prize to the first man or woman who discovers and donates a lost or legendary technological invention of historical significance to her majesty's British Science Museum in honor of her beloved Prince Albert. An additional £500,000 will be awarded for the most rare and spectacular of all submissions. Address all inquiries to P. B. Waddington of the Jubilee Science Committee.

Simon absorbed the significance, the possibilities. "Bloody hell."

"I assume you're reading what I'm reading," Jules said. "News like this must have hit the front page of every newspaper in the British Empire."

"And beyond." Simon fixated on the headline, specifically the words "FAME AND FORTUNE." He wanted both. For his family. For himself.

"Pardon the interruption, sirs." Contrite, Harry had reappeared with three small envelopes. "It would seem sorrow regarding the loss of Lord Ashford has muddled my mind. These were in my pocket. I picked them up at the post whilst in the village this morning." He handed an envelope to each of the brothers, then placed the third near their sister's place setting. "This one is for Miss Amelia," he said. "That is, if she joins you this morning."

Since their father's death, Amelia had been grieving in private.

"We'll see that she gets it," Jules said. "Thank you, Harry."

The man left and Simon struggled not to think of their young sister locked away in her bedroom, mourning, worrying. Yes, she was a grown woman, twenty years of age, but she'd led a sheltered life, and though obstinate as hell, Amelia was tenderhearted. At least half of Simon's worries would end if she'd relent and marry a good and financially stable man. Alas, Amelia's fiery independence was both a blessing and a curse. Frustrated, Simon focused back on what appeared to be an invitation. "No return address."

He withdrew the missive in tandem with Jules and read aloud. "Given your family's reputation as innovators, adventurers, and visionaries—"

"—you have been specifically targeted and are hereby enthusiastically invited to participate in a global race for fame and fortune," Jules finished.

"Royal rejuvenation."

"Colossal monetary prize."

"Legendary technological invention," they said together.

"Is your missive signed?" Simon asked.

"No. Yours?"

"No." He glanced from the mysterious note to the *Times*. "Apparently the anonymous benefactor thought us worthy of a personal invitation. Do you think it is because of our association with Briscoe Darcy?"

"Yet again it's assumed that because Papa knew the Time Voyager, he must have had significant knowledge regarding the infamous time machine."

"Also natural to assume Papa would have passed along that information to us," Simon said, "which he did not."

"No, he did not."

"Unless . . ." Simon looked at the envelope next to Amelia's empty plate.

"If Papa had pertinent information regarding the construction and design of Briscoe's time machine, he wouldn't have burdened Little Bit with such knowledge," Jules said. "Too dangerous."

Indeed. No invention was more historically *significant* than the one constructed by their distant cousin Briscoe Darcy. A time machine used to catapult Briscoe into the future (1969), thereby enabling a group of twentieth-century scientists, engineers, and artists known as the Peace Rebels to dimension-hop back to the past (1856) in a similar device dubbed the Briscoe Bus.

Intending to inspire peace and to circumvent future atrocities and global destruction, the Peace Rebels preached cautionary tales throughout the world, most notably in America and Europe. Unfortunately, a few Mods (twentieth-century Peace Rebels) were corrupted and soon leaked advanced knowledge that led to the construction and black market sales of anachronistic weapons, transportation and communications. The globe divided into two political factions—Old Worlders and New Worlders. Those who resisted futuristic knowledge and those who embraced it. The Peace War broke out and the nineteenth century as it should have been was forever changed.

The Victorian Age meets the Age of Aquarius.

For years and for political reasons, Simon and Jules resisted the urge to explore anything to do with Briscoe Darcy or time travel. Not to mention time travel had been outlawed. However, this Race for Royal Rejuvenation, coupled with their family's unfortunate circumstance, motivated Simon to break their childhood pact. "It is true Papa never shared any secrets with me regarding Briscoe. However, I do have an idea of how to get my hands on an original clockwork propulsion engine."

Jules raised a lone brow. "As do I."

"Are we in accord?"

"We are. But first, let me teletype this P. B. Waddington as well as a personal contact within the science museum. I want verification that this treasure hunt is indeed official."

Simon's heart raced as his brother left the room. With

every fiber of his being, he knew the response would be affirmative. His brain churned and plotted. Only one of them needed to find and deliver the clockwork propulsion engine in order to avenge their father's name and secure the family's fortune. But, by God, Simon wanted it to be him.

CITY OF LONDON
THE LONDON INFORMER

"Willie!"

Wilhelmina Goodenough, known socially as Willie G and professionally as the Clockwork Canary, refrained from thunking her forehead to her desk at the booming voice of her managing editor. She did, however, roll her eyes. She could always tell by the timbre of Artemis Dawson's bellow if she was being summoned for a good reason or bad. This was bad. Given her foul mood of late, this could well mean a bloody ugly row.

As lead journalist for the *London Informer*, Britain's most popular tabloid, Willie had a desk in close proximity to Dawson's office. Lucky her. Or rather *him*, as was public perception.

For the past ten years, Willie had been masquerading as a young man. Sometimes, she was amazed that she'd gotten away with the ruse for so long. Then again, she was slight of frame as opposed to voluptuous. What womanly curves she did possess were easily concealed beneath binding and baggy clothing. Her typical attire consisted of loose linen shirts with flouncy sleeves, a waistcoat one size too big, and an Americanized duster as opposed to a tailored frock coat. Striped baggy trousers and sturdy boots completed the boyish ensemble. When outdoors, instead of a bowler or top hat, Willie pulled on a newsboy cap and tugged the brim low to shade her face. She'd chopped her hair long ago, a shaggy style that hung to her chin and often fell over her eyes. She was by no means fashionable but she did have a style all her own.

And not a bustle, corset, or bonnet to her amended name.

Once in a great while, she yearned for some kind of feminine frippery, but she was far more keen on surviving this intolerant world rather than feeling pretty.

"Willie!"

Blast. "Right, then. Best get this over with," she said to herself, because no coworkers were within earshot of her somewhat sequestered and privileged workspace, and even if they had been, she wasn't chummy with any of the blokes. Willie had two confidants in this world: her father and her journal. One hidden away and one locked away—respectively.

Abandoning her research on significant technological inventions, Willie pushed away from her scarred wooden desk. Her home away from home, the desktop was crowded with stacks of books, piles of documents and files, scores of pens and pencils, her typewriter, and her personal cup and teapot. Dawson often wondered how she found anything, but she did in fact know the precise whereabouts of any given item. Organized chaos—just one of her many gifts.

On the short walk to her boss's office, Willie breathed deep, seeking solace in the familiar scents of the newsroom—ink, paper, oil, cigarette smoke, sweat, and assorted hair tonics. Scents she associated with freedom and security. This job enabled her to pursue her passion as well as provide for herself and her addle-minded father. Forsaking her gender and race had seemed a small price to pay in the beginning. But lately she teemed with resentment. Bothersome, that. She had no patience for self-pity.

To her own disgust, she stalked into her boss's office with a spectacular chip on her shoulder. "You bellowed?"

Dawson looked up from his insanely neat and orderly desk. "Where's the story on Simon Darcy?"

Bugger.

Certain her palms would grow clammy any second, Willie stuffed her hands into the pockets of her trousers and slouched against the doorjamb. "What story?"

Dawson's eyes bulged. "The story I asked for days ago. The story that's *late*. The interview with Simon Darcy regarding the collapse of Project Monorail!"

"Oh, that."

"Yes, *that*."

"The timing seemed off."

"Off?"

"He's been away, attending his father's funeral, comforting his family."

"Yes, I know, Willie. The father who blew himself up whilst building a blasted rocket ship! Two Darcys suffer ruin due to two fantastical projects one day apart. One week before a global race is announced that promises to stir up interest in *outlawed* inventions—if you know what I mean, and I know that you do!

"The timing, dear boy, is *perfect*! Pick Simon Darcy's brain whilst he's vulnerable. Get the scoop on his failed project and his father's bungled invention. Probe deeper and dig up buried family secrets. Go where no man has gone before and ferret out never-disclosed-before details regarding Briscoe Darcy and his time machine. If anyone can do it, you can!" He pounded his meaty fist to his desk to emphasize his point.

Willie felt the force of that blow down to her toes. Her temples throbbed and her pulse stuttered. Yes, she could do it. But she did not want to. The subject of their discussion was too close to her spectacularly well-guarded heart. Though she said nothing, Dawson clearly read her reluctance due to her obviously not so guarded expression.

Narrowing his bloodshot eyes, the portly man braced his thick forearms on his desk and leaned forward. "Close the door."

Gads. This was worse than bad.

Willie did as the man asked, then slumped into a chair and settled in for a lecture. Meanwhile her keen mind scrambled for a way to get out of this pickle.

"*The Informer* is no longer the most popular tabloid in the country. We've been edged out by the *Crier*."

"The *City Crier*? But that's a Sunday-only paper. We are a daily. Not only that . . ." Willie tamped down her pride, snorted. "You're jesting."

"Our investors are not happy," Dawson went on, sober as a judge. "The publisher and executive editor are not happy. Which means . . ."

"You are not happy."

"Get the dirt on Darcy or dig up something even more titillating." He jabbed a finger at the door. "Now, get out."

Although Dawson could be a curmudgeon, he'd always had at least a sliver of good humor hiding beneath the guff. Willie sensed no humor now. The pressure from above must have been severe, indeed. Pausing on the doorstep, Willie voiced a troubling notion. "When did I stop being your favorite?"

"When you went soft on me. That original piece you typed up on Ashford's death was fluff. And the revision wasn't much better. Our readers want sensational, Willie, not respectful. They can get that from the quality press." After a tense moment, Dawson sighed. "You've had a good long run at the *Informer*, Willie. Some people think you've gotten too comfortable. Too arrogant. Most people don't know you as well as I do, and even *I* don't know you that well. But I do know that you have a special gift. I'd hate to lose it."

Sensing freedom and security slipping away, Willie spoke past her constricted throat. "You'll get your story."

Amanda Bonilla

Blood Before Sunrise
A Shaede Assassin Novel

Having found the half-crazed Oracle who tried to overthrow the Shaede Nation, Darian and Raif now face a possibility too painful for Raif to imagine, and too enticing for Darian to ignore.

Determined to reunite Raif and the daughter he thought was dead, Darian is willing to risk everything—though she could lose her lover Tyler in the bargain. Soon, Darian finds herself caught between the man she loves like a brother, and the man whose love she can't live without.

Don't miss the first book in the series
Shaedes of Gray

"Awesome action, as well as raw romance...
one of my favorite heroines of 2011."
—Heroes and Heartbreakers
(on *Shaedes of Gray*)

Available wherever books are sold or at
penguin.com

facebook.com/ProjectParanormalBooks